The Fatal Child

John Dickinson
AR B.L.: 4.7 Alt.: 743
Points: 20.0   UG

THE
FATAL CHILD

John Dickinson

David Fickling Books

OXFORD · NEW YORK

A DAVID FICKLING BOOK

Text copyright © 2008 by John Dickinson
Illustrations copyright © 2008 by Assheton Gorton

All rights reserved. Published in the United States by David Fickling Books, an imprint of Random House Children's Books, a division of Random House, Inc., New York. Originally published in Great Britain by David Fickling Books, an imprint of Random House Children's Books, a division of the Random House Group Ltd., London, in 2008.

David Fickling Books and the colophon are trademarks of David Fickling.

Visit us on the Web! www.randomhouse.com/teens

Educators and librarians, for a variety of teaching tools, visit us at
www.randomhouse.com/teachers

Library of Congress Cataloging-in-Publication Data is available upon request.
ISBN 978-0-385-75110-0 (trade) — ISBN 978-0-385-75111-7 (lib. bdg.) —
ISBN 978-0-375-89367-4 (e-book)

Printed in the United States of America
September 2009
10 9 8 7 6 5 4 3 2 1

First American Edition

Random House Children's Books supports the First Amendment and celebrates
the right to read.

For Amanda

Beyah

Hayley

Tareeny

Aclete

Beyah

Hayley

Tarceny

Jent

Velis

Pemini

Tuscolo

Trant

Develin

Tuscolo

Lackmere

Contents

PART I

THE LANTERN

I

Sack!

he wall was down, the breach taken. Buildings were on fire. In the courtyards the men had turned to murder. They peered through armoured eye-slits at the figures who ran before them. They bellowed in their visors with the lust of the chase. Screams hung like the smoke in the air.

Among the sheds near the palace gardens some fugitives were cornered. They were servants – unarmed scullions and barrow-boys. But the attackers in their madness saw only living flesh. They hunted after them through the little rooms, overturning the pots and barrows and flinging aside the stacks of hoes to catch the squirming, rag-clad bodies that hid there, and to hack and hack and hack and stand grunting, even laughing, over the bloody figures at their feet.

One of the sheds had been barricaded. An armoured man, covered in dirt and blood, was flinging himself at the door. It shuddered at each rush but inside there were bodies pressed against it. It did not give way. The attacker roared like a drunk, '*Here, here!*' and threw himself at the door again. Others were beginning to gather, clutching weapons that dribbled with fresh blood.

'Fire it!' cried one.

'An axe, an axe!' bellowed the madman at the door. Another yelled and lunged at a little window where a pale face had shown itself fleetingly from within. His blade prised the shutter open. He reached through to flail at the people inside. They must have recoiled, for suddenly the door was giving and the men battering at it were tumbling forward in a clatter of arms and swearing.

More cries, from behind them now! Another group ran up, yelling '*Quarter!*' in voices already hoarse from shouting. They were armoured, too, with mail and open helmets, but carried only staffs. Frenziedly they seized on the knights in the doorway and pulled them back.

'Quarter!' screamed one, kneeling on the chest of the fallen madman with his nose an inch from the man's helm. 'In the King's name!'

The madman thrashed and bellowed but his sword was gone and he was pinned. The newcomers clustered around their leader, blocking the doorway. One looked within.

'They're alive still,' he said.

'Quarter!' cried the man on the fallen knight's chest. He was a fat, red-faced fellow with greying brows who glared at the murderous men before him. 'In the name of the King.'

'King?' groaned the knight on the ground. 'Who calls on the King?'

'Thomas Padry, King's chancellor,' said the fat man, sweating in his helmet and coat of iron. 'The King promised me every man, woman or child over whom I laid my staff.'

The knight was silent for a moment, as if the things that made him human were reassembling slowly in his brain.

'He did,' he muttered. 'He did. Let me up.'

Slowly they picked themselves off the ground together and looked at one another. The bloody knight towered over the fat chancellor. His face, enclosed in his helm, could not be seen. His surplice was gone, torn from him in the fight, or perhaps he had never worn one. His shield was gone, too. There was no device on him but the streaks of blood on his mail.

The chancellor stood his ground and held his staff. All around them the air drifted with smoke and the sounds of screams.

The knight bowed his head and turned. 'Come,' he said to his fellow murderers. 'There is more to do.' With a slow clatter of arms and the faceless glances of helms they followed him away.

Thomas Padry stood at the door to the shed. He could see, above the line of the rooftops, the battlements of the great round keep. Up there, tiny but clear, the dark heads of the defenders moved quickly in and out of the cover while the delicate *flick, flick* of arrows flew around them. Down below there were shouts and the sound of running. Beside him someone was giggling – a high, hysterical sound that broke into sobs. Some of his companions had begun to coax the survivors out of their refuge and into the dreadful sunlight. Others were checking the remaining sheds, pausing cautiously in the doorways and calling within – into the seeping, responseless dark where murder had been done.

He leaned against the doorpost, shaking with exhaustion. His throat was hoarse and his skin was soaked. He felt the weight of his armour settling heavily on him. Armour! By the Angels, he hated it almost as much as the things it was supposed to protect him from! The padded leather coat rucked and heaved with every move he made, rubbing his skin sore in a dozen places. And the shirt of iron rings he wore over that dragged him down so that his shoulders and knees sagged. He could not run so much as waddle, and he could not see so much as peer through the frame of his helmet like a poor carthorse trying to look past its blinkers. He was sweating like a roast in an oven. He could have drunk a bottle – no, a butt – of water without stopping for breath. Come to that, he was short of breath as well. But there was no time to rest or think or drink. There was more to do.

One of his men hurried white-faced from a shed, propelled by something he had seen there. He dropped to his knees. A second later he began to vomit.

Padry heaved himself from the doorpost and lumbered over to the kneeling man. He knew he should have told them. He *had* told them, but he should have told them better, the things that really

6

happened when men had iron in their hands. These boys were not warriors. They were clerks and priests who spent their days copying his documents. They had volunteered when he had appealed to them, but they had had no idea what it would be like. And it was too late to tell them now. Now they knew, and they would never forget. They had seen men pinned to doors by arrows through the ear or tongue or testicles. They had seen a babe still mewing bloodily on the point of a pike. They would carry the images in their heads for ever, as he did.

All he could do for them was . . .

'Be glad if your stomach turns, Master Ricard,' he said, patting the clerk's shoulder and speaking in what he hoped was a kindly, jovial voice. 'For it is a sure sign that you are still with us.'

The man climbed slowly to his feet, pointing into the shed. He could not speak. Padry, who had no wish to look on this particular horror himself, took him gently by the arm and steered him away.

'The one in there has no need of us, I take it,' he said.

'No, master,' grunted the young man. 'No.'

'Well then,' said Padry, as cheerfully as he could, 'let us busy ourselves with those who have. And if your heart is the heavier, why, your belly is the lighter now. So you may make the same speed as before!'

'Yes, master,' said the clerk, still shaking his head.

Yes, master, thought Padry. And tonight, my boy, you will tell your fellows it was not the blood that made you gag but your master's wordplay. And they will all say, *Oh aye!* and together you will repeat all the other things I've said to you while these things embraced you. And you will roll your eyes and mock me, imitate my voice and my walk, and laugh until you are sick once more. And I forgive you for it. I forgive all of you, for you have followed me out of love and I know it.

Besides, if a man could not laugh today, he would surely scream.

'Well done,' he said, patting the man's shoulder again. 'Now— What? What?'

Someone was pulling at his other arm. It was a woman, one of the survivors from the hut. She was dressed like a high-standing servant. Her face was narrow and bird-like. Her accent was so thick that he could not understand what she was saying to him. But she was speaking the same words, again and again, and pulling at him.

'It's all right,' he said, as soothingly as he could. 'We won't harm you.'

Still she was pulling at his arm and saying the same thing, urgently. Still he could not understand her. She must be one of the hill people, he thought – the heathen, wretched folk who lived in the mountains and the march west of Derewater. What was she doing here? What fate had brought . . . ?

Again she pulled at him, almost shrieking now. And she pointed away behind her.

'Hold on, hold on,' he grumbled. 'I'm coming. Lex!'

'Yes, Chancellor?' said one of the young priests with him.

'I'm going with this one. You'll have to get the rest

of them out of here. And spare some to keep looking, will you? Find every one we can.'

'Yes, Chancellor.'

He followed the hillwoman in a daze of exhaustion, out behind the sheds and down a short mews. There was a wall ahead of him. Beyond it was the keep. Angels send that she did not want him to go in there! The mines below it had been fired hours ago. The props would be down to ashy nothing by now. It should have fallen already. Looking up, he wondered if the stonework was indeed beginning to sag as its foundations were eaten away.

The woman led him on, down the mews, straight towards the keep. At the far end he could see a flight of steps leading up to a little postern door. His nerve failed him. 'Stop!' he cried. 'We can't go in there!'

They would shoot him from the roof even if he tried! Whoever was still in there was going down to the bitter end.

But she screamed at him and pulled at his hand. He followed, feet stumbling. There was a body lying face down near the foot of the steps . . .

In the left wall of the mews was a little iron-grille door. The woman ran to it, looked through and called. Then she turned to Padry and beckoned urgently.

Padry glanced fearfully upwards. They were within easy shot of the keep. Dark slits looked down on him. Anyone behind them with a crossbow . . .

Hurry!

He came to the door and peered through. He blinked.

For a moment it seemed to him that he must be looking through a window in time to another place. It was a place he knew well. It was the small walled garden in Tuscolo, where he would walk when he needed to clear his mind, and where no murder had ever come. There were colonnades about it and pavements lined with pots of sweet-smelling plants – all the things the fevered brain needed to calm it and set it on the path of contemplation. And in the middle of the court there was the same old fountain with the same wide stone bowl, like a great cup belonging to some giant of legend.

By the fountain, looking away from him, was a child. She wore a dress of rich blue. Her hair was long and dark. She was standing quite still.

Padry gripped the bars. This was no vision. The garden was like the one in Tuscolo, very like. It was bright and calm in the sunshine. But it was here in Velis, and beyond its walls the plumes of smoke drifted and screams still tortured the air. This little pocket of Heaven was surrounded by a hell that would consume it in minutes.

Beside him the hillwoman bent and called urgently through the bars of the door. The word sounded like 'Atti!' The child must have heard her but she did not look. She stood with her dark plaits falling over her dress and ignored them. She ignored everything that was happening around her.

Padry cursed and tried the door. It was bolted from within. He tried to force his hand through the bars but the fine iron tracery would not let him. *This is*

Heaven, it seemed to say. *It is not for you.*

He shook the bars again. Useless. He must not panic. The just man should not panic. Nor should the philosopher weep at the pity of the world.

'Atti! Come!' called the woman beside him.

He bent and called, too. 'You must come,' he hooted. 'It is not safe!'

The child did not look at them.

'*Atti!*' wailed the hillwoman.

'Atti!' he echoed, assuming this was the child's name.

She did turn, then. And it seemed to him that it was at his voice that she turned – perhaps simply to see this stranger who presumed to call her so. He beckoned urgently.

'Come. Come, dear.'

For a moment she turned away once more. She stood in the sunlight by the fountain with all the war and fury around separated from her only by the thinness of a garden wall. But then she seemed to change her mind. She faced them, and came walking slowly down the flowered paths towards the door.

And Angels! There were arrows falling in the garden, dropping from the tops of their arcs near the keep roof! They fell like single spots of rain. The sunlight flashed on them as they tumbled from the sky. But still the child walked towards him, keeping her eyes on his face.

'Can you open it?' he said, and shook the gate again.

She looked at him with dark brown eyes. She might have been no more than eleven years old. She was fine-boned, small and solemn. Her skin was pale, her brows beautiful and dark, her nose finishing delightfully in a curve that was not quite snub. He saw that in a very few years she would be enchanting indeed – if she lived. And he knew who she must be.

'You have to open it,' he said. 'Quickly!'

She put out her hand and drew the bolt. The door to the little Heaven opened. Scarcely believing the grace that had been granted to them, Padry reached and took her hand. It doesn't matter who she is, he thought. She is a soul like any other, and more innocent than most. Angels, only let me get her out of this!

She was ignoring the hillwoman, who must have been her maid. She was ignoring her with the childish determination of a girl who had quarrelled and had not yet forgiven. Of course the maid would have been trying to hide her, but the girl, frightened, must have run away to lock herself in the fountain garden while the King's warriors stormed through the stronghold and murdered everyone they could.

'Come!' he said, glancing upwards at the keep. (Umbriel! Was it about to fall?) Still keeping hold of the child's hand, he hurried back down the mews with the hillwoman at his heels. Lex and a couple of his fellows were waiting at the sheds.

'I've another one!' said Padry. 'Lex, I've another one!'

'Another wordplay, master? Or a soul?'

Padry looked down at the girl, who still held his hand. 'Oh, it is a soul, I think.'

'Angels! Isn't that the Baldwin child?'

'I think so. Can you take her to the breach?'

'We should take her to the King.'

'To the breach first,' said Padry, panting. 'There will be time to find and tell the King later. Also . . .' He hesitated. 'Also,' he went on, 'I *think* it would be wise to let Gueronius forget that I sat on his chest, before I see him again.'

Lex's jaw dropped. 'That bloody knight? That was the King?'

'None other.'

Lex shook his head in disbelief. He said something. But his words were lost in the long roar of the keep falling.

II

Chess Pieces

t sunset King Gueronius was in his tent in the dunes above the sea. He had put off his armour, bathed and then oiled his young beard with scents. He wore blue silks with the great yellow sun of his house gleaming on them. He had a cup of wine in his hand and had himself poured another for his chief ally, the marshal Orcrim, who captained the troops of the Lady of Develin.

The marshal was a white-haired giant of a man whose age had robbed him of the use of his legs. He lay propped on cushions on his litter, frowning over a chessboard on which black and white pieces stood locked in silent combat. But the King (who was losing) appeared to have forgotten the game. He paced to and fro, laughing, talking, pausing now and then to gaze out at the glowing horizon.

'Do you see?' he cried, pointing across the bay. 'Do you see all the jewels of Velis that they would have kept from us? Now they shall belong to us – and not only to us, but to all men! The sea is ours again, as it should be. *So Wulfram came from the sea, with three ships, four Angels, seven sons and one thing!* His finger swept the wavetops. In the long light of the summer evening they glittered like jewels indeed.

'A salty prize,' said Orcrim drily. He jerked his chin. 'I should have said the city itself was a greater reward for this day's work.'

Across the bay rose Velis, the second city of the Kingdom, on its pair of round hills. Its walls glowed in the low sun. Heavy smoke still trailed from the castle, blown southward by the sea breeze. Where the keep had ruled the skyline there was now only an absence. Without it the city looked unbalanced. Its spires and towers clustered awkwardly like witnesses at the death of a friend.

'Velis is a prize, yes,' said the King. 'But where does her wealth come from? From the sea. Orcrim, in my city of Tuscolo I have found treaties drawn in secret by past kings, with Velis – with Velis, as if she were an equal power and not a subject of the Crown! To Velis alone was granted the right to trade with merchants from other lands, provided that they met in secret places, neither their land nor ours, and that no Outlander should set foot in the Kingdom itself. Orcrim, did you know there were other lands beyond the sea?'

'I did not suppose that Wulfram was born on a wavetop. Nor that the silks I have had from Velis in happier times were woven here.'

'And yet you never thought to ask where these lands might be, or what manner of men lived there! It is vile and heinous that such things should be hidden for the sake of profit! Now the secrets of Velis will be ours. We shall meet with these merchants. Maybe we shall even travel to their lands, far beyond the water. My lord, when you look over this bay, you see a city. But I see the world!'

Again he pointed out over the glimmering wave-tops, into the far distance where the sea and sky blended into one.

'I see what a man can hold,' said Orcrim. 'No man can hold the world.'

'Hold it? I dare say not. But to know it – to go and go, to push the skyline back with each step and open new sights to the eye! Did Wulfram himself do less, when he set out in his three ships? *So Wulfram came from the sea!* Did not his sons, when they took the Kingdom for their own? *Hah, Dieter!*' he cried, throwing up his arms in a kind of ecstasy. '*Hah, keen-eyed Lomba!*'

'Your Majesty speaks the truth, as the stories tell us. In their youth, so they did. And (permit me to say it) Your Majesty is a young man also. Young men long to push skylines, even to seize kingdoms, if they are able. But a man who will have something to keep must learn how to hold it – a king most of all. Now I have not had the use of my feet for nine months, but—'

'Oh aye! To see you riding in your litter to the breach this morning – it was the bravest sight in the world! I shall have new verses written in *The Tale of Kings*. And by Heaven, sir, one will be for you!'

'Your Majesty does me honour. But fighting men must know where their captain is. I did not mean to let mine—'

'That is right!' said the King quickly. 'They must know where their captain is – by the standard, in command. I did not forget it, sir. Not in the very thick did I forget it!'

'I am certain of it, Sire,' said the marshal impassively. 'Although in truth I was so tossed about in the press that I had no eyes but for my bearers and barely a word but to bid them hold me steady. It is not good to go without legs into a fight. May Heaven allow that this will be my last.'

'The last and the greatest,' said the King. 'This morning, when the stewards refused our summons to surrender, I tell you I all but wept for joy. Was there ever such a fight, Orcrim? I killed all who came against me! Tell me truly, of all the fights you have seen, was this not your greatest?'

Orcrim frowned over his wine. 'Greatest? Four years back, when I restored my Lady Develin to her house and lands, we struck barely a blow. Yet with speed of horse and a mob of peasants we chased her enemies from Develin in a month. Was this not all that a fighting man could hope for?'

'A feat indeed, but hardly a fight. I mean your fiercest, or most desperate.'

'Whenever I face a man with iron, it is desperate. But . . .' Orcrim looked into his cup again, as though he might see something there. 'But I stood in an affray a little before the taking of Develin. That was the worst, I think.'

'Tell me.'

'It was a small matter,' said Orcrim reluctantly. 'I

had but twelve knights with me, and two women and a boy.'

'And how many men had your enemy?'

'Men? Two, only.'

'By the Angels, sir! You mock me!'

'Your Majesty asked how many *men*. There were others that were not men. And by the Angels you name, Sire, I would face any number of pikes sooner than look into those eyes again!'

The King gave him a long, hard stare. 'What do you mean? Witchcraft?'

'So some might call it.'

At length the King shrugged. 'If all I have heard is true, a man who once served Tarceny must have expected to meet such things.'

'So I believe it is said, Your Majesty. At all events I no longer serve Tarceny but my Lady of Develin. And through her fealty to you, I serve yourself.' Orcrim looked up. 'Now here is another servant who has changed houses, I believe. Only this one is the teacher who quit Develin for yours.'

A small party of men were picking their way up the strand towards the tent. At their head was Thomas Padry.

When a teacher falls among lords and killers of men, what is he to do?

Why, teach, where he can – where they have children they will set before him. And when those children grow and take power themselves, then teach them again – only this time call it not 'teaching' but 'counsel'.

Teach them, all the time, that there is a Path they must follow. The Path is not easy and not always clear, but every living moment brings a choice between following it and straying from it. And once the soul has strayed it is harder than ever to return to the right way.

Teach? Beg, plead, wheedle, cajole . . . When they listen, then beg some more. And if they share a little of their power – if, say, they make you their chancellor because you were once their teacher and seemed wise – then use the power you are given. Write the laws, give judgement, seek agreement and then once again beg your man of power to endorse it. And when all else fails, then yes, even put on armour and follow him through the breaches to stay his hand from slaughter where you can. Every moment is another step along the Path.

Thomas Padry, trudging bone-weary across the soft beach-sand, supposed that it might indeed have been through the act of some Angel that he had become first tutor and then counsellor to the young Gueronius diTuscolo, who would now be undisputed King. He had not thought the Angels had such a wicked sense of humour.

'Ho, Lord Chancellor,' cried the King gaily. 'It has been a good day. For you I trust also?'

'Your Majesty,' said Padry, bowing.

'The marshal and I were debating,' said the King. 'But the old man and the young do not agree. Now you stand between us in years. What do you say is the greatest prize we have won today?'

19

Padry frowned. 'Why, Your Majesty,' he said carefully, 'I suppose . . . I suppose it must be our blisters.'

'Our *blisters*? How?'

'Your Majesty, I do not think we dream of blisters. Nor do I think there can be blisters in Heaven. Therefore, since we most certainly have blisters, we may know that we are neither dead nor dreaming but are alive at the end of this day. And that is a prize worthy of thanks.'

'Amen,' said the King. 'I had not thought to give thanks for my blisters.'

'Well . . . It may be that I have accrued more than Your Majesty. For I swear I have them on every limb and part of me. Even so I am grateful, since by this I may know that all my parts are still joined to me and that I am not in any sense diminished. Indeed,' he went on, theatrically wiping his brow, 'since they swell according to their nature, I may even claim to have increased a little.'

'You are still joined to your tongue, it seems,' growled Orcrim, with a face like a severe old abbess in whose presence the conversation has turned to sex.

'Nor will he let it rest, until he breathes his last,' said the King.

Padry would have added that it was surely *bliss ter* be alive. But he glanced once more at the marshal and stifled his pun with regret.

'Your Majesty,' he said, 'I have the terms of the city's surrender for your consideration.'

'They have agreed to unseal all their charts and

records of sailings, and to put their mariners and shipwrights at our disposal?'

'Among other things, Your Majesty. The fine—'

'Enough. I will consent. Tell me of your morning,
Chancellor. What success had you?'

Dear Heaven! thought Padry. *Enough! I will
consent* . . .

It was possible to be fond of Gueronius. In fact it
was not difficult at all. He had the charm of a young
bear. He had no use for subtlety, but the warmth and
loyalty he showed to those around him was real.
And he was willing to do what men thought right
when his attention could be brought to it.

But – was it too much to ask for *just a few seconds* of
his ear?

While others were resting after the fight Padry had
gone to meet with the aldermen of Velis. Still sweating
and clinking in his mail, he had spent hours in a
stifling room haggling with a pack of frightened,
stubborn, miserly old men who had twisted and
turned and wormed every way they could before grant-
ing anything that might conceivably satisfy the
morning's victors. Were all his demands and com-
promises, the drafting and re-drafting of words worth
thousands of crowns, now to be granted with the wave
of a hand? But Gueronius must know what it was he
was consenting to, or he would surely find some fault
with it later on.

'If Your Majesty pleases, perhaps we should
consider—'

'We shall consider that which is most important.

For a fight brings many things, yet I never heard of stranger deeds than yours. Tell me of your morning. I command it.'

'Aye, sir clerk,' said the old marshal, rolling his eyes. 'Tell us. Did you talk the King's foes to death when you met them?'

No, thought Padry crossly. But now I must talk away the King's battle-madness, so that he may be better pleased with himself.

'You do him injustice,' said the King (and Padry heard something uneasy in his chuckle). 'My "clerk", as you call him, was on his knees to me before dawn, begging that he and his priestly friends should don mail and follow us into the breach. Not to strike a blow for Our Person, no. But to bring Our Clemency to all whom they could, once the defence was broken, and so make Our day's work pleasing in the eyes of the Angels.'

The marshal stared. Padry set his teeth.

'I have seen sack, my lord,' he said softly.

'And so have I!' said the marshal. 'And it is better to walk among wounded lions than to go crying peace among armed men with the blood-lust on them. What was this for?'

'Before you came to Develin I was a master at the school there. I was in the house the day the soldiers of Velis took it by treachery.'

'And someone spared you?'

(*Spared* me, sir? One of *your* kind, spare me? I would laugh if I could, but I cannot!)

'My lord, I hid in a chimney. So did one other

22

below me. When they came to search it they poked my companion with pikes and he fell down among them. They cut him to pieces. I heard . . .'

Padry looked down at the sand between his feet, groping for words to describe how the screams of the man, an honest house-servant, had echoed in the stonework around him those five years ago. He wanted words that would protest to the marshal and to the King against *all* sack, *all* blood-letting everywhere, including the murder they had done that morning. He wanted to jar them to the core of their iron-blinkered souls!

But the words would not come. And other instincts rushed to haul him back, reminding him that he was tired, and that he must not – must *not* – appear to criticize Gueronius before a witness without being very, very sure of what he was doing.

'They – they busied themselves with him. But they never looked further up the chimney to see me there. So I lived and owe my life to the Angels. And so' – he shrugged, and finished as quickly as he could – 'so I do what I can, my lord.'

'Aye,' said the King, whose eyes had wandered out to sea. 'And for two years as my tutor he dinned it into me also. Do what you can. Hide not from the world, for it will find you out and betray you. So do. And today we have done, have we not?'

'Indeed, Your Majesty,' said Padry woodenly.

'An honest thought, but foolish,' said Orcrim. 'You were lucky to come away with no more than blisters. And in all that rout I think you will not have saved more than a handful – six at most. Am I right?'

'In truth it was almost a score, my lord. Mostly of low rank, it is true. I do not count those that men may have taken for ransom—'

Orcrim's eyes narrowed. '*Mostly* of low rank?'

(A pox on all bloody men with more brains than they had a right to!) Padry had not wanted it to come out like this.

'Um ... Indeed, my lord.' He coughed. 'Your Majesty will wish to know—'

Gueronius turned back hastily. 'Aye, it is well done. Padry, I am to have new verses sung in *The Tale of Kings*. And for this day's work you, too, shall have one.'

'But *I* want to hear—' said the marshal.

'Your Majesty is gracious,' said Padry hurriedly. 'But you would wish to know that among those spared – through your clemency – we have found the child Astria, daughter of Tancrem of Baldwin whom your uncle King Septimus slew in Tarceny.'

'Very good,' said the King, nodding.

'No, Your Majesty!' said the marshal, raising his hand. 'It is *very* good. I was wondering what had become of her. And now I think your clerk may after all have done you greater service than any fighting man who climbed through the breach this morning. If you will permit it, I shall give you some advice.'

Padry gritted his teeth. He could guess what was coming.

'Gladly,' said the King.

The marshal heaved his huge frame upright among his cushions. 'Your Majesty asked what prize we have

24

won today. It is plain. The child Astria is the heir to
Baldwin and to Velis. So, if you would have your
victory last, you will bring her to Tuscolo, have her
cared for, and when she is of age you will wed
her. Then no power in the Kingdom will be strong
enough to challenge you. We shall see such a peace as
we have not known in thirty, maybe three hundred
years. We may rebuild what we have destroyed. We will
till the earth, year in, year out, and never lift a weapon
against one another. *This* is the greatest prize.'

The King frowned at the old warrior. 'I had not
given thought to marriage, Marshal,' he said.

'Then it is time that you did. Again, it is a matter of
holding what you have. And let me tell you that
the holding is often harder than the gaining . . .'

Padry's fingers clenched and unclenched themselves around his staff. He looked down at his feet,
trying to harry his wits into order. His head was singing
with exhaustion. He could see the individual grains of
sand speckling upon his toes. And deliberately, in his
mind, he pictured himself reaching out to take hold
of his anger. Anger did not lead along the Path. Above
all, he must not be angry because the marshal had
advised the King before he himself could! In one way
the advice was not bad at all. She lives and we have her.
Let us use her *so,* like a pawn at chess, and our position
is strengthened. If he had not seen her he might have
counselled the same thing.

But she was not a chess piece. She was a soul, as he
had said to Lex. In his mind he saw again how she had
walked across the garden with the spent arrows

dropping out of the air, and how she had looked at him through the barred door to the fountain court (those delicate, wary eyes, which already seemed to know how much evil there was in the world!). Her house had been torched and the people she knew slaughtered. Yet she had drawn the bars at his word and put her hand in his. This morning he had saved an innocent from the fire. If there was one thing among all others in all his life that he could hold up to the Angels, it would surely be this!

He gripped his staff, pushing the butt end sharply into the sand. He knew better than to blurt out his feelings in council. The King was reluctant in any case. There were subtler ways of doing it.

'With your leave, Your Majesty . . . ?' he murmured.

'On the same?' sighed the King. 'If you must.'

'The marshal speaks well of peace,' Padry said. 'A lasting peace is the prize. With peace there may be law. In older days the High Kings made such law that a man who carried a purse of gold might go from one end of the Kingdom to another without fear—'

'Aye, this I will do also!' said Gueronius.

'Only for that reason, Your Majesty, the matter of marriage must be carefully weighed. Your hand may only be given once. And there may be more than one possibility. The Lady of Develin herself might be considered. Baldwin may or may not rise again. But as things stand Develin is second in strength only to the royal house itself.'

The marshal eyed him coldly. 'Is this a considered

proposal, Sir Clerk? For when my lady gave me the charge of her soldiers she let me have no word on what I might say to this.'

'It is the first I have heard of either idea,' said the King.

'Well then, Your Majesty,' said Orcrim, 'I do not think your chancellor's *other* former pupil would thank him for this thought. It is well known that she mourns one she has lost and that she will take no man until her mourning is past.'

'Not even if I commanded it?' said the King sharply.

The marshal looked into his wine. 'If it lay between marriage and war,' he said slowly, 'I suppose she would choose marriage. She has said as much to me. If it were to save the Kingdom when another had imperilled it . . .' He shrugged elaborately and affected a glance at the chessboard. 'Why, Sire,' he exclaimed in a tone of surprise, 'I believe it must be your move.'

The King ignored him. 'Is it the command that imperils the Kingdom then?' he insisted. 'Or is it the answer? Tell me, Marshal. Whom does Develin truly serve?'

Orcrim met his look. 'She had put her hands between yours. Her dead lie with yours in this morning's breaches. Is it necessary to have her body as well, before you are sure of her? Whereas Baldwin—'

'That is no matter. Marriage I shall consider at a time and place of *my* choosing. Now I speak of loyalty. You tell me that hers is to me. Indeed. But one cannot serve two kings. What of this hedge-king we hear of, who holds no land and yet will give judgement on all? Is her loyalty not to him?'

'That one? I have heard of him, I suppose. But surely Your Majesty jests—'

'Do I? Why has she not sent him to me in chains, then?'

The marshal eased himself back into his cushions. He looked less comfortable now, thought Padry with some satisfaction. This would pay the old brute for making the child into a pawn – and for calling an honest chancellor 'clerk' to his face!

But Padry was also curious. He, too, had heard of the so-called 'Hidden King', or 'Prince Under the Sky' (Prince Under the Sky? Strange name! Did it mean that the fellow was so poor he had no roof over his head? Or so rich that all the lands under the sky were his?). At all events he seemed to be a figure of some authority, in a land where all authority must be united in the King. And Padry guessed that Develin knew more about this person than the marshal was admitting.

'Shall my lady hunt through the ditches of the land and send to Tuscolo every ragged prophet she finds?' growled the marshal. 'Is all the blood that Develin has spilled for you mute beside these hedge-whispers? This man is not in Develin's country, but in the March of Tarceny – beyond our reach and, I suppose, beyond even yours, Your Majesty.

'And permit me to say another thing about kings, Sire, since I have seen more than one. A king must beware, yes. Always. But if he looks too hard for enemies then he may find enemies indeed. And not only in his own head!'

The two men glared at one another. Then the King shrugged a shoulder.

'If you say so, Marshal. I am not going to make enemies today. That *and* marriage can wait for another time.'

And he turned. Putting his hand on an awning pole, he went back to staring at the sea.

The sun was sinking to the water, spreading its light in a great flare of gold. The last of the sea breeze sighed in the tent-ropes. No one spoke. The marshal frowned over the chessboard. He tried a few moves of the King's pieces, shaking his head and replacing each in turn. The King ignored him. Padry watched them both. At length he coughed, signed to one of the clerks to bring him a scroll, and unrolled it. 'The terms of surrender, Your Majesty. The city has agreed to pay a fine of fifteen thousand in silver—'

'So little?' interjected the marshal. 'Must my men go unpaid on their march home? Unfed, too?'

'As to the feeding of them,' said Padry, 'the city has undertaken to provide—'

'It is well, Marshal,' said the King, still standing with his back to them. 'It is well.'

For a moment Padry and the marshal waited, thinking that he would add some order or correction. They could hear him murmuring as he stood and stared at the sunset. But he was not speaking to them. Padry recognized the opening verses of *The Tale of Kings*.

'*So Wulfram came over the sea,*' chanted the young man softly.

'*With three ships, four Angels, seven sons and one thing.*

'*And the thing was Iron . . .*'

And iron in the hands of men, thought Padry, had never brought the Kingdom peace.

III

The Woman of Develin

elissa always remembered the day the King came.

She was about six, then. Dadda was out somewhere in the great woods that surrounded their clearing. She was sitting in the hut, cleaning the pot. And Mam rushed in, frightened. Someone was coming up the path.

Melissa wanted to run and see who it was. (Anything was better than cleaning the pot!) But Mam hushed her and dropped the shutters. They sat quite still in the dark of the hut, holding each other, listening to the hooves and pretending that they were not there.

Then a fist banged hard on the boarded window. Mam decided that it was better to open after all.

There were two of them: an old man who rode a huge horse and wore a coat of metal rings, and a tall, dark-haired boy of about thirteen on a mule. The old man had a sour face and Melissa did not like him. The boy was different. He spoke cheerfully to Mam and politely to Dadda when Dadda came home that

31

evening. Melissa watched him all through the meal that they shared together. Afterwards she realized that the two visitors were going to sleep with them in the hut that night. It was something that had never happened before.

Melissa was put to bed against a wall, not in her normal place near the hearth. Mam and Dadda and the old knight lay down, too, and went to sleep. Melissa did not sleep. She lay awake, still watching the boy sitting by the fire.

He had traded with Mam for a black cloth, which was Melissa's shawl, and a pale cloth that had once been a sleeve of Dadda's. Using a knife and working by the light of the flames, he cut first the shawl and then the old sleeve into shapes. Then he took a needle and thread that Mam had given him and slowly stitched a piece of the pale cloth to the black. As the fire sank Melissa watched him bend lower and lower over the cloth to see what he was doing. At last he reached over and put two more logs on the hearth to give him light. When he turned back to his work he found he had lost his needle. He sighed and fumbled for it in the darkness.

'It's by your foot,' Melissa whispered to him.

'What?'

'It's by your foot.' She had never spoken to a stranger before.

He found it and said, 'Thank you.' Then he went on working in the firelight and she went on watching him.

His face was long and his dark hair fell down over

his ears almost to his jawbone. His cheeks were smooth and his brows arched over careful eyes. He was frowning a little, peering at what he was doing as though it were somehow very, very important. Now and again he would look up and see her watching him. Then he would smile – a quick smile at the corners of his mouth. From time to time he stopped and looked thoughtfully at the shadows as if they held things she could not see.

When he had finished he held up the black cloth in his hands. In the red-brown light of the embers Melissa saw that he had stitched the pale cloth into the centre of it. The pale cloth was a circle, but the circle was not whole.

'There's a piece missing,' she said.

'Yes, there's supposed to be.'

'Why?'

'It's the moon,' he said. 'You are looking at the moon on a dark night. But there's something between you and it, so you can't see all of it. That's what the black bit means. I don't know what it is yet, but I'll think about it.' He smiled again. 'You should go to sleep now.'

In the morning the two visitors rode away together. The boy carried the black cloth tied to a stick that he slung from his shoulder. Mam and Dadda looked hard at it. Afterwards they told her that it had been a flag. It meant that the boy was the Lord of the March.

'What's the March?' Melissa had asked.

'It's the land, my lovely. Where we live and all around us.'

'And over the hill, too?'

Mam laughed. 'Much, much more than that. All the way to the lake, and north and south as far as the lake runs. And if he's Lord of the March, he should be the King, too! And that means lord of all the land on the far side of the lake as well!'

Melissa had heard of the lake but had never seen it. She could not imagine that there was even more land on the other side of it.

'I hope he doesn't go there,' she said. 'I want him to stay with us.'

Dadda snorted.

'It's a fair wish,' Mam told him. 'If only he'll keep the peace and make us safe.'

'Lords bring taxes and trouble,' said Dadda. 'Here, we stand on our own feet.'

Some time later – it may have been months, or a year – Melissa and her mother were outside the hut one evening. Mam was on her hands and knees by the fire. She had got the little flame going and was carefully putting the smaller twigs into place around it.

Melissa asked, 'Why isn't Dadda a king?'

Mam looked up and laughed. 'But he is, my lovely! King of the clearing, the stream and the woods on either side. And I'm his queen and you're his princess.'

'I mean a real king,' Melissa said crossly.

'Oh, but he would not want that! The woods are what he loves. Keep going, sweetheart, or it'll never be done.'

Melissa had the basin on her knees and the

millstone in her hand. She was grinding at the cornmeal to break it down into flour. It was hard work for her, and also boring, and she could only hear or draw breath to speak when she took a rest.

'But don't you want him to be one?' she asked a minute later.

Mam looked at her sideways. 'A man's no good if he's not happy, now, is he?' she said.

'He'd have all that land and a crown. Wouldn't that make him happy? And you?'

'No, my lovely. I can't make him what he's not. And I can't be what I'm not either. He's my stoat and I'm his blackbird. That's the way we are.'

The answer annoyed Melissa. Of course Dadda was lithe and brown and silent, and very clever at catching small game in the woods. But it was silly to say that he was a stoat. He wasn't a stoat any more than he was a king. Anyway, stoats didn't marry blackbirds. Melissa had slept in the same room as her father and mother all her life. She knew what man and wife got up to in the night. The only thing a stoat could do with a blackbird was eat it.

'What am I, then?' she asked grumpily.

'Whatever you want to be. But always our lovely.'

Across the clearing the huge shapes of the forest were grey-blue and cloudy in the evening. Dadda was out there still. At this time he might be checking his snares. The moon, pale and silver, was rising over the leafy hillside. Melissa looked up as it began its climb into the sky. The fire hissed and the sweet smoke drifted in the air.

Mam was watching her. Her eye was as bright as a little bird's and there was music when she laughed. 'Can't touch the moon, can you?'

'No,' said Melissa. 'But I can see it.'

'Can't feel it, though. Not warm enough, is it?'

'No.'

'Look.'

Carefully Mam drew one of the longer sticks out of the fire. She held it pointing down so that the flames at its tip could lick up along the unburned wood. She put the palm of her other hand near the glowing end.

'You can feel that, can't you?'

'Yes,' said Melissa, copying her.

'It's not big, like the moon. It doesn't shine all over everywhere. But you find it, you keep it close, it'll warm you like the moon never could. And give you a little light, too, maybe.'

'Yes,' said Melissa.

'That's what you've got to do,' said Mam.

'Yes,' said Melissa again.

But she did not stop thinking about the King. In her daydreams he would come by again and she would speak with him properly, because she was older now (by a year, by two years, three . . .). She remembered how he had smiled at her. His smile had said a lot in a very little. It had told her that although he had many, many things to think about, he also had time to think about her. She thought how he might smile at her again and ask her what she was doing. And then she would take extra care with whatever it was (whether it was sweeping, or gathering wood, or milling corn), just in case he did come at that moment, riding up with the old knight at his side.

Mam often said she was a good girl.

The seasons passed, one after another. He did not come. But Melissa beamed and hugged Mam and Dadda with delight when baby Clara came instead. Then she ran out and hugged the goats and told them about her new sister. And that winter she helped Mam with the long, hopeless battle to keep poor Clara alive when the chill had got into the baby's lungs. She took her turn to hold Clara as the little thing coughed and coughed into the nights. Mam did not think Clara would live and neither did Melissa, because there had been a baby before, baby Penni, and Penni had not lived either. And Clara did not. At the end Melissa and Mam sat and held what was left between them for a long, long hour after Clara had ceased to stir. Then Mam silently prised the body from Melissa, kissed her on the forehead and took the thing away.

Dadda fished, cut wood, hunted. The three of them all worked together over the strips of crops that grew in their clearing. Melissa toiled day in, day out. In the autumns she might spend whole days out in the woods picking nuts and berries, but she never went further from the clearing than that.

People did come by – mostly hunters, or the men from families up or down the stream. Father would speak with them and learn about things that were happening elsewhere in the March, or maybe on the lake. Once or twice the passers-by were hill people. These were the little folk with narrow, bird-like faces who came down from the mountains to trade for things like buckles and knives that they did not make for themselves. They always looked hungry and spoke few words that Melissa could understand. She was sorry for them. She was sorrier still if Dadda sent them away without making a trade. But the goods of the hillmen were often poor. There was no point giving away things that were needed if there was nothing to be had in return. Besides, Dadda said, the hill folk were heathen. They did not believe in the Angels.

And one day in the summer of her thirteenth year, when she was gathering yet more firewood under the trees, she heard noises down in the clearing. She picked up her bundle and hurried down the slope to see who had come. As she rounded the back of the hut she heard Mother call to her anxiously. But she ran on.

On the far bank of the stream were two men on horses.

Two knights!

They were not the King and his friend. Not even after all this time. They were two grown men, wearing red cloth over their armour. One of them had a big yellow beard.

Dadda was standing on this side of the stream. He had been cutting hay. Now he was holding his long hayfork in both hands, pointed towards the newcomers. They were talking to him and he was answering. Melissa could not hear what was said. She thought the bearded knight was trying to sound friendly, but it was not the sort of friendliness she liked. Dadda, when he answered, did not sound friendly at all.

One of the knights stirred his mount and rode it into the stream. Dadda shouted and pointed his fork at the animal. He looked as if he would stab it if it came within reach. The knight stopped, rested his arms on his horse's neck and smiled. Dadda did not move. The points of his fork were sharp and bright. They wavered just slightly as he gripped the shaft, like twigs stirred in a light wind. The water frothed around the legs of the horse and whirled away downriver.

The bearded knight said something. The other knight turned his horse to climb back out of the stream. Together they rode away. Dadda watched them go, all the way to the cover of the trees. At the very edge of the wood one of the knights looked round and waved cheerfully at him.

'*Be back.*' The words carried faintly to Melissa's ears.

Dadda was angry that night. He frowned and tore at his bread over supper, saying nothing. Mam, too, was tight-lipped. Melissa knew better than to ask who the knights had been or what they had wanted. Neither of her parents paid her any attention. At length Mam murmured something to Dadda. He snorted.

'I don't need 'em. I stand on my two feet.'

'What if they do come back, then?' Mam asked.

'They won't,' he said. 'I'll have their hides if they do.'

But they did.

Two years after the fall of Velis, and on the most desperate mission of his life, Padry the chancellor returned at last to Develin.

It was a strange feeling, rather terrible indeed, to ride up the river road and see the long white line of the outer wall and the buildings around the upper courtyard, as if nothing had changed in all that time. In the old days he had made many homecomings like this, returning from Jent or Pemini or Tuscolo with new books for the Widow's library or new scholars for her school. Now he came with the sun banner of Gueronius over his head, six men-at-arms at his back and the seal of the lord chancellor in his pouch. And before him was Develin, just as it had been, just as if his fellow masters – Pantethon, Grismonde, Denke and the rest of them – would be there to greet him as he rode into the courtyard, and the old Widow herself still waiting for him on her throne.

The red-and-white banners flew over the gates. The guards wore the same checked red-and-white tabards and they sounded the gate-horns in the same way. But the faces were different. Padry looked into the eyes of the gate-sergeants who asked him gruffly what his business was. They were strangers. The men he had known had perished in the sack seven years before. So had almost everyone else.

The Widow they had killed in this very courtyard, he thought as he dismounted at last in the upper bailey. Grismonde, white-bearded Grismonde, they had cut down at his altar in the chapel over there. Denke had thrown himself from his own window as they had broken down his door. Pantethon? He had a mental image of Pantethon lying somewhere, with his favourite peacock-blue-and-gold doublet all soaked in his own blood. He could not remember where it had been. The scholars, the servants, the officers of the house, even the animals . . .

The courtyard was busy. There were scholars, servants, animals, all doing as they always had done in this place. They were not the ones he had known.

The keep and the hall towered over him. Their outlines were familiar, yet at once he was aware of changes that were both subtle and real. The old hall roof had sagged in two places. Now it did not. And the tiles, though weathered, were no longer the old dingy brown that he remembered. All that side of the upper courtyard had been burned in the sack. The roof had been replaced since. Presumably the floors of the living quarters had been, too.

The school was unchanged – a plain rectangular building, jutting into the courtyard. At his back rose the Wool Tower, also unchanged. There, in the big guardroom chimney, he had hung for hours with his eyes weeping from the faint fumes and his heart jumping every time someone entered the room below. His muscles and fingers had screamed to be released, until all his world had shrunk to the simple, agonizing battle between body and mind. Even now, looking up at the blunt circular shape of the tower, he imagined that he could still feel those pains: the torture of Develin, and the torture of Thomas Padry as he hung in the soot.

Sweating, he wiped his brow on his sleeve. His memories disturbed him. At the same time the thought of his mission gnawed at him. He was agitated, more than he should be.

41

'Tell your mistress that the King's lord chancellor begs for an audience as soon as may be,' he huffed to the gate-guard.

'Yes, sir.'

'*Now*, man. At the run!' He turned to his escort. 'Go to the stables. Find us fresh horses. You may drink and unbuckle, but be ready to ride again as soon as I appear.'

'How long, sir?'

'Heaven knows. But not long, I hope.'

And that was all he could do. All, except to calm himself as far as he could, and wait.

He took himself to the old school building. Automatically his feet climbed the stair to the first floor where the library of Develin was housed. The library was the same: a long chamber with rows and rows of great open cupboards and a passageway down the middle. The scholars at the benches looked up as he entered. Their eyes held no recognition. He was a stranger here. Yet some of the best hours of his life had been spent in this very room. He paced fretfully up and down, peering at the books chained to their places. Some were new. Others were like old friends whom he was seeing again after years of exile, and yet with no time to renew their acquaintance. Some, indeed, were ones he himself had recovered from Tuscolo or Velis, where they had been taken by the men who had pillaged Develin. Yet others were still missing. There were many gaps in the shelves.

A woman's voice sounded in the stairwell behind him. Footsteps were approaching – dozens of footsteps, crossing the landing from the living quarters. They were entering the library in a great bustle. Students were rising from the benches, startled by the sudden invasion. He turned.

'Well! Thomas Padry!' cried the Lady of Develin as her councillors crowded in behind her. Padry bowed. She came to take his hand.

'Now I give thanks to Michael that he has guarded you,' she said formally. 'And to Raphael, for he has guided your way. For you are safe come. Padry, I could hardly believe it when they told me you were here.'

'Nevertheless, my lady, it is true. And I am grateful indeed that you are able to receive me.'

He straightened and looked at her.

She was the same. She might have been just that bright, fair, wilful sixteen-year-old who had driven him to exasperation twice a week seven years ago. The Lady Sophia Cataline diCoursi Develin. The same, except that like her mother before her she now wore black.

And . . . He looked more closely.

There was – perhaps – the slightest fullness to her face, the slightest strengthening of her features, that hinted at a much greater strength within. This was no longer a girl who was becoming a woman. This was a woman in full. There was steel in her now. (Perhaps there was too much. But how could it be otherwise?) And there was something else in the way she looked at him, pleased but wistful, which hinted at a quality he did not remember. He knew it at once. That was grief: grief for all of lost Develin, and also for a man who had died.

Grief, too, at the passing of the years.

'You are older, Padry.'

'Less fat, but more grey,' he said, smiling ruefully. 'And a martyr to my teeth, my lady.'

'You are great in the Kingdom, too.'

'Not that. I am suffered to use my skills for one who has them not, but who has become great in spite of it.'

'Indeed. And is it for his sake that you are here? I presume so.'

Padry spread his hands disarmingly. 'I cannot say so much, my lady. It is more on my own account. I have brought – a gift.'

'A gift? Oh, Padry! Have you found another? Have you?'

Padry's smile broadened a little. 'Not just any other, my lady.'

He had carried it here himself because he would trust no other with it. Now he took it from his satchel reverently, and lifted it in both hands. The council of Develin – all men in rich doublets – clustered round to see. He saw their eyes and heard their indrawn breath. They knew at once that its value was immense. Its vellum pages were made from the hides of three hundred calves – a princely sum by itself. But the worth of the words written on them was far more.

'It's Croscan's book!' said someone.

'It is the Arc of the Descent,' breathed Padry. '*The Path of Signs Illuminating the Arc of the Descent of the Spirit.* "The First Sign is Fire. Fire is bright, and yet it is formless, ever-changing. It gives light, and light is truth. Therefore . . ."'

' "Therefore Fire is a sign to us of Heaven, of the unknowable Godhead that lies beyond the world," ' said the lady. 'How you dinned it into me! And where did you find it, Padry? Where was it?'

'It was in Velis, as we supposed. Forgive me that I have not returned it sooner. I have had copies made so that it is no longer the only one. Now it is my privilege to bring it home.' And he passed it to her.

She took it, and turned it in her hands. 'We are more grateful than we can say. But – the other volume, Padry? The Ascent?'

Padry shrugged. 'Alas. Some other looter must have taken it. We must go on looking.'

'They *separated* the two? How could they?'

'Ignorance, my lady.'

Quite possibly the brute men who had squabbled over the loot of Develin had not been able to read at all. To them a book was a book, valuable, sellable, but no more. (I'll have *this* one, you have *that* one, and you can have the pretty dress off the woman who we—) So one half of the great work of the sage Croscan, describing the descent of the sparks of Godhead from the very highest to the very lowest order of creation, had been found. But its companion volume, which told how each spark then yearned upwards, guiding the soul on its long path to reunion with Godhead, was still lost and might be lost for ever. And without it the book in the lady's hands held only half of the truth. Less than half, for in its final chapter the Path reached the Abyss, the last place of all where the soul should leave it, for in the Abyss all hope was lost and faithfulness was brought to nothing.

Padry had known the Abyss, here in Develin before the end. He had returned to it more than once in the grim years that followed. And now he was near to it again, treading on the very lip, refusing to look down only because he knew that it was there.

'We must continue to hope, my lady. We *must*,' he said.

She looked at him. He realized that he had spoken with more emphasis even than the fate of the lost work might justify. To cover himself, he added, 'If all else fails I could write it from memory – if I had the time.'

'You may be the last man in the Kingdom who could. And yet . . . time is so precious, is it not? Especially for the King's chancellor.' She passed the book to a man who stood behind her. 'Padry, you shall sit at my right hand at table tonight. We will talk of happy memories. And – of anything you wish.'

Ah, Sophia! No longer the pupil! He had dangled the great work of Croscan before her eyes and she had not been fooled. Chancellors did not come long distances just to return stolen goods. Any gift they brought would just be an excuse, or more likely a bribe. *We shall talk of anything you wish.* So, Thomas Padry, you want something. It shows in your face and your voice. What is it? Why are you really here?

He coughed. 'There is, um . . .'

She waited for him.

'. . . a matter on which I would speak in private. And as soon as may be.'

She raised an eyebrow. Then she looked around at

46

the staring scholars and at the councillors behind her.

'Very well,' she said.

She led them all out of the library, across the stair-well and down the passage to the keep and the living quarters. The corridor was busy. People crowded out of the lady's way and stared at Padry as he passed. Guards saluted. An elderly, round man in a rich doublet waited at the antechamber door.

'My lady—'

'I am occupied, Hob. Is it Gisbore?'

'It is the bailiff from Gisbore.'

She looked around at the expectant faces of the men who had followed her and gave a little exasper-ated sigh. 'Beg him to wait yet a quarter-hour. The lord chancellor himself has come to see me.'

'Very good. And the council?'

'The council must wait also.'

'Very good, my lady.'

They withdrew. The guard opened the door to the antechamber. A maid was in there, making up the fire.

'Leave us,' said the lady.

The maid went. At a jerk of the lady's head the guard followed her. Padry looked around the room that had once been the centre of his world. The tapestries had changed but the new ones had the same red colours as their predecessors. There were the old silver candlesticks. The chair – not the old one, but one much like it – stood in just the right place by the window. Empty.

The Widow's daughter settled herself into it.

'So,' she said, fixing him with a look. 'Shall I guess?

When Orcrim returned from Velis two years ago he brought with him a story of something you had said. You had made a proposal about the King and myself. He was minded to advise me to accept. I must tell you that I was not pleased, either with him or with you.'

Embarrassed, Padry looked at his feet.

'I hope you have not come to revive the possibility, Thomas.'

He shook his head. 'I have not, my lady.' And, a little insistently, he added, 'As I said, it is a private matter.'

'What is it?'

He swallowed. His fists tightened at his sides.

'Where may I find the Hidden King?'

'Who is he, Uncle Thomas?' Atti had asked him.

They had been sitting together in the cloister of the convent in Tuscolo. It had been a warm, late summer day. A pigeon had been cooing somewhere among the orange trees.

'Truly, my dove,' he said absently, 'I do not know. Why do you ask?'

She sat like a little statue beside him, her back rigid. She was even paler than usual today. There were marks below her eyes. Nevertheless it was pleasing to see her: her face framed in her novice's hood, with the fullness of her long black hair in the shadow within. He looked at the delicate curves of her cheeks and lashes and eyes and his mind played with thoughts such as: *O Powers that framed the Dome of Heaven/No greater work didst then or now/Than trap the* (something)

48

starlight's glisten/And set it on a child's brow! (Well – some work needed perhaps, but in moments such as these he felt nearer to poetry than at any other time of his day.) It was a while before he realized that she had not answered him.

'Why do you ask, my dove?'

'He spoke to me,' she said.

'Oh? When?'

'Last night, when I was asleep.'

'I see. Do you want to tell me about it?'

'No.'

No. She never did.

'I'm sorry you still have nightmares,' he said. 'You must try to remember that you are safe. No one here will harm you.'

She said nothing. Her face was solemn, her thoughts secret. Brown eyes, pale skin, all in the dark surround of the hood – what did her young mind see when it turned in on itself so? Something was in there, some idea or plan forming in her brain. It might be a new way of avoiding the attentions of the convent mothers. It might be some revenge upon another girl, for something silly or spiteful that had been done. And one day soon it would become action. He knew her well enough to be sure of that. But she would not share it with him until it did.

Poor thing, he thought. She needed comforting, yet it was always difficult to comfort her. He said nothing but reached across to take her hand.

In the cloisters the hillwoman maid Gadi was coughing – a light, plaintive sound. They had told him that Gadi was not well these days. She was often feverish and lay in bed. Nevertheless she seemed to have dragged herself from her pallet and put on her convent servant's gown to come and watch over them. That was proper, he supposed.

It was quite unnecessary of course. He would never dream of harming Atti. But it was proper all the same.

He pointed upwards. 'Look,' he said.

Above them, hard against the blue of the sky, the walls and roofs of Tuscolo castle rose one above another to the keep, where the banners of Gueronius hung in the windless air.

'Count along from the end of the big hall-building. One, two, three windows. That's mine. That's the room in which I work. I'm always there, looking over you.'

'Yes, I know,' she said.

'So you are quite safe, you see.'

Her hand rested in his own like a thing with no life. 'This one wasn't a nightmare,' she muttered.

'That's better then, isn't it? No more screaming in the night, eh?'

He looked at her anxiously, wondering if the convent mothers were still beating her each time she woke the dormitories. By the Angels! If they were, after all he had had to say on the subject, he'd make them wish they had paid better attention! Convents were convents and rules were rules, but there were things a chancellor could do with his pen that made even bishops tremble.

'No,' she said.

'That's better, then. Even so . . .' he mused. 'Cloisters may cloy, orders be odious and nuns none. I have been wondering if this is the best place for you. I do not think you are happy here. I will look around for something better. There is never any space up at the castle but – well, maybe you could lodge with me for a while.'

She did not answer. Behind those beautiful cheeks and lashes her face showed nothing. Maybe her hand tensed a little and pulled slightly against his fingers, but that was only Atti being Atti. He held her wrist, leaned back and looked at the sky. Really, these visits to the convent were the only oasis in his waking hours. Up there in the castle, behind that impassive façade, all his time and energy was given to others. All the muttering and copying and scurrying – all the piles of paper heaving on his tables within! In a few minutes, just a few minutes, he must be back to it. Heigh-ho! One day, maybe, the King would appoint him Bishop of Tuscolo, or Jent, or one of the other great sees. He could take the vows, have a tonsure and become not only a priest but a prince overnight. It was something to know the worth of what you did, but it would be *nice* to have a reward for it, too.

'Is he here, in the city?' murmured the girl suddenly.

'Who? The Prince Under the Sky? No. If he is real at all, he is on the other side of the lake. Or so I believe.'

'Is it a long way?'

'A very long way, my dove.'

Silence again, in the cooing air. They sat side by side until the bell chimed the hour. He felt her hand slip from his own.

'You must go now,' she said. 'There is a service.'

She said it as though it were an instruction. But, alas, it was indeed time to go. The King's business waited for no one.

'Yes,' he said. 'Cheer up. I will come again to-morrow, and we will talk some more about where we might place you.'

And he had come, smuggling some forbidden sweetmeats in the folds of his robe. Rules were rules, but he had wanted to see her smile.

He had come, but she had not been there.

The Lady of Develin searched his face. 'She *dreamed* of him?'

'So it appears. We could find none among the sisters or servants who had spoken to her of him.' Not though the convent mothers had plied their canes with a will.

'And now she has run off in search of him.' She frowned at the fire. Her fingers were drumming on an arm of the chair. 'I find this disturbing. For more than one reason.'

Padry nodded. 'You see the urgency of my mission.'

'My reasons may not be yours. This dream – what did she see?'

'I know only that she thought he spoke with her.'

'And what does Gueronius know of this?'

'The King? Nothing, my lady. He is in Velis.'

'So I had heard – and this disturbs me also! The Kingdom is barely won. Two summers of peace do not make men forget war. Yet the King plays shipwright and dreams of adventure beyond the seas. Is it true he will captain this expedition he plans?'

'Oh,' said Padry (noting how firmly she had changed the subject), 'we will persuade him from it, my lady. The Kingdom cannot afford his absence.'

'It cannot. I hear he would make the lords Joyce and Seguin co-regents in his absence. We would have power struggles and blood spilled within six months of his going. Such . . . *folly* in a man for whom I have given the lives of my soldiers! The Kingdom cannot be his plaything, to be left on the shelf while he amuses himself with other toys! It tries me, Thomas. And it tries me that you do not see it so! You should be there, not here. You are the one man he has the wit to listen to for more than a minute at a time!'

'I *will* go to him, my lady,' he said soothingly. 'As soon as I have finished—'

'Thomas Padry!' she cried.

Padry jumped.

'Do you forget what men are? After what you have seen in this very house? And I have been giving thanks every evening that it is you who advises the King! But now I see you have dropped your pen and run off in a direction opposite to the one in which you are most needed – on a goose-chase here in the south after some brat of a dead lord! Men have not changed in two summers, Thomas. Feud breaks out like pox wherever I look. Faul's men raided a village of mine last month – under this King's peace! Must I go to war with Faul because neither King nor chancellor can tear themselves from their fancies?'

'All men know the value of peace, my lady—'

'Do they? Yet they take up iron whenever there is dispute. We are cursed with it – cursed by Heaven, and blessed with too few who are willing to heal it!'

Padry was shocked by the blasphemy. 'My lady,' he said slowly. 'If you ask me from my heart, I say that I do not believe we are cursed. Although I do believe that we must know evil as well as good, so that we may know the difference when we go to the Angels. It would be a terrible crime to return to Paradise as innocent as when we were sent from it.'

'A dry answer, sir. I thought your heart had grown since you left this house.'

'I hope that it has, my lady. But it still tells me the same. As for my request to you . . .'

He noted the flicker in her eyes as he returned to the subject she had avoided.

'. . . I can only say that it is of *great* importance. I ask for your trust in this.'

'A matter of state? Yet you have not spoken to the King of it.'

'You will forgive me for my presumption, my lady. I had thought that I might more readily obtain your help if I came to you in secret. And also if I promised you that I would neither harm this "Hidden King" nor tell anyone else of his whereabouts, so long as I might safely return with the child.'

'You have not lost all your wits, then,' she said.

You have not lost all your wits. That was her mother, indeed!

She was looking at him, thinking. He waited.

'You realize that there is every chance she will die on her journey? Indeed that she may already be dead?'

Another diversion. He shrugged it off. 'Perhaps not. There is some hope. Her maid accompanied her. They stole provisions from the convent kitchens and a mule from the stables.'

'So. But her chance of finding the one she is looking for is that of finding a feather in straw.'

'I think – it will depend on whether her dreams were more than mere dreams,' he said carefully.

Silence.

'Say what you mean, Thomas.'

'*Witchcraft*, my lady.'

He should have guessed it. The moment Atti had spoken of a dream that had not been one of her nightmares, he should have been alert. He should have put the thought of this Hidden King, who might be somewhere in Tarceny, together with the memory that in past days Tarceny had dealt with black evil. Vexed by the hundred daily urgencies of the King's court, he had not – until it was too late. The thought of that failure was like a goad. It had burned in him all the way here, to the one person he could think of who might tell him what he needed. And she had leaped at him, not when she had heard that he had a mission but when she had learned what that mission was. That confirmed his thought. The Lady of Develin knew something that was dangerous to speak of.

What do you know, my lady, and how? And how far will you trust me, Thomas Padry, whom your mother would have trusted to the death?

Out in the passage he heard the murmur of voices, the shuffle of feet. Familiar sounds: councillors waiting to be admitted, swapping whispered guesses about what it was that had brought the lord chancellor so far to the south. Beyond them rose all the other noises of the castle: feet on boards overhead, horses in the courtyard, a harsh voice calling something to someone, the drone of the breeze in the open casement. Two hundred people had made their living under the old Widow's roof. It did not seem to be less than that now. And he stood eye to eye with the Widow's daughter, and the shadow of witchcraft was between them.

'I think it possible that you are right,' she said at last.

'And this . . .' She sighed. 'This is what disturbs me most of all. Not for your sake or hers, but for his.'

'Then you do know of him?'

'Yes, I do. And yes, I suppose he may know where this child is.'

Her fingers tapped the arm of her chair, once, twice.

'I have your promise that you mean him no harm?'

'Absolutely, my lady. My life on it!'

'Good, Thomas. But have you a man you can trust for this? Someone you can trust as much as I am trusting you? I should warn you that the road may be harder than you would think possible.'

He thought, and nodded. 'I have. One, only. But yes.'

'For you must *not* go, Thomas. That is my condition. You must return yourself to Gueronius. *He* is your duty. Each day that passes without you at his side is dangerous for all of us. Your conscience should tell you that, but if it does not prick you then let me be the other spur. This house has suffered enough from the whims of kings – as you know.'

'My lady, I know. And I will go.'

'As swiftly as you can, Thomas. I shall not sleep well until I know you are in Velis.'

'Trust me, my lady,' he said, and bowed.

His conscience did prick him then. It told him that if he were truly the just man he thought himself to be, the man who trod squarely in the centre of the Path, he would draw breath, risk all, and tell her plainly that although he would join Gueronius as soon as he could, he would not do so at once. Because the man he had spoken of, the one man whom he would trust to go to the Hidden King, was himself. There was no other.

He said nothing.

IV

The Haunted Knight

elissa dreamed a wonderful dream of food.

She could smell it: a beautiful stewy smell, steaming in the hut where Mam (yes, Mam alive and well and smiling) was stirring it with a ladle. Everything was warmth and bright colours.

Can I have it now? she begged. *I'm so hungry.*

Soon, said Mother, and smiled, and stirred the pot (thick with rich bits of meat and carrots and herbs!). *It will be very soon.*

Please! begged Melissa, reaching for the ladle. There was fresh bread on the table, crusty and smelling like honey. Mam just smiled again.

Then – Melissa did not notice the change, but there must have been one – she was no longer in the hut. She was in a landscape of brown rocks under a dull sky. She could not smell the stew any more. Two people were watching her, a little way off among the stones.

There, said one (a hunched figure, indistinct in robes and a great hood). *By the path in the forest.* The voice was so deep that the ground beneath her ear seemed to tremble with it.

The other was a tall young man with a long face and dark, curling hair. Melissa thought she knew him. But he seemed so much older than she remembered.

Who is she? he asked.

One who is looking for you, the deep voice answered.

The young man picked his way among the stones and knelt down beside her. He looked closely at her. *You should eat,* he said.

I don't have any food, she thought.

Where is your home? he asked.

I don't have one any more.

He frowned. He seemed to understand what had happened. He seemed to understand it better than she did.

Please, she thought. I'm trying to find you. But I don't know where you are.

Who did this? the King said, still frowning.

She could not tell him.

Did they wear a badge? A sign?

Red, she whispered. And she heard her own voice in her dream. *Their things were red.*

The young man looked up at his companion. *Bavar's folk,* he said. *Again.*

The hunched figure loomed over them. It was not a man or a woman. A face like a mask peered out of the hood. A mouth, which seemed impossibly wide, moved to speak.

She will die, said the deep voice. *Do you want me to bring her to you?*

If she is weak, said the King, *your journey might kill her anyway.*

Perhaps.

In one swift movement the King rose to his feet. He seemed to fill the Heaven above her, a creature of tremendous lightness and power. She saw how his fists had clenched at his sides. She saw the lines of his face, dark and clear against the sky.

I have a better idea, he exclaimed. *Show Bavar to me instead!*

The companion bowed. Melissa looked up at the King and he looked down on her. *Hold on,* he told her. *We are coming.*

Then they, too, were gone. And so were the brown rocks, and so were the sounds and warmth and smells. She was lying by the trackside where she had fallen yesterday. Her body was chilled to the bone. She felt too weak to lift herself. The pains in her eyes and head had come back again.

She lay there because she could do nothing else. It had been days since she had run from her home. Days and days of wandering in circles from the smoking hut, where Mam lay stripped by the stream side and Dadda had been hanged by a rope from the tree.

Padry dreamed of petitions, and the morning brought them for real. It brought them with the sound of hoofs in mud and a man dismounting. The door to the little pilgrim house opened and Lex – his own assistant Lex, who should have been thirty leagues away in Tuscolo –

flung into the low room where Padry and his escort were having their breakfast.

At once he banged his head on a beam and dropped to his knees, cursing.

'Rise, my boy,' said Padry peaceably. 'Your sins are forgiven.'

Lex dragged himself to the bench. 'Am I bleeding?' he asked, examining his fingers.

'Not yet. For which we may be grateful. You have enough mud on you to displease my host as it is.'

'Angels!' groaned the young man, still feeling his head. 'This comes of riding all night.'

'I am a little surprised to see you here, indeed. How did you find us?'

'Hither and thither. At Develin they said you had returned to Tuscolo, but I had come down that road and knew you were not on it. So I looked further. I have woken every village between here and the river by banging on doors in the small hours.'

'Hum. I am also surprised that you risk the roads alone and in the dark. What is the matter?'

Lex opened a satchel and drew out a paper. He handed it across to Padry. 'Lord Joyce demands an answer before the end of the week,' he said. 'And he will take no satisfaction from me.'

Padry sighed. 'Lord Joyce? I re-Joyce to hear from him,' he said. 'In return I bequeath you my breakfast, since I guess you have had none of your own.' He pushed his half-finished bowl of broth across to his subordinate. His body groaned at him, *That was mine!* But he bridled his hunger as a just man should. The

61

innkeeper might or might not have more to offer, but there was no doubt where the greater need lay.

'My thanks,' said Lex, and fell on it.

'So,' said Padry, scanning the paper, 'it is on behalf of his man Delverdis, who claims rights over the market at Pemini, is that it?'

'Exactly.'

'And is there a counter-petition from Pemini?'

'Not yet. No doubt it is on its way to us, citing ancient rights and freedoms and charters. You could write the sort of thing in your head.'

'I could. I was born in Pemini. Didn't you know that?'

Lex shook his head vigorously. His mouth was full. When he could speak, he said: 'I never asked myself where you came from.'

'You thought I had sprung full-formed from a library bookshelf, I suppose. But I was a child of muddy alleys, just like you. Glad indeed to leave them. And yes . . .' He frowned at the page. 'Yes, Delverdis had some rights, as I remember. But this! This is pure theft!'

'Will you say that to Lord Joyce?'

Padry sucked his cheeks. 'He will protest to the King, who will give him whatever he asks simply to be rid of him. We must be more cunning.'

He knitted his brows over the petition, trying to think his way back to the chancery of Tuscolo and to the busy wharves of Pemini far beyond.

After a minute or so he sat back and put his heels on the table. He had a theory that this tilted the blood to the brain and so helped him to think better. It was certainly more comfortable.

Pemini, a town beginning to grow back to its former wealth. A greedy lord. A long history. Two years ago this would have been settled with knives. Now at least they were sending to the King first, to see if they could get their way without the trouble. But the knives were still there. They were everywhere, as the Lady of Develin had said. If either side thought it had lost too much in the judgement, or even if they grew tired of waiting, the iron would be out in an instant. And Thomas Padry, former schoolmaster, regretting his lost breakfast in a wayside inn, had the key to lock the iron away.

He scratched his head. Well, he *ought* to have it. But he was badly placed, like a piece in the wrong part of a chessboard. He needed to be with the King when the judgement was given, to forestall any appeal. Right now Gueronius and he were almost at opposite ends of the Kingdom. And he was moving further away.

'Nothing for it,' he sighed. 'We must play for time.'

Lex, mouth full, raised an eyebrow. Yes, even that was dangerous. It needed just one young hot-head on either side to take matters into his hands and then the blood would be flowing. The parties could not just be told to be patient. They had to be given something to be patient for.

'We will appoint a panel of "right men" to judge the matter. Of which I will be one. And we will set a date. Ho, there!' he called over his shoulder to the kitchen. 'Are there such things as pen and ink in this house?'

Wordlessly, Lex produced an ink bottle and a quill from his satchel.

'Thank you,' said Padry again. He turned the petition over and began to write on the back of it.

'I have paper, too,' said Lex.

Padry shook his head and went on writing. 'Let us spare our king's coffers another coin. He will need every groat for his shipwrights. Are there more matters like this a-waiting?'

'They arrive every day. Some have already come to blows. But only Lord Joyce, so far, has put his dagger between my eyes to have me make haste. When will we have you back in Tuscolo?'

'I must join the King as soon as I am done here.'

'But at least you can pass by us. When will you be done?'

'Oh, I should think . . .' Padry looked at his thumbs. 'Perhaps in a week.'

'A week!' Lex rolled his eyes.

'You forget yourself,' said Padry coldly.

'Your pardon,' said Lex. 'If I forget myself, it is because I remember things as I have left them. May I at least ask what the business is?'

'You may ask, but I may or may not answer.'

'It's the Baldwin child, isn't it? I know that much. But why does it have to be you, personally?'

'Because I, personally, understand the importance of the case,' said Padry harshly. 'Also I have some idea how to pursue it.'

'I see.'

Lex's eyes were full of questions. Padry clamped his jaw firmly shut.

'Very well,' sighed Lex, pushing the empty bowl away. 'At least tell me where you go from here.'

'I must be in Lackmere tonight.'

'Lackmere? Do you know the way?'

'Is it hard?'

'It is thorn-forest. Easy to lose the path.'

'Excellent!' said Padry. 'Can you lead us there?'

'I can. I will, if it means we get you back sooner. What about Lord Joyce?'

'We will send three of my men back with this. That will leave us another three for the rest of our journey. It is not many, I know. But while we are so near to Develin, the roads should be safe. After that we must put our trust in the Angels.'

'Amen.'

Melissa was still lying beneath the tree. Her world had shrunk to the few square inches of ground that she could see with her eye, and to the aches of hunger and cold. A beetle heaved itself over a dead twig and was lost to sight behind her fist. An ant, or something, was crawling across her cheek. She lay still. In her fingers she held a leaf, dropped from a branch up above. It was broad and green, and the edges were crinkled. Some time after her hand had closed on it she realized that it was an oak leaf. She went on holding it even though it seemed to be difficult for her fingers to grip anything any more.

She was lying with her ear against the ground. So she heard the horse long before she saw it. She heard it like a steady, dull thudding in the earth, which slowly became louder and clearer and crisper, so that she could hear the edges of the sound, the click of pebbles and the squelch of mud. Her hearing was so much better than her sight now. She could pick out the squeak of leather and the jingle of harness, the blowing of the horse, the flap of a pennant in the wind.

She saw it.

It was a great brown animal with a man on its back, pounding up the narrow path along which no one had come for days. What were they doing here? The horse was caked with dried sweat, like flecks of stale foam.

It stopped, blowing hard. The rider must have stopped it. He looked up and saw the oak. He looked around. He was searching for something. It seemed to be very important to him to find it.

His eyes fell on her. She knew him.

Him!

She knew the big blond beard, like a spade. She knew the red vest over his armour and the red pennant on the end of his lance. This was one of the men who had attacked her house. This was the one who had stood at the edge of the woods with his bow, shooting arrows after her and laughing as she dodged between the trunks, while the others had hauled Dadda into the tree.

Her brain yelped. Urgent messages went to her legs and hands, begging them to get up, to push her off the ground, to run, run, run, as she had run all those days before. Nothing happened. Her limbs were heavy and barely stirred.

Again she tried. *He's getting off his horse. He's coming over!*

Her arm moved, a fraction.

He was standing over her. He was fumbling at his belt. She turned her head, just a little, to look up at him. There was a knife in its sheath.

'N-n—' she said.

He frowned and knelt down beside her. There was nothing she could do.

Maybe she would see Mam again now.

Something popped – a bung, coming out of a bottle.

'Drink,' said the man.

He was holding it before her lips – a water bottle. She could smell it. Suddenly she knew how thirsty she was.

'Drink,' said the man, more urgently. 'You must drink.'

I can't drink while I'm lying down, she thought.

He seemed to see that. Setting the bottle on the earth, he took her by both shoulders and propped her against the trunk of the tree. Then he lifted it again and poured it gingerly at her mouth. Water splashed on her lips and down her front. She caught a gulp of it and choked.

'Not too much,' grumbled the man.

She put a trembling hand on the bottle, steadied it against her lips and drank some more. Again she choked. She lost her hold and between them they dropped it. The man muttered angrily and returned the bottle to his belt. He stood up, looking down at her. She wondered if he would get out his bow and arrows again and tell her to run through the trees. She knew she could not run. She did not think she could even crawl.

He reached up to his shoulder and undid the brooch that held the red cloak. He put it round her. It was warm from his body. He picked her up and slung her over his shoulder.

'You stink,' he said.

So do you, she thought, with her head hanging down against his back.

He carried her to his horse. Again she felt herself lifted, up and across its shoulders. Her face was against its hide. Her head, upside down, seemed a horrible distance above the ground. The man climbed up behind her.

'He says we must go to him,' grunted the man. 'Both of us, together.'

'For all the Angels!' cursed Padry. 'Where are they then?'

Again the man-at-arms banged at the castle door.

'Ho there! Lackmere! Open for the lord chancellor!'

There was no answer from inside.

Night was coming early. Heavy, dry clouds hung low over the land, dimming the light to a feeble yellow in the west. Already the details of the thorn forest out of which they had climbed were dissolving into shadow. The rocks of the crag on which Lackmere stood were a dull grey-brown, and the walls of the castle were the same grey-brown colour, rising above their heads to a line of battlements and squat towers against the gloomy sky.

The man-at-arms set his shoulder against the gate.

'It is barred from within,' he grunted. 'There must be someone inside. Unless they are drunk, or dead now.'

The castle was a single enclosure, constrained by the narrow hilltop on which it was sited. Surely no one inside could fail to hear them. But there were no lights, and no banners on the walls. To left and right the gate towers peered down on them. Black arrow-slits showed nothing within.

'Try it again.'

'Ho, Lackmere . . .'

Lex was looking out over the shadowy waste like a shipwrecked sailor at the sea.

'It is wolf country,' he said. 'If we camp, we must hobble the horses.'

'There's someone coming,' said a man-at-arms.

Padry held his breath. Yes, unmistakably, there was someone coming after all. A long, slow step sounded from within, approaching. It reached the door and paused.

'Who is there?' a voice said through the boards.

There was something indistinct about the words. Padry wondered whether the speaker was indeed drunk.

'I am Thomas Padry, Chancellor to the King,' he answered.

There was silence inside.

'I do not know you,' said the voice.

'Bones of Angels!' exploded Padry. 'Will you leave us to the wolves? I tell you I am the King's lord chancellor! And I bear letters from Develin!'

Again there was silence behind the door.

From above their heads another voice spoke.

'Let them in, Highness.'

Padry looked up. No head showed there against the sky: only the silent battlements, and the slow clouds drawing by, so close, it seemed, that they must scrape themselves against the flagless poles above the towers.

Clunk! went the door bars, reluctantly. A black crack split the gate from top to bottom. It widened. Nobody bid them enter. A curious, watery smell flowed out from inside.

Muttering an oath, Padry shouldered through the narrow gap and into the darkness of the gate-tunnel. There was a figure there, a tall man, standing in the shadow behind the door. Instinctively Padry stepped away from him. He retreated further to make way for Lex and the men-at-arms as they coaxed the horses into the strange-smelling place. The tall figure swung the gate to and dropped the bar again.

'We ask for lodging for the night, and an audience with the master of the house,' said Padry. 'In the King's name.'

'The master of the house is not here,' said the figure, in the same slurry voice. He did not seem at all impressed by the name of the King.

'To whom may I address myself, then?' said Padry. 'You?'

'His son will attend you.'

70

The figure pushed past them in the darkness. Again Padry stepped away, repelled by the dank smell that seemed to flow from him. The tall man led them out into a small courtyard. In the light of the fading day Padry saw that he wore a great closed tilting-helm that completely hid his face, and a ragged cloak that dropped all the way to the ground. His movements seemed slow but he covered the ground in great, stalking strides. Padry and his followers hurried after him, stumbling across the uneven paving.

'You may stable your horses in there,' said the doorman. He pointed a long arm – it seemed incredibly long – towards a low, dark building. 'Then you may go up to the keep. I will see that they have hay and water.'

There were no lights in the courtyard. There was no sound of any man or animal, other than the strange doorman. Padry squinted in the dimness. The castle was a mean place. Walls bulged with age. The spaces were narrow. He thought the roofs were in poor repair.

'What about my men?' he asked.

'They should go up, too.'

'Is there no watch? No guardroom?'

'No.'

The castle seemed almost deserted. Padry and his followers felt their way into the rude stable and found that it held only two horses, shifting and snorting in a line of stalls that could have accommodated ten. Dull light filtered in through gaps in the roof where slates were missing. They tethered their mounts, patted them and removed their harness, all

71

in the near darkness. Then they returned to the dim courtyard. The doorman had disappeared. In the keep a light was burning.

'Come on,' said Padry as his men hesitated.

A narrow flight of steps led up the outside of the keep to a door at the first storey. The door was open. Firelight and lamplight glowed from inside. Padry led the way in.

He stood in a square chamber, the full width and length of the keep. There was a fire in a big hearth and a trestle table set near to it with places laid. Other tables and benches were stacked against the walls. The room was hung with arms and hunting trophies – antlers and wolfskins.

Two men were crouching by the fire. One was the doorman, still in his cloak and his great helm. He was feeding vegetables into a pot that hung on the hearth. The other rose as they entered.

'Welcome, in my father's name,' he said. 'I am Raymonde diLackmere. I have charge of this house until my father returns.'

He was a short man with straggling brown hair and slanting brows. He wore a faded doublet and a knight's belt. His cheeks would have been clean-shaven after the fashion of the provinces, but he had allowed the stubble to grow for some days. His tone and stance offered no welcome, whatever his mouth said. And he did not bother to invoke the Angels.

His face, sour and triangular, tugged at Padry's memory. Yes, he looked like the Baron of Lackmere, whom Padry had met once or twice in his Develin days. But it was not only that . . .

'We are grateful to you and your father,' Padry said. 'Will your father return tonight?'

The man smiled bitterly. 'He has not set foot in his house for a half-dozen years.'

A half-dozen years: the words were spoken as if they were all the explanation Padry should need. Again, Padry struggled with his memory. There had been something, some evil thing that had happened here. There had been . . . there had been *two* sons. And one had killed the other, and . . .

'Angels' Knees!' exclaimed Padry. He stared at the man in front of him.

This was the brother-killer! And not only that . . .

'You – I have seen you before,' he stammered. 'You were one of Velis's men! You were at the sack of Develin!'

The man's face had hardened. 'I was,' he said.

As Padry fought for words, the man shrugged. 'I counselled him to do it,' he said.

'You have a letter for me,' he added, when Padry could not speak. 'From my Lady Develin.'

His hand was out. Padry stared at it. He could not look at the man's face. He could not see the room. His eyes were fixed by that hand – that hand that had killed the man's own brother. The hand that had done – what? to whom? – at Develin. He thought of Grismonde and Pantethon and Denke – all that learning lost, all those scholars, those young men of promise! And the Widow, too, and all her folk, dead in the senseless, shameful wreck of old Develin. *I counselled him to do it.*

The hand was held before him for the words of Develin's daughter.

'I was not told this,' he muttered.

'You said you had a letter.'

'Not that. Not that,' he said.

The road may be harder than you would think possible, she had said.

'Give him the letter,' he mumbled to Lex.

He turned and walked to the wall. His head seemed to be singing. He heard the rustle of paper being handed over. He heard the seal being broken – a light, slight sound. He put his hand out to steady himself. His palm touched – not stone, but fur. He looked up. A wolf mask, dried and pinned to the wall with rusty nails, grinned back at him.

'She writes only that the bearer of this letter is looking for the Prince Under the Sky, and that I am to help them if I will,' said the man.

Padry stared at the wolf mask, willing the shock to clear from his brain.

'How has she forgiven you?' His own voice sounded harsh in his ears.

'To tell you the truth,' said Raymond diLackmere with a chuckle, 'I do not know that she has.'

'Good,' said Padry.

'So? But you have come for my help and you have come to my hearth. You may, of course, change your mind and set your fellows on me – if you think they will win. Or you may leave, if you think that will make you better than I am. Or you may break bread with me. I am willing, although we had prepared for two and must now stretch to seven.'

The bristles of the wolfskin were harsh beneath Padry's right palm. The fingers of his left hand had reached instinctively for his belt. They touched the walnut shapes dangling there. They closed on one and knew it. It was the one carved in the shape of the dragon. He gripped it, hard. The philosopher is not slave to passion. The just man keeps his eyes on the Path. As the way darkens he keeps them on it still.

Atti was in the wilderness somewhere, alone, searching. He *must* find her.

He pushed himself away from the wall. Still with his fingers on his sign, he turned to face the man of blood.

'I will stay – and eat with you.'

'I am glad that Talifer's labour is not in vain. Is it ready, Highness?'

'It will serve,' said the doorman.

It was the poorest meal that Padry had ever tasted in such a setting: a watery gruel – *very* watery indeed. It seemed that the doorman had simply added a pail to the pot when he realized that there would be seven to supper. There were lumps of vegetables in it, some of which had barely cooked. There was bread but not much of it. There was cheese and salted meat, which were more welcome. Raymonde diLackmere neither apologized nor asked for thanks for what he had put before them. He sat at the head of the table. Out of rank, Padry was obliged to sit at his right. Lex sat opposite. The three men-at-arms took the lower places. No one spoke.

The doorman served them all. Padry felt himself shrink involuntarily as the man came behind him to reach a skinny arm past his ear. He wondered what facial disfigurement was hidden inside that helm. And what was the fellow called? Talifer! What a princely label for such an unpleasing creature! A name of legend from the first founding of the Kingdom. Perhaps that was why his sour master nicknamed him 'Highness'. In this place all natural order seemed to be upside down.

At length Talifer left the room by the outer door, no doubt to see to the horses. The men-at-arms stared after him. One let out a long breath. Still no one said anything.

Padry stole a glance at the man on his left, at that wolfish face brooding over a bowl at the head of the table. So much evil was there, behind those slanting brows. What good could ever come of him? The man was making no effort to entertain his guests as a host should. The quiet did not seem to trouble him. Did he eat like this in silence, every night? But in a way Padry was glad. He did not think he could have brought himself to converse with this murderer. Let him only learn what he needed, and then he would be gone.

'Sir,' said Lex suddenly.

The knight looked up. 'What's that?'

'Are there no other men in your house?'

'None. No women either, or children. There are men-at-arms quartered in the village, if I need them.'

76

'Strange that you surround yourself with so few, and but one servant.'

'Talifer is no servant,' said Raymonde. 'But of course, it is because of Talifer that – for the present – I do not keep others in the house. They find it hard to endure him.'

'And is he a man?' asked Lex.

Padry looked up sharply. He knew that he had had the same thought, and yet had stifled it. He had stifled it because he had feared what the answer might be.

'Oh yes. He is, mostly. And much more so than he was.'

Lex was watching him. They were all watching him, trying to guess his meaning. The knight grinned as though he were enjoying himself.

'If this is a riddle, I do not understand it,' said Lex.

'He has lived a long while, in another way,' said Raymonde. 'He forgot much, and was changed much. But he did not altogether lose himself. No man will do that this side of death. Now the more that he lives as a man, in the house of a man, and eats men's food, the more he becomes again what he once was. Mind you, he does not *need* to eat. Such a one eats only because it helps him to remember. Although . . . you will have noticed that he prefers not to let you see him at his meal.'

'But what—' began Lex again. Then he broke off. They heard Talifer's long step on the stair outside.

Step, step, step, coming up to the door. Bones of Angels – was he climbing them three at a time?

The door opened. The silence at the table was so

thick Padry was sure that the helmeted man must have felt it as he came in. He was carrying a keg under one arm, and a leather bottle. From the bottle he poured wine for Raymonde, Padry and Lex. From the keg he poured ale for the men-at-arms.

'Thank you,' said Padry, tasting the wine and finding it surprisingly good. He looked up curiously.

The blank eye-slit stared down on him, expressionless.

Nothing more was said until the meal was finished. The men-at-arms were dismissed to sleep in the room below. They went hurriedly, looking over their shoulders.

Once again Talifer poured wine for Raymonde, Padry and Lex. The fire cracked and spat. The wavering light played on the men's faces. The air droned in the high slit windows. Far off some beast (a dog? a wolf?) was giving tongue. The floor creaked as Talifer came to stand behind Raymonde's chair.

Raymonde was looking into his bowl, swilling the wine slowly round and round. Then he sipped it and spoke. 'You wish to find the Prince Under the Sky.'

Padry cleared his throat. 'As swiftly as possible.'

'At this moment I believe he is back in Tarceny.'

'Tarceny!' groaned Lex. 'It is too far.'

'Not too far,' said Padry. But his heart was sinking. (Tarceny? The wasteland that had once been the March of Tarceny was huge. They might spend a month combing it without finding the one they looked for!) 'However, we must hurry. We must reach him as soon as we can.'

'I see.' Raymonde frowned into his bowl. 'This is important?'

'An innocent life depends on it. And much else.'

'I think I understand why you were sent to me,' said Raymonde. 'Well, yes, I may be able to help you. I suppose I should warn you that there is a price, of a sort.'

'Name it,' said Padry wearily.

'Only that you are willing to accept my help.' He looked at Padry and smiled wickedly. 'Which you may not be.'

Padry swallowed. He thought of the burned roofs of Develin. And he thought of a child, in a dull novice's habit, walking in pursuit of a phantom king.

'I am willing,' he said.

'Well done,' said Raymonde, and went back to studying his bowl. Without looking up, he said: 'Highness, you should sit with us.'

Wordlessly, the cloaked and helmeted figure of Talifer settled on the bench a little way down the table. He sat with his head bowed.

'You have heard what these men need?' said Raymonde.

'Yes,' said voice within the helmet.

'You will take them to him?'

The figure hesitated. Then 'Yes,' it said again.

'Why is it not—?' began Padry. Raymonde stilled him with a lifted finger.

'It is a week's journey to the man you are looking for. To where I suppose him to be. Talifer could take you there in a day and find him more surely than I – if you are willing to go with him.'

'How?' said Padry sharply.

'He has a way. I should warn you that it is not a comfortable way. In fact men like you and me should not take it at all, unless we are desperate.'

'Men like . . .? In the Angels' name – then what is he?'

The bowed figure did not answer.

'Highness, I think you should remove your helm,' said Raymonde.

'I do not wish to,' said the voice.

'I know that you do not. But you are bidden to serve and these men need your service. Before they accept your service they must see you as you are.'

For a moment the figure gave no sign. There was no sound but the hiss of the fire. Then, slowly, the figure put its hands to the helm and lifted it.

'Angels!' gasped Lex.

The face that turned towards them was a mask – a living mask, for the eyes that blinked from it were alive and human. And yet . . .

It was long, impossibly long, from crown to chin. And pale, and wrinkled like skin that has been exposed to water. High on either side of the head were great bumps that looked like the wounds left on a cow's head when the horns had been cut from it. The colour of the skin was a slate grey. Around the brow was – of all things – a simple circlet of gold!

Padry forced himself to breathe again. His heart was thumping hard. His fingers had gripped the rough woodwork of the table, and his knuckles were white.

'You are looking at Prince Talifer, son of Wulfram the Seafarer,' said Raymonde harshly. 'One of the seven princes who first founded the Kingdom. Do not despise him. He has lived these past three hundred years in a hell you could not imagine. Only lately has he emerged from it. He will be your guide, if you are willing to follow him.'

'I – I . . .' gasped Padry.

The pale head turned towards him as if Padry were a king passing sentence. And Padry stared at it open-mouthed. Thoughts tumbled in his head: the horror of the thing before him; the names, Talifer and Wulfram, the great names of the Kingdom-founders, linked in the glory of song; and the words of the murderer beside him – *three hundred years in a hell you could not imagine.*

He almost shrieked and fled the room. But as his hands gripped the table, another, stronger image rose in his mind – of Atti, wandering blindly into shadows. It was these things she was groping towards, these things that had suddenly leaped to life in his sight. They were calling her from the darkness. And she was going to them – feeling her way into the pit where nightmare creatures roiled and watched her come . . .

Atti!

His mouth was open. His lungs drew air. As if from far away he heard his own voice speak.

'I – will follow,' he said.

V

Tears

t is witchcraft,' said Lex in the darkness.

'I know,' said Padry.

'The men will not do this.'

Of course they would not. Padry was not sure how he would either. He lay wide-eyed in his blankets on the floor of the hall of Lackmere, which was the only sleeping space the house could afford him. His mind seethed with doubts.

I will follow, he had said, but he could not see the Path.

Atti had gone ahead of him. He would have given his life to save hers. But could he give his soul? Witchcraft! He would have to acknowledge powers that were not the Angels. He was already acknowledging them. He might already be lost. And no power could offer him her soul in return. He was trying to bargain where no bargain could be made. What could he do?

'Will you?' he asked.

Lex stirred in his blankets. By the light of the fire

embers Padry could see his outline, propped on one elbow, looking away into the obscurities of Lackmere. Around them the hall glimmered faintly in the glow from the hearth. There was no sound but the low wind in the wall-slits and passages of the castle.

'I admit I am becoming curious,' mused Lex. 'About this "King" who has no land, no men-at-arms as far as we know, who tells ancient princes to serve murderous knights, and to whom people from all ranks and places go in secret for judgement. I should like to see him, even if it puts my soul in peril.'

'Do you think we are in peril?' (Angels! Why could he not sound as calm as his own assistant?)

Lex's grunt might almost have been a chuckle. 'As a priest, it is my duty to teach that this is the very gravest peril of all. But I wonder. Can witchcraft *never* do good in the sight of the Angels? I do not know. There is peace between Lackmere and Develin, it seems. How was this done? Also the peril to my soul seems somehow less real than the danger to my body if I return to Tuscolo without you. Lord Joyce will want my hide. So, no doubt, will a dozen others. I think I will come.'

'Good. It will be a comfort to me if you do. I confess . . . I do not like this at all. The more I press myself into this thicket, the more its thorns drag at me.' He frowned up at the rafters. 'It was hard, to meet the killer of so many friends.'

'I could tell. I have never seen you go so pale.'

'Do you not feel the same?'

The outline of Lex shrugged. 'Remember I left Develin before the massacre. I had my reasons. Also I have seen many things since. And I do not think our host is at peace with himself.'

Not at peace? cursed Padry in his thoughts. Nor should he be! The man should burn with guilt for the rest of his days. And then he should burn in Hell!

He lay on the hard boards and looked up at the ember-glow on the ceiling. Everything seemed impossible. It seemed impossible that he should be here – fat old Thomas Padry, staring at his enemy's roof, unbelieving of the things he had already seen and quivering like jelly at the thought of what might happen next. It seemed impossible that he should accept the help of the young diLackmere; impossible that he should ever find Atti. Impossible, above all, that he could ever rest again. Sleep was far away.

'Why did you leave?' he asked suddenly.

'What?'

'Why did you leave Develin?'

Lex took his time about replying.

'I am not sure what happened,' he said. 'Perhaps I simply got drunk. But if so, no amount of drink has ever done it to me again. There was a moment on one of the Widow's winter progresses – it must have been her last. I was sitting at a table, listening to the talk, and all of a sudden I seemed to be seeing the whole of the world from the inside out. I felt – ah well, it was different. I cannot describe it. It felt as though I was seeing things far more closely – almost as though I was inside them. And at the same time I could have seen everything, as though I was far, far off, and yet had the eyes of an eagle. And all the big things we worry ourselves over – kings and wealth and long years and good crops – I saw that none of that mattered. What matters is little things: laughing when you want to cry; putting an arm round a stranger – that kind of thing. And it matters at some times and not at others. Vast things, things we cannot understand, may turn because a man helps an old widow with her load. But only if it's *that* man in *that* place and *that* widow. I don't know if I'm making sense. I could not make sense of it at the time. But I left the school. In fact I had a horror of it. Everyone had become so depressed . . .'

'I remember.'

'And I followed my nose for a bit. I became a clerk in orders. And, well, that's the story.'

'And now you administer justice which you think is not important, for lords whom you think are not important, in the name of a king whom you think is not important.'

'Like our three-hundred-year-old prince, I must serve. To serve, I must use the skills I have. My skills are those that Develin gave me. You know that half your clerks passed through the school at one time or another.'

'True.' And typical of Lex that he should rank himself no higher than his colleagues, when without doubt he was worth any ten Develin-trained clerks. There was something unshakeable about him. Padry had seen that at the taking of Velis. He saw it much more clearly now. Perhaps it came from this very experience the lad described, back in the days when (as far as Padry had been concerned) he had been the chief ruffian and trouble-maker among the scholars of the middle studies.

The just man follows the Path. He should follow it without fear wherever it leads him. Certainly he should not be quivering with fright when he is still safe, warm and (relatively) comfortable! Padry sighed and turned to try lying in a different position. His mind would not rest. He was angry – yes, angry – at the impossibility of it all! The chancellery, Lord Joyce, the Lady of Develin, Gueronius and his wayward wish to sail off into the distance – all the urgent voices that called him back! They had no *right* to stop him, blathering on about charters and all! What was the Kingdom beside a human soul? And if he was putting his own soul at risk, was it not fair to stake the Kingdom, too . . . ?

Why, why, why had she gone wandering off like this? This mad adventure! Her life was not hard. She had one of the most powerful men in the Kingdom watching over her. She was not stupid. She knew all that well enough. At fourteen she was almost a woman. Was she bewitched? Possibly. Who knew what witchcraft might do?

But it was also possible that she was doing this of her own accord. It was *like* her to think about something all by herself, decide whether it pleased her, and then act on what she had decided! And he never knew what she thought until he found out what she had done about it. Like the toys he had brought for her last year, and had later discovered deliberately broken and tossed out with the rubbish. (Oh, Atti!)

On the edge of sleep his mind seemed to divide. One part went on raging and sulking as if he were a prisoner kicking at the corners of his dungeon. But another just lay and watched himself stupidly, like a helpless observer who happened to be chained to the wall of the same cell. And he wondered, as if it were a question of no real importance, who it was here that was really bewitched. Was it Atti, or was it himself? He had heard the warnings. Still he was going forward. He was like the soul that meets the Demon by the Path, who sees the evil and yet cannot help himself from hearing its voice. Eyes wide, mesmerized, he inches closer and closer to the fascination of his death.

In his dreams the Demon wore the face of the child. And she said to him, '*Thomas Padry, in this you have no will at all.*'

Melissa lay in a big house. It was the biggest she had ever known.

It had one big room and lots of little ones down below. And then on top of those it had more rooms, reached by wooden steps running up from the lower floor. In one of these, on a pallet of straw, she lay all by herself. She had never slept alone in a room before, but the red knight had shouted at the people in the house until they had let him have one to himself, and then he had shouted at them again and buried the point of his knife in a table to make them let Melissa have one, too. '*I've got to see she's safe!*' he had roared, thumping his fist at every second word. '*That's safe from everyone!*' Melissa had been terrified because she knew what he could do. And now it terrified her to hear him bellowing drunk in the house below in the evenings, and to hear his snores through the thin wooden wall by her head at night. But at least she did not have to sleep in the same room as him.

Outside her window there was a big green hill rising to the sky. That was all she could see. On the other side of the house, she knew, there was much more. There were huts and houses, lots and lots of them, covering an area bigger even than the whole of the clearing at home. And round them was a great wooden fence, taller than the red knight's head. And beyond that was the water – a huge, sparkling lake of water, running on and on to the horizon. She had not known that it was possible to have so much water in one place.

The woman who kept the house brought broth in to her. She did not let Melissa have very much but said there would be more tomorrow. It tasted very good and Melissa wanted more of it. She lifted her head so that her eyes could follow the pot. The pot was still in the room, because the woman who held it had stopped in the doorway, waiting for someone in the corridor to pass.

It was two of the other women of the house. They were carrying an older woman who seemed to be sick. Behind them walked a girl about Melissa's age.

At once Melissa's eyes left the pot and followed the

girl, for the instant that she was framed in the doorway. Her face was pale and her dark gown was in tatters, but she walked (Melissa thought) like a proud buck deer. She was not helping the others or saying anything to them. She was letting them lead the way for her. Melissa remembered her long after they had all gone.

She remembered the girl's face clearly, smooth and pale and . . . well, it had made itself noticed, the way that a forest flower did peeping through the ragged ferns with its bright colours and shaped petals exactly in place. Mam had once told her that when people died and went to Heaven they all had beautiful faces and were never hungry again. Melissa, who had seen so few people her own age in her life, wondered quietly if somehow she had just glimpsed herself in Heaven, and if so, how close to dying and going there she was now.

Knocks and noises and voices sounded all the time. The house was full. And outside, in the other buildings, there were yet more people. Some of them lived here. They farmed the fields, herded the animals and went out onto the lake in boats. And then there were even more people, who like Melissa and the red knight and everyone else in the house did not live here but had come to the town to wait. They were all waiting.

They were waiting for the King.

'Now Michael guard us,' said Lex in the cool air of the dawn.

'And Raphael guide our way,' agreed Padry. 'For we are far from home.'

They left the stable, where their men-at-arms were preparing in silence for a return to Tuscolo, and led their horses across the courtyard to the gateway of Lackmere castle. Raymonde was waiting for them. He ran his eye over the mounts.

'You must lead them today,' he said. 'It is not good ground for horses. They will be happier if you are at their heads.'

Lex and Padry exchanged looks. What – walk, leading a beast, the day long? What kind of ground was this?

'Highness?' said Raymonde.

'I am here.'

The gaunt shape of Talifer emerged from the darkness of the gate-tunnel, which Padry could have sworn had been empty a moment before. He was again wearing his helmet. But the cloak hung loosely about him and in the early daylight Padry could see for sure how long his limbs truly were – long, and thin like a spider's. No man had arms and legs like that. Padry guessed that for all their frail look they might be very strong.

'These are the land-dues for my father,' Raymonde said, handing the ancient prince a purse. 'And say to him also that his house and his son still wait on his homecoming.'

Talifer nodded silently.

So, thought Padry. The Baron Lackmere was at the side of the 'Hidden King'. What did that signify? A holding like Lackmere's would not tip the scales of power in the Kingdom. But it was not nothing, either.

Raymonde looked at Padry. Words did not come easily to either of them. An air of embarrassment hung between them.

'I bid you fare well, Master Chancellor,' said Raymonde eventually.

'I – am grateful to you for our night's lodging,' Padry managed.

'Are you? I am glad to hear it. Maybe one day you will yet be grateful that I breathe and walk the earth.'

There was nothing Padry could say to that. He took his horse's reins.

'Follow me,' said Talifer.

Raymonde himself lifted the bar on the gate and pulled the great door inwards. They started forward. Lex, leading, stopped with an exclamation.

The land had changed.

They were not looking down on the thorn forest through which they had ridden the previous day. They were looking across a plain of dry brown boulders under a colourless sky. In the distance, in all directions, the ground rose and rose into what seemed to be a great wall of mountains, so that the horizon was far above their heads. The air was thick and heavy, a perpetual twilight. There was a strange humming in the air, so low that Padry could not so much hear it as feel it rising through his bones.

Their strange guide had walked ten paces into the rocks and turned, waiting for them. Padry looked around helplessly.

'That is your way,' said Raymonde, grinning at him.

With a dry clatter of hooves Lex led his mount forward. The sounds were distorted, as if the air through which they travelled were as thick as water.

'What is this place?' Padry heard him say.

'It is the world as its mother sees it,' said Talifer. He looked back at Padry. 'Come.'

'Those lights . . .'

There were two lights, burning close together like low stars on what seemed to be a distant mountain ridge. One was a little brighter than the other.

'Oh, that's the dragon,' said Raymonde, grinning more broadly. 'But don't worry. He doesn't eat travellers. He's too busy holding the world together.'

A *dragon*? Padry took a step back. His eyes searched the dimness. He could see nothing – nothing that might not have been mountain wall, and the two lights that burned on the very rim like huge and distant fires.

Dragons were an idea, a myth! They were an image for meditation. A dragon carved from walnut dangled at his own belt. They should not be a *thing* – a thing so vast that it could circle the whole world! What was this? It must be some trickery! It must be . . .

Witchcraft.

Panic rose in him as he dithered in the gateway. He gripped his horse's reins. Lex and the monstrous guide were waiting.

'Come,' said Talifer again.

With a jerk of will Padry stepped forward. His mount followed. The gate of Lackmere clattered shut behind him and disappeared. He stood in the middle of a brown waste that ran in all directions. There was no Path before his feet.

She could not lie down for ever. She was not made that way.

Melissa crawled from her pallet. The floor was smooth, but dusty and stained. For the first time she looked properly at the boards. Someone had cut those things from wood, she thought. They must have cut a whole tree to do it, and then cut the trunk into flat bits. How had they done that? You couldn't do that with just an axe. And *then* they had somehow smoothed the flat bits down so that when she ran her finger over them, drawing a pattern in the dust, they were silky and splinterless to touch. She had not seen wood like this before.

Last night she had wondered if she were near Heaven. But this wasn't Heaven, was it? It wasn't Heaven just because there were things she had not seen before.

Her palms pushed the boards away beneath her. One hand went to the wall to steady herself. She got her feet together under her. She could not have said why she was doing this, when really there was no longer any reason to do anything any more. But she had spent every waking moment of her life doing things. Her body felt wrong, lying down when it was not sick. Besides, she had heard noises.

In that strange day in a strange house, she stood on her own two feet.

She was still wearing her smock – the same smock

in which she had run from her home when the raiders came. The red knight had said that she stank. She supposed she must stink even more now. But there was no stream to wash in. She pushed the hair back from her eyes. She had nothing to tie it with. She listened.

It was mid-morning. Daylight had come hours ago and she had gone on sleeping, just like the day before. The house was not quite still but she could tell that most people were out. This was the time when everyone was busy.

Not everyone. She heard it again – the noise that had made her get up. It sounded like a harsh giggle, coming from one of the rooms nearby. But it wasn't a laugh. It was something else.

The giggle broke into coughing, and then became a thin whimpering that wavered and faded but would not die away.

Melissa did not cry much herself. Until a few days ago she would have said that no matter how bad things were, they always got better after a bit. And when she did weep – with pain after a beating, or something – she would do it silently, because if she had made too much noise when Mam or Dadda were angry, she might have been beaten again. '*What's the use of crying? Crying never fed anyone.*' And that was true, so she would always stop as soon as she could.

She did not like this sound. It was so weepy and so . . . so . . .

She just did not like it.

The press of the floorboards felt strange beneath

94

her bare soles. Her knees shook but they held her. She stepped out into the corridor. The noises came from an open door a few paces away. She tiptoed unsteadily to it and peered in.

It was a long room in which many people had spent the night. Their things were all over the floor. But only two people were in it now. One was a woman, still lying in a pallet bed. A hillwoman. Melissa knew the look. And she could tell, too, that the woman was sick. The thin little face was even thinner than it should be. It turned restlessly this way and that on the rough bundle that pillowed its head. The eyes were screwed tight. The mouth was open, and from it came the thin wails that had brought Melissa limping down the corridor.

The woman was sick. She was in fever. One hand was fumbling uselessly at the rough blankets that were drawn over her. Was she too hot or too cold? Too hot, probably. But she could not push her coverings away. Maybe she couldn't even hear the noise she was making.

On a low stool beside the bed sat another figure, wearing a brown habit and hood. It was sitting very still with its back very straight. At first sight it seemed smaller than a person should be, so that Melissa wondered if it was not some strange object cut out of wood.

Then the head turned. The Face looked at her.

It was the girl she had seen in the corridor the day before. She knew it because of the Face. Those strong brows, those eyes – they jumped at once in her mind.

95

She was the same age as Melissa, or maybe a little older. But she was also smaller. Melissa had always thought that the less you got to eat in your life the smaller you were. This girl looked as though she had always had enough to eat. Her skin was good and what Melissa could see of her hair and nails was good. Her clothes were plain but there was no roughness on her hands. She was just small and that was that. She was pale, too. And – when you looked closely – her mouth was pulled down just a little at the corners and there were marks below her eyes, as if she had not been sleeping so well. Immediately Melissa wanted to know her and also to comfort her. She hobbled forward, ignoring the woman in the bed, for she was drawn to the girl like a moth to flame.

'Are you all right?' she said. 'Do you need help?'

The girl did not reply. She turned her head away and sat just as she had been sitting when Melissa had first looked in.

Melissa crouched down beside her. She found it easier to kneel on the floor than to stand on trembling legs. 'What's the matter?' she asked.

There was no answer.

'Is that your – your friend?' Melissa asked, nodding at the figure in the bed. She had been going to ask, *Is that your mother?* But the girl beside her did not look like one of the hill people.

'It's my servant,' said the girl. Her voice was empty.

Melissa looked at the still figure in the pallet. She had heard about servants – people who dressed and looked after other, very rich people, and were able to live in big houses, eat well and wear wonderful clothes because of it. She had thought that servants must be very lucky.

And the girl must be one of the very rich people herself – one of the people whom Melissa had always thought must be very happy, because of all the luck they had had and because they would never ever be cold or tired or hungry. And instead of being happy she was sad. What could make a person with so much luck so unhappy?

The hillwoman had stopped her noise. Her breath was coming in short, uneven gasps. Her face was so thin that Melissa could see the shape of the skull within it. She seemed neither to see nor hear what went on in the room. One hand still plucked at the blanket. And a corner of Melissa's mind wondered why, if the woman was too hot, the beautiful girl beside her had not just reached out and turned the blanket back.

'She's dying,' said the girl.

She said it crossly, as if she thought the woman was stupid for dying and Melissa was stupid for having to be told.

Melissa hesitated. Then she put an arm around the girl, meaning to hold her as she and Mam had held one another when poor baby Clara had at last gone still between them. But the girl's shoulders were lumpy and hard. 'Don't touch me,' she said.

And then: 'You must go away.'

Melissa felt helpless. 'Do the people here know—?' she began.

'It's horrible here,' said the girl.

Meaning *No, they didn't*, Melissa supposed. Maybe the girl had tried to tell them and they hadn't understood. Or maybe she thought they, too, ought to know without being told.

'Shall I go down for you?' she asked.

She remembered that the red knight might be down below. He might be angry if he saw she had left the room where he had put her. But she wanted to do something for these people – for the sick woman, and above all for the girl beside her. Red knight or not, she had offered to go down. She had meant it.

'They've been kind to me,' she said when the girl did not answer. 'They brought me broth and a blanket.'

The girl said nothing.

Melissa was hurt. Yes, the woman was sick. Yes, she might be worried about that. But to ignore people – even when they offered to help – that wasn't fair! It was so rare for Melissa to meet other children that she felt they might at least pay *some* attention to her when she did. She opened her mouth to say something rude, but shut it again, telling herself that it wasn't right to be hard on someone who was already sad. She waited for the girl to show some sign. Then she realized the girl would not.

At the last moment, just as Melissa was drawing breath to snap, *Well, if you're busy I'll just get out of your way shall I?* the girl said, 'Yes. You do that.'

'What – tell them downstairs?'

The girl nodded.

'All right,' Melissa sighed. 'If it'll help.'

She looked again at the woman on the bed. She put a hand out and felt the skin. As she had thought – far too hot. Gently she folded the blanket back.

'You can pull it up again if she starts to shiver,' she said.

There was no reply. The girl sat like a carved thing. Looking back from the doorway, Melissa saw her still sitting there in the bright daylight from the windows and the woman lying on the pallet before her. The whimpering sound had begun again. It seemed to fill the whole room, and yet both of them were so still that it was hard to tell which it came from – the figure on the pallet or the one that sat straight-backed on the stool, with its head a little bowed as if in pain.

Melissa began to hobble back along the corridor. The short distance seemed a very long way. Before she reached the stairs she found it easier to get down on her knees and crawl. She kept going.

'Someone is weeping.'

That was Lex's voice, Padry thought.

The air in this place distorted sounds. It made thinking difficult. Padry's head was swimming. His brain was repeating *Step, step, step* to itself, as it seemed to have been doing all his life. Step, step, step, on this journey without beginning or end.

It had been Lex. He had stopped and put his head to the ground. The figure of Talifer was standing over him. Padry toiled up to them, gasping in that heavy, dead air. He shook his head but still the low throbbing filled his ears like a sound on the very edge of hearing. He hated it. He hated all this dry, dull land and the pale sky under which nothing ever seemed to change.

'Listen,' Lex said, still bent to the ground.

Padry sank to his knees and put his head to a stone. The harsh, powdery surface scraped at his ear. It was when he felt things like that – when he stumbled, stubbed his toe through his boot or scraped his palm on some boulder – that he knew he was not dreaming. That he was really where he seemed to be.

'Can't hear,' he muttered.

'The earth is crying,' said Lex. He lifted his head. His eyes stared and his mouth was a short, thin line.

'That is her,' said Talifer. 'That is Beyah, whom the hillmen say is the mother of the world. She has wept for three hundred years.'

'Why does she weep?' said Lex.

'Because we killed her child.'

Padry could make no sense of the sounds. He climbed slowly to his feet. The face of Lex, the helm of Talifer, swam in his vision. 'I need to rest,' he gasped.

'We must go on,' said Talifer's voice.

'How far is it?'

'Not far.'

Not far. But every step was far, and every step must be followed by another and another, and all the time with this feeling in his ears. He lifted his head and blinked at the dreary land. Nothing had changed. Nothing had changed since he had first set foot here, a lifetime ago. There was no sun but the pale sky, no moon or star but the light of the distant dragon. And spread beneath them was the sea of brown rocks and the far mountain wall that never came any nearer. There was no path for his feet or his soul to follow.

'We must go on,' said Talifer.

Lex's face passed – it might have been Lex, or a man much older, grim and drawn. Padry saw the shape of Lex's horse, plodding patiently after his master. They were leaving him. He stumbled after them. He wished he could catch up, but no matter how his feet pushed and struggled on that uneven ground he never seemed to close the gap. He was seized with fear that he might fall behind, become lost and wander for ever with this weeping in his ears!

'Angels,' he muttered. 'Look down on me. Walk with me.'

His fingers had crept to his belt. They found the dragon there. It was one of the signs he himself wore. He knew that. He had always known it. He wore it as an object of meditation, since, since . . . There had been an important moment. One that now he could not remember.

The dragon had meanings. That was why he kept it at his belt. It was a sign of eternity, and of faithfulness in the sight of the Angels. It should have been a comfort to find the dragon here . . .

But to see its fire! To feel the tears of the earth throbbing in the air! It changed everything, all meaning. That was what the Demon did. That was how witchcraft turned truth into lies. The things he clung to would be the things that most deceived. He understood it now. He almost understood it. The dull, trembling feeling came from all directions, up from the very rocks themselves. The hill people sacrificed their children to appease their goddess, he had heard. Stumbling among the rocks, he could understand why they did. In the end almost anything would be worth it to silence that voice.

How many million tears had fallen? These rocks should have been a sea-bed. And every tear was another grief, another cruelty in the world he had come from. It was appalling to think of. It was madness, eating into his mind. It was the Abyss itself, the last sign of the Descent. A little more of this would drive him to . . .

Step, step, step. The fire of the dragon burning distantly. His hand at his belt, feeling for the comfortless signs: the dragon; the lantern; the leaf; his mind groping for the meanings they had once held for him. The Lantern: it lit the path from the Abyss. The Leaf (where was it? He fumbled. There!). The Leaf grew towards the light. The Dragon: did not loose his hold for pain . . .

It seemed to be darker now. He had not thought the light ever changed in this place.

Again. The Lantern, a light on the Path. (Path? There was no Path. But yes, strangely, there might almost be one now – pale and twisting before him on the rough ground.) The Leaf grew. The Dragon did not loose his hold.

The Lantern, a light . . .

There was a light ahead of him.

For a moment he thought it must be the distant

dragon-fire again. He must have lost his direction and gone stumbling off towards the rim of the world. In his fevered state it would have been easy. But no, the others were with him. And there was just one light, not two – a light very like a lantern, jigging ahead of them.

By the Angels! It *was* a lantern, held low in someone's hand!

Suddenly it was quite dark. The ground beneath his feet felt different. It was still stony, but of a more familiar quality. The path – yes, it was indeed a path – seemed to float like a ribbon on the night-clouded terrain. The ground sloped down to his left. He could see the branches of trees, moving against the starlit sky. He could feel the air on his skin. He was hearing wind among leaves and, from somewhere below them, the sound of a stream. He was on a wooded hillside in the ordinary night of the world.

'Praise be!' he heard Lex exclaim.

The lantern was on the path ahead of them. It was waiting for them at the top of a low rise. As they approached, it lifted. Padry saw that it was held by a tall man. There was another, shorter man beside him.

'Who is there?' called the tall one.

'It is Talifer.'

'Greetings, Talifer,' said the man, in a tone of mild surprise.

'Greetings, brother,' said someone else from the darkness beyond the lamp, in a voice deeper than the deepest bass Padry had ever heard.

'And who the devil have you got with you?' said the short man.

'Two who seek the Prince Under the Sky.'

The lantern-bearer came forward, lifting his light. He was young and clean-shaven. His face was long but delicate, framed by dark, curling hair. He looked curiously into Padry's eyes.

'Master Padry!' he said at length. 'I think you have had a hard road. But if you are indeed looking for me, you have now found me.'

'I am glad,' panted Padry. He did not know how this young man knew his name, but after all the strangeness of the day it did not seem strange. He did recognize the companion, however – that short, sour, wolfish face. That was Aun, Baron of Lackmere, sure enough. The old brigand did not seem to have changed much in half a dozen years.

'I bring you silver from your house, lord,' said Talifer.

'Good,' said the baron. 'We need it.'

'And a message from your son, if you will hear it.'

'I will not.'

The young lantern-bearer looked at the baron but said nothing.

'Sir,' Padry said to him (not at all sure how to address a king whom he could not possibly acknowledge, but from whom he needed help). 'I – I am searching for my charge, who is the daughter of the house of Baldwin. I believe she has been trying to make her way to you. Have you seen her?'

Again the young man studied Padry's face. Padry stood before him, pleading silently in his heart for the words he needed to hear.

'I think she is at the inn at Aclete,' said the Prince Under the Sky. 'We are going there now. You may come with us, if you will.'

Behind Padry, a third figure lurched from the darkness of the hillside – a hooded, crouching shape that fell into step beside Talifer. The tall guide bent his head as though in recognition. Lex muttered something and led his horse forward. Padry followed him along the path. And the King went before them with the lantern in his hand.

VI

On the Knoll

n one sense this 'Prince' was well named, thought Padry the next morning. He held his courts under the sky.

They were on the broad summit of the hill above the town, high up and exposed to a rough north wind. The clouds were moving fast and the surface of the lake was a heavy grey. The eastern shore, the heart of the Kingdom, was just a dark, featureless line on the edge of sight. The breeze rushed in the branches of a wood and stroked the grasses silver. There had been one rain shower already this morning. There would be more.

Padry had seen at least two big buildings in Aclete, the town at the bottom of the hill. Either of those would have had enough room for at least the immediate protagonists in each case. All the rest of this crowd could have waited their turn in other rooms, or huddled for shelter against the wall outside. Padry knew many a baron who preferred to sit in judgement under a roof. But here in Tarceny, it seemed, justice must be heard by everyone.

Nevertheless, Padry was grateful for the weather. The big breeze was the perfect antidote for the shadows in his mind – the nightmare memories of the place of brown rocks, which had pursued him in his sleep and still lingered in the corners of his brain. Cold air, wet wind – brrr! *This* was what he needed, after a night spent tossing on his straw! Better still, it gave him an excuse to huddle in his cloak and bring his hood well forward over his face. He did not want too many people recognizing the chancellor of Gueronius, or gossiping among themselves about why he was attending this upstart 'King' in Tarceny. That sort of rumour could be very uncomfortable if it ever came to court.

In the middle of the circle sat the Prince Under the Sky.

The ragged, lantern-bearing young man of the night before was squatting cross-legged on the ground with the Baron of Lackmere and a handful of other villainous-looking advisers standing around him. The boy wore a workman's jerkin, cloak and leggings, with a thin, plain circlet of gold perched incongruously on his head and only a goatskin between his seat and the dank grasses. The crowd gathered around in deference.

'You know who he is, don't you?' Lex had said as the two of them breakfasted in the mean hut where Lex had arranged their lodgings.

'Not really,' Padry had replied, wolfing bread and root soup.

'I thought no master ever forgot a pupil. He was in

Develin with us, in the last winter there. He nearly stuck a knife into me – I'm not likely to forget that.'

'A knife? In Develin?'

'Oh, I probably deserved it. His name was Luke, then, although he seems to be calling himself something else now.'

Padry's next morsel of bread had stopped halfway to his mouth.

'Luke.' Of course! And no wonder the young man had recognized him when he had lifted that lantern on the road!

'Luke': the name that the council of Develin had chosen for him, because it had been thought too dangerous for his real name to be known – Ambrose, the heir of Tarceny, one of the seven great houses of the Kingdom, and possible pretender to the throne. Padry remembered a haunted, hungry-looking thirteen-year-old, who had come on rather well in that winter while Develin had sickened around them, and whom he had thought dead with all the others in the sack.

So here he was, the Lord of Tarceny, a man of twenty years, holding court in the wasted remains of his father's lands. Above him was the standard of the Doubting Moon, white on the black cloth of his big banner, with the black break in its disc that might have been a shadow or might have been a thing, and you never knew which. In the circle around him stood the people who had come for his judgement. Everyone was wearing brown or grey hoods and wraps against the weather. He could see only noses and chins and the occasional eye, rarely the full face. They were like a tattered choir of monks waiting for the cantor to begin. Say about a hundred. The court of a minor baron might draw that many. But the baron's people would all be local, come from the manor he was visiting. There would be some in the circle around this 'prince' who had come from much further afield. Atti for one, although he had not seen her yet. Himself and Lex. And others.

Yes, come to that, just who else here was hiding in their hood under the pretext of the weather?

Now this knight – this big, spade-bearded brigand of a fellow with makeshift red livery, just leading his horse into the ring – now *he* did not live within a stone's throw of this place, for sure. Those saddlebags were enough to have sustained him for a good two to three days' journey.

On the back of the horse sat a gawky, half-starved peasant child; a dirty, waif-like creature with the big eyes of hunger and masses of filthy light-brown hair. Under a red cloak, which must have been the knight's, she wore only colourless rags. Her feet were bare. What was she doing up there, riding above them all like some bride or trophy? Whatever this was, it did not look like a matter of water rights or short weight.

The horse had halted. The knight dropped to his knees before his young lord. Padry edged a little closer. Witchcraft, politics, even Atti – those thoughts were all in his head, but they could wait. For the moment he was just curious to see how a former pupil would do.

'Bavar,' said the King, 'why did you come?'

'You called me, my lord,' said the red knight, without raising his eyes. 'I came as quickly as I could.'

From her perch on the broad back of the knight's horse Melissa looked down on both of them. She hated sitting up above them all with everyone staring at her. She did not know what was going to happen. She did not know what all these other people were doing here.

What she did know was that the red knight was afraid.

It was the way he had sworn at the inn people that morning and cursed her for being clumsy when he had lifted her on the horse. She had felt his fear as he had reached past her for the reins. They had climbed the hill and she had seen so many others, all heading the same way, all going up to see their lord. And behind her she had felt the red knight growing more and more tense. She had realized that something big and terrible was going to happen. The red knight knew what it was. All those people trudging upwards ahead and behind them, they also knew what it was. She did not, but she had felt the fear of the man at her back. And although she hated him, she had begun to be afraid, too.

'Tell your story, so that it may be heard,' said the King. There was no expression on his face or in his voice.

'Three – three nights ago you came to me in a dream, my lord,' stammered the knight. 'You told me where she lay. You said to find her and bring her to you.'

'Have you seen this girl before?'

The knight paused before replying. He was looking for a way to answer the question. But all he said was: 'Yes, my lord.'

'When?'

Melissa's heart sank as she understood what the King wanted the knight to say. It sank and went on sinking, into darkness, coldness . . .

'Ten days back,' said the knight, still looking at the ground. 'My men burned a house. I – I was with them.'

'I knew that house, Bavar. There was a man and a woman there. They showed me hospitality once. Where are they now?'

'Lord . . . you know.'

(*You know, he knows*, begged Melissa silently. *That's all. Please – don't say any more!*)

'Tell it, so it may be heard.'

'We hanged the man from the tree.'

'The woman?'

Melissa's shoulders were hunched and her head turned away. She wanted to put her hands over her ears. She wanted to shout aloud, *Stop it! Stop asking him!* Asking him was making it happen again. She could see it again. Shut places in her head were breaking open. Voices were beginning to scream. *It wasn't like that! He's not telling it all! They laughed! They laughed when they pulled Dadda up into the tree!* She could see again how Dadda had kicked and kicked at the air as the rope had dragged him upwards. She could see the knot of red-clad men around Mam, and Mam

111

wrestling and screaming among them. She saw the red knight look round, grinning, and how his grin had widened as his eye fell on her, staring from among the trees. And he had put an arrow to the string of his bow, and lifted it . . .

'The woman, Bavar?'

The horse beneath her would not move. She wanted it to carry her away but it was staying where it was, held in its place because it could see its master the knight kneeling in front of it. And the knight was held by the eyes of the King. He was looking at the grass a yard from his own nose.

'What did you do, Bavar?'

At last the knight's right shoulder seemed to shrug. 'As men do, my lord,' he said hoarsely.

There was silence.

Melissa found she was shaking – shaking with rage and tears. She thought that that night, when the red knight was asleep, she would creep into his room. And then she would *squeeze* his eyes out! She would do it if he *killed* her for it!

The King said, 'Why did you do these things?'

The knight drew breath. 'The cotter was a stubborn one—' he began. But he stopped, seeming to think better of what he was going to say.

After a moment he tried again. 'I did not know that you knew them—'

Again he checked himself. He shook his head, and bowed it.

The King looked around. At his right hand stood an old man in armour, wearing over it a white-and-blue

112

shirt with the mask of a wolf embroidered onto it. Melissa remembered him. He was the sour-faced knight who had come with the King to her door all those years ago.

'What would he say, Aun?' asked the King.

'If a man would be a lord, he must pay and feed his soldiers,' said the wolf-knight. 'Pay and food must come from the land. If a landsman yields what is demanded, the lord's soldiers will protect him. But if he does not, they must do the other, or no man will give to them.'

With tears on her cheeks Melissa looked at the wolf-knight. How could he speak like that? He saw her looking, but his face was hard.

'I think he does better to hold his tongue,' said the King.

'I ask for pardon, lord,' mumbled the red knight.

'Pardon,' repeated the King. 'Why should I take your crime on my shoulders? It shrieks to the Angels. Do you fear the Angels, Bavar?'

'Yes, lord.'

Yes, thought Melissa bitterly. *Now* he does.

'If I saw what you did, Bavar, how do you think that the Angels did not? Why should I take your crime in their sight? Why should I not avenge it?'

The knight said nothing.

Melissa looked down at him and then at the King. She found the King was looking at her.

'I remember you,' he said. 'But I never knew your name.'

'M-Melissa, sir.'

'Melissa. What would you have me do?'

Do? thought Melissa. What did he mean, 'Do'?

What could anyone do? They were dead. Home was gone. There was nothing left. How could anything she said change that? She had thought that he would know. He had been the only thing she could turn to. Now she was here before him – above him, even – and *he* was asking *her* what to do!

'Pardon, or vengeance?' the King prompted.

Squeeze his eyes out, said the voices in her mind. But they were weak now.

She shook her head. The only thing she knew was that she wanted never to see the red knight again. She wanted never to be hungry again, never to be sad again. She did not see how anything she might say could give her any of those things.

The King sighed. He opened his hand to look at something he held in his palm. From her seat on the horse's back Melissa could see that it was a small white stone. His fingers closed over it again.

'Bavar,' he said.

'My lord,' said the knight hoarsely.

'Take her down from your horse. Then take yourself and your horse away from me. In the place where your crime was committed, build a house of good stone. There you will install a priest, whose tasks shall be to pray to the Angels that they forgive what you did, and to care for all travellers, no matter how poor, who pass that way. Take no profit from the place, whether in tithe or tolls, but give all over to the keep of priest and travellers and the poor. I

114

will come within a year to see that it has been done. If it is done and done well, then I shall pardon you.'

Wordlessly the red knight climbed to his feet. He lifted Melissa down from her place. Melissa saw that his face was pale and that there was sweat upon it. He climbed into his saddle, bowed to the King, and wheeled the horse away. The crowd parted to let him go.

Melissa faced the King. His eyes had shown her nothing while he dealt with the knight. Now she looked into them and saw that they were sorry – sorry for her, she thought. Maybe it wasn't going to be so hard now. And at least they had stopped talking about it. She tried to square her shoulders.

'Do you have anyone you might go to?' he asked her.

'No, my lord.'

'Nowhere that might become a home for you?'

'No, my lord.'

'What will you do?'

Do? Everything had been smashed and taken away. Now even the red knight was gone. She had been put down into a different world.

'I cannot give back to you what you have lost,' he said at last. 'But for the moment we will see you sheltered and fed in Aclete. After that, if there is anything that you would ask me for, and it is in my power to give it to you, I shall.'

Melissa looked at the ground. 'Thank you,' she said.

Thank you, I suppose, she thought.

Fascinating, thought Padry. And sinister.

The boy sat with no trappings of power. There were no trumpeters, no banners, no rituals. There was just one weather-stained knight in his following. He was clothed as roughly as the poorest of the people who waited around him. From the lean look of his face he fed no better than they did either. Yet they came to be judged by him with every appearance of intending to abide by what he said. And although he had imposed a fine, he had taken no profit for himself. He seemed to embody a philosophical ideal: a wisdom that walked in a tattered robe.

And yet there was power there. No doubt of it. There *had* to be power before there could be law. Part of it might be founded on the consent of those who came to him. But that was not all. It was not the threat of some village rabble that had brought that red-coated cut-throat crawling here on his belly. He had come at a word, bundling from his nest, picking up that peasant child as evidence of his own doings, and had thrown himself on the mercy of a ragged and distant overlord. By the Angels, the fellow had not even brought an armed following with him!

It had been fear – fear of the boy himself and of what he might do. Witchcraft! Tarceny had a long and evil reputation. This boy had appeared in a dream, the knight had said. He had spoken of crimes the knight had thought hidden; threatened him with – with what? What else could he do? Padry did not know. But not knowing only made it the more fearful. He remembered the sudden and unexplained deaths of two recent kings – found torn with an unspeakable savagery as if they had been set upon by beasts. The shadows of his journey still hung in his brain. He swallowed, and his palms had begun to tingle. Atti had had a dream, too.

Atti, my child. What are we coming into?

And now they were calling her name.

'The Lady Astria diBaldwin.'

Melissa was sitting among the group of men around the King. Someone had thrown a heavy cloak over her shoulders. It was still warm from the wearer's body. The red knight was gone. She had nothing to do but wait and listen. She wondered who would approach the King next.

'The Lady Astria diBaldwin.'

They were calling, but no one was answering. People in the ring were looking around. No one stepped forward.

They called again. Again no one answered. Melissa heard the King murmur to a man beside him: 'Well, move on to the next one. We can find her later.' She wondered if whoever it was had slipped away rather than face the King.

Then, just as the man beside the King was looking down at his scroll again, someone in the crowd threw back their hood and walked into the ring. It was the girl who had been sitting in the long room. She walked without hurrying, all the way across the middle of that space, and stood before the King. And she looked at him as if there was no one there but the King and herself.

'Forgive me,' she said. Her voice was light but firm and very clear. 'I had thought you must be calling someone else. I am the Princess Astria Anthea Aeris diPare diBaldwin.'

She said the word *Princess* so that it stood out just a little.

'I am not certain of the rank of the knight in your last case,' she said. 'If he was your father in disguise, or perhaps some royalty of whom I have not heard, you will of course have done right to call him before me.'

'I hear people in the order that they come to me,' the King said. 'Bavar and Melissa reached Aclete the day before you did. That is all.'

Melissa saw the princess look at him, and the way the King looked back. She thought, *They know each other. They've met before.*

'Did you come just to teach me protocol, or was there something else?' said the King.

'I came for the justice you promise,' she answered.

'I promise you the justice that is in my power – and yours – to find.'

The girl raised her voice and spoke to the whole ring. 'I seek justice,' she said, 'against the house of Gueronius, for the deaths of my father and his brother, the robbery of my lands and the murder of my people.'

There was a moment's silence on the hilltop.

'Is that all?' exclaimed the knight at the King's side.

'You want us to cross the lake, march on Tuscolo, seize the throne and put you on it?'

The girl looked only at the King. 'I ask for justice,' she repeated.

'Angels' Knees!' cried the knight. 'What justice? Your father and uncle were rebels against his house. Your uncle put *his* uncle's head on a spike when he took the throne! Damn me, I was there! Do you think we want the same to happen to us?'

'One moment, Aun,' said the King quietly. He was prodding at the ground before him with a finger. He seemed to be thinking. After a little he looked up.

'I did not know you would ask this,' he told the girl.

The girl watched him. She was daring him to refuse her.

'I'm sorry,' said the King. 'I am not Gueronius's overlord, and I can't judge him if he does not come to me for judgement. Which he won't, of course.'

Silence.

'But I want to help you if I can,' said the King. 'Is there not something else besides Gueronius that is troubling you?'

The girl's eyes went down to her hands, and then back to the King. She said: 'I have asked for what I want. And you say you won't give it to me.'

'Sometimes,' said the King, 'when we say we want something, it is because we want something else that we cannot name. I think you do. Can you tell me?'

She turned her head. For the first time she looked around her, at the ring of people all looking back at her. Melissa thought she wanted to turn and walk away without answering. But their eyes held her in her place. She seemed very small in the middle of all those people.

'I ask for your confidence,' said the King.

Her cheeks were colouring. Coldly she lifted her chin. 'You want me to tell you something you can give me?'

'Yes.'

'Can you give me justice against *your* house, then? The house of Tarceny?'

Somebody swore under their breath.

'My grandfather and his eldest son both died at Tarceny's hands,' the princess said. 'I am the last of their line. For their sakes you should grant me justice against yourself!'

The King looked hard at her. Then he turned to the knight at his side. He was angry now. Both men were angry. Melissa could tell from the way they looked and the hiss of their whispers.

'. . . wants a good spanking,' she heard the knight say. 'That, or duck her in the lake!'

'No,' said the King.

'You cannot pay blood-money to every old enemy of your house! Damn me, if you did, *I* could have a claim on you!'

'Again, no,' said the King.

He turned back to the girl who stood before him, waiting.

'This is not what I was thinking of either,' he said shortly. 'We are getting further from the matter and not nearer to it. But since you say this here, I will tell you that my father, who was guilty of these things, is dead, and that I have long ago disowned what he did.

'Nevertheless,' he went on, 'I think you may have a claim on me because of him. I shall have to decide whether you are right, and if so what there is that I may offer you.'

The girl nodded slightly. Her expression did not change.

'But I have a question for you now,' the King said, leaning forward. 'It is this: I think you did not come here alone. Where is the one who helped you?'

'I did come alone – unless you mean my servant.'

'That is who I meant. Where is she?'

'She is sick. She lies in the inn.'

'Did she fall sick on the way?'

'She was ill to begin with, but she has become worse.'

Melissa wondered why she did not say that the woman might die.

'How long has she been your servant?'

'As long as I can remember.'

'Was it her choice that she should come with you, or yours?'

The girl looked puzzled by the question. 'I was coming to find you. Of course she came with me.'

'Remember that I did not ask you to come. And I did not ask you to bring one who was sick and might suffer on the journey.'

The girl said nothing.

'Who is caring for her now?'

Again the girl did not answer.

'I believe,' said the King, 'that your servant has given many years for you. I fear she may now be giving her life. You should give what care you can to her in return. Shouldn't you?'

The princess looked at him coldly. 'Is this your judgement?' she asked.

'Not yet. Later, when we know what becomes of her, I will judge both you and me.'

She did not bow or grovel as the red knight had done. She turned and walked back to her place in the circle. She looked small and alone, but also, Melissa thought, very, very fine. She had not been frightened at all. And she had spoken so beautifully – all the time! She had even stopped the King, who seemed to know everything, and had made him think. How wonderful, to be able to speak like that!

Melissa's eyes followed the princess in the dark-grey hood. Even as she admired her, she felt sorry for her. Because the King had been right. She was very calm and strong on the outside but still there was something wrong. Melissa knew that. She remembered the way the princess had sat in the long room with the wails of her servant filling the air around her. She hadn't been lifting a finger to help. She had just been sitting there, as if she were fixed by some great, quiet pain and were as feeble as the woman on the bed. Maybe it was just knowing that the woman was dying. Maybe it was something even worse. Melissa could not guess.

She wanted to go after the princess, to comfort her

if she could and to tell her that she would help look after the hillwoman at the inn. But her legs were weak. She did not know if she would be allowed to get up from where she had been made to sit. And the princess had not stopped when she had reached the edge of the circle. She was still walking away, followed by two men from the inn. Melissa knew she would never be able to catch her without help.

She watched the small, hooded head and shoulders disappear below the brow of the hill.

VII

Over Wine

ay I speak to you,' said Padry, 'as a master to a former pupil?'

'Certainly,' said Ambrose of Tarceny.

They were at supper together outside the big stone lodge that stood on one side of the bay at Aclete. Lex was there. So was the Baron Lackmere, who had brought Ambrose's invitation just as Lex and Padry had been contemplating another meal of root broth in their mean lodgings. Now there was pale wine in the bowls before them, and on the table were olives, fresh bread and spitted lake-fish that gave off a delicious scent of seared oils. The wind had dropped (thank the Angels!). Only the lightest airs stirred the vine-leaves above their table. A little warmth had stolen into the evening. The great hillside across the bay was alight with the sunset.

'Well,' said Padry, 'as a master, praise first. I have seen many a lord hold his court and I could have wished that some of them had been with me in yours today. Too many lords judge as if justice were an instrument of their lordship. Others treat all judgement as a waste of their time and a demand on brains that they do not like to use. You, however, judge as if justice were truth, and it is your task to find it. This is good.'

'If you flatter me, Master Padry, I shall flatter you back. Develin taught me. I try to follow as I was taught.'

Padry nodded. Even now, supping with this young witch-king, he could feel the little glow of a teacher who sees evidence of his own work in the man before him.

'I have two more points,' he said carefully. 'Will you listen to them?'

'I will.'

'My first is the Lady Astria diBaldwin.'

'Yes,' said Ambrose wryly. 'I did not think to be put so firmly in my place by a twelve-year-old.'

'She is fourteen, although she looks younger. She is of great interest to the King.'

'Really?' said the Baron Lackmere. 'I thought that pup was interested in nothing this side of his harbour wall.'

'The King,' Padry said rather grimly, 'is interested in everything that he should be interested in. To some extent this is the duty of his advisers.' And he wondered just how widely in the Kingdom Gueronius's hair-brained dreams of exploration were known.

'I see,' said Ambrose.

'My advice — my very firm advice — is that you have nothing to do with her suit and that you return her at once to Tuscolo. My colleague and I can escort her, at least until I can command better protection. If you choose to send messages of loyalty to the King at the same time, I suspect it is possible that the King will in return confirm you in your ancestral holding of the March of Tarceny, and perhaps even your mother's manors around the fortress of Trant.'

'This is the sort of gift that costs a king nothing but paper and ink,' growled Lackmere. 'The March, such as it is, is beyond his reach. And Trant is waste, and the fortress a ruin. If we were to part with the heir to one of the seven houses, particularly *that* house, it would not be for less than' – the baron knitted his brows – 'fifty thousand crowns.'

'Out of the question,' said Padry promptly.

'Why?'

'Because it would cost the King less to come and fetch her – and hang any who stood in his way. Of course' – Padry shrugged elaborately – 'it is not impossible that the King might agree to defray any costs of the child's keep that a loyal subject had incurred, but—'

'We can't send her back,' said Ambrose.

'Why not?' said the baron.

Indeed, why not? thought Padry, carefully putting down his wine bowl. He had been prepared for a ransom demand (although how he might slip fifty thousand, or even five thousand, out of Gueronius's starving treasury was another question!). He had also weighed the risk that his hosts might imagine he himself would be worth a ransom.

But he did not at all like the finality with which the young lord of Tarceny had spoken. She must come back. One way or another, she *must*.

'She appealed to me for justice against Gueronius,' said Ambrose. 'Before witnesses from many places. Gueronius will consider that treason. The penalty for treason is—'

'But these were the words of a child!' Padry protested. 'A child well-schooled in speech, to be sure, but she knows nothing of politics. And Gueronius does not execute children.'

'Children can be made to die without ever climbing a scaffold,' said Ambrose.

'True,' said Lackmere. 'Although at fourteen a child is old enough to marry or stand trial as may be. And *I* would say that one who calls for justice against a crowned king must accept what follows, be they child or no.'

Padry gritted his teeth. The baron was right. Atti would have known exactly what she was doing. After the fate of her family, after seeing the storming of the castle at Velis herself, she knew that death came swiftly to those who meddled in politics. It was dreadful to think that she valued her present life so little that she was willing to risk it on a wild adventure.

Atti! *Wilful* child!

'She will not be harmed if she returns,' he said. 'You have my word on it.'

'And what is your word worth?' asked Lackmere.

'In this case, my life,' said Padry.

They looked at him curiously.

'I myself rescued her from the sack of the citadel at Velis,' he said. 'In a sense I adopted her. I arranged for her to be placed in the convent at Tuscolo. She was not happy there. I was thinking that perhaps I should take her directly into my own care, but . . .'

Their faces hardened. And of course there were difficulties. He knew it as well as they did. He had not the time. And a clerk, however exalted, could hardly be given charge of the raising of a young aristocrat – well, except as a very temporary measure, perhaps. (How stupid the world was!)

'She knows me as "Uncle Thomas",' he said.

'I see,' said Ambrose carefully.

They did not trust him. He could read it in their eyes.

'I think . . . Despite what you say, Master Padry, I do not think she should return to Tuscolo. I am sorry.'

'May I at least see her and speak with her?' Padry pleaded. 'It may be that of her own free will—'

'No.'

Padry sat back slowly and looked out over the water. The sun was down and the bay was in shadow. But the top of the broad knoll opposite still glowed that bright yellow gold that earlier had touched his heart. No longer. He remembered the name of the hill. Talifer's Knoll: named, presumably, after that same gaunt, deformed Talifer who had led him through the witch-world to this place.

All that misery, all that trial, for nothing!

'I swear,' he said, aware that his voice was trembling. 'If she returns with me, she will come to no harm.'

'It is in my mind to ask you, Master Chancellor,' said the baron, 'if she returns with you, what you think might and might not count as "harm".'

'I forgive you your vile insinuation,' said Padry heavily. 'Although I do not like to be lectured in morals by a man who feuds with his own son.'

Lackmere glared at him. 'Blood of Angels! If you were a knight—'

'Stop!' cried Ambrose, slamming the table with the flat of his hand so that the crockery jumped. Padry jumped, too.

'Master Padry,' said Ambrose, looking hard at him, 'there is peace between Aun and his son – peace, if perhaps no embrace. And you have strayed from the Path, I think. You should apologize.'

Apologize! Padry gasped. Apologize for reacting to that filthy, base, *shameful* charge! He would sooner—

Someone else was standing by the table.

It was a woman, dark-haired, in a plain dull robe that hung all the way to her feet. There was something immediately familiar about her – a likeness to the young Lord of Tarceny, who was looking up at her in surprise. Her face was more oval than his and less long. But the stamp of the eyes and nose was the same. An elder sister? A half-sister? Padry had not heard that there was one.

And he had not seen her approach. Suddenly she had just been there.

'I beg your pardon,' she said. 'I am late.'

'You come in your own time,' said Ambrose as the

men all rose to their feet. 'And I give thanks to Michael and Raphael that you have. Mother, may I introduce Thomas Padry, who is chancellor to King Gueronius, and his colleague Lex, who was once a student with me in Develin?'

'Thanks to the Angels, sirs, that they have guarded you on your journey here.'

'Amen,' said Padry automatically as he rose from his bow to take her hands. He was thinking: *Mother!* So now this journey had brought him to meet not only a pair of ancient princes, but also Phaedra of Trant, once infamous in the Kingdom as the runaway bride of old Tarceny! Inwardly he was still fired with anger and outrage, but in her presence there was nothing he could do with it. It was embarrassing that such a woman, of such a name, should have appeared and caught him with his feelings running so far ahead of his wits, as if he were a schoolchild with a tantrum.

His second feeling was one of awe.

To meet her in the life was extraordinary – this solemn-eyed woman with a lightness to her touch that was . . . well, not frail, but less substantial than it should be, as if she were not altogether flesh and bone. He studied her curiously as she turned to greet Lex. She looked young – or untouched by age, at least. Certainly she seemed younger than she should be, to be the mother of a grown man.

They settled in silence around the table again. Ambrose did not call to the house for a place to be laid for his mother. He simply passed down the bread.

She took it, broke off a small piece and put it into her mouth, chewing slowly. She was watching them. She looked as if she knew exactly what was going on. Perhaps she did. She had made her appearance, pat, just as matters at the table had started to slide towards disaster. And her interruption had given Padry the chance to think again.

'Sir,' he said slowly to the baron, 'I spoke in haste. I beg you to pardon it.'

The baron looked hard at him, and then nodded grimly.

Now he could begin once more. (Even though the wretched man had not offered a word of regret for the far, far worse things *he* had said! Really! But control yourself, Thomas Padry. A philosopher must not be slave to passion. You are here for a purpose.)

'I understand,' he said to Ambrose, 'that you would refuse me.'

'For her safety – yes.'

'Well,' said Padry, taking a deep breath, 'I had three points. On this, my second, I think you are choosing to offend against the King. Will you hear my third?'

'Of course.'

At the end of the table the woman broke off another small piece of bread and held it in her fingers. She looked at him as if she could hear his thoughts spoken aloud. Words jumped in Padry's memory: *Such a one eats only because it helps to remember.* Her face was like a pool that hid secrets below its surface.

'It concerns the practice of witchcraft,' he said.

131

The men eyed him warily. He put both his hands on the table to show that he held no iron in them. Tonight, his weapon would be his tongue.

'I need not remind you that witchcraft is abominated by the Church,' he said coldly. 'And that the Church has the ear of King and noble alike. Even in Develin – you may not have been aware of this – we were occasionally troubled by querulous bishops who felt that our studies had gone too far in certain directions. Your house, of course, has the reputation of having gone much further. The manner in which I was brought here confirms to me that this reputation is not unfounded. The manner and willingness with which that man Bavar came to put his head on your block says the same. I believe I heard him say you had commanded him in a dream.'

'I did. Although I would not call it witchcraft.'

'What would you call it, then?'

Ambrose shrugged. 'If any speak of it in the March, they give it the name "under-craft".'

'A name that only conceals its nature,' said Padry harshly.

The hands of the baron had slipped out of sight. Padry knew there could be a knife within inches of his belly. Still he did not care. There was just one thing that he was playing for. She must come home. He would risk everything – himself and Lex, too, if he must – for that.

'The Lady Astria has seen you in dreams also,' he said. 'I know this.'

'So now you are threatening me,' said Ambrose.

'I am saying that if you choose to make enemies, you give your enemies the chance to work a great alliance against you.'

At the end of the table the woman sat very still. But she was not looking at him any more. She was looking at her son.

'Ambrose,' she said, 'is this true?'

He glanced at her, and shrugged again.

'About Astria? Yes.'

'Then – I agree with your guest. I think she should not stay with you.'

Ambrose frowned. Padry almost cheered.

'Why not?' said Ambrose. 'You think she should go back to Tuscolo?'

She looked at Padry, and his heart sank once more.

'No,' she said.

No. Again! *Why* were they so set against him?

'But she has no claim on you either, Ambrose,' the woman said.

'I think she may have.'

'Why? You were right this morning. You were right to deny her suit and you were right about her. What thought had she given to her servant, who had come all this way with her? Does she grieve that the woman might die? No. But that she might lose the last thing she controls – yes, that gives her grief, it seems!'

'I thought so, too,' said the baron.

In a daze Padry wondered how they could be so unjust to Atti. Gadi was the girl's last link to her old life. Now she might lose her. She would need him now more than ever, he thought. And they would not let

133

him go to her. They would not let him!

Ambrose was looking at his mother. A slight smile played around his lips. 'The judgement – you saw all that?'

'I did.'

'Hah! And yet if I get Rolfe to show me things, you start to worry.'

'It is different, Ambrose. You know that. And if you have approached her in a dream, then yes, I worry!'

'Don't. Or if you must worry, worry about something that needs worrying about. Astria has lived well, at least outwardly. But take that other girl they brought to me today. I remember her when she was six. She'd been helping her parents in their fields and in their hut since she could walk. She's never known anything else. Of course, you say. That's always been the way, and there are tens of thousands like her across the Kingdom. But it hasn't always been the way! The priests used to run schools that even the poorest could go to. All that has been lost. Why? If I wore the crown in Tuscolo I could do something about it. Here, I can't even begin. And now she's an orphan, because of a stupid, petty act of brigandage that almost went unnoticed. What's to be done about orphans? That friary we set up today—'

'It isn't the poor, Ambrose. It isn't the children. It's you.'

'Me?' said Ambrose cheerfully. 'All right. Then maybe you should worry about this.' He picked up his drinking bowl, turning it so that the pale liquid swirled around the rim. 'Wine. This is the only place in the March I can get it, and I can't get enough. I'm sick of lying on wet ferns and drinking well-water that tastes of someone's lavatory. Does Gueronius drink wine every day, Master Padry?'

'Ambrose!'

'*Yes*, Mummy?'

'Amba, please listen – even if I am your parent! You must not think of going to Tuscolo, for Astria, or for any reason. You must not.'

'You would be hanged,' said Lex, speaking for the first time.

'Quite possibly,' said Ambrose, still smiling, but more grimly now. 'And no, I am not going to Tuscolo, Mother. I know my limits – or at least, I know what's good for me. He told me what would happen, long before any of you.'

('He'? thought Padry. For the word had slipped in through the fog of his misery.)

'He is dead,' said Phaedra quietly.

'His words live on,' Ambrose tapped his head. 'In here. *Go to Tuscolo, and you will die.* I don't forget that. Although I often wonder what he meant by "die".'

'I know of only one meaning,' said the baron.

'You should not listen to him,' said Phaedra. 'Even in your memories. What you will hear are his lies.'

'He lied expertly, by telling the truth,' said Ambrose simply. 'But no, I will not go to Tuscolo. I will curb my pities and bridle my thirst. And if it will make you happier, I will agree that Astria diBaldwin should neither stay in Aclete nor travel with me

135

round my various damp, filthy-watered hidey-holes. It might kill her anyway. We will have to think of something else.'

The woman gave him a long look, as if she wanted to believe him but was not sure that she could.

'Thank you,' she said.

'Indeed. And you can reward me for my good behaviour by persuading Master Padry here that he should not after all raise the standard of holy war against us when he returns to Tuscolo.'

They all looked Padry's way, then. Their faces were in shadow. The evening was deepening and the colours of the lakeside were fading into grey. The little lights on the tables seemed brighter now, flickering with the slightest movement of the air. Padry gathered his scattered wits. He felt sour, depressed and cheated. They had hardly listened to him. His plea had been rejected for reasons that seemed incomprehensible. Angels above! Did they think he could not handle Gueronius?

Or was it he himself that they did not trust? Must he defend himself even for liking to look at the child? For taking her hand when she needed comfort? They would not say. They would not tell him the truth. There was something hidden here. He could sense it. It was as if the Demon were with him again, walking unseen beside him on the Path. But he could not think what it might be.

'Very well,' said Phaedra. 'Although I will begin by speaking to both of you. I will say to you, Ambrose, that your guest is right. Under-craft, witchcraft, call it what you will, but it is indeed poisonous. It is poisonous because it is power. The more power you assume, the more you poison yourself. When you were a child you knew that. I wonder that you can have forgotten it . . .'

'I haven't,' said Ambrose. 'But there are many poisons. Need is a terrible poison, and power is the antidote. If I need to bring a petty warlord to heel, I must have power to do it. And a man like Bavar fears his dreams more than any drawn sword . . .'

'Nevertheless, Ambrose, an antidote is also poison, to be used sparingly if at all. And when you speak of "need", you must be sure that it *is* need, and not just something that makes things easier – or that gratifies you.'

'The step you most want to take is the one that strays from the Path,' said Padry.

'Oh indeed, Master Padry,' said Ambrose. 'Indeed.' And his look was so direct and grim that Padry felt a little uncomfortable. He wondered again whether he had missed something.

'And now I must address you, sir,' said Phaedra.

They were all looking at him – all of them, even Lex. Their heads and faces were becoming round grey shapes in the dusk. The lamplights rushed in a gust of wind.

'Tell me, sir. Of all the things you have learned in the past days, which seemed to you the greatest?'

Padry frowned. He did not like to follow when he could not see where he was going. He sucked his cheeks warily. But there was a clear answer. An obvious answer. He should not be afraid to give it.

'I suppose . . .' he said. 'The weeping voice.'

(The voice! The voice of the weeping earth. The pity of it! How could he have forgotten it for an instant? How could any hear it and not be changed?)

'I do not know if she is truly a goddess, or if she truly made the world,' said Phaedra. 'But she is the land that we live in. All the things you call "witchcraft" stem from the tears she weeps. You have seen Talifer and his brother Rolfe. Near to this place there is a miserable creature you would not recognize as a man. He is Prince Lomba – keen-eyed Lomba of our legends – the father of the house of Bay. Like his brothers he was held in a pool of Beyah's tears for three centuries until my son was able to call him out. He has been learning speech with me. Tonight for the first time he will speak with his King, and one day he will be a man again.

'The other sons of Wulfram – Dieter and Galen, Marc and Hergest – live on in the same pool. We will free them in time. But these are small victories. Still she goes on weeping. And while she weeps she poisons all our hearts. We hear her in our deepest dreams. She cries "*Let them eat their sons*", and we will. Today's truce is only a respite from tomorrow's war. So long as she weeps we will turn the iron that we brought into this land against one another. Perhaps she will never stop. But I believe it possible that she will. She is waiting for something. We do not know what it is, but one day we will find it.'

'Sometimes I think that it may be my death,'

said Ambrose ruefully. 'I am after all the very last father-to-son descendant of Wulfram there is.'

'Do not say it, Amba – please!'

'The heathen appease their gods by sacrifice, don't they? What other sacrifice, now, would appease Beyah? If she can be appeased at all.' He shrugged. 'All right. We don't know. But we are where we are. Will you have more wine, Master Padry?'

He did not wait for an answer but poured the sweet liquid into Padry's bowl.

'The point is,' he said as he served first the baron and then Lex, 'that if you have ever wondered why our people are so prone to war against each other, it is because we are driven to it. So my mother and I are looking, all the time, for the thing that might make the World-Mother cease from weeping. In the meantime I make it my task to bring peace wherever I can, and protect and help whomever I can. And I honour those who do the same. Sadly there are not many among the mighty of the land. Sophia at Develin is one.'

Padry looked up sharply. There was something in the way he had said her name that implied he had not simply picked her as an example.

'She is not the only one,' Ambrose went on. 'I would also name Raymonde diLackmere if his father would allow it. And until today I would have named you.'

The jug finished its round with a light thump as Ambrose set it on the table. He looked at Padry levelly. Night was almost on them. The boy's face was a shadow but his eyes glinted in the lights.

Padry cleared his throat. 'You have heard from Develin?'

'Today, concerning you.'

Develin was almost a week's journey away. The only way a message concerning him could have reached here was by the same way he had come – by witchcraft. And the Lady of Develin would know that he had deceived her. This might be awkward. Very awkward. Padry shifted in his seat. He felt tricked, trapped . . .

'I agree with Sophia,' said Ambrose, gently but firmly. 'You should not be here. You should be with Gueronius. You should go to him now. One way or another, you must persuade him not to cross the ocean.'

'I shall say this to him when I see him, and so will his other advisers.'

Ambrose shook his head. 'But you have not yet understood what I am telling you. *Why* must he leave off this adventure? It is not only to preserve his authority and keep the Kingdom at peace. He must do those things if he can, yes. But there is more. When Wulfram came from over the sea he brought great evil with him – iron, and the love of iron – all the things that make the World-Mother weep. It is for their share in it that his sons have suffered such torment. It is because of our share that she calls for us to eat our sons in turn. Now Gueronius will go over the sea, and what will come of it? Yes, I am afraid that he may go and be lost. But I am more afraid that he will go *and come back*. He will bring an evil as great as Wulfram did when we first came to this land.'

His eyes were like dragon-light. His forefinger pointed straight at Padry's heart.

'You have heard her. You know what the first crossing brought. You must go to Gueronius at once. *That ship must not sail.*'

VIII

The New Servant

hat can we do?' asked the princess.

'Not much now,' said Melissa. 'Only wait.'

They sat together in Melissa's bedroom at the inn, by the pallet on which they had laid the hillwoman. The window was shuttered against the night. A single rush burned low at the bedside. In its sickly light the face of the servant already looked like a skull.

Melissa had watched both her own little sisters die. She had not seen such sickness in a grown woman before. She did not know if the end would be the same.

She had done everything that she could think of. She had held the woman's hand, removed her blankets and wiped her with wet cloth when her skin burned, and wrapped her in them again when she started to shiver. She had talked to her, although there was never any answer. She had done all that through the long hours of the evening. But there was nothing she could do to stop the coughing. There was nothing to do but wait.

The princess sat with her at the bedside until

darkness. What did she feel, watching her servant die? Grief? Guilt? Anger, at the trouble of it? Melissa had felt all those things at her sisters' deaths. But the face of the princess was so very hard to read. And it grew harder still as the light failed. When she rose with a murmur and went to lie down on her pallet against the other wall, Melissa only thought, Good for her. There was no point in both of them staying awake all night. It might end before dawn, or it might not.

She sat in the darkness, holding the hillwoman's hand, listening to the uneven breaths for any sign of a change. As the inn around them fell silent she heard the breathing of the princess too. She heard it deepen into sleep. She began to doze herself.

In her doze she thought of her sisters, who were gone, and her mother and father and the hut, all gone. And she thought of the red knight who had brought her here, and he was gone, too. They had all left her. They had left her in this place where she had no place. The King had promised her something, but she did not know what it was yet, and neither did he.

She had nowhere to go. She did not want to go back to the clearing. She couldn't anyway, if they were going to put a priest there. In her mind she wandered and wandered in the darkness, just as she had wandered and become lost after her parents had died. She did not know what to do.

A hand gripped her own. She jerked awake.

Had she slept? How long? The light had gone out.

For a moment she could not think where she was. Her legs, curled on the floor, were numb from their position. Someone was gripping her hand, hard. Who . . . ?

A rustle of straw beside her. It was the hillwoman. It was her. She was awake.

She was awake but she said nothing. From the sounds in the darkness she was trying to lift her head. She was not even breathing. She was holding her breath.

She was listening.

Melissa listened, too. And now she thought that someone had been speaking in the moments before she had woken. There had been words, mumbled and indistinct. They had woken the hillwoman. What had they said? Melissa could not remember.

Then the words came again. It was the princess, loud but indistinct. 'Keep him away.'

She's asleep, Melissa thought. Asleep and dreaming. Is it . . . ?

'Keep him away,' begged the princess.

And '. . . following me.'

She's talking to the King, Melissa thought. She's talking to him in a dream, like I did.

'He's following me!' the princess repeated.

If the King answered, his words never entered the room. And still Melissa held hands with the hillwoman in the darkness. She heard a sigh from the pallet.

'Atti – Atti,' a hoarse voice said.

'She's asleep,' she whispered back. 'She was just dreaming. You should sleep, too.'

The hand gripped hers harder than ever. It was pulling her closer. She bent to listen.

'Look – after her,' the sick voice gasped in her ear. 'You must look after her.'

'I will,' she said.

'She is – so . . .'

A slow, hoarse breath. And another. And then: 'Look – after . . .'

'Yes,' said Melissa. 'I promise.'

She remembered to add, 'Till you're better, anyway.'

The gasping breaths resumed. One after another they struggled on into the night, like weary, lost footsteps that no longer knew where they were going. Melissa shifted her position. She went on holding the hand.

When she woke it was sunrise. Bleary and aching, she got to her knees. She was exhausted from the long watch and her days of eating nothing. She bent over the hillwoman to see if she was awake, and saw that she would never wake again.

The princess was sitting upright against the other wall, looking at the bright sky beyond the window. Melissa turned to tell her, then realized that she already knew.

'You must dress me,' the princess said, without taking her eyes from the light.

Dress her? thought Melissa. Was she too upset to dress herself?

'I'll try,' she said. 'Do you want to dress here?'

(Here – with the dead woman in the room?)

'Yes.'

145

Melissa dragged herself over and began to rummage for the princess's other gown.

'You stink,' said the princess dully.

'I'll wash when I've done you,' said Melissa.

Padry was dictating letters in the mean lodging hut when Lex put down his pen.

'I must say this,' he said. 'This is not good.'

Padry stared at him in astonishment. 'On the contrary,' he said when he had found his voice. 'We must tell Gueronius we have had an audience with Tarceny, or he will hear it from some other source and assume that I have begun to plot against him—'

'I don't mean *this*,' exclaimed Lex, jabbing his finger at the half-written page. 'I mean that we should not be writing letters at all! We should be going ourselves. We should be in Tuscolo. We should be in Velis. That's where we are needed. Not here!'

'We have not finished here.'

'We have done as much as we can, surely. We can't bring the child back but we know where she is. And we know she's safe.'

'Do we?' said Padry.

'He has said so, and for my money he's honest in this. In any case, the danger isn't in Tarceny. The danger is what's happening to our precious King's rule while our backs are turned.'

'I am not so sure.'

'Everyone else seems to be. You said it would take no more than a week, remember? We are right at the end of that now.'

'If you are keen to return to Tuscolo, do not worry. You will carry these letters, since I have no one else to send.'

'I'm nothing. It's *you* they need. You were his tutor. You must go and tell him that he cannot leave!'

Padry paused in the doorway. Their hut was right against the landward stockade of Aclete. All the little township lay between him and the big house at the waterside where Atti had her lodgings. He might have walked through the alleys and been with her in three minutes. But he could not do it. There were men guarding the house now. Ambrose of Tarceny had put them there to prevent him from approaching her. As if he would have dreamed of abduction! Really it was an insult: a rank injustice, and one he would be slow to forgive!

(Atti, Atti. What are you doing now?)

'Enough of this,' he said, turning back into the room. 'Please resume: "Wherefore, Your Majesty, if you see fit to accept my humble advice, you will forth-with have copied for your seal a letter to the March-count requiring . . ."'

Lex had not picked up his pen. He was holding his head in his hands, and breathing heavily. 'I walked through a bad dream to get here,' he said. 'Now it's a nightmare.'

He lifted his head to look Padry in the face.

'I thought it was a matter of state. I thought you knew she was going to appeal for help against the King.'

'I had no idea she would do that.'

'No. You didn't. It's never been about politics, has it? It's about *her*.' He drew breath. 'I'm sorry. I've been pleased to follow you. I've even come to admire you. But there was a question you did not answer when they put it to you last night. I've got to ask it again. *What is this child to you?*'

'What do you mean?'

'This . . . infatuation with her!'

'I am not infatuated with her.'

'Your mouth denies it. But what you do reveals it! Everything must wait. Everything – King, Kingdom, Justice, all so that you can have her back! Do you think we don't see? Didn't you ever see how your clerks smirked when you went out for your "walk in the cloisters"? And I'd say to them, "No, you don't understand. He sees himself as her guardian, that's all." And you'd come back with a light in your eye and a spring in your step and I'd say to them, "He just needed to clear his head." Master, please, for your own sake – what is it you think of, when you think of her?'

His eyes held Padry's. Neither spoke. Then Lex burst out: 'You are a good man! Why are you letting this happen to you?'

'ENOUGH!' roared Padry.

In utter silence they glared at one another.

'You are mistaken,' said Padry coldly. 'No philosopher could trammel himself with such an attachment – as you should know. Now please resume: "Wherefore, Your Majesty, if you see fit . . ." '

Wordlessly, Lex picked up his pen and began to write. He said nothing more while the letters were finished. He packed them into his satchel and his other belongings into his bag. He lifted them onto his shoulder.

'I'm going to sell the horses,' he said grimly. 'Then I will go down to the harbour. If I can get a boat today, I will take it.'

'I may only be a day or two behind you,' Padry called after him. 'I must hear how he judges her, that's all.'

Lex did not look back.

The next morning the two girls stood again before the King on the hilltop.

'Astria,' he said, 'I am sorry to learn that your servant is dead.'

'I have a new servant,' said the princess, with a slight nod towards Melissa.

All around them stood the circle of people. Some faces Melissa remembered from two days before – especially the hard-faced knight at the King's right hand. Others seemed to be new. The air was warm. Most of the watchers had thrown back their hoods and cloaks. Again Melissa felt awkward to be standing before all of them, even though it wasn't really her they were looking at but the princess. They had called the princess out first today. Perhaps the King did not want another argument about the order in which he listened to people.

'You must be sad to have lost a companion who has been with you for so many years,' said the King.

'I have had many servants who have died,' said the princess.

Melissa could not see her face. She had decided that the princess really was sad but would not say so to anyone – least of all to someone like the King. Melissa understood that. It was like not wanting to weep too loudly in case you were beaten again.

'Astria,' said the King, 'you asked me for judgement on two matters. On the first, I said that I thought it would be wrong to take up your quarrel against Gueronius. I have considered my words and I am sure that they were right.'

The princess said nothing.

'On the second, I admit that you have some case against my house . . .'

Melissa saw that the old knight beside him was looking away across the lake. His mouth was set in a short, straight line as if he knew what the King would say but did not agree.

'. . . I cannot, of course, give you back the people who were lost. I cannot even offer blood-money, since I live myself by the charity of those who please to call me their lord. All I can offer you, for the present, is the freedom of the March, my protection, such as it is, and food and shelter so long as you choose to stay in places where I may supply them to you. Will you accept this?'

Still the princess said nothing.

'Will you accept this?' repeated the King. 'If you do, there may come a time when I can offer you more. But if you do not, the only course I see for you is that you return to Tuscolo. And that I do not believe you want to do.'

'I will accept it for now,' said the princess.

'That is good. And I think it would be best if for the time being you went somewhere where it will be hard to find you, at least until your journey from Tuscolo and the reasons for it have been forgotten.'

'Where do you mean?'

'My mother has agreed to take you into her home. She has a house in the mountains beyond Hayley. She left last night to prepare a place for you there. If you are willing to go to her, I will see that you are guided and guarded on the way. I will also let you have mounts, since it is a hard journey through the March and your new servant is still recovering her strength.' His eyes fell on Melissa. He looked thoughtful.

'Thank you,' said the princess.

Melissa had thought she might be angry because she was not being given anything that she had asked for. But it did not show in her voice. Perhaps she was just glad now that someone was telling her where to find food and safety. Melissa was.

'It is not a rich place, where I am sending you,' said the King. 'My mother, whose line is as good as yours, worked with her hands for many years to win her keep from the mountains. So did I.'

'I do not care,' said the princess. 'I hate Tuscolo. And your lodging house has fleas.'

'Very good,' said the King. His eyes fell once again on Melissa. 'May I speak now with your servant?'

The princess glanced over her shoulder. Her face said nothing, but Melissa guessed that she was surprised.

'If you wish,' she said.

'Come forward, Melissa,' said the King.

Melissa came forward and knelt without being told to.

'You have taken service of your own free will?' asked the King in a low voice.

'Yes, lord,' she said.

'Why?'

Melissa shrugged. 'Don't know what else I'm to do, lord.'

'Very well then.' He glanced up at Atti, who was standing back a little. 'Help her for me,' he murmured, 'because I care about her. But remember that I care about you, too. I have promised you that if there is ever anything you wish, and it is in my power, I shall give it to you. I will not forget that. Neither should you.'

'I will not, lord,' she said, although she could not think of anything to ask for from him.

'Very well then,' said the King, lifting his voice and addressing both of them. 'For your safety you should go as soon as you can. Your escort is waiting for you among those trees, with mounts. Do not fear him. He is hard to look upon but he will keep you safe on your journey. Now Michael guard you and Raphael guide you on your way.'

And then they were alone, two girls walking across the open space towards the trees. Behind them in the ring another name was called. The sound of voices was diminishing with each step they took. The trees were coming closer. Melissa watched them loom up and over her – great smooth green-brown trunks, a carpeting of dead leaves, moss gathering on fallen branches. She could see only a little way among them.

It was gloomy. The branches wove and rustled in the light air. Everything was green and orange and brown. She hesitated. She could not see any guide or mounts. The princess strode on.

Wait a moment, thought Melissa as she hurried after her. Wait up there! I'm supposed to be looking after you.

But it did not feel to her as though she were looking after the princess. She felt helpless, blind, as though she were walking into mist. She was walking into her future and had no idea what it would hold. She could not imagine the place that she was going to. Only the princess, walking a pace ahead of her, and the memory of the King's voice, gave her any direction at all.

Deeper they went into the wood. The open space behind them was lost altogether. The ground was uneven and ran with roots. Something blew, hard, and Melissa jumped.

There! Behind a low bank she saw the back of a horse – a horse, and a mule beside it. They were saddled, with bags hanging from them. There seemed to be no one else. The two girls scrambled over the bank and stood by the animals. They looked around. Melissa wondered whether she should call out for the guide.

Then something lurched forward from the shadow of a trunk. Melissa screamed.

It was a monster – a terrible thing, half man, stooping, with long trailing arms and legs that bent the wrong way like a hideous bird's. It was wrapped in shreds of grey rag that concealed half its face, but she saw its eyes and the sagging, drooling mouth that cooed at them like a dove. She saw, with the sudden clearness of a nightmare, how its limbs were covered in a film of water that gathered in dull droplets at its talons and yet did not fall to the ground.

She shrank back, crossing her arms before her to shield herself from the thing. The mule lifted its head and looked at her, as if to ask, *Why are you behaving like that?* And the princess stood before the monster.

'You must take us into the mountains,' she told it clearly. 'He has said so.'

At about noon Padry emerged from the oak-wood and found a little hut at the foot of the northern slopes of the knoll. There was a landsman sitting at the door binding an axe-head to a shaft. Yes, he had seen two girls this morning. They had come out of the wood on horses and taken the road to the north. No, he had not spoken with them. Matter of fact, he had had to go indoors as soon as he had seen them. He couldn't remember why.

And had the girls been alone?

Maybe, maybe not. The landsman couldn't say, somehow.

Padry tossed a coin onto the earth. The man looked at it, but made no attempt to pick it up. No, sir. He couldn't remember.

154

'I see,' said Padry, and looked up at the sky.

Noon. It was time to go.

It was past time. Even if he set sail the moment he returned to Aclete, he would barely finish the crossing before dark. Somewhere in Aclete bay was a fisherman whom Lex had engaged to wait for him and carry him across the lake. The man must be impatient already. Perhaps he would even shake his head and say the crossing was impossible now and they must wait until tomorrow. He would say it to wring more money out of Padry, in addition to whatever it was that Lex had paid him to stay and wait.

And beyond the lake was the journey to Tuscolo – a good three days of it, travelling like a tinker in whatever gaggle of pilgrims he could attach himself to for safety. Perhaps Lex, if he reached Tuscolo unharmed, would have an escort sent back along the road to look for him. And then the piles of the King's business that he had been neglecting in his absence, and the journey north to Velis to talk sense into Gueronius. How long before that wretched ship was ready? They might even be loading it now. He was running late, late, and he knew it.

He knew it was urgent. If he did not go, then none of it would be done. But – but it could wait just a little longer, surely. He could look just a little further. That was what he had to do now.

They had not let him speak with her! They had guarded her, taken her up to the hilltop and then spirited her away! He had been there, muffled carefully in his cloak and hood, to see her second appearance on the knoll. He had watched her, willing her to look his way in the hope of passing some sign to her. He had a cold, depressing feeling that she had known he was there and still had not looked. (Wilful child – *just* like the twelve-year-old he had led from the smoking garden!) And perhaps the Lord of Tarceny and his men had known he was there also. He had felt the need to be careful, and in being careful he had delayed too long. By the time he had slipped away she was gone. There had been no sign of her among the oak trees. She was on her way to the mountains beyond Hayley.

He had heard the King say she would have a guide. But would that be enough in this wild country?

And what sort of guide was it that this landsman was insisting he had not seen? Padry thought he could guess. He did not like his guesses at all.

At least she was travelling by the ordinary roads of the world. That was good. No child should walk in the place of brown rocks. No one should go there at all unless in the most desperate need. Ambrose understood that.

And they were going to Hayley. Padry had a vague idea that Hayley was a keep in the far north of the March. The Kingdom had never stretched beyond that point, so far as he knew. The mountains were peopled by no one but the wretched, heathen hill tribes. Atti was being sent to the very edge of the known world. And why?

To keep her out of his reach! It was unfair! Unjust!

They did not trust him when they should. What were their feelings for her, beside his?

What hurt most was that she had gone willingly. And that he had not had the chance to speak with her before she went.

If he had . . .

He gripped the staff and prodded the dusty earth at his feet.

His boat was waiting. The man would have been waiting all morning while Padry first went to the hearings, then searched the oak woods and then sat on a root with his head in his hands. He would go on waiting while Padry walked back to his hut to gather his belongings. And when Padry finally appeared on the quay the man would spit, say it was too late, and they would begin the long haggle for a passage all over again.

Maybe it was indeed too late. The sun was inching past noon. The man could not land his boat in the dark, surely? So Padry might now have until tomorrow to spend on this side of the lake.

How many roads were there to Hayley from here? And how far could a child, even mounted, have travelled in a morning?

He prodded the dust again with his staff.

He had no food with him, of course. He had his purse but no food. Perhaps – perhaps the sensible thing would be to . . .

No, not sensible. He was tired of being sensible. There was only one thing he wanted to do. Even if it came to nothing.

With a strange lightness in his heart he turned his back on the Kingdom. He turned his back on his King, dreaming crazy dreams of adventure across the sea. He followed the path to the north.

The path ran along the lakeshore. The ground was hard. But where it dipped to cross the mouth of the stream, Padry found hoofprints in the mud of the far bank. And with them he found something else: a curious, trailing mark, more like the print of a huge bird's foot than of any animal he knew.

Casting along the path on the far side of the stream, he found the mark again. He found it sunk in a broad, flat stone: a long, clear stroke, with smaller ones at angles on either side of it. The depressions in the rock were damp and stained a brown colour. There was a strong, watery scent to it, which screamed at once to him of the gateway at Lackmere.

A little way further along the path he found another.

With his heart in his mouth now, he began to hurry.

IX

The Abyss

fortnight later he was in the mountains beyond the last borders of the Kingdom. He had eaten little more than berries for two days. There was still some dried fish in his pack but he was saving that. Down in the wooded March, on the road to Hayley, there had been little huts or hamlets where people had accepted his coin for food and a night's lodging. (He had developed a trick of pretending to count out his last coin each time, just in case his hosts were tempted to murder him for his purse.) Up here the people were even fewer. He did not trust them. These were the hill folk, traditional enemies of the Kingdom: poor enough, he guessed, to kill a man for the clothes on his back. Besides, he did not know if they had any use for coins. He avoided their settlements when he could. He had nothing to guide him but the marks of that awful foot and the rare, blessed sight of old horse-droppings by the path.

He had missed the trail more than once. He had lost count of the days. The Angels might know what the King was doing but Padry did not care. He could guess at the words Lex and Lady Develin were using about him, and what they would say to him when they saw him again. But he did not care about that either. He thought that perhaps he would never go back. At nights he dreamed of Atti and held her hand. By day he rehearsed the talk he would have with her: what he would say and what she would, how he might persuade her, how he might make her see.

Indeed they were beautiful, these mountains. He had never been among such peaks in his life before. They rose, sharp-edged, clear against the hard blue of the sky. Their lower slopes were coated with brush, their heads and shoulders were yellow and grey rock. Carrion birds drifted in lazy circles above the hillsides. Insects buzzed thickly among the thorns. As the day drew on, clouds grew above the peaks and settled on their shoulders in long, foaming masses that poured silently down the slopes at evening. He would sit and watch them, with his legs weak, and hungry and aching from the day. Above him the ridges would darken, going purple against the sky, and then fading into night. One by one the stars would come out.

They were beautiful but they were deadly. From the tops of the ridges, when he climbed them, he could see far away the higher peaks where the snow would never melt. And as the year wore on those snows would come down, falling in blankets over all this country and stifling it of life. Already the air seemed to be cooler in the evenings. Winter was coming. And then where would Atti be?

Come back, Atti. Come back to life. Come back to me.

Or shall we both die in the mountains?

He was following a path; a narrow, winding track no wider than rabbits make. To his right the hillside climbed steeply to a high crest. To his left it fell a giddy depth to the valley floor. A stream ran there, narrow and muddy brown. The path sloped upwards. It might take the rest of the day to reach the ridge top. His limbs were weak. His muscles strained with the slope. He was panting. His ears were full with his own breath.

He stopped and listened.

For a moment – he could have been imagining it, but it had seemed very real – for a moment he had heard footsteps that had not been his. Yet there was no one on the path with him. There was nothing but the great, empty hillsides, sweeping barrenly up to his right and down to his left.

He shook his head. His ears were not ringing. They seemed to be hearing perfectly clearly.

After a moment he walked on, listening intently. He could hear nothing but the gasp of his breath and the rattle of the stones under his thinning soles. He was leaning heavily on his staff with his head bowed as he went. He was nearly exhausted. Very nearly. At the ridgeline he might rest. Or perhaps before that. But he would keep going a little further. Just a little.

Then—

'Who's there?' he gasped.

'I am,' said a voice behind him. A woman's voice.

He levered himself round to face her.

161

She was alone, standing on the hillside where a moment before there had been no one but him. She was just as he had seen her at the table in Aclete: dark-haired, slim and too young for her age. She wore the same dull robe that hung all the way to her feet. She was looking at him solemnly. He looked back into the face of Tarceny.

'You were following me,' he said. His voice sounded like a croak in his ears.

'Not long, and not so that you would see me. But yes, I have been watching you.'

He leaned on his staff, and looked at her. 'By witch-craft, I suppose?' he said.

'You may call it that. I have to tell you that you are near the end of your journey. But you will not get what you want by it.'

There was nothing harsh or forbidding about her tone. She sounded a little sorry for him.

'Is she close?' he asked.

'Yes.'

'Guarded?'

'Yes.'

He pulled himself upright and gripped his staff.

'By many?' he insisted.

'She is guarded by Lomba, brother to the princes Talifer and Rolfe. Lomba has only recently come out from the pit, although we spent a year calling him. He is much more a monster than either of his brothers, with a monster's pitilessness and strength. You would not prevail against him.'

'That has yet to be tested,' Padry said.

She took a step closer. Her eyes looked up into his. 'What poison is it, sir, that drives the brain to madness? This pretty thing with her delusions of a throne! Would you of all people risk a bloody death for her?'

'Poison! She is not poison to me!'

'No, my Lord Chancellor? How is it then that you stand here? She had barely set foot in my house before she had warned me that you might follow. And you have.'

Angrily he struck his staff on the stones of the mountain. 'May I not simply care for her? How is it *poison* to want to save a child from the wilderness?'

'If you wish, I will show you.'

In her hands there was a large stone cup, with a stem like a goblet. The stone was roughly carved, and winding around its rim was the vague form of something like a snake, or a long-bodied dragon. The bowl was half full of dark water. Where had it come from? She could not have been carrying it beneath her cloak like that, water and all, surely?

But undeniably it was there.

'Look,' she said.

He looked at the water and . . . Well, it was water, with the sky reflected at one level and the brown, pitted bowl showing through at another. He glanced up at her, perplexed, and down at the water once more.

'I don't—' he began.

'Look,' she said again.

There was something in the water – floating? A

163

scrap of waste or cloth? Or was it another reflection? All these thoughts chased through his mind in a moment. Then the thing wavered and turned, and it was a ship.

It was a ship: a big, two-masted cog such as the merchants of Velis used. The image of it floated there on the surface of the water, seeming to grow as he looked. It was moving gently out of a bay. Its sails were set, curving to catch the light and the wind. There were banners flying from the masts, long, floating banners, and even at this distance he could guess at the device, the great sun of Tuscolo.

Gueronius.

'He has gone, you see,' she murmured. 'Without you, they could not hold him. He has left his throne and judgement hall empty. And where now is all the work you have done, since the day that Develin fell?

'The mind deceives itself, Padry. Even as it blunders into darkness, gratifying its desires, it will tell itself that it is on the true Path. Yes, you did a good thing when you saved her from the sack. Perhaps it was wise, too, to have placed her under the convent mothers, so that should you be tempted you could at least not act on your temptation. Still she was there, under your window every day, for your eyes and thoughts to dwell upon. Why did you remain in Tuscolo when Gueronius returned to Velis? What good-seeming reasons did you find, to mask the one in your heart? You hid it well – well enough at least that you never needed to admit it to yourself.

'But your eyes betrayed you. When you let them rest

on her, that beautiful little thing, she guessed. She knew your heart better than you did. You never saw how she shuddered. And then you spoke to her, and said that you might take her from the convent and into your care. You have thought that saving her might be the one good thing you had done in your life. If she has done one good thing in hers, Padry, it may be that she saved you by fleeing from you. But she could not save your duty. And many people will pay the price.'

Padry's eyes were fixed on the ship. He could see it so clearly that he felt he could almost call to it. But no, even if he had stood on the shores of the bay itself, surely it would have been too far. He watched it heel as the wind took it, drawing it gently beyond all reach, out into the ocean. As it began to diminish, he looked up.

'He will – he will have made provision for the Kingdom,' he said. 'There will be regents. When I return to Tuscolo, I can—' He stopped.

'Will you return?'

'I . . . Of course.' He gripped his staff. 'But I must see Atti.'

'You cannot take her with you.'

'I will take her if she will come.'

'She will not. Understand me. It is you that has driven her here. She will not go with you. And if you would save yourself you will make her dead to you in your thoughts, return to Tuscolo, and see what can be remade from what has been broken.'

Padry looked at his hand, at the uneven colours of

his ageing skin. He seemed to see it very clearly, as her words sank slowly into his heart. Anger, a horrible weak anger, rose in him. It was unfair! Lies! It was a trick to keep him from her. *It should not be like this!*

And wrapped in his anger was the fear that it might be true.

Atti, looking away from him. Atti, not seeing him, determinedly. Each time he had stood there on the hilltop she had not seen him. Even in the convent garden, even when he had taken her hand and stroked it soothingly, her face would have been turned away, looking among the bell towers or the shadowed cloisters. Only the curve of her cheek, like the crescent of the new moon. Atti . . .

He almost stamped in his frustration. Day after day on the roads, and his duty in ruins – for nothing? 'I must see her! I can't help it – I must *see* her!'

'Very well,' said the woman at last. 'Follow the path to the ridge. You will find a house. She is there. You may speak to her if she will listen. Do not attempt to touch her, even if she seems to be alone.'

She turned, still holding the cup, and seemed to walk into the hillside. In an instant she had vanished. Padry was by himself, high in the mountain valley.

He reached the ridge at sunset, when the valleys were lakes of deep shadow and the ridges, yellow in the last light, were like islands in a rising sea. Before him, across a great gulf of air, was a high, snow-covered peak, wreathed in cloud. The air was chilly. He shivered.

At his feet the path ran on, downhill now, along the very crest of the ridge. There at the end of it, where the ground fell steeply on three sides, was the house. It was a strange sight to see here in the mountains, with a little squat-towered gatehouse, roofs and terraces clustered on the sharp spine of the rock. It was not big, and yet he had seen nothing more than the mean, circular huts of the hill folk since passing the ruined keep at Hayley. On that huge arm of rock the scale of it seemed all wrong.

Voices came distantly to his ears – the voices of girls from within those solemn walls. He heard one of them laugh. There was something chilling about that laughter – about the thought that a girl could be happy without him, not even knowing that he was close. With a growing feeling of dread in his heart he limped down the path to the gate.

The doors were ajar. The gate-tunnel was deep in shadow. He did not call. He did not dare risk raising his voice. He slipped through the open leaf of the door and crept inwards.

On the far side was a small courtyard, bounded on three sides by buildings and on the fourth, to his left, by a low wall that looked out over the valley. There was no one there. The voices came from beyond an arch-way opposite. He recognized Atti's, speaking in a low, serious tone.

He stole across the open space and stood in the shadow of the second arch.

He was looking through a colonnade, like the cloisters of a convent, or— No, it was more like the columns around the garden at Velis where he had first set eyes on her in the middle of the smoke and battle. There were no plants or pots or pathways here – just a simple paved space – but there in the middle of it was the bowl of a fountain, exactly like the one he remembered. Beyond it was something like a throne on a raised platform. Between the fountain and the throne stood the two girls.

They were playing a game. One of them was the gawky peasant girl he had seen on the hilltop at Aclete. She had a cup and ball in her hand. She was trying to catch the ball in the cup. She was not very good at it. Atti, standing with her, was saying, 'You must keep your eye on it. No, not like that. Let me . . .' and she took it, and showed the other girl how to catch it one-two-three, with easy flicks of her wrist that saw the ball landing neatly in the cup again and again. She gave it back to the other girl and watched while her companion tried and tried and failed. The peasant girl laughed again. Atti did not laugh. She never did.

Padry stood in the shadows and watched. It was so long since he had seen her! He wanted to rush forward, to have her eyes on him, to see her smile in joy as he would smile in joy. And yet . . .

And yet he did not want to move. He did not dare to break the moment that he saw, two girls together. He was afraid of what would follow if he did. He was trying to imagine Atti smiling at him, and could not. He could not remember ever having seen her smile. Even now, as the other girl giggled at her own clumsiness, her face (as much as he could see of it) was solemn, watching. She was calm, but . . .

Why could he not see more of her face?

Atti, dear Atti – turn and look at me! Do not make me come bumbling out of the shadow to you. Turn and show me that – that at least you are pleased that I am here?

She did not turn. But as he watched he saw the other girl's eyes fall on him and the laughter drop from her lips. She said something in a low tone to Atti. Atti answered. Two words – he did not catch them, but they might have been *I know.*

She did not look round.

She knew he was there. She would not look at him. She stood just as she had stood in the garden at Velis, looking away, very, very still – still as a statue, while he pleaded to her back. Oh, Atti!

There was no gate, no bars here. He could step into the courtyard. He could walk across and take her by the arm, look her in the eyes: *Atti, do you see how you wrong me?*

But the shadows were deep in the colonnades. The girls seemed to be alone, yet in the darkness close by something was watching him.

It was forbidden. And now even his own soul forbade it.

He let himself cast one more look, one long look, down her. His eyes traced her cheek, pale as the sickle moon; the subtlest curves of her young breast and hip, just showing under her gown: the woman swelling within the child's frame. He knew his own corruption.

He knew it at last and knew that it had always been with him.

He caressed it once in his mind. Then he turned and shuffled back into the outer courtyard.

Phaedra was standing by the low wall. She said nothing as he approached. He said nothing either but walked slowly with his head bowed. He could not help it that his eyes screwed up, hot and moist and burning, or that his throat seemed to block and choke as if he had swallowed sweet embers. And the Path was lost, lost long ago. And every word he had spoken was a lie.

He reached the wall and stood beside her.

'You see,' she said to him.

He could not speak.

In a moment, he supposed, she would tell him where he might sleep, and whether he might eat, and how he might begin his journey home. He did not want to think about that. He thought that he might even jump from the wall, if he could find the will.

She must have read his thought, for he felt her hand gently grip his arm. He shook his head, meaning *I'm not going to be that silly.* He did not want to look at her, although she must know very well that he was weeping.

He looked out and down, into the cold shadows of the valley. The hillside sloped away, a long, barren plunge of rock and thorn. His eyes blurred as he stared at it. He wondered if it had a bottom at all. The wall between him and the gulf was little more than waist-high. So little, and the fall beyond so very deep.

He was back, back in the Abyss where nothing had meaning any more. At his belt hung the carved wooden figures: the Lantern, the Leaf and the Dragon. But his fingers seemed to be numb. He did not touch them.

Behind him the peasant child laughed as the girls resumed their game.

PART II

THE LEAF

X

Night Talk

he dream was of the safe place, the girl's childhood home, the great house filled with sunlight. There were tall windows and high rooms and brilliant, beautiful, smiling people who passed her and spoke to her with love.

She had dreamed it many times before.

A face swam by, a face she remembered, one of the hill people who were servants in the house. She tried to speak to the face and could not. Another came, a beautiful woman in pale silks with long brown hair who smiled and spoke. She knew that the woman was dead.

She had dreamed all this before. She knew what was coming. She knew it because this was the safe place and the safe place was not safe. Very soon it would not be safe for any of them and they would all be dead. She tried to speak to the faces that passed her. She tried to tell them what would happen. But her tongue was that of a child so little that she could not say the words. The people smiled at her as they passed. Their faces were already darkening.

The colours were changing. The rooms were not bright but a purple haze in which black shapes of people moved, hurrying now. She could hear the voices crying aloud. She cried aloud, too. She cried to them not to forget her, not to leave her, but she could not say the words. Father stalked by, angry in his black armour, and it was too late.

Now the shapes and faces and cries gathered into one. And she knew that there had only ever been one – one shape, only one, close, all the time, just beyond the curtain. The curtain was behind her. She could not turn. She could not face it. Now it was drawn aside, slowly. She could not face it but she knew that it was drawing aside.

The killer entered and all the voices became a single scream.

'Atti! Atti!'

The cries had stopped but Melissa's ears were still ringing. In the darkness she fumbled for the body that writhed and kicked like an animal beside her.

'Atti – you're having a nightmare! Can you hear me? Atti!' She found the shoulders, gripped them and tried to shake them.

'*Get away from me!*' Something hit Melissa hard in the mouth. She lost her hold.

'*Get away!*' Atti screamed. She still had not woken.

'Atti – it's Melissa! You're all right – it's just a nightmare!' (Just? She was thrashing in the darkness and shrieking like a rabbit in a snare. What was happening to her?) 'Atti! Can't you hear me? *Atti!*'

Atti's breath was coming in long, shaking gasps. Gently Melissa reached out and risked putting a hand on her arm again.

'Atti? Are you awake now?'

Atti groaned.

'You poor thing,' whispered Melissa. 'What was it?'

'No!'

'It's all right! It's all right . . .' Melissa fumbled around, found the blanket and dragged it up over their knees. Then she put an arm round Atti's shoulders and they sat together with their backs to the rough, chilly wall of the sleeping chamber. The only light came from the open square of window, which showed a patch of night sky decked with stars. The moon must be down. It was somewhere beyond midnight.

Her lip throbbed where Atti had struck it.

'Cold, isn't it?' she said at last, and as cheerfully as she could. 'Getting colder, too. I suppose when winter comes we should sleep in the kitchen after all.'

Atti had not wanted to sleep in the kitchen. People like her did not sleep in kitchens. But it was the only working hearth in that strange stone house, and it drew the warmth into its walls. Melissa already knew that winter in the mountains was going to be far colder than either of them were used to. She was beginning to worry about how they would cope with it. Even now the night air chilled her neck and shoulders.

Sleep dragged at her brain. She wanted them both to snuggle down under the blanket and sink back into warmth and darkness. But Atti wasn't going to sleep. Not yet, anyway.

'It's back,' she said.

'What is?'

'The dream.'

'You've had it before?'

Atti did not seem to hear the question.

'Someone's going to *kill* me,' she said quietly. 'That's what it means.'

Melissa was astonished. 'No one wants to kill you, Atti!'

Atti drew breath. Then she let it out again in a long sigh.

'I've had it ever since Velis,' she said. 'I'm *remembering* things – things that happened when I was little. And then I'm seeing something that's going to happen. Something ... I don't know if they're going to kill me, or just kill everyone else and destroy everything and leave me there. But that's what it means. And it's ... I always think it's—' She stopped.

Then, quietly, deliberately, she said, 'I think it's someone I know.'

Melissa, dazed with weariness, didn't believe a word of it. Her fingers tested her lip and found it was swelling up fast.

It was just a *dream*, Atti ...

But she didn't think it would help if she said that.

'Maybe you should talk to Phaedra,' she mumbled.

Atti stiffened. 'Why should I?'

'Because she's supposed to help us.'

'I shall do nothing of the sort.'

'But she might—'

'*No!*'

Suddenly Atti was beginning to shake again. More astonished than ever, Melissa tightened her hold around her shoulders. 'Atti! What's the matter?'

'She's a witch!' Atti hissed. 'Hadn't you noticed?'

'No, Atti!'

'She doesn't sleep, she doesn't eat, she's there when you can't see her! She doesn't even need to open the door when she comes into a room. And she ought to be much older than she is!'

'She doesn't mean to—'

'I hate the way she looks at me!'

Melissa nearly said, *Oh, go to sleep!* But she didn't. She knew that Atti was scared and lonely. Really, really lonely. So she went on holding her, as if this princess who by day might barely speak, barely allow herself to be called 'Atti', was in the darkness one of Melissa's lost little sisters who had somehow lived and grown after all. Melissa had never thought that a sister might try her so.

'My fingers are bleeding,' Atti said.

'You hit me in the teeth.'

'Does it hurt?'

'It's all right,' said Melissa, testing her swelling lip.

'You should be angry with me.'

'Why? You didn't know what you were doing.'

They sat together in that narrow, dark chamber with the window-square of night sky above them and all the vastness of the mountains outside.

'Do you ever dream of your home?' asked Atti.

Melissa tensed. 'I dream of my mam sometimes,' she said reluctantly. 'She tells me things.'

'But you don't dream of what happened?'

'No.'

Silence.

'I'm the worst thing on earth,' said Atti.

Sleep was in Melissa's brain. Her swollen lip was making her mouth clumsy. Her shoulders hated the cold. But there was still that aching loneliness in Atti's voice and Melissa knew she had just made it worse. Cross and tired as she was, she had one last try.

'What do you mean? That's stupid, Atti! That's really stupid! You're wonderful! I wish I was like you. You're clever, and brave, and—'

She stopped before she said *beautiful*, because of course that was what she really wanted to be. But Atti heard it all the same. Her head turned in the darkness.

'You only see my face,' she said. 'You think that's what I'm like. Everybody does. But you'll learn.'

'Oh! Go to sleep!'

Melissa did not sleep well herself after that. She did not sleep because of the things that had stirred inside her when Atti had asked *Do you ever dream of your home?*

She knew why Atti had asked it. Maybe it was the only thing they could have talked about that would have done Atti any good. But Melissa did not want to talk about those things – the stream, the hut, the goats, Mam, **Dadda** . . . She had shut all that away. If

180

she thought about it she would find herself thinking –
Why?

(And – what did they feel, when it happened to
them?)

She could not know the answers. If she did they
would only be worse than the questions.

Why? No answer.

Dadda would have told her to stand on her two feet.
That's what she would do. She would not think of
home and she would not dream of it either. She never
would.

Who'd want to dream like Atti, anyway?

No wonder Atti had wanted Ambrose to make her
Queen. If she was right up there, right up at the top
with guards and armies and everyone obeying her,
then everyone would have to look after her. No one
could come breaking in and destroying everything
then. Too bad they couldn't all be kings and
queens, then none of that sort of thing would ever
have to happen to anyone!

(Dusk in the clearing, the smell of woodsmoke, and
her own voice asking, *Why isn't Dadda a king?*) She
stopped herself. She wasn't going to think about that.

Then Atti spoke in the darkness and made her
jump.

Atti was talking in her sleep. Her words were loud
but muddled. Melissa remembered the night that
Gadi had died in the big house at Aclete. Atti had
spoken in her sleep then, too. She had been speaking
to the King.

She's speaking to him now, Melissa thought. He's

right there beside me, in her head. What's he saying?

Why doesn't he speak to me?

She waited, but nothing more happened.

Something happened the next evening. Atti came into the kitchen and found Melissa gutting some fish she had caught in the stream at the bottom of the valley. She stood with her hands on her hips to watch while Melissa took off a head with one stroke of the knife, slit the belly with a second and scraped out the dark innards with a third. Melissa dropped the rest into the basket, picked up another and began again – head (one) belly (two) insides . . .

'Here, let me,' said Atti.

Surprised, Melissa let her have the knife. Then she got up from the rickety old stool and let Atti settle herself, put the clay platter on her knees, pick up a fish and take aim with the point of her blade.

'Um,' said Melissa.

Then she said, 'That's right,' and tried not to wince at the waste of flesh as the head finally came off.

'Will we eat these tonight?' asked Atti, without looking up.

'One of them, only. We thread the others on sticks and hang them up to dry for the winter.'

'Dried fish,' groaned Atti. 'How lovely!'

They'll be lovely when we get to them all right, thought Melissa. We'll be wanting them that badly in a month or so. But she didn't say it. She just stood and watched. It was the first time Atti had ever helped with something like this.

'What did he say?' Melissa asked.

'Who?'

'The King. You spoke with him last night.'

'Why should he have said anything?'

Because you're gutting fish, Melissa thought. You, the princess. And looking at you, I'd say you've never done it before in your life.

Atti kept on working. After a moment she said, 'I was getting it again. I was back in the room with the curtain behind me. It was about to open. And then Ambrose ... It's hard to describe. He was standing beside me, looking as if he had heard me and had come to see what the matter was. It's something he's done before. Three or four times, now. That was why I left Tuscolo to find him ...

'And he says the same thing each time. I have to turn round and speak to whoever is behind the curtain. I can't, of course. It's not like that. Then he says he will stay with me and we will meet whoever it is together, but I still can't. Then he asks me if I would just like to wake up. So I say yes. And I do. Last night I woke in our room and you were lying beside me. And he said – I won't say what he said about you. But you're right. We should sleep in the kitchen from now on.'

'He can't get you, you know,' said Melissa.

'Who?'

'The man who followed you here. That's who you're dreaming of, isn't it?'

Atti frowned over the next fish. 'It's not him,' she said. 'Not any more. He was just a silly old fool.'

'Who is it then?'

Atti neither looked up nor answered. Her knife sawed furiously at the fishhead.

Fine, thought Melissa. You know, or you think you know. But you won't tell me so I can't help you. You'll let the King help you, but you won't let me.

And what was it he said to you about me? Was it just *Try to help Melissa if you can?* Or was it more than that? You won't tell me that either.

'There,' said Atti. 'Is that all?'

'I only caught the four,' said Melissa. 'I'll do better when I can make some traps.'

Atti put down the knife and lifted her hands. They were filthy and slimy with the insides of fish, and fresh fish blood had dribbled to her wrists. She looked at them for a moment, turning them to see both the backs and the palms. And watching her, Melissa was caught by the Face again. She saw it as if for the first time – the pureness and brightness of it, the simple curves of brow and nose and cheek that would never be lost even in a starving mountain winter. It sat on her head like a mask, separate from the person within, and seemed only a little sad that the world would never be as perfect as itself. Melissa stared at her, forgetting for a moment everything else. Can this be true? she thought. Can someone like this really be alive?

Then Atti dropped her hands with a light, weary chuckle. It was the nearest Melissa had ever heard her come to a laugh.

XI

Mountain Home

hill boy got them through the winter.

He appeared one day in the autumn, leading a donkey up the narrow path that led back down the hillside and out to the rest of the world. He was small – no taller than Atti – but then all the hill folk were small, so among them he might have been ordinary. His hair was black and shaggy, his narrow face was brown and already wrinkling at the eyes from the sun and wind, but his teeth were white and good so Melissa guessed he was not much older than she was. He smiled a lot. He did not speak a word that Melissa could understand. But he pointed to the bags on the back of the mule and opened them for her, and there she found meal, a sack of roots she did not recognize, dried berries, dried fish and even a little dried meat.

'For us?' she said, astonished. 'You're joking!'

He was not joking. He unslung the bags from the donkey's back and put them into the room in the outer courtyard that was used as a storehouse – he seemed to know just where it was. Melissa watched him open-mouthed for a moment. Then she said, 'Wait!' and ran into the inner courtyard, into the kitchen, and took one of the blankets that she had folded up that morning by the hearth.

Fair was fair, she thought. You got something, you gave something. But also she thought that if there was going to be a trade for the food then she would be the one who would say first what it was worth. She ran back to the boy and held out the blanket. He shook his head and smiled. She had expected that.

'What's the matter with it?' she said loudly. 'It's a good blanket. It'll keep you warm.' At the same time she was thinking she would try two blankets next, and then the smaller of the two iron knives from the kitchen. And she wouldn't offer more than a blanket and a knife together, even if he put the whole lot back on his donkey and walked off with it again.

He didn't want any of it. He waved it away with his hand, grinning as though it were all a big joke. '*Puka halalah*,' he said. '*Puka halalah*.'

'What's that?' said Melissa. But he couldn't tell her.

He accepted a drink of water for himself and his donkey. (He did not like to go into the inner courtyard with the fountain and the throne, so she had to bring a pail out to them.) Then he smiled at her again, took the donkey and led it back out of the gate. When he reached the point where the path dipped out of sight, he turned to wave and she waved back at him.

He came four times that autumn, and twice in the winter during brief, bright spells when the cloud suddenly lifted and the horrible wind was no longer driving sleet and snow along the mountain sides for days on end. By then she was calling him 'Puck', because of the words *Puka halalah* that he always said when he showed her what he had brought. She always talked to him, even though he never understood. 'You're like the sun,' she would say. 'We don't see you often enough these days.' And he would grin and be gone again soon after, for the walk back to his village was a long one and not even the hill people seemed to know how long the weather would stay clear. And she would put his sacks in the storeroom, thinking of the risks he was taking for them, and take the blankets (for he brought her blankets, too) back to the kitchen, where Atti crouched shivering by the low fire.

It was a long, lonely, dreary time. The two girls spent hours and hours huddled together under blankets, listening to the wind. Atti screamed in the night and was silent by day, and the coldness between her and Phaedra grew. One day Melissa looked up from rooting in the storeroom and found Phaedra watching her, sitting on a log in a dark corner of the room which had been empty a moment before.

Phaedra did not live in the house. Much of the time the girls would not see her at all. She seemed to spend most of her days up on the other side of the ridge, where there was a pool sunk in a horseshoe of rocks with great white stoncs around the top. Melissa knew the pool had something to do with the princes. She preferred not to go up there herself. But unlike Atti she did not mind it when Phaedra came down.

'How are you, Melissa?'

'We're living,' said Melissa shortly. Cold made her tired and hunger made her cross, so she did not feel much like speaking. 'We'll do. The hill boy came last week. He brought us this lot – look.'

Phaedra looked at the basket of roots. Melissa realized that she, too, was tired. Not from hunger or cold, but from whatever it was she was doing all this time up by the haunted pool. Perhaps she had come down for a rest.

'They are kind, in that village,' said Phaedra.

'I wish they'd take something from us all the same.'

'They will not accept a trade. The food is a gift, for my son's sake. Ambrose has asked them to help you as far as they can.'

'They don't have much, though, do they?' said Melissa.

'Not much. But you cannot repay them. Just remember it. Do the same for another when you can.'

Melissa thought of the times that poor hungry hill people had come trying to trade with Dadda in the clearing that had been her home.

'How is Atti?' said Phaedra.

Melissa shook her head. 'Can't seem to do anything for her.'

'Yes, you can. You are keeping her alive.'

'Oh, that. But it's the dreams.'

'Worse?'

'Yes. Happening more often, anyway. And Ambrose – he helped her once, but—'

'I have told him he must not.'

I'd say she knows that, thought Melissa. I'd say she knows, and it's not helping. Maybe she thinks it's you behind that curtain now.

But all she said was: 'I don't know what to do.'

'Neither do I,' said Phaedra.

Spring came at last, suddenly, and long after it must have crept into the wooded valleys down in the March. It came with a change in the air; stiller, clearer days and waters running off the mountains. Melissa could see them on the far side of the valley – three, four, five delicate threads of falling water, spilling down the slope to join the brown torrent below. And one evening when she was in the outer courtyard she heard a sound that took her back at once to the clearing by the stream where she had grown up. It was the cry of a goat.

There, coming through the gateway, was Puck. He was shooing five of the animals ahead of him and leading his donkey with one hand. The goats spilled bleating into the outer courtyard. They were smaller, darker, uglier things than Melissa was used to, but they were goats all the same. Melissa whooped with delight when she saw them. Puck closed the outer gate behind him. Atti appeared from the inner courtyard to see what all the noise was. She was in time to see the boy catch one of the goats and pin it between his knees, pulling back its chin with his left hand.

It was a yearling. Melissa saw what was going to happen a moment before it did.

Puck drew a long, heavy knife from his belt. Quickly

and firmly he cut the animal's throat. Blood spurted in a wide arc across the courtyard stones. The animal shook between his knees. The other goats set up a great bleating and bolted for the inner courtyard. Atti screamed and followed them.

Melissa left Puck holding the dead animal up by its hind legs to drain the blood. She made her way into the inner courtyard where the goats were huddled in the far corner, looking at her with their goaty eyes. She found Atti standing stock-still in the kitchen.

'How could he *do* that?' Atti gasped.

'It's for us,' said Melissa. 'Haven't you seen it done before?'

Atti did not answer. She did not turn round. Melissa did not know what to say. Dadda had always killed a yearling kid when the spring came, as long as there was a male one to spare. It had to be a male, because the females were too useful. Anyway the flock became difficult to manage if you had too many males in it. And that meal had always been the best of the new season. She'd have been whining at Mam for weeks about when it was going to be. She hadn't ever dreamed that the hill people would send one up to them, but since they had . . .

'Didn't you see how beautiful it was?' said Atti.

Melissa realized that Atti was weeping. 'Yes,' she said. (Yes, she remembered being upset the first time she had seen a goat killed. But she had been about four, then, and Atti . . .)

'It was *cruel*, it was *brutal*, it was *wicked*!' exclaimed Atti through her tears.

190

It would barely have felt anything, thought Melissa. All its blood had gone out of it, whoosh, like that. And you don't usually even look at animals, Atti! You don't see the birds overhead or the little hares among the thorns. You can't have laid eyes on that kid for more than a moment! And don't tell me you don't like meat, either. You're always on about how dull it is to eat nothing but fish and roots and meal!

'They've sent it up for us, Atti,' she pleaded. 'It's really, really good of them. They can't have many—'

'I won't touch it!'

But it's *meat*, Melissa thought. The best thing there was – tender flesh and smells that made the mouth water! After all that winter, too! Why all the fuss over a dead animal? Because it was beautiful?

She hesitated a moment more, torn between Atti's sadness and the hill boy's goodness. And her stomach made up her mind for her. 'Well,' she declared, 'I suppose I'll just have to eat for two, won't I?'

Puck was in the outer courtyard, butchering the kid. He looked up as she approached. She gave a helpless gesture. 'Sorry,' she said. 'It's just you and me.'

He said something, a question, and pointed to the inner courtyard.

'Sorry,' she said again. 'She just won't.' She laid a hand on his arm and smiled to show that it wasn't his fault. 'It's to do with something she dreams about, I think.'

Puck still did not want to go into the inner court himself, so the two of them built a fire in a corner of the outer yard and cut strips off the haunches to roast.

The air was cold. The night was full of the sound of water, rushing from the hillsides and roaring down in the valley as snows melted. Puck had a blanket, and the two of them sat side by side under it while the meat sizzled on long sticks over the embers and the smells set the juices running in their mouths. They listened to the water and watched the moon rising, and because they could not speak a word of each other's language they made goat noises to each other and laughed until Melissa got the hiccups. And when the meat was ready they tore into it with delight.

It should have hung first, Melissa thought, as she burned her tongue on her first mouthful. Dadda would have hung it for three days. But after all that winter, who was going to wait? It was good – warm and juicy and very, very good. She ate more than she would have thought possible.

Puck leaned back with a sigh. He hadn't said anything for a while. His face was thoughtful. She knew what it was. You killed the goat, you ate on it, but you felt sorry for it, too. And grateful. That was right. That little life had been closed off so that you could go on. And Atti was also right. It had been beautiful.

Funny thing, beauty. Always getting where you didn't want it.

Puck had begun to hum, or maybe sing – Melissa knew so little about the hill tongue that she could not be sure if there were any words in the sounds he made. She stopped licking her lips to listen. She had not heard anything like it before. It was a low, slow, sad tune. It made her think how very small the two of them were, here by their spark of a fire, and how around them in the night were the great mountains – huge, cold things that had stood long before she was born and would be here long after she was dead, and each year they wept their melting waters into the torrents below. It made her think of Atti, and the beauty she wept for, and the horrors that surrounded her as coldly as the mountains themselves.

She wondered what the boy was thinking now, and whether he had ever slept away from his village before. He must have known, when he set out with those goats, that it was going to take him all day to get them here. And he'd have had to get them across the river somehow, and up the narrow path which would have been cut every few hundred paces by another streamlet off the mountainside. It was good of him. It was more than good.

She huddled a little closer to him for warmth. She suddenly felt very aware of him – the strange press of his shoulder against hers and his thigh against her thigh. Her blood seemed to be turning upside down inside her, slowly. She almost put her head on his shoulder but did not quite feel she could. She thought she might put her arm around him. Or he might put his around her. And then . . . Then what would she do?

It was a little like looking over one of these mountain cliffs, down at the great drop below her, with her stomach tingling with the strange, awful delight of it. And what she always did was wait there for a moment, then turn and walk back to where there was firm ground all around her, and she wouldn't look again.

She lifted her head as the song ended. 'That was nice,' she said. 'Thank you – I'm going to sleep now.'

She got to her feet without waiting for an answer, smiled at him and let her feet take her firmly back towards the kitchen, where Atti would already be lying in a silent heap under her blankets. She walked quickly, and after the first few steps she knew that she was safe. He would not follow her.

He would not follow her into the inner courtyard, where the stone fountain and the empty throne stood like the ghosts of another time.

The arrival of the goats meant more work. The girls had to take turns leading them to pasture and watching them there, to be sure that they did not stray or get taken by mountain beasts. But Melissa did not mind this. It was worth it for the goats' milk alone. There was more time in the earlier mornings and later evenings to fit in other chores. And goats were goats, not only useful but funny and good for the temper.

She was watching them one summer afternoon, about a year after her first arrival at the house. The sky was clear, the sun was on the mountainside and the wild flowers bloomed like little fountains of colour wherever they could in the rocky ground. The goats moved on the sloping hillside, pulling at the sparse green with their big lips. And a stone went rattling down the hillside a hundred paces away.

Her eyes jerked away from the herd. Someone was coming up the path. Could it be Puck again? But he had come only a few days ago. And she could not hear a donkey bell or hooves. Who could it be?

More stones rattled. A man's head and shoulders bobbed into view and disappeared again. Then he rounded a boulder and stepped into full view.

It was the King!

He saw the goats first – one had just emerged from a clump of thorns below the path. He stopped and shaded his eyes. Then he saw her, too, and waved a friendly hand. And he began to pick his way down to her.

Melissa started up in confusion. She couldn't believe it was him – really him, coming down the steep hillside towards her in his rough cloak and jerkin and leggings, smiling with unshaven lips and coming nearer every moment! She had thought him a hundred miles away in the March, judging all the people who needed to be judged. And he was here!

'Melissa,' he said. 'It is good to see you again. Are you well?'

'Um – yes, lord,' she said, and wondered what else to say.

'Don't call me "lord", Melissa. You'll only swell my head.'

'Um . . . yes,' she said. If he wasn't to be 'lord' – or 'sir' or something – she did not know what to call him.

'You've grown,' he said. 'I think the mountains must be good for you.'

'Um,' she said, and looked at her feet.

He must have seen that her tongue was tying itself into knots. But he said nothing about it. He looked around the pasture like a man who had at last come home. 'Goats,' he said. 'I used to do this.'

And when she did not answer he asked: 'Do they behave themselves?'

'Mostly, lor— Um. Mostly, yes, they do.'

'Mostly. There's a villain in every goat, isn't there?'

Sunlight, and pasture, and a little purple hill-flower sprouting between the stones at her feet. And the tallest, handsomest, wisest man in the world had suddenly appeared before her! Why couldn't she say anything?

'And what do you do if a wolf comes? Or a lynx?'

She pointed to her long stick, the sling and the pile of carefully chosen stones. 'They're no trouble.'

'No trouble, so long as you see them first. Is that a sling?' He bent over and picked it up. 'I never had one of these. I know the hill folk use them, though.'

'They gave it to us. They give us lots of things.'

'There are good people in that village. Can you use it?'

She nodded.

'Show me.'

It was never going to be a good shot, not with him standing there. Puck would have rolled his eyes – maybe even rolled on the ground, beating the earth in mock despair. But the King nodded as her stone skimmed the top of the bush she had aimed at.

'That would scare them, wouldn't it? So. How are things?'

'Well enough, lord.'

'Do you like it here?'

She did not know what to say.

'Do you miss the March at all?'

She thought about it, and nodded. 'Winters are harder here.'

'Hum. Is Mother up at the pool?'

'Don't know where she is, exactly,' she said, and managed not to say '*lord*' this time. 'You come to talk with her?'

'Yes. About various things. She says another of the princes in the pool is ready to hear us now. So there's that. Also . . .' A rueful smile played over his lips. 'Well, there's Atti.'

Atti. Her heart sank. 'You going to talk to your mother about her?'

'Yes.'

'Um . . .'

He looked at her, and her mouth shut itself at once. (*I'm sorry, sir, but they just don't like each other?*) She could not say it. He would want to know why. And she couldn't tell him that either. It seemed to have started even before there could be a reason.

Ambrose grinned sourly. 'Older woman, younger woman,' he said. 'It's eternal. You would think Mother of all people would be above that now, but she isn't. Not when she thinks it's about me.'

In the end Melissa's tongue failed her again. She could only shrug and say, 'Maybe.'

'Well, let's go up and see what we can do. I'll give you a hand with the goats, shall I? How do you call them? Cu-cu-cu-cu . . . ?'

It was too early to bring the goats back in. There was an hour of good daylight left before dusk, which was the most dangerous time for wolf and lynx and that. But Melissa could no more have told him so than she could have flown. She stood up and gave the long, dropping whoop that her mother had taught her, years ago in the clearing by the stream.

'That's a March call,' said the King, surprised. 'Didn't these come from the hill people?'

'They did, lord.'

But they're *my* goats now, she thought.

The goats did not behave.

It was the old mother-goat who was the worst. She knew she was being cheated of an hour of pasture. She made the two of them do more running and shooing on the steep slopes than Melissa normally had to do in a week. Melissa would have felt bad about it if the King had not enjoyed himself so much. He laughed and leaped about the boulders as if he were trying to be a goat himself. And when they finally had the animals all assembled on the path, he waved a thorn branch like a banner over his head and called, 'Ho, knights – to the Dark Tower, ride!' Of course the goats bolted and scattered, so he ran after the leading pair, laughing and swearing at his own stupidity.

That left Melissa to round up the stragglers, including the mischievous old mother, who had taken herself off to catch another few mouthfuls. Melissa chased them and cursed them, aware that the King was getting further ahead all the time. She cursed herself, too, for being so surprised and stupid when he had appeared.

Why couldn't she have said all the things that fine people said, like *I give thanks to Michael that he has guarded you on your way* and so on?

Why couldn't her slingshot have hit the bush, *whack*, as it should have done? Why couldn't she have told him all the things that had made her laugh in the last year, so that he could have laughed, too? He would have, if she had given him the chance.

You have grown. Why couldn't he have said: *You have grown pretty?* But she'd probably have died on the spot if he had.

She reached the house at last, shooing the wretched goats along before her. As they approached the gateway, Atti came out.

'They're arguing,' she said.

'Oh! Why?'

'About me.'

She walked past Melissa and looked out over the steep drop to the valley floor. Melissa faced the doors. Loose thoughts in her brain wailed that a wonderful moment was being spoiled – spoiled because of Atti! Grimly she shooed the goats into the house.

Phaedra and Ambrose were facing each other in the inner courtyard. Ambrose had his hands on his hips. They were both angry. Melissa knew it at once, although they did not shout or shake their fists at one another. She could hear it in their voices, as cold and distant as the mountain snow.

'. . . but I do *not* judge her, Amba. I *might*, but I do not.'

'So why does she have nightmares still?'

'How do you know that she does?'

'It doesn't matter how I know,' said Ambrose. 'The point is, she is having them. You know that.'

'I do. But *I* have never chosen to disturb her sleep.'

'She's scared of you. That's the truth. Why?'

'I give her no reason to be scared.'

'It's not about reason, though, is it?'

Melissa fled into the kitchen. She couldn't get between the two of them but maybe a little supper would help. People often stopped being cross if they were given something to eat, didn't they? Maybe Ambrose was hungry! He'd have been walking all day and for many days before that. Maybe that was the trouble. Anyway, she felt better working for him with her hands than trying to talk to him with her tongue. Her fingers could do her talking for her. He would see that.

The embers were still warm and rekindled quickly. Melissa found the pan, the vegetables, the water, the knife. The bread was old but there was goat's milk in the pantry and fish drying on the frame. She could put something together that would please him.

She wanted to keep busy. She wanted to have something to do. Anything not to have to listen to the voices out in the courtyard – those cold, angry voices, of people who should never be angry with one another. She put the water on and then scraped and chopped the vegetables. She did more than usual because of the extra mouth, and more again because it was him. It was early (for a summer's day) and there was still plenty of light to see by.

Check the fire. Let it begin to work its way back down to embers. What next? The broth was on and would need watching, but she did not want just to hide in the kitchens.

Water! She should refill the jug. She picked it up and carried it out into the courtyard. Even before she stepped into the light, she knew something had changed. The voices had stopped.

Ambrose was still there. He was walking by the low wall that ran along the open end of the courtyard above the steep slope to the valley floor. But the person beside him was not Phaedra. It was Atti.

Ambrose was explaining something to her, waving with one hand as he walked. He was looking at Atti as he spoke, as if he were anxious about what she might think of what he was saying. Atti was nodding slowly as she listened. What struck Melissa most was how small she was compared to him. She did not even come up to his chin.

Phaedra was standing in the shadow of the columns. She was also watching them, with hard eyes.

'He thinks she should leave,' she said flatly.

'I got that much,' said Melissa. 'And go where?'

'Back to the March. He wants to move some families into the old castle of Tarceny and make it his home.'

'Oh,' said Melissa again. She tried to imagine it. 'A castle like this one?'

'Much bigger.'

Bigger? thought Melissa. Even bigger than this?

Ambrose and Atti reached the end of the wall, turned and began walking slowly back again. Melissa noticed that Ambrose was still doing most of the talking. Atti would nod, or ask a short question, and then Ambrose would answer, saying lots of things, and saying them eagerly as if he had so many things to tell her and wanted her to be excited by them, too.

'I do not like being told that we have failed,' said Phaedra softly.

'Did he say that?'

'Not in words.'

Atti would go, Melissa thought. Of course she would go. There was nothing for her here, living like a peasant in the hills. She had said so often enough. It surprised her that Ambrose was having to do so much talking to persuade her. Then she realized that he would already have persuaded her, and that they were now talking about something else. What? Her dreams, of course. Why did her dreams mean so much to him?

'You do not have to go with her,' said Phaedra. 'You must choose for yourself what to do.'

Melissa nodded. She was thinking that Ambrose had never talked quite like that with her – never so eagerly or for so long. When she had dreamed of him, starving, he had saved her with a few words to the red knight. He had thought little more of it. Was Atti so much more needy than she had been?

'You must not let her rule you,' said Phaedra. 'You are young but not a child any more. Whatever your birth, you are a woman as much as she is.'

You must stand on your own two feet, Dadda would have said.

But . . . but what choice was there, really, if Atti went? Melissa did not want to stay here by herself, with only Phaedra and the occasional visits of Puck to look forward to. If she did not go with Atti, she would spend all her time wishing she had done – gone with her to where the King lived, to be in his house with him nearly every day.

The King every day or a hill boy only twice a month? It was not even worth thinking about.

'I'm her servant,' said Melissa finally. 'That's who I am.'

'Because you choose it. Here, you can choose. Down there it will be more difficult. And she will need you less than she does now.'

'He wants me to look after her.'

'Does he now?' Phaedra murmured.

Ambrose and Atti were crossing the courtyard towards them, side by side. Whatever they had been saying to each other was hidden in Ambrose's smile. Atti curtseyed formally to Phaedra. She almost never did that.

'So . . .' said Ambrose.

'So?' said Phaedra.

'I will prepare the supper,' said Atti. She went on into the kitchen. As she passed, Melissa saw her face break into a smile of its own – that smile of hers which was as rare as honey-dew. There was a clank from inside as she took up the ladle.

'I imagine that I am not going to be surprised,' said Phaedra coldly.

'No,' said Ambrose. 'You will not be.'

'Well, then . . .'

They looked at one another in silence. At last Ambrose gave an embarrassed shrug. 'Well – the pool, next?'

'As you wish.'

'Um – supper will be ready in half an hour,' Melissa blurted out, anxious that some credit at least for their meal should come to her.

'Thank you, Melissa,' said Phaedra.

Mother and son turned and started walking towards the outer courtyard. They walked side by side. Neither spoke to the other. There seemed to be a great distance between them.

XII

Firewood

he girls left the mountains the next spring, after the weather had lifted and the torrents had done their worst. And the March welcomed them. It embraced them with its warm air and its scented, tree-covered valleys where the little streams rushed unseen in the thickets at the bottom. Melissa's heart ached as she travelled through it, so comforting and well-known it seemed after the cold peaks. And the castle at Tarceny was the biggest house she had ever seen.

It stood on the spur of a hill above the olive groves. The ground fell steeply on three sides from its walls, covered with great thickets of black and white moon roses. It had a large outer enclosure, surrounded by a wall that had been pulled down in two places, and an inner courtyard with tall buildings and towers around it. In the days of Ambrose's father it must have held more than a hundred, possibly two hundred people. But the wars that had devastated the March had cut its population to a handful. For the last half-dozen years it had been abandoned altogether. Now Ambrose and his friend the Baron Lackmere had brought nine families to the place. These were younger sons and daughters of landsmen elsewhere in the March, who had had to move away from their homes because there was nothing there for them. There were children among them – nearly as many as the adults – and no elderly people at all. They brought with them small herds of goats and other animals, which were kept in the outer courtyard. Because the castle gates had long vanished, the outer and inner gateways were barred at night with rough thorn hurdles to prevent the herd from straying.

Suddenly, after the long silent days among the mountains, Melissa's world was crowded. The adults and the older children worked in the abandoned olive groves and fields below the castle during the day, but even so there was laughter and shouting and bustle among the old brown walls as the younger children fought and played, and supervising mothers scolded them. And there were always a couple of the men knocking and banging away in corners as they tried to repair bits of the castle, replacing stones and timbers that had crumbled or had been taken for building materials by the handful of cotter families who still lived on the land nearby. The upper floors of the keep were judged too rotten to be safe, so Ambrose and his friend the baron slept in the first-storey room when they were at home. A stretch of the roof of the living-quarter building was repaired so that Atti and Melissa could have two adjoining rooms there. Ambrose told them they had once been his mother's.

'They were my father's, too,' said Atti as she watched Melissa stop up crevices in the walls.

Melissa looked up, astonished. 'You lived here before?'

'My father held Tarceny for King Septimus, after the fall of Ambrose's father,' said Atti simply. 'Then Septimus wronged him and they went to war with each other. Septimus killed my father and destroyed Tarceny, which is why it is like this now.' She looked around. 'This must be the room I dream of. Only it seemed much bigger then.'

'It's *this* room?' Melissa gasped. She looked at Atti, alarmed. 'Will you be all right here?'

'I suppose so,' Atti mused. 'I wonder where the curtain was – across that door, I expect.'

She was sitting on the end of her pallet bed, teasing gently at the ends of her long hair and speaking as if she thought it was the most unimportant thing in the world that she should be sitting in the very place she saw in her dreams. Melissa watched her nervously, wondering if at any moment a fit would come on her and set her thrashing and screaming there in the sunlight.

'There would have been tapestries,' Atti said, almost dreamily. 'And joined furniture. And everything in bright colours.'

'Tapestries?'

'Like rugs, only beautifully woven. They would hang on the walls so you could look at them.'

And hang them across a door, maybe? thought Melissa. Yes, to stop the draughts, of course. And then any time anyone wanted to come in . . .

'Don't stare at me so,' said Atti coldly. 'And close your mouth or I'll put something in it.' She stomped to the window to look out at the view across the wooded ridges north of the castle.

'They're giving me a headache,' she said.

She was sulky now. But she did not sound as if she were about to scream. She was just being Atti – normal Atti, if there was such a thing. Melissa shrugged and got back to her wall.

She herself had grown used to the constant hammering of the carpenters. She was grateful to them for the new roof above her. Of course they had to move on to the other buildings in the courtyard now. She could hardly expect them to stop, just because she and Atti would be in the dry! And at least the men were working. What she didn't like was when they found an excuse to stop work and drink the strong drink they brewed in the outer sheds. Then they sang and swore and fought each other, and not even Ambrose could do anything with them. It had been horrible, the first time she had seen a man who could not speak clearly or walk in a straight line. It had made her angry. Dadda had never brewed anything that made him silly when he drank it! But these men were not like Dadda. They did not stand on their two feet. They leaned on each other, more like. Yes, it got you great big roofs that no one man could have made by himself. But it got you a lot of other stuff, too.

The clay was cold and sticky on her fingers. It was also heavy. Melissa had a whole pail of it, which someone else – bless them – had carried up from a stream bank for her and others to use. She would need nearly all of it. After years of no one living here there were cracks wherever she looked, and any of them could house large spiders or scorpions, or the little lizards that flickered along the walls and out of sight whenever they saw you move. She did not mind the lizards but they made her jump.

'You must call me "Your Highness", Melissa,' said Atti suddenly. 'It's important, now that we are with other people again.'

Melissa's thumb smoothed one more blob of clay into place.

Your Highness. That was what she had just said.

Atti, we've been living cheek-to-cheek for two years! You wouldn't have lasted a month up there if I hadn't . . .

Her fingers dabbled once more in the pail. Her lips moved.

'Yes,' she said.

'Yes . . . ?' Atti had not turned her head. Neither did Melissa.

'Yes, Your Highness.'

'So how is Atti doing?' asked Ambrose.

Hey! thought Melissa. I didn't go to all that trouble just to talk about *her*, did I?

She had caught him perfectly. She had been watching him from the shelter of the gate as he harangued a drunken and surly settler who was late on his way to the fields. She had seen him turn and come back towards her and had timed her appearance from the woodstore, struggling with an enormous armload of firewood, so that as he strode frowning in under the arch he had almost run into her. (*Whack*, hit! It had worked just as she had wanted it to, like a stone flying true from a sling!) He had smiled at once and had taken half her load. Now they were walking back towards the living quarters side by side, moving at Melissa's pace, which was as slow as she could manage without letting him guess that she was being slow on purpose.

Except that he wanted to talk about Atti, and Melissa didn't. She wanted him to talk about – well, about herself, if she had the choice.

(Anyway, saying whether Atti ever *liked* something was always a bit difficult . . .) 'She was glad to leave the mountains,' she said.

'And now?'

Melissa thought. 'Could we get her some tap . . . um, tapeasies . . . ?'

'Tapestries? You think that would please her?'

'For a little, maybe,' said Melissa truthfully.

He paced on beside her. Melissa wondered if he had guessed at the things she hadn't said – all those little complaints about Atti that she told to no one except the lizards on the walls. (Why couldn't the girl be happy with what she had? Why wasn't anything ever good enough for her?) Maybe he was sorry that she thought them.

'Didn't know this was the place she dreamed of, sir.'

She said it to show that she was still trying to look after Atti, as he had asked her to.

'Didn't you? She did, and yet she still wanted to come. Is it affecting her, do you think?'

'Not that I've seen.'

'No. In a way I was hoping it would. I thought it might help uncover things. But the dream – the memory itself – isn't the trouble. It's just the clothes that the trouble comes in. I mean, yes, her house was destroyed. Twice, in fact. Once here, when she was very little, and then again in Velis a few years ago. You know how bad that can be. But it's not the past, for her. I can see that now. It's the future. She's convinced that it's going to happen again – or something like it. You know, sometimes I wish I could set her up in a high palace, surrounded by minstrels and knights in shining armour, so that wherever she looked she could see she was adored . . . But I can't, of course. The best I can do is see that there's a roof over her head and meal in the bucket and clean water in the bowl. Which is hardly . . .'

His voice tailed off thoughtfully. He was looking up at the living quarters. The unshuttered windows looked back down on them like a row of blank eyes.

'Water,' he said. 'That reminds me. Those carpenters still haven't done the winch for the well yet. I swear my arms are an inch longer than they should be from hauling heavy water buckets up hand over hand. And Aun keeps saying we have to get them to build us a proper gate, or one day someone we don't want will come riding straight in on top of us and catch us here like rats. That's a huge job, though.

Sometimes I despair of ever getting everything done. So . . .' He pulled a face. 'At least let's get this lot up to your rooms. We want to keep you warm, don't we?'

She clumped after him up the stairs. He knocked at the girls' door but there was no answer. He led the way in. Atti was not there.

'Where shall we put it?' he said. 'There?'

'Tapestries?' he mused aloud as they stacked the wood together. 'They'd have to come from Watermane. And just one would cost us all we could produce in a harvest, I guess. But fire's cheap, and on a dull night it's prettier than any tapestry. Let's look at the things we have and be thankful. We'll help as many needy people as we can, Melissa. But we'll see ourselves warm and fed at the same time.'

'Yes, sir . . .' said Melissa.

They were kneeling side by side. It was now or never. 'Um . . .'

He looked at her. She felt the blood rising to her face.

'I've got something for you, sir,' she said.

She held it out – the little four-pointed moon-rose flower, with its three white petals and one black, that she had picked from below the walls that morning.

He looked it at. Slowly the smile returned to his face.

'Now there's a thing,' he said softly. He touched it with his fingertip. 'Why did you bring me that?'

'Because it's like the moon on your flag,' she said. 'Black and white, see?' She looked at him earnestly, wanting him to remember that first time they had seen each other – the firelight and the hut, and the needle that had fallen to the ground.

'Yes,' he said. 'But the moon had a piece missing. This says something different.' He touched it again. 'This isn't a piece missing, is it? It's just a petal that's black, not white. What do you think that means?'

'Sir?' she said, still holding it out to him. (Oh, take it! Take it, please, for me . . .)

'Here, the black is part of the whole thing. It says you can't have the flower without it. And even the black leaf grows towards the light.'

'Um . . .' said Melissa. Her heart was going *flip-flip-flip* because he was so close to her. Her tongue was sticking to the roof of her mouth, because she had used up all the things she had thought of to say to him, and it was hard to think of any more. (Take it. Oh, please take it . . .)

'You show me this,' said Ambrose. 'And thinking about Atti . . . Do you know who I mean by Beyah?'

'The mountain, sir?'

'The mountain near my mother's house is called Beyah, yes. But it's not just a mountain. It's also a woman. A spirit. She's been weeping since – well, for a long time, anyway.'

'Um, yes. Your mother said.'

'Did she? Did she show you the Cup?'

'A cup? There were bowls—'

'No. A stone cup. She keeps it for me up there. If you have the Cup, you can make Beyah's tears appear in it. And then you can do various things. But of course they are tears – sad and cruel. They're everywhere: in the Cup, in Rolfe and the other princes, in Mother. To some extent they are in all of us. And I think that when Atti was very little Beyah must have wept a tear straight into her heart. It's still there, colouring everything for her. I can almost smell it.

'You see, Melissa, if I could find out what to do about that tear inside Atti, I might know what to do about Beyah and her tears wherever they fall. That's very, very important. It's the most important thing there is. But is it a piece missing? Or is it part of the whole? I don't know. I need to think some more. Thank you, Melissa,' he said, taking the flower from her hand at last. 'Now I'd better get after those carpenters, or they'll be down behind the woodpile with a bottle of that wretched ale and no use for anything for the rest of today . . .'

He was rising, turning, smiling, and leaving through the door. She saw him put the flower away in a pocket as he went.

And then he was gone. His footsteps clumped down the bare boards of the passage and clattered away down the stairs. The glory she had felt went with him, leaving her as dull and flat as a muddy river-bed after the spring flood had passed. There had been no meaning in his smile.

Sometime this evening, she thought, he would put his hands into his pocket again. He would find the flower there, wilted and forgotten. It had already been wilting when she gave it to him, because she had had to pick it hours before. He would see that. He would know that she had planned the whole thing, and that the firewood had just been a way to catch him. Perhaps he had known that the moment he had seen her carrying it. And he had gone and helped her anyway, because, because . . .

She thought back over all they had said together, and saw that it had all been about Atti. Even while he'd been talking about carpenters he had been thinking about her, and that was why his talk had gone back to her when she had showed him the flower. And she remembered the way he had looked around as he had stepped into their rooms, expectantly, as if hoping that Atti would be there. She wondered if he had used the firewood as an excuse to visit their chambers, just as she had used it as an excuse to be in the outer court-yard when he came in through the gate.

With a sinking feeling she decided that he had.

Tonight he and Atti would play chess together again, moving all those knights and bishops and queens around on their chequered board in a way that Melissa could never understand. And barely a word would pass between them, but they would speak to each other with their eyes over the pieces. It took a different sort of mind to do that, thought Melissa. And their minds were the same.

Her hands had started to rearrange the firewood, not because it needed it, but because she needed something to do. It will help to keep you warm, he had said. She picked up a stick, and looked at it. She remembered another stick, years before, with the flame licking around its end.

How could it keep her warm, when the moon was out of reach?

XIII

Iron on the Wind

he woke suddenly, in the darkness of the living-quarter chamber. She had heard something in her sleep. She knew that. She did not know what it was.

She listened.

She heard the wind in the trees beyond the walls – a watery sound, rising and falling.

And a low *chink-chink* sort of noise, like metal, coming from somewhere on the slopes below the window.

What was that?

Was that what she had heard?

There were noises inside the castle, too. A man was speaking quickly in a low tone. Wood scraped, as if something heavy were being pushed against or away from a door. Footsteps were hurrying along the corridor from the keep.

She sat up, her heart beating hard, with the blanket wrapped around her. The knock came softly.

'Up, both of you,' whispered Ambrose urgently from the corridor. 'Get dressed and come to the fighting platform. Don't show any light.'

He was gone, like a breath of wind into the darkness. Atti was standing at the door to the inner chamber where she slept. Melissa could not see her face – only the black line of head and hair and shoulder against the paler dark from the window beyond. But she knew. They both knew.

Her home was destroyed, too, thought Melissa.

The two girls stared at one another. *Chink, chink, chink* came the sounds from beyond the window. And then the unmistakable noise of a horse, blowing within a hundred paces of the walls.

'Quickly!' hissed Atti.

They hurried into the inner chamber. Melissa groped for Atti's gown and threw it on over her night-dress. She left the fastenings for Atti, who fumbled with them, muttering in the dark, while Melissa hunted for Atti's cloak and shoes. Then Atti was moving for the door, saying urgently, 'Come on!' Melissa, still in her nightdress, her feet bare, felt her way back to her pallet and groped for her own clothes. *Don't leave me!* she thought. But Atti was already gone. Melissa listened, heart beating hard, but she could hear nothing more from outside.

She left her gown, her shoes – all of it. She found her cloak and hauled it around her shoulders. Barefoot, she hurried through the corridors in the direction the others had gone.

The stairs led up, twisting, past the old war room to the fighting platform at the top of the bastion. She emerged breathless among the battlements of Tarceny. The great keep looked down on them, flat and black against the sky. For a moment she thought she was alone.

'Don't show yourself!' said Lackmere's voice, low and urgent.

They were crouching against the parapet on the north side. Atti was there with them. The figure of a man – it must have been Ambrose – was peering round a battlement at the hillside beyond. The others were keeping down.

'Among the trees, about level with us on the ridge,' he said. 'Horsemen, for sure. I think there are others down among the groves.'

'Posted to watch the postern,' growled Lackmere. 'Whoever they are, they know this castle. And the main force will come in through the outer courtyard. Damn, but I knew we should have got those gates repaired!'

'Who are they?'

'Armed in the night? Enemy, of course.'

'Rolfe's not far away,' said Ambrose. 'If we had him with us we could just follow him through a wall and come back into the world wherever we liked.'

'Call him then. But if he doesn't hear you—'

A shout broke from the inner courtyard.

'They're in!' exclaimed Ambrose.

A second shout: '*Ho, Tarceny,*' followed by a horn-call.

Carefully the four of them peered over the inner battlements.

There were lights in the inner courtyard, held in the hands of armoured men. Around the yellow pools they cast Melissa glimpsed horses, armoured limbs, the glint of steel. The place seemed to be crowded. She could hear more horsemen filing in through the gate from the outer courtyard – so many! The light fell on the buildings of the inner courtyard. It showed the faces of the settler families appearing in doorways and windows.

'Keep back there,' bellowed the voice in the court-yard. 'Keep your heads in.' And then again '*Ho, Tarceny!*'

'The postern,' hissed Lackmere. 'And as soon as we're out, scatter!'

They hurried down the twisting stair, down past the war room, down past the chapel and the living-quarter corridor. Down . . .

Ahead of Melissa, Ambrose stopped abruptly. She almost bumped into his back. There were men in the postern corridor below. She could hear them hurrying along it, clinking in their mail. Ambrose turned on the stair.

'Back!' he hissed to them all. 'The keep!'

'They're up there!' cried a voice below them.

Melissa turned and bolted up the stair. The others were already running before her, stumbling up and along the living-quarter corridor. She ran after them. She heard armoured feet clattering up the stairs behind her. Her nerves were screaming with the memory of the red knight, the whisper of his arrows as she had dodged among the trees. *Don't look back!* Ahead was the door to the keep. Lackmere had it open. Atti was through it next, looking back at her.

She reached it and threw herself into the tower chamber. She heard Ambrose slam it shut behind her, the feet pounding beyond it, the scrape of old bolts going home and something heavy slamming and rattling into the wood from the other side.

'Bolt the other door!' cried Lackmere, throwing his weight with Ambrose against the boards.

'Rolfe!' called Ambrose into the air. 'Rolfe!'

'The other door!' yelled Lackmere again, glaring over his shoulder at Melissa.

The other door! The door down to the bottom chamber! She was closest. She picked herself up and scurried across to it. It stood open at the top of the steps that curled up inside the wall from below. She looked down it – into the eyes of the armoured man, climbing the steps towards her with a flaming torch in his hand!

She screamed and threw the door shut. Desperately she put her weight against it, wrestling one-handed with the bolts. They would not go. The lower was rusted into place. She fought it and it would not budge. She tried the upper. It moved – reluctantly, scraping . . . and then it jammed!

As if in a dream she saw it, lit by her enemy's torch through the cracks in the door. The door timbers had warped. The bolt rested against the rim of the bolt-hole. The bolt-hole was a black crescent, tantalizing and useless as she slid the bolt against it again. It would not go. Her enemy's foot scraped on the stair, inches away. And then the door slammed in against the side of her head, and everything was black.

Voices were shouting and her head was singing. She could not see. She was lying on her side in the chamber and a man was standing over her.

'Put up your iron!' he roared. 'Put them up, or I'll have this one in a heartbeat!'

Cold metal rested against her chin. Her vision was clouded, dark and sparkling after the blow. There were more footsteps coming up the stairs. Someone was beating on the other door.

'Damn you, I'll not put up on your say-so!' That was the Baron Lackmere.

'What about on mine?' said a new voice above Melissa's head.

'Caw!' she heard Ambrose exclaim.

'Greeting to you from Develin, my lord,' said the voice, clipped and hard, as if the words it spoke were pebbles dropping from its mouth. 'I knew you would try to sneak out if we gave you the chance. But we've come a long way for you and I don't mean to lose you now. All right!' he bellowed suddenly. 'You can stop that racket! We've got them.'

The pounding on the other door ceased. Bolts were drawn back. More people were entering the room.

'Sophia sent you for me?' said Ambrose.

'My lady sent us, yes. But not only her. I believe you also know the lord chancellor here.'

'My lord,' said someone else.

'Yes,' said Ambrose, and his voice sounded colder than ever. 'You've come for Astria, is that it?'

Melissa's sight was clearing. She opened her eyes. There was torchlight in the room now. She could see floorboards and the boots of many men. She tried to lift her head. As she did so she felt the touch of metal against her neck again. She froze.

She was looking up the long blade of a sword, held point-down at her chin. The man who held it had dark, cold eyes. He was the soldier she had tried to shut out of the room. The torchlight played on his whiskered cheeks and on the fringe of his black beard. The point of the sword held her locked where she lay.

'My lord, no,' said the someone else who had just arrived. 'But we have a petition for you to hear.'

'What is it?'

'A very delicate matter. If you will put your swords away and agree to listen, we will stand our men down. They will not molest your people.'

'We will listen,' said Ambrose warily.

'And no tricks,' said the pebble-voiced man. 'That one on the floor there will be our hostage. If you go walking through a wall on me it will be the worse for her.'

'I'll talk to no one under threat of murder,' said Ambrose. 'There's no need for it.'

'No need,' agreed the third voice, 'if we have your word that you will hear us and give us a fair answer. No, it is enough, I think, Sir Caw. It is *my* message. Let *me* set the conditions for this parley.'

'You have my word,' said Ambrose.

Lying fixed as she was, Melissa missed the exchange of looks. But suddenly the blade was gone from her neck.

* * *

Padry settled himself on a rough wooden stool – one of the few bits of furniture in this bleak tower chamber. He tried to ease his limbs. It had been a long, hard ride from the spot on the lakeside where Caw, the new marshal of Develin, had brought their mission to land. He himself would have preferred to send a small party ahead with a flag of truce and come on with the main body at an easier pace. But that was not Caw's way. 'Do that and he'll just give us the slip,' he had said. Caw knew Tarceny and he knew their quarry. Moreover Develin was providing two-thirds of their force.

To give Caw his due, they had tracked the young witch-lord to his lair and caught him before he could escape. Now they just had to make him listen. The air in the chamber was thick with anger.

Ambrose and the Baron Lackmere stood by the hearth, whispering to one another. The baron was fingering the hilt of his sword. Caw was in the doorway, giving instructions to his men about stabling the horses, setting guards and all that. Padry knew he was still furious about being overridden on the hostage (really, this new marshal of Develin was even more difficult than his predecessor Orcrim had been!). The hostage herself – a peasant girl whom Padry vaguely remembered – was on her knees before the hearth, coaxing flame into the fire she had just built. He tried to give her a reassuring smile. She ignored him. After being banged on the head and having a sword held to her throat she must hate the lot of them. He could not blame her.

223

And Atti was there, too, standing against the wall. Padry fixed his eyes on his feet.

He had wondered if she might be here, camped with this young brigand-lord. He had sworn to himself that if she were he would not look at her. Not a hint of reproach, not an effort at recall, would escape from him. She would only treat him with the contempt he deserved. All he could do was bear himself with dignity in front of her so that she should see that there was nothing to fear from him any more.

He was holding rigidly to his determination.

Still she bulked in his mind, the strongest presence in the room. Sixteen years old she was now. No longer a child but a young woman: dark-haired, full-breasted, slim and beautiful – beautiful, with a forbidden grace that made him writhe inwardly as he looked at his toes. Ah, Thomas Padry – you used to think you were so wise and enlightened; and then you behaved like a slobbering old fool over a child a third your age! And still, two years on, sadder, more weary in your labours, you are vulnerable. You are wiser only in that you know your own weakness!

And did they know what it was like for him to be here? Did anyone? That he should come crawling back on his belly to these actors in the most shameful scene of his life! Wasn't it enough that he should hate his own self-deceit? He carried it every day like an imp clinging to his back and whispering in his ear. It was with him when he rose in the mornings, when he lay awake at night, whenever he sought to clear his mind. Wasn't that enough? Or was the drunk only cured when he was made to sniff at the bottle and then could walk away?

Here he was, with the two of them again. The last of the men-at-arms had gone. The guards had been posted within call, but not within hearing of a low-voiced conversation. Caw remained, seated on a block of wood by the hearth. So did the baron and the maid. But they were insubstantial – creatures of smoke and shadow whose understanding would never matter. Atti, standing there at the corner of his sight, was a thousand times more real than they were. And so was the young man who settled cross-legged before him with suspicion in his eyes.

So you don't like me, thought Padry bitterly. That's fair enough, my boy. I don't like you either.

No, I *don't* like you! I don't like your handsome face, your clear look, your clean, jowlless jaw. I don't like the way you see into a man's heart and find there the things that he hides even from himself!

And why should I? Why should I? Why should *you* be the Just, when I thought that I was? I saw the look in your eyes when you thought I had come for her. I felt it, like the stab of a knife! Can you truly be Just, if you feel like that about her?

(Ah, Thomas Padry . . .)

The flames were beginning to lick around the logs. Everyone was looking at him. Padry cleared his throat.

'It is quite simple,' he said. 'We need a king.'

No one spoke.

'It is two years since Gueronius sailed,' he went on. 'There has been no word of him. The mariners of

225

Velis have spoken with merchants from foreign lands at their usual meeting places. His ship has not been sighted since the first winter after he sailed. We are now approaching the third. Our seafarers say that ships cannot survive the winter storms. Even if his did, the last of his stores will have been exhausted long ago. In Tuscolo we have continued to say that he will return, because if we did not we would be kingless and on the brink of chaos. All but the most witless now know that we are telling a lie.

'The two regents – I do not know how well you know my lords Joyce and Seguin?'

'Not at all,' said Ambrose coldly.

'They are as honest as most lords of the Kingdom, which is to say that neither will trust the other, neither will give way to the other, and neither will wait for ever. The Tuscolo faction is split. Already blood has been shed among their supporters—'

'Why are you telling me this?' broke in Ambrose.

Padry lifted an eyebrow. Wasn't it obvious?

'He said they need a king,' grunted Lackmere. 'They want it to be you.'

Ambrose scowled at the fire.

'If matters in the Kingdom are allowed to run their course, there will be war,' Padry persisted. 'One party will win – eventually. There may be peace for a while. But once again the throne will have gone to the strongest. And every strong man in the Kingdom will think that he may seize the throne at the next opportunity. You, on the other hand, are the last heir of Wulfram. Your house has worn the crown more than once before this. You have what no other possible contender now has – legitimacy. Kingship *with law* is the only kingship that may last.'

There, he thought. I've done it. I've offered him the throne. And he'll be good. He'll be good at it, this boy who dragged me through the mud. Umbriel, write what it cost me!

'My lady is convinced of this,' said the gaunt-faced marshal of Develin. 'Also, she remembers you well and thinks you a better choice than either regent, or any other. Her strength – which is not small now – she will lend to you, if you will agree.'

Still Ambrose would not look up.

'My lady also bids me say,' said the marshal slowly, 'that *if necessary*, and for the sake of peace, she would now be prepared to offer to a good king not only her soldiers, but herself also.'

Ambrose sprang to his feet. His stool clattered on the wooden floor. 'Yes,' he said, glaring at them. 'Yes, you were right. If I had known what it was you were coming for, I *would* have slipped away!'

'For the sake of peace in the Kingdom—' Padry began.

But Ambrose did not listen. He strode to the door and out of it. The wood banged. They heard his feet thumping down the stairs towards the hall.

In the silence Lackmere chuckled. 'I could have told you he would do that.'

Padry heaved a long sigh. Caw said nothing.

'It's not just fear for his neck,' said Lackmere. 'Though that may be part of it. He doesn't like

227

Tuscolo, he doesn't like what comes from kings, and he most certainly doesn't want to be one. Which is why he lives in rags and ruins and takes no profit from his courts. You'll have your work cut out to persuade him otherwise.'

'Persuade him we must,' said Padry, wiping his brow with his sleeve. 'Or carry him back with us in a sack for my Lady Develin to persuade, if we cannot.'

'She's set on it, is she? Very good. But who else is with her? *He* may or may not care for his neck, but I do. I'm not having him adventure after a crown unless there are very good odds on his side.'

'I have letters from the bishops of both Tuscolo and Jent.'

'Show me.'

Padry fumbled inside his shirt and drew out the wallet he carried next to his skin. From it he drew the letters that the bishops, meeting in secret, had written for him with their own hands. He broke the outer seals and handed them across. Lackmere peered at them.

'They are discreetly worded, of course,' said Padry.

'It doesn't matter how they are worded, since I don't read,' said Lackmere. 'But I know their seals and I judge that there's enough in here to hang a man.' He folded the letters away inside his tunic. 'So. You have the Church, or a good part of it. They must want us badly indeed if they are willing to overlook certain matters in Tarceny's past. Last time I saw you I think you were threatening us with a holy war.'

Padry swallowed and nodded. He knew that he had

just let the old baron pick his pocket. Yes, in the wrong hands those letters could certainly cost the lives of two princes of the Church! He should have been more wary. If he hadn't been so obsessed with Atti and Ambrose, he would have been. Damn it, Thomas Padry! Wake *up*!

'Times change,' he said. 'Or rather, they bring new necessities. And – whatever one may think of your lord's practices – his public doings over the past few years have made him a number of friends east of the lake.'

'What kind of friends? Who would come out for him, if we landed?'

'For a good, lawful candidate, backed with enough force – many. Even the regents might give way. Lord Joyce has said as much to me.'

'Joyce? He's a bantam – all crow and no kick. I suppose he is weaker than Seguin, and his fear of Seguin is greater than his hope to come out on top. Did he know what you had in mind?'

'He – may have guessed.'

'Well then,' said the baron, and pursed his lips. 'Well, it may be worth the gamble. We will need to let the boy calm down first. Try him again in the morning. But if I were you, I would not mention the possibility of marriage. Not unless he does. No disrespect to my lady, but I have a notion that his affections lie elsewhere.'

Padry could not help himself then. He looked for Atti. But she was no longer in the room. She must have slipped out after Ambrose had left them.

The maidservant had gone, too.

XIV

Moonlight in Tarceny

elissa saw Atti leave, and followed.

Atti had made no sign to her. She did not even look round to see that Melissa was there. But Melissa did not want to stay in the tower room with those scheming old men. The side of her head still throbbed from the impact of the door.

Atti led the way down the stairs to the hall gallery. There was a sentry here, one of the intruders, with his weapon in his hand and a lamp at his feet. It was the very man who had put his sword at her throat.

He caught her look. 'Sorry about your ear, girl,' he said, and winked. 'Better now, eh?'

She ignored him.

Atti led on, down into the long hall itself. The tall windows were pale with moonlight. The light gleamed on the chequered black-and-white flag-stones of the floor, so that the white tiles seemed to float in a sea of darkness. And Atti floated across them with no sound but the rustle of her gown and the whisper of her feet. She stopped in the middle of the empty room, looking around her.

There were two doors out of the hall. The further led to the upper courtyard, the other – the nearer one – to the fountain court. The fountain court was one of Ambrose's favourite places.

Melissa pointed towards it. 'He'll be—'

Atti was already moving. Melissa followed her out into the night.

It was past midnight. The old moon was high above them, its crescent like a crooked finger beckoning the hidden sun. The black outlines of the living quarters, the hall and the high keep bulked against the sky. The paving showed faintly in the dull grey-silver of the light. The colonnades were deep in shadow. The great crumbling pots with their half-dead herb trees threw shadows, too.

He was there.

He was there, sitting with his back to the fountain and the bowl curving outwards over his head. His head was sunk onto his chest. He was fiddling with something – some small white thing – in the fingers of his left hand. He did not seem to be aware of them. They crept closer.

He did not look up until they were almost at the fountain themselves. Atti knelt down beside him.

'Ambrose – what is the matter?'

He gave an impatient gesture. 'Damn them,' he said. 'They don't know what they are asking of me. Or maybe they do – Sophia should – and yet they want me to do it anyway.'

'Would they ask if it was not important?'

'No. They wouldn't. But that doesn't mean I'm going to do it.'

'Why not?'

He sighed. 'Atti – I don't like being cold or poor or hungry any more than anyone else does! But what I do here *works*. One of the reasons why it works is because we do live like this. It means nobody wants my place and I don't have to fight too hard to keep it. And so I can do things the way they need to be done. If I go over there and put myself at the head of the Kingdom, then I would have to start fighting – with laws, taxes, favours, and yes, if it came to it, with swords, too – just to stay on the throne. All kings have to.'

She looked at him thoughtfully. 'Isn't that better than another war?'

'Maybe. Who can say what would happen? But I wouldn't be doing what needs to be done any more. I'd be part of the problem. That's what I'm afraid of.'

'Afraid? How?'

He frowned and looked again at the white thing in his hand.

'There was a man called Paigan,' he said at last. 'He was a brother of Rolfe and the other princes. He told me that if I went to Tuscolo I would die. It was almost the last thing he said to me. And . . . I'm not afraid of death. But I remember him as he said it – how he looked at me and seemed to know everything I thought and would think and would ever do. I could see myself in his eyes, doing worse and worse, and finally dying a wasted death when all I had ever hoped for was in ruins. Yes, I'm afraid of dying as he saw me die. Very much.' He let out his breath. 'I still dream of him sometimes.'

'And what happened?'

'Oh.' Ambrose gave a short, bitter laugh. 'We killed him.'

'So why are you still afraid?'

When he did not answer, she went on softly, fiercely: 'Ambrose – what have you been telling me? Night after night you wanted me to turn round and see who it was coming through the curtain. Do you know how hard that is? I can't do it when you're not there. I can't do it even when you are. But sometimes I've felt that I almost could, because you were there and *I thought you weren't afraid.*'

She leaned forward and her head was close to his. He turned his face away. But she did not give up. More softly than ever now, she said: 'How can *I* turn when you will not?'

'It is not the same thing, Atti!'

'Isn't it? Isn't it exactly the same thing? I have demons. I can't hide that. But you have them, too. You hide it well but I know what it looks like! And what it feels like! And I know you can't do it alone. *You* told me that.'

He looked at her sharply in the moonlight. 'What are you saying?' he said.

'You would be a good king, Ambrose. They wouldn't have come out here if they didn't think so. I think so, too—'

'Not that,' said Ambrose. 'What are you saying about you and me?'

'That . . . that we can help each other.'

'How?'

She hesitated. 'By – by showing each other how.'

His voice hardened. 'And if I don't go to Tuscolo?'

'I can't help you if you do not turn.'

Suddenly he chuckled. 'Yes, I see. Well done. You've neatly dosed me with my own medicine. But . . .' He ran his hand through his hair. 'It isn't the same. Not really. And yet what you said just then – what you almost said – it nearly changed everything. Do you know why?'

'Tell me.'

He said nothing for a moment. Then there was a faint click as he put down whatever it was he had been holding in his fingers. Melissa watched, with a slow horror dawning on her. She knew what he was about to do. And he did it.

He reached across and took Atti's hand. 'I'm in love with you,' he said.

The court was so still that Melissa could almost hear the pulse in her own neck; the dizzy wail in her stomach as it dropped away into nothingness.

'Ambrose,' said Atti at last. 'You must not love me. Don't love me. You don't know what I'm like.'

'I know you better than you think.'

'You must not!'

'Atti – don't you see? If you hate yourself, all your days will be hateful. But if you let yourself be loved, you will be lovely – I swear to you! Atti, you *must* let yourself be loved. And you must love, too.'

'I don't love anyone.'

'Said without thinking! But without love the soul dies. Think, Atti. I've looked into your eyes so many times. And you have into mine. You need power to beat your demons. Love is a power. Love is the best power there is. Do you love me? Could you love me?'

Atti looked down at the hand that had taken hers, as if she did not understand what he had done.

She'll take it away, thought Melissa. She won't let herself be held.

As the moments lengthened, Melissa thought: She'll wait a little. She'll talk about something else. Then she'll slip it out of his fingers. She'll do it as soon as she thinks she can.

Atti was still looking down. Melissa could see she was frowning slightly, as if she were debating something with herself. The face of the man was hidden in the shadow.

'You asked me for justice once,' said Ambrose. 'I could not give it to you then. If – if we went together – perhaps I could give you all you were asking for.'

Went? thought Melissa in mounting horror. Went where? He's not going off to be King after all, is he – for her?

Atti had still not taken her hand from his. 'You must not do it because of that,' she murmured.

'No,' said Ambrose. 'It's a bad reason. But I'll do it to face my fears – if you could love a man who was able to do so.'

She lifted her face to his. 'Ambrose – I don't know. I think I could try. But . . .'

'But?'

'But yes,' she said in a rush, as if something within her had given way. 'Yes, let's go.'

'You are sure? *He* would be there – Padry. Had you thought of that?'

'He's nothing. It's not him, now. He doesn't bother me any more.'

'That's good.'

They were silent in the moonlit court under the dry fountain, holding hands with their heads bowed together as if it were the only thing they ever wanted to do. Melissa saw Atti look up at Ambrose. She saw the wondering look in her eyes. Then his head came forward slowly and hid hers.

They kissed one another lightly, and looked, and kissed again. The air was so still that Melissa could hear the sound of a night bird, hooting away in the olive groves below the outer walls. She could hear the scrape of a sentry's foot as he shifted at his post somewhere in the castle. She heard the murmur of voices within the hall and the clinking steps of an armoured man coming closer.

The man was coming into the fountain court.

Ambrose and Atti looked up. Their hands parted. Atti rose to her feet as the newcomer emerged from the black maw of the hall.

It was the man Caw, the captain of the intruders.

'I have one more message for you, my lord.'

'Yes?' said Ambrose coldly.

'It is from Orcrim.'

'I thought he was dead!'

'He is – these past three months. But I spoke with

him in his illness, and I was there when his mind turned to your father and to you. He said there had been only one thing in the way of your father being such a king as he should have been. It was that he wanted the Crown too much. Orcrim hoped we should one day be ruled by a Tarceny who had not wanted the Crown at all.'

For a moment Ambrose said nothing. Then he sighed. 'Very well,' he said, and got slowly to his feet. 'I will come. You may tell them I will come to Tuscolo, Caw.'

'Good – Your Majesty.'

'Rolfe?' said Ambrose suddenly.

'I am here,' said a deep voice in the shadows of the colonnade. Melissa jumped.

'You have taken your time,' said Ambrose.

'I came when I heard you call.'

'I need you for something else now. You must go to my mother and ask her to come to me. I have things to tell her.' And he took Atti's hand, and drew her to his side. 'They are important.'

'I will go,' said the voice from the shadows.

The voice was followed by silence.

Still holding Atti by the hand, Ambrose walked from the fountain court. Caw fell in with them. As they passed her, Melissa heard him mutter: 'A word of advice – Your Majesty.'

'What is it?'

Caw jerked a thumb over his shoulder to where Rolfe had been. 'There must be none of *that* when we are east of the lake.'

* * *

237

And so it was all going to change again, thought Melissa dully.

She stood in the moonlit court, looking at the bowl of the fountain where Ambrose and Atti had been.

Two years in the mountains, among the great valleys and the high, clear peaks. Two years as Atti's companion: Atti, watching bird-like as Melissa ground small quantities of grain, because she had known that she must take a turn at it and did not know what to do. Atti, shivering beside her under the same blanket during the winter nights. Atti, smiling that smile which was as rare as honey-drops when Melissa showed her . . . (What? Some little trick of living that grand ladies never learn; like gutting a fish, but it hadn't been that. The moment was gone. Only the smile was unforgotten.)

And Ambrose.

Melissa thought how eagerly he had talked of the new families that would come. Of getting the gate mended. Of the new winch for the well. Now he was going to leave all of it – for her.

Why did he love *her*?

Oh, of course Atti looked wonderful – almost always. She spoke wonderfully, too. Melissa knew she could never speak like Atti. And she couldn't play chess. And she did not have the Face.

But surely that could not be everything!

They would go to Tuscolo. Melissa could not imagine it. It was a big city, she had heard. Bigger than Aclete, she supposed. How many people lived there? Five hundred? A thousand even? She had no idea.

It must be very big if someone like Ambrose dreaded it. Maybe the houses covered the ground just as the forests did here in the March. And maybe there would be carpets and tapestries in the houses, and other things that Atti knew but she did not. There would be other servants, too. Not just her. There would be people like Gadi, who had been servants all their lives and who knew how things should be done. Would Atti even want her as a servant still, when they came to Tuscolo?

What did they think of Melissa? She had been with both of them just now. And they had said all that to each other in front of her. All that. They had spoken like strangers, with words she could not have imagined them using but that must have been there inside them all the time. They had said it all as if she had not been there.

They had not even thought what she might feel about it!

Something shifted in the darkness of the colonnade, close by.

'Rolfe?' she said, and found to her surprise that her voice was hoarse.

'I am here.'

'Shouldn't you be on your way? He told you to go.'

'I stayed for you. I think you are sad.'

'I suppose so,' she said.

I suppose so. That was just what Atti would have said. *I suppose so.* Not *Yes, I am sad.* Not *This is what I feel;* but always the wary answer, so that you never knew for sure what she was thinking. Even just now: *I could try.*

Melissa screwed up her eyes but she could not stop

the tears. She hiccupped. Abruptly she sat down and put her hand to her face.

She heard Rolfe settle on the paving beside her. He was still smaller than a full-sized man should be, but he was very heavy. She felt the paving shift slightly, as if a great weight had pressed upon it.

'Do you know why you are sad?' Rolfe asked.

She nodded, speechless.

'You love him, too,' he said.

She nodded again.

'Didn't know he *loved* her,' she managed to say. 'Should have done, I suppose, but . . .'

'I am sorry.'

'He doesn't look at me!'

Rolfe was looking at her. She could see him at the edge of her sight as she blinked back her tears. His great wide face peered at her from under the cowl he always wore. His big mouth – still far bigger than a man's should be, although no longer the frog-like satchel that it had been – was set like stone. She could not read his face. But yes, she could feel he was sorry. It helped her a little, feeling that. It helped her to weep some more.

'Did you ever love anyone?' she asked after a bit.

'I think so. It is hard to remember. I think I did not love them as much as I should have done.'

'Other way round, with me,' she said. 'There was a boy in the mountains,' she went on. 'He brought us food from the hill village across the valley. We wouldn't have managed without it. He would smile at me every time. Maybe *he* liked me.'

'What did he say to you?'

'Don't know. I couldn't understand his talk. He'd say something like "*Pukkalalla*" and he'd point to the food. He always began that way.'

'*Puka halalah.* It means "For the King." Ambrose is their King, too, you see.'

'Didn't know that either.' She wiped her eyes on her cloak. 'Looks like everyone wants a piece of him, then.'

'Yes.'

She sniffed. She drew a long, shaking breath. She looked around at the court. 'I liked this bit of the house,' she grumbled. 'I liked it because there's a place in the mountain house that's just the same. Only that one's got a throne in it, too, and you can see out of one side of it, over the valley.'

'I know. And in my house there was one also. I had it built when I was prince there. It pleased me, and I never knew there was another like it. Then I came here for my brother's wedding, three hundred years ago. I walked into this place.'

His sentences followed one another in a voice as flat and sibilant as shoe-leather on stone.

'I cried out when I saw it, for it was the same as my own. In jest I accused my brother of having a spy in my house. He denied it and said the idea was his. I grew angry. The other princes came running at our cries. They saw the court, too. And each swore that they had built one the same, without knowing another existed.

'We had seen it, each of us, in the depths of our

dreams. The court, and the cup in the centre of it. And we had each built it, in Ferroux, in Tarceny, in Tuscolo and Velis, in Trant, Baldwin and Bay. And by this fountain we looked at one another. Our eyes were wide with fear. We knew that some spell had been laid upon us all. But it was already too late, then. Knowing it did not help us. One after another we came to the pit.'

Melissa looked at the great stone bowl, waist-high on its stem.

'It's a cup, then, is it?'

'Of course.'

'And there's one in Tuscolo, too, is there?'

'Yes.'

'Maybe I'll go there when I want to weep.'

Rolfe did not say anything.

Melissa cleared her throat. 'I'm going to hug you,' she announced. 'It'll help me.'

He neither spoke nor stirred as she put her arms around him. His cloth was as dank as old canvas. Beneath it his body was hard as rock. She rested her head on his shoulder for a moment. Then she got to her feet.

'Thank you,' she said. 'I suppose you should go now.'

'Wait,' he said.

She turned back to him, wondering if he wanted her to hug him again. But he was sitting exactly as he had been, with his eyes on the paving below the fountain.

'There is something there,' he said. 'Do you see it?'

It was a white pebble, plain on the gloomy flagstones.

'He was playing with it when we came up,' she said. 'I suppose he forgot it when . . .'

When he went off hand in hand with Atti.

'You must pick it up,' said Rolfe. 'I cannot touch it.'

She walked over, bent, and plucked the thing from the moonlit stones of Tarceny. It was the King's white pebble, small enough to fit into the pit of her palm.

'Take care of it,' said Rolfe. 'It is cut from the tooth of the dragon.'

There seemed to be lines chiselled into it. She traced them with her finger. They were not letters, she thought. She knew what letters looked like, even though she could not read them. They looked as if they were part of a pattern. The pebble had been cut from something bigger.

Cut from the tooth of a dragon? What dragon?

When she looked up from it to ask, Rolfe had gone.

XV

Oak Wreath

n the fifteenth day of the new year Ambrose crossed the lake with a handful of followers from the March. He made his landing under the ruined walls of Trant castle, which had once been his mother's home.

All the land around Trant was war-wasted. The hillsides were empty. Wild beasts scurried in the thickets and a cloud of crows lifted from the untended olive trees. There was not a plough team or goat flock or fishing boat to be seen. The castle walls were green with ivy and brown from weather, and its windows were as dead as the eyes of a corpse.

But there were men there, all the same. Hidden in the ruins was a troop of knights, drawn chiefly from Develin, but also some sent from Lackmere and from Jent. Their captain was Caw, the lady's marshal, and he led his men out to drop their lances at the feet of their ragged King. They had spare mounts with them, and news, plans, and more messages. For half an hour the men spoke in quiet voices under the banner of Tarceny. Then the horses kicked the dry earth with their feet and the dust rose behind the cavalcade as it pressed inland.

Messages were sent ahead to Tuscolo, demanding that the city declare itself. But neither Caw nor Aun of Lackmere would wait for a reply.

'Our necks are already in the noose,' Aun said. 'Delay now and the other side will start to reckon the odds. March boldly and they will think you already crowned – if they have time to think at all.'

They covered twenty-five miles the first day, and at the end of it found a baron of the north, Lord Herryce, waiting with another two-score men-at-arms to pledge his allegiance. On the second day they forced their pace, marching thirty-five miles closer to the capital. They passed by three castles, including one belonging to the regent Lord Joyce, but no one opposed them. They halted that night within five leagues of Tuscolo.

Again riders went out, demanding yet more from their horses. They were under the city walls by dawn, hammering at the gates and shouting the arrival of the new King with a great force. But Ambrose's party did not break camp the following morning. They rested and fed their mounts, repaired their harness, sharpened their weapons and put on their armour with care. Only when the sun had begun to decline and the heat of the day was past did they mount and move warily towards the city.

Messages dribbled back to them during the afternoon: from Lord Seguin, defiance and a demand that they surrender; from the Lord Chancellor Padry, to say that the treasury was secured for Ambrose and had been removed to a secret place; from Lord Joyce, proposing a parley before the walls and also that a Great Council of the nobility and clergy should consider Ambrose's claim to the throne; from the Bishop of Tuscolo, urging that there be no bloodshed; from a city burger called Wrathmore, begging that the new King consider urgently his case against the Mercer's Guild as soon as he was installed in the city.

They pushed on. Aun of Lackmere had his men stop every traveller coming away from the city and make them march back towards it in Ambrose's train. They pressed donkeys, carts and drivers from the fields to join them, too. The column straggled back for a mile along the road, raising a great cloud of dust on the sun-blasted earth, which drifted high into the sky for the watchers of Tuscolo to see.

Another report came, from one of their own outriders. The city gates had been closed. Some of their men, already in the city, had been cut off. The citadel was flying flags with the devices of Gueronius and Seguin. At that, Caw ordered a halt and Ambrose called a council of war. But even as Caw and Aun were arguing about what to do, more horsemen arrived. The gate was open again. Moreover, Lord Joyce was now bidding them come with all speed. A crowd was said to be gathering on the walls.

'Quickly then,' said Aun. 'We must be there by sunset or our moment will have passed.'

On they went. The sun dipped behind them, throwing great shadows of the horsemen forward on the road. They topped a rise and there was the river and the city itself on the near bank. Its walls and towers were bathed orange in the long light. There were banners drooping in the air, and a crowd massing by the gate. The road led down towards it. People were beginning to gather at the wayside, landsmen hurrying from their fields to gawp at the passers-by and townspeople come out from the gate to call blessings on the new King or shout their own petitions for when he should come into his own. Rough garlands were hoisted up on sticks to the leading riders. Ahead of them the gates were indeed open.

'Now cheer, you dogs!' cried Aun. 'Ambrose Umbriel – King!'

'*Hurrah!*' bellowed the escort. And the cheering spread back down the line to the followers they had forced to come with them, and ahead to the crowd at the gate, dissolving into a shapeless, endless barrage of noise as Tuscolo, a city of ten thousand souls, welcomed its new master home.

In the gateway stood the bishop, with the keys of the town. On his right, in armour, was Lord Joyce, a small man with a huge plume and a little rat face peering out through his open visor. On his left was the chancellor, Thomas Padry, with a wreath of oak leaves in his hand. Hastily made banners were waving among the crowd: the black-and-white Moon of Tarceny, the Sun and Oak Leaf of Trant, and banners of any colour with the letters AU stitched upon them, which stood not only for 'Ambrose Umbriel' but also recalled Aurelian, the last High

King, whose reign a century before had been counted a golden age.

Before the doors Ambrose dismounted. He knelt for the bishop's blessing, then stood to receive the keys and the wreath. All three men bowed to him.

'Welcome, Your Majesty,' they said. 'Welcome to your city.'

'Where is my Lord Seguin?' demanded Ambrose.

'Your Majesty, he left by the east gate an hour since,' said Lord Joyce. 'He had but few followers with him. Loyal men hold the castle of Tuscolo for you.'

'Then may the Angels be praised,' said Ambrose. 'For there will be no blood shed today.'

And on foot, with crowds around him and armed men at his back, he entered the city of kings.

Melissa reached Tuscolo with Atti a week later. Even before she arrived her head was in a whirl. She had crossed the lake by boat, which she had never done before (water all around her – as far as the eye could see!). She had passed strange fields, with few trees, yellow grass and pale brown earth all cracked and baked hard from the sun. And now she was in the city, where there were houses and more houses, people and more people, stalls and street criers and smells that punched into her nose; walls further around even than those of Tarceny; buildings with their own towers, some of which were called chapels and were supposed to be holy; whole streets in which only meat was sold, or only leather goods, or only iron. When she lay down at night, all the images of the day went on

248

going round and round in her mind, chasing her into her sleep and tumbling among her dreams.

But there was no time to stand and gawp, because from the moment she arrived she was running errands for Atti. These were mostly messages for this person or that to find the things Atti wanted for the apartments that had been set aside for her, or for clothes, or for someone or other to come to see Atti instantly because there was something she needed to discuss with them. And Melissa would hurry through the great castle, getting lost and finding her way again, asking and finally tugging on the person's sleeve to get them to stop what they were doing and listen. And then when she returned there would be another errand, and another.

'I shall need a lady-in-waiting,' said Atti to the mirror on the third morning while Melissa was arranging her long hair for her. 'At least one, and preferably six. Find me pen and paper, and I shall write to my Lady Joyce and my Lady Faul for their help. I shall need a clerk, too, I suppose.'

'Can't I be your lady-in-waiting?' asked Melissa, frowning at the plait in her fingers and trying at the same time to remember what a *pen* and a *paper* and a *clerk* were, and where she was supposed to find them all.

Atti's head turned slightly. 'No, Melissa. You cannot be.'

A lady-in-waiting, Melissa discovered, had to be a lady herself. Lady Something diThis, or Lady Somebody of That, with servants of her own to look after her. Some of them could be young – the daughters of any important Lady Whoever. But the chief lady-in-waiting had to be someone important in her own right, and a lot older than either Atti or Melissa. Melissa did not feel so bad about it once she had understood that.

But it was hard nonetheless, on the day of the betrothal, when she and the half-dozen other servant girls whom Atti had employed stood back from their mistress (on whose hair and face and hands they had been working since dawn) and watched the young Lady Someone give Atti her fan, and the Lady Thingummy pick up the baby lynx that Atti had been given, and other ladies lifted Atti's train, and the chief lady-in-waiting swept her eyes over all of them, nodded, and led the way out of the apartment towards the great hall.

And Atti was gone – gone out to her destiny, with him. Melissa could not go with her. She could only train the hair, clean and trim the nails, and see the beautiful thing she had helped to make walk itself away, surrounded by women who had never heard her cry in the night or felt her shiver under the same blanket in the mountains.

'We can watch from the gallery,' said one of the other servant girls. 'No one's going to need us before it's over.'

That was the thing, thought Melissa – knowing when you were going to be needed. In among the running around there was beginning to be quite a bit of waiting, too, sitting on stools in small back rooms and listening to the talk of the other servant girls with whom she had so little in common. Once she had told them all she cared to about Atti, there was hardly anything left to say. But no one was unfriendly, at least. And now they assumed she would go with them. So she did. She had never seen the court before.

She followed the others along unfamiliar, unlit corridors, knowing that if she lost them she would be lost altogether. She could hear them ahead of her, whispering to one another, giggling as someone tripped, and a mock-cry of pain as someone else stubbed her toe. She followed them left and right through the shadowy passages, hearing the distant murmur of the court swell ahead of her. She waited at the back of the group while the leading girls fumbled at a door. She saw the light crack around it as it opened, swinging away. The clamour of a crowd rose from beyond.

They emerged one after another onto a narrow wooden gallery that ran along one wall of a huge vaulted room. Others were here before them but there was still a little space. Melissa pushed her way to the rail and looked down on the court of the King.

Below her was the crowd – knights and barons, nobles and ladies, packed against either wall so that the long aisle was clear. The air was warm with the press of bodies. Everyone down there seemed to be talking, lifting their voices so that their neighbour might hear them in the clamour. Guards in polished armour stood shoulder to shoulder at the front of the crowd, holding long weapons in their hands. They lined the central path all the way from the double doors on her left to the throne itself.

And there he was, Ambrose, sitting on a high seat at the top of a short flight of steps at the right-hand end of the hall. There were banners above him and richly dressed men around him, and on the wall above the throne was a great golden sun, to which had been added, in fresh green paint, a giant leaf of oak.

He sat there amid all the clamour. He was wearing a tunic of blue edged with gold. His new little beard was trimmed to a point after the fashion of the capital. But the same simple circlet that she remembered was on his head, and there was the same thoughtful look on his face that she had seen on the knoll.

He hasn't changed, she thought suddenly. He's here to do just what he was doing before. All the rest of it's fancy dress – no more than that.

He was waiting for something.

A trumpet blared. Melissa jumped. It had come from the door on her left. Armed men stood there, wearing yellow shirts over their mail, marked with a black bird flying over a black tower. The babble of the crowd was subsiding. Up and down the hall people were craning to see. And now other people were coming through the doors – ladies carrying garlands, and then . . .

And then came Atti herself, in her long pale dress, standing out among the bright colours of her escort like a diamond in a golden ring.

They had dropped that stupid veil over her face,

thought Melissa crossly. No one would be able to see all those jewels she had pinned into Atti's hair that morning, or the whiteness of her skin or the fine lines of her brows that two of the others had spent all that time perfecting. Her head was the main thing after all. Why hide it?

Slowly Atti and her escort advanced down the hall. When she was ten paces into the room the last of the ladies carrying her train were still emerging from the door. When she was twenty paces into the room she stopped. Her escort stopped with her. Again the trumpet sounded.

'The Lady Astria Anthea Aeris diPare diBaldwin, heir of Velis and of the house of Baldwin, Princess of the Realm!' cried one of the men in yellow shirts.

And again they moved forward, pacing slowly down the room towards the throne. Before the steps they halted, and again the trumpet blew.

'The princess will do homage to her King!' cried the herald.

Atti walked forward and knelt before Ambrose. Her hands were between his. A man was reading words from a scroll. Atti was repeating them. Now Ambrose was replying. And now he was rising from his throne, taking her hand, raising her to her feet. They faced the crowd together. More trumpeters came forward. On their tabards they wore Ambrose's arms, the moon quartered with an oakleaf. They sounded their brass down the hall. Another voice bellowed that the King now offered his hand to the princess, for the love that there was between them and for the peace of the land. If the princess willed it they should be wed on the day of the King's coronation and crowned together in the cathedral of Tuscolo.

Atti nodded to her own herald, who roared her reply. 'The princess wills it!'

'Hurrah for the King! Hurrah for his Queen!'

And all the crowd bellowed, '*Hurrah! Hurrah!*'

One of the girls was pulling at Melissa's arm. 'They'll leave now. We'd best be back before them.'

'Coming,' said Melissa. The others were already ahead of her, slipping quickly out of the gallery door.

Standing just inside the doorway was a woman in a dull cloak and hood. She must have come in after the serving girls to watch the procession from up here. Now the other girls were pushing past her, ignoring her in their hurry to be back at their posts before Atti returned to her chambers. The woman moved a little to be out of their way but there was not much space. Melissa looked up at her as she passed.

She stopped.

Then she put her hands together beneath her chin in the way the hill folk did, and said: 'Thanks to Michael, lady, that he has guarded you, and to Raphael that he has guided your way, for you are safe come.'

And Phaedra of Trant and Tarceny, mother of the King, smiled sadly at her. 'Thank you for your greeting, Melissa. I did not suppose that anyone in this place would know me or notice me. But you did.'

'You come to see him betrothed, my lady?'

(In the hills she would never have called her *my*

254

lady. Here, it felt wrong to call her anything else.)

'Betrothed and wed and crowned,' said Phaedra. 'What mother could miss it? I shall do my best to be happy for him.'

'Wedding and crowning's going to be another month, my lady. There's so much to get ready.'

'You will be busy, Melissa.'

'I suppose so.'

'And are *you* happy?'

Happy?

Melissa shrugged. 'I'm not sick,' she said. 'They feed me every day – as much as I want, pretty well.'

'And now you know that isn't happiness after all. Not after you've had a chance to get used to it. I was sorry to lose you from the mountains, Melissa. They are emptier places without you.'

Melissa said nothing. She did not feel comfortable talking about herself with Ambrose's mother. She never knew what Phaedra did and did not guess.

Phaedra was looking down at the court again. So they both stood there and watched together as Atti and her attendants walked backwards, train leading, down the long aisle in the middle of the chamber. They were walking with their heads bowed out of respect for the King, but also so that they could see where they were putting their heels. They moved even more slowly than when first they had entered. The rear of the train had only just reached the great double doors. Atti herself still had twenty short paces to go. At the other end of the hall the King sat still. His eyes had never left his bride.

'I nursed him through the shadows,' said Phaedra softly. 'And through the mountain winters. He was my world for thirteen years. What does he remember of that? But he was a child then, with a child's strength. He strove with an enemy of Angels and did not fail. Now he is a young man. His weakness is that of all young men. And he does not want for his mother.'

'He does love her, my lady,' said Melissa. 'And she him,' she added stoutly.

'And I loved my husband when I married him,' said Phaedra. 'And I betrayed him to his death. Did you know that?'

'No, my lady! No, you never said.'

'It is not a story I tell. But one day maybe . . . Even before his whole court, if I must.'

Atti was still backing down the aisle. Melissa could hear the slight jingling of her jewellery as she moved. The doors stood wide like the mouth of a great frog. The train withdrew into it as if it were a silken tongue, carrying the pretty thing on its tip. All eyes were on Atti as she disappeared. Then the doors closed. A murmur of voices rose in the hall.

'Um . . . Does he know you are here?' said Melissa.

The question pulled Phaedra from her thoughts. She smiled ruefully. 'He does not, yet. It is ironic, Melissa. I can see far and speak far and pass where no one should be able to pass. Yet in none of these ways can I approach my son. There are too many people around him. There is always someone to hear and see. And until he knows I am here I cannot even walk up to him like a supplicant. Truly I think that a king's flatterers must be the thickest and most impenetrable of all defences. Can you bring a message to him from me?'

'I can give it to someone who gives it to someone who gives it to him,' said Melissa. 'That's the way it works here. At least,' she added, glancing at the doorway, 'I can when I find my way out.'

The corridor was empty. The girls who had led her to the gallery were gone. Down in the hall the court babbled on, waiting for the next thing.

'Do you not know the way?' said Phaedra.

'No, my lady.'

'Neither did I when I last came up here. I was no older than you are now. Let us see if we can remember it together.'

She held out her hand and Melissa took it. Her skin felt very cool, almost damp. Together they felt their way forward into the dimness, and the trumpet blared in the court behind them.

XVI

Wulfram's Crime

 did ask if we might speak in private,' sighed Phaedra to her son.

Ambrose glanced around the chamber. And that, thought Padry, was the last straw.

It wasn't so much Ambrose himself. Padry could work with Ambrose (albeit with gritted teeth), because when it was about lands or laws or charters, Ambrose was willing to listen to him. And so far Ambrose had not once referred to that disastrous episode in the mountains. So far.

But the presence of Phaedra shrieked at him. It transported him back to the very moment of his humiliation, two years ago, when he had stumbled out of that courtyard, knowing himself for what he was. He could not look at her. His eyes went to his writing table, to the window, to Ambrose – to anything but the woman in her drab, colourless gown who stood in the middle of the room. Waves of shame and self-disgust pulsed through him like a headache. It was as bad as when he had to be in the presence of Atti herself. Worse, because she had come without warning. And because Atti had turned her back, that day in the mountains. But she – *she* had seen into his naked and quivering soul.

And they wanted to speak in private! These people – did they know nothing about kingship? Why, for this audience he had virtually emptied the room! He had almost been on his knees to the suspicious, jealous lords of the council, begging them for a half-hour's indulgence while the King met with his mother, and assuring them that no matter touching the Kingdom or the royal estate would be decided in their absence. He had packed off all his assistants apart from Lex, all the guards bar two and all the servants except for one whom he had kept back to pour wine if that should be desired. Did they *know* what it cost the King's authority?

'This is as private as it's ever been,' said Ambrose.

'Can it not be more so?'

'That depends.' His tone was wary, almost harsh. 'Do you want to speak to me as mother, subject or counsellor?'

Phaedra lifted an eyebrow. 'As mother and counsellor, if you like. I have not come to ask for anything for myself – since there is nothing you can give me.'

'Is it about Atti?' said Ambrose grimly.

'It is not.'

'But you don't approve.'

'Does it matter whether I approve or not, since you did not ask me before you bound yourselves to one another? Nevertheless,' she added, perhaps with some difficulty, 'I, too, made a marriage without my parents' let. When I see you together, you shall both have my blessing.'

Ambrose let out his breath. 'Thank you,' he said, sounding a little more at ease. 'So I suppose you want to scold me about becoming King?'

'Do you think you deserve a scolding?'

'No – and yes.'

'And could anything I say persuade you that you should not be King after all?'

'No.'

'Then what use would it be for me to scold you? If you need a scolding, you may scold yourself. You remember as well as I what Paigan said about coming to Tuscolo.'

Ambrose swallowed and nodded. 'I do.'

She looked at him with eyes that said, *Well?* But he looked back defiantly.

'He was a liar. Always,' he said. 'Anyway, I'm here.'

'So. And do you like being King?'

'Like it?' Ambrose laughed bitterly. 'There's never any time to think whether I like it or not. But we'll do good things, Mother. We will re-settle Trant and restore the castle. Aun says I have to have lands east of the lake. At least this way I can have them without taking them from someone else. We'll do the same for Baldwin and Bay if we can. After twenty years of war there's a need for healing wherever you look.' He ran his hand through his hair. 'I just had not realized that so much of it would be about money!'

Padry exchanged a long-suffering look with Lex.

Money? Of course it was about money! Almost everything a king did must be about wealth in some form or other – who got it and who should be deprived of it, and above all how the royal coffers were to pay the next fee when demand always exceeded revenue! Didn't he understand that yet? He could do with some more house-training, this boy.

'I sent for you as soon as I decided to come here,' Ambrose said.

'I know. But I was occupied with one for whom you have been waiting.'

'And?'

'I will bring him to you now, if you are willing.'

'Now?'

'He is ready. He can speak. He remembers who he was.'

Again Ambrose ran his hand through his hair. 'Very well.' He looked at Padry. 'Clear the room.'

Padry gaped. 'But Your Majesty—'

'Clear it! *You* may stay, but all others must leave.'

It took Padry a moment more to realize what was about to happen. And to understand that yes, if it was going to happen – here, in Tuscolo of all places – then no one must see it! Grimly he signed the guards and the wine servant to the door. He took the paper and ink bottle from Lex, and muttered, 'Come back in half an hour. No, better still, remain in the corridor and see that no one listens at the keyhole. I will call you in when I have leave for you to return.'

Lex nodded and rose. Tight-lipped, Padry drew the pen and parchment across to himself. His fingers were

261

trembling. Angels! Was he not tried enough already? Wasn't it enough that he must serve, day in, day out, a king and queen whose very presence made him hot with shame? Just a moment ago he had been thinking what further house-training this pup needed. Well, when this was over there would be words – very frank words – between them! He must *not* spring something like this on his council! Gueronius might have had his faults as King, Padry thought bitterly, but at least he had never indulged in *this*!

His palms were sweating and there was the same hollow feeling in his stomach that he had felt when the news of Ambrose's landing had burst upon the capital. It was not anger. It was fear. It was that sudden lurch of the pulse when events started to move at a pace he could not control. And now there was nothing he could do.

The door closed. Footsteps and low voices faded in the corridor. Padry held his breath, listening. There was silence.

'Come,' said Phaedra.

For a moment nothing happened. Then a man stepped – it seemed from nowhere – into the room. He bowed silently to Ambrose. Padry knew the long figure at once. It was the Prince Talifer.

The air seemed to thicken. A dank, watery smell stole upon Padry's senses. Memories surged in his brain and made him shudder. Three more figures loomed from nothingness, silently. They took their places before Ambrose's throne. Two were clothed, with hoods that half concealed their faces. One of these was a broad-headed, slouching man – yes, man, for Padry could see the stamp of humanity beginning to emerge in its eyes and nose and chin. The other was more stooped, longer-faced, and with joints that seemed to bend in a way no man's should.

Between them they led, or held, their companion. It was a wretched, pitiful thing, smaller than any man and wrapped in some shapeless dark cloth or . . . Padry blinked, peered hard, and could not be sure whether he was actually seeing *through* the creature that was there. Wherever his eyes rested – on its hood, its wrinkled fingers (black as wet tree roots), or its robe, it seemed solid enough. And yet, again and again as he stared at it, he seemed to glimpse the wall hanging or the floor beyond where it stood.

It was hiding its face in its hood. It was hiding deliberately, staring at the floor. It did not want to be looked at. It did not want to meet the eye of the young King, seated on the throne before him.

'Welcome, Talifer, my ancestor,' said Ambrose calmly. 'Welcome, Rolfe and Lomba. Each time I see you, you are more like the men you were. This is good. Will you present your brother to me?'

'My lord,' said Prince Lomba, in a voice like rushing wind. 'This is our half-brother Marc, youngest of the sons of our father Wulfram's first marriage.'

'Welcome, Marc Wulframson,' said Ambrose. 'Will you greet me?'

A sound like high-pitched weeping broke from the shadow. It took Padry a moment to realize that the thing was weeping indeed.

'Do you know me, Marc?'

The thing did not answer.

'You came to me among your brothers, years ago in the garden at Ferroux. With them you pleaded to me. Do you remember? You came to me and I did not know you. I know you now. What is it you would ask of me?'

The weeping subsided. The thing stirred. A delicate, transparent hand reached towards the throne.

'Lor' . . . Gi' me 'eh.'

'I will not give you death, Marc. Each of your brothers asked me for death, one after another, when they came from the pit. I refused them. Just as the things that you have done cannot be undone, so what you have suffered cannot be taken away.'

The thing bowed its head and seemed to shrink. Padry, looking on, felt that he could almost smell its pain: an immeasurable weight of guilt and grief, shame at what it had been and horror at what it had become. His mind backed away, revolted. Why had they brought that thing here? Really, it might be kinder to kill it! At least they would not have to look at the wretched—

And then the creature raised its hands again. It raised its black, wrinkled, dripping hands, pleading to the boy on the throne. And as if some Angel had reached out and jerked at an eye-muscle, Padry's gaze fell to his own hands, fat and soft and stained with ink on the table before him.

A terrible feeling swept over him – a feeling that

these hands, which he knew so well, were one and the same with the twisted talons that were lifted to the King. They were joined by just such sinful bones to a mind as black with corruption as that of the creature crouching there. It was not only a forgotten prince who was begging oblivion. It was Thomas Padry himself. It should have been – it *was* – Thomas Padry who was on his knees, whining for release while the things he had done towered over him like black cliffs about to fall – the neglect of his duty, the blinding of his conscience, the insane and lustful pursuit of a child! He squirmed in his seat and put his ink-stained fingers to his temple, thinking: Who is the most shameful thing here? That thing or I? Oh, dear Angels! Dear Lord . . .

Coolly in the room he heard the voice of the King. 'I have three commands for you. Fulfil them, and I shall hold you forgiven. Do you listen?'

Miserably, the thing nodded. In his heart Padry nodded, too.

'You shall learn to be a man again. That is one. And for the rest of your days, until by some chance death meets with you, you shall serve all the people of this Kingdom in any way that I direct or that you shall otherwise find is possible for you. That is another.

'But first, you shall tell me your story. Talifer and Rolfe and Lomba have told theirs, but you are the only one so far who was born before Wulfram's landing. You remember what they do not. You were present when they were not. Tell me what you saw.'

Again that high-pitched, horrible weeping broke from the creature.

'Tell me, Marc,' said the King.

'Lor' . . . wha' 'oo wan' know?'

'Tell me why Beyah weeps.'

Sweating, Padry caught Lex in the corridor afterwards.

'What did you hear?' he muttered.

Lex looked at him darkly. 'Not much. But enough to bring back bad memories.'

'Did anyone else?'

'I don't think so. But the councillors are getting restive in the hall down there. They're saying Seguin has sent to offer his submission. They want to discuss it.'

'Has he, by the Angels!'

'So when can we let them back in?'

'Not yet. We're going to move straight to Grand Audience in the hall. If Seguin's sent us a message we'll hear it there and discuss it later. *Meanwhile* you've got to get the Privy Chamber aired. There's a smell in there that's bound to start rumours. And find another carpet.'

'Carpet? What happened?'

'That creature they brought with them . . . I didn't realize it, but the damned fabric shrivelled under its feet as it stood there! Get it changed. Give out that it's my fault because I sent the wine waiter away and then spilled the wine when I tried to pour it . . . That's a good idea, actually. Tip over the wine jug while you are at it. It may help hide the smell. And clear everything

266

yourself. Don't let anyone help you. And *burn* that damned carpet!'

'And what do we say?'

'About what?'

'What was said in there?'

'Oh.' Padry chuckled slyly. His horrors were passing. His mood had lifted. Now he felt light-headed, gleeful, ready to leap from danger to victory in an instant. (Seguin wanted to submit, did he? Good! Just give Thomas Padry the chance and he would squeeze that old ruffian until . . .) 'We tell the truth, of course.'

'Are you mad or am I?'

'*Part* of the truth. My lady presented His Majesty with an account, by an ancient prince, of an event that occurred during Wulfram's conquest. It is, er, rather sensitive, because it differs from that given in any version of *The Tale of Kings*. In particular, it does *not* show our founder Wulfram in a good light. Which could be damaging for the authority of the Crown itself' – Padry theatrically put his finger to his lips – 'if it became too widely known among the common sort. You understand? We must ask for discretion from our fellow councillors. Of course we can tell *them*, but it must go no further. You understand me?'

'The games we play!' groaned Lex. 'Very well. And where is this account?'

Padry handed him the scroll of jottings he had made as Ambrose coaxed the creature's story from it. 'Here. Once you've seen to the room, you can copy this for me. I want one for the library here, one for myself, and one to send to Develin.'

(Tell your story, the King had said. It had not been Padry's story to tell. But he could see that it was not forgotten. He could serve. He, too, could become a man again.)

'Very good,' said Lex.

'Burn the notes when you've finished!' added Padry over his shoulder. And eagerly, relieved beyond measure, he hurried down to the royal hall to take Grand Audience by the horns.

She dreamed of the safe place, her childhood home. Sunlight poured through the windows and filled the high rooms. The people were passing her, brilliant and smiling, and she looked among them for him.

There was the beautiful woman with the long brown hair, who smiled and did not answer when she asked for him. There was Gadi, tight-lipped and bustling away, and she called after her but Gadi did not turn round. She knew that Gadi was dead.

Where was he?

She knew what was coming. This was the safe place and the safe place was not safe. Very soon it would all happen again. She tried to speak to the faces that passed her. She tried to ask for him, to get them to make him come so that the dream would stop before it happened. But she could not say the words. The people smiled at her as they passed. Their faces were darkening.

Where was he? The colours were changing. The rooms were a purple haze in which black shapes of people moved, hurrying now. She could hear the voices crying aloud. She cried aloud, too. She cried aloud for him. Where was he? He should be here now! She needed him now! And the curtain was behind her. She knew it. And the faces and the cries were gathering. Father stalked by, angry in his black armour, and it was too late.

The curtain was behind her. She could not turn. She could not face it. Now it was being drawn aside, and behind it was blackness, and the figure that moved in the blackness, and it was – it was . . .

The scream tore Melissa from sleep.

Sick with the suddenness of it, head swimming, she was on her feet and blundering in the darkness before she remembered that she was no longer in the mountains. She was in the King's castle at Tuscolo, surrounded by hundreds and hundreds of other people. And Atti no longer slept in the same room. It had been a year since this had last happened.

The scream came again, muffled by oak doors, but she knew it at once. She groped for the door handle. In the room the other girls were stirring. Someone half asleep asked a question. She left them. In the passage the torches lit the faces of the lady-in-waiting and the guard who were hurrying to Atti's door. Melissa reached it before them. As she put her hand on the latch the door opened inwards. Another of the ladies-in-waiting stood there, pale and trembling.

'It's the princess!' she gasped. 'She's—'

'It's a dream she gets,' said Melissa shortly. '*You* aren't needed,' she told the guard. And she pushed past them as they stood wide-eyed in the doorway.

The outer room was empty and dark, but the door to Atti's bedchamber was open and the dancing glow of candles showed from beyond. As Melissa strode across the room she heard Atti scream again.

She was there, kneeling on her bed with her shoulders hunched and her forearms tight up against her chest. Her eyes were open but she did not seem to see. At the foot of the bed yet another lady-in-waiting stood trembling, begging as if she herself were in pain, 'Your Highness . . . Wake up, please . . .' It was she who held the candle. And if she didn't look out, thought Melissa, she'd have the bed curtains on fire in an instant.

Atti drew breath again. Melissa scrambled up onto the bed and put an arm around her shoulders. 'Atti,' she said. 'Atti, it's just the dream! You're all right! Hear me?'

The scream burst in her ear, so loud that it hurt. Atti's shoulders were as hard as wood. It was like trying to hug a tree trunk. This was a bad one, Melissa thought. She held her more firmly, rocking the two of them together on the mattress, and said again, 'Atti, it's Melissa. You hear me?'

The scream broke into sobbing. Melissa felt the shoulders ease a little under her embrace. It was still bad. She couldn't remember it ever being this bad before. Atti would not sleep again tonight. Oh, and tomorrow they'd be starting all the things they had to do for the crowning, and all . . .

Now that the crisis was passing Melissa could feel

her exhaustion coming back. She had been deep, deep asleep, unconscious in the few hours allowed to her between the end of duty last night and the pre-dawn rise tomorrow. Tomorrow? Today, probably. To judge by the silence from the King's rooms Ambrose was either already up or hadn't managed to get to bed at all. There was so much to do. And she, too, was up now.

The room was full of faces, all the Ladies This-and-that looking at her. Looking frightened, looking angry, looking at her. Well, none of *them* had nursed Atti through her nightmares before this, had they? Perhaps they should start to get used to it. And next time it could be one of them that jumped up in the middle of the night and tried to talk her out of it!

'Meh . . . Meh . . .' said Atti.

She was trying to say 'Melissa'.

'I'm here,' said Melissa. And then she remembered to add: 'Your Highness.'

'It was him. It was him!'

'Him? The King?'

Atti nodded.

'Did you turn? Did you see him?'

'No,' she whispered.

'Then it won't have been him, will it? It was the dream, that's all.'

When Atti did not reply, she added: 'You'll be see-ing him again tomorrow. The real him. You love him, don't you?'

It was the question she had wanted to ask for weeks and never could. And now it was easy – oh, so easy! It had slipped out of her as if it were just another word of comfort. Why had she done it now?

A slight shifting of the shoulders told her that the question had announced itself in Atti's brain. She had done it now. It was in there, in Atti's mind, calling like a voice in a dark cave. *You love him, don't you?* Atti opened her mouth but did not speak.

'You do love him,' Melissa said, rocking her again. 'You love him.'

Atti beat at the bedclothes with clenched fists. 'Why did I have to put my hands between his? *Why?*'

And some stupid, stupid Lady Something said: 'Because he's the King, Your Highness. Everyone must submit to him.'

Atti's shoulders shook and she was weeping again. The ladies murmured and glanced at one another.

'Don't be afraid. You mustn't be afraid,' said Melissa.

And of course that was a useless thing to say. Of this one thing Atti would always be afraid: that however high she was, there would be one who could come suddenly and destroy everything again. She would always fear anyone who could do that to her. Even if it were the best man in the world.

Because he was the King, and she had put her hands between his.

The scroll that Lex handed Padry the next morning read:

A copy of the account by Prince Marc, son of Wulfram, that was presented to His Majesty King Ambrose Umbriel by his mother

272

the Lady Phaedra of Trant and Tarceny, in the first year of King Ambrose's reign.

In the third year after his landing, Wulfram seized a great city of the Artaxalings (who are now the people of the hills). He slew their warriors and their high priests and took their palace for his own. And from the city he took hostages, nine hundred in all, and held them in the outer courts of his palace lest the city should rise against him.

There came to him a woman of the Artaxalings, richly dressed with bands upon her arms. She begged to him that the hostages be released, for they were well loved in the city. In their place she offered him tribute in gold, and she stripped her bands from her arms to show that what she said was true.

Wulfram smiled upon her, and said, Tribute in gold will I take this year and every year hereafter. But I will not release the hostages, for I fear that the city will rise.

Then give me but half of them, said the woman, and our love for the rest will keep the city from rising.

Half will I not give, said Wulfram.

Then give me but ten, said the woman.

Not even ten will I give, said Wulfram. But if you ask it, I will give you one, he said.

And the woman named her own son, who stood among the hostages.

And Wulfram had her son brought to him, and he slit his throat with a knife, and gathered his life-blood in a cup. He gave the cup to her, saying, This is the hostage I have released because you asked it. Drink this cup and tell the city what you have seen.

And the woman drank it and went away weeping.

* * *

Lex tapped the last line with his finger. 'I suppose she is weeping still,' he said.

'I think we heard her, didn't we?' said Padry sombrely.

'How does a woman, be she princess or priestess, become a goddess?'

'It is a mystery,' agreed Padry. 'And unlike anything the Church teaches of Heaven or Godhead or the Angels. But . . . Do you remember you said to me once that things so big that we cannot understand them may turn because someone takes pity on someone else?'

'Yes.'

'It may have happened in this case. Or, to be exact, it may have happened because he did not.'

Lex sucked in his cheeks, looking at the manuscript again.

'What did our King say?'

'Not much,' said Padry. 'I think he had guessed some of it. But he made our . . . visitor repeat himself three times at one point in the story. When Wulfram offered to release just one of the hostages. He seemed very struck with that. He said someone had said that to him, too, once.'

'Coincidence?'

'He seemed to think it was fate.'

XVII

The Scholar

n Atti's wedding night they took the jewels from her hair. They removed her gown, her under-dress and the clothes she wore next to her skin. Over her naked body they dropped a long shirt of purest white silk. Two maids, one on either side of her, began to brush the dark tresses that fell from her head to her waist.

They prepared her in her antechamber and not in her bedchamber. Her bedchamber was separated from the King's only by a wooden door. In the King's room councillors were already gathering with lights and solemn faces. By long custom the wedding night of a king or prince had to be witnessed by trusted men, so that it could be sworn, if it came to it, that the marriage had been made complete and that any heir would therefore be royal. There was no help for that. But the women did not think it decent that the men should overhear the Queen's preparations, or the things they said to her as they made her ready.

'Oh, you look lovely, Your Majesty,' said one. 'He'll swoon at the sight of you, to be sure.'

'It's hard waiting now,' said another. 'But once you're in there and it's started, you'll be all right.'

'We all envy you so, Your Majesty!'

Melissa, working one of the brushes, bent and whispered in her ear: 'He loves you, remember?'

Atti's head turned a little at her words. Now she stared at a different patch of wall from the one she had been staring at before. That was how Melissa was sure she had heard.

Brush, brush, brush. The hair slipped like silk under her fingers. She tried to make the strokes as gentle as possible. Long, gentle touches were calming. Calming mattered more now than brushing out any tangles.

Atti stood like a statue under their attentions. She did not speak to any of them. She did not look at any of them. Her hands were wrung together before her. If she had not held them so, they might have been shaking. The door to her bedchamber was open. On the far side of it was the door that would lead to the King. They could all hear the voices of the men as they murmured to one another, waiting.

'He loves you,' whispered Melissa through set teeth. 'Nothing else matters, does it?'

Atti nodded, mute.

'Your Majesty?' said the chief lady-in-waiting.

'I am ready,' said Atti quietly.

A maid slipped through the bedchamber to scratch at the King's door. It opened at once. They could see heads, bearded faces, the gleam of gold chains. Eyes glinted in lamplight, looking their way.

Atti stepped forward, and stopped. Her shoulders were shaking. Her hand groped blindly and Melissa caught it. She was trembling.

But there was only one thing she could do. He was waiting for her. The men were waiting for her. The women were around her, willing her on. There was no possibility of hiding or turning away. This was the moment she had chosen. Slowly she lifted her head and squared her shoulders. She released Melissa's hand. She walked forward across the short breadth of her bedchamber. The door of the King closed behind her and shut her from the women's sight.

'That was brave,' said one. 'When you think how scared she is.'

'It'll be easier for her next time,' said another. 'And there won't be all those nosey old men to make it worse.'

'If it doesn't get easier,' sighed the chief lady-in-waiting, 'it'll get harder. That's the way of things.'

Melissa said nothing. It was not her place.

Success meant more business: more audiences, more petitions, councils and ceremonies. More business meant more preparation and less time in which to do it. By the second month of the reign Ambrose, Padry and Aun of Lackmere were meeting at sunrise in an attempt to master each day at a time before the torrent of affairs overtook them.

And the problem with meeting the King at sunrise,

thought Padry, was that you got all the ideas he'd had in the middle of the night.

'. . . But Sophia sits in judgement, doesn't she?' said Ambrose.

'Develin's different,' snapped Aun. 'It's been ruled by a woman for twenty years. Everyone knows that. We can't have the Queen taking your place for however long. The barons won't put up with it.'

'Not even if I'm away on progress or something?'

'Again, no. The court follows you. That's why you go on progress – to take justice to the provinces. Put the Queen in your place and you'll make yourself a laughing stock. Worse, you'll make yourself enemies.'

Ambrose ran his hand through his hair, as he did when he was agitated. 'I just think it would help her! If she could see that she was in control of *something* it wouldn't be so bad.'

'Maybe not. But she'd be so busy being in control that she'd turn everything upside down. She could do you more harm with a day in court than Seguin could in a year of plotting on his estates.'

'You're not being fair to her, Aun!'

'Aren't I? Ask someone else then. Ask anyone you like, except those besotted dandies who swarm round her with their lutes and caps and feathers! You'll get the same advice.'

Ambrose looked to Padry for support but Padry had seen it coming. He mumbled something and fixed his eyes on his feet. Privately he sided with the baron. Not so much about women in general – he could think of several abbesses who were just as much lords of their territories as the lady was at Develin. But yes, Atti, with her opaque thoughts, her scorn and her quick tongue – to set her up in court would be to risk disaster. When it came to judgement there was no tyranny worse than caprice. Couldn't Ambrose see that?

He did not speak, one way or another. He had an absolute rule with himself that he must not speak on any matter to do with the Queen. No one would have forgotten his mad pursuit of the girl to the mountains. They would always think his words would be coloured by that. And they might well be right. Whatever the stakes, the baron must fight this one alone.

Fortunately he seemed to be winning. He was winning because in his heart the King knew he was right.

'I know it would mean so much to her,' Ambrose groaned.

'You can't do it,' said the baron flatly. 'Justice is too important.'

'Nothing's more important, Aun! Not to me. Don't you understand that? If I can't help her I can't help the Kingdom either, and nothing I do will be any good. All right, I'll try to think of another way. But there's got to be something. Because she still thinks she's powerless. That's how she sees it. That's why she's not sleeping well. She's still the victim.'

'Well, that makes it worse, doesn't it? Never put a victim in judgement. Never.'

'Sometimes I will, you know,' said Ambrose quietly. 'When I've got the villain on their knees in front of me, I turn to the victim standing there, ask what they would do.'

'And every time you do it my heart's in my mouth. Just remember this. Victims make the worst villains there are.'

'You can love whom you like,' he added when the King did not reply. 'You can be sorry for whom you like. But only trust whom you can.'

Melissa had given up counting the people in the castle. There were too many.

There were courtiers and ladies and priests and servants. There were clerks and gold-chained officials. There were cooks and scullions and butlers and stable hands. There were heralds and minstrels, men-at-arms and armourers, blacksmiths and tanners, bowyers and jailers. There was a man whose only duty was to pluck and serve the royal swan, and a woman who could do the same for the peacock. There was a dressmaker, a milliner and a jeweller who worked only for the Queen. There was a special baker who made short, thin loaves of a particular shape that made the ladies giggle and whisper to each other that they would never guess, but Lady Somebody-or-other had actually *tried* it – yes, really! And there were people who seemed to do nothing at all, and yet were paid and fed for it all the same.

There were quite a lot of these – especially around the Queen, Melissa thought. Rebelliously she included in this all the Queen's handsome young men, every last one of her ladies-in-waiting, and even a number of the maids, who she thought spent far too much time shirking the job and chatting about men and bits of men and all the very improbable things that men and women could invent together in bed. She also included the men-at-arms, who at another time would obviously have been useful but who seemed to have nothing to do these days except stand in their armour and make eyes at poor busy maids as they passed.

Dadda wouldn't have given a stick for the lot of them, she thought. Not one of them stood on their two feet. They all leaned on the King. But then so did the ten thousand people in the city, from the abbess in the convent to the ragged and deformed beggars in the streets. And so did the – how many? – thousands and thousands and thousands of others living around the Kingdom, even the ones who had never petitioned him or laid eyes on him in their life. They needed him to make laws and rules about weights and measures. They needed him to keep order among the barons. They needed him to go after the ones who cheated or stole or torched the homes of honest folk. And they needed him so that they could blame him (or at least his advisers) when they felt things were going wrong. Melissa saw all that.

There was a gate sergeant one day, standing under the middle arch with a mug of ale in his hand. 'They need their heads examined!' he was saying loudly to a circle of his followers. 'That's what. Whoever's talking to him needs their head examined! I've a mind to tell him so myself.'

The other guards nodded dutifully.

'All this going to and fro,' the man complained. 'It makes no sense. If they're going to *study* up here, then make them *sleep* up here. If there's not room for them to sleep up here, then make them do their studies in the town. But letting them go in and out every day – how'm I going to know who's coming in with them? What if someone with a grudge puts on a hood and walks through with them? And then goes and pushes a knife into the King? And who'll catch it for that, hey?'

That was how Melissa heard about the founding of the school.

At the King's command the old barrack building in the middle courtyard was cleared to make space for a library, a lecture hall and writing rooms. And soon (whatever the guards thought about it) scholars in hooded, monk-like robes began to appear in the castle, processing in and out in a great ragged troop every morning and evening. Melissa saw them day after day as they crossed the upper courtyard in twos and threes with writing slates in their hands or spilled out from their hall in a laughing, shouting mob after some lesson or other had finished. She did not know what they were for. She supposed that it was their job to read all the books in the new library (who else was going to do it, after all?). But she could not see what good that would do. And she made her way firmly past them and paid no attention if they started making eyes at her like the men-at-arms.

Until the day she walked by a group that were

on their way to a lesson, and some of them smiled and winked at her, and she kept on walking, looking straight ahead of her as always. And then she stopped.

She turned round, picked up her skirt and hurried after them. The one who had caught her eye was looking back over his shoulder and saw her coming. His face was heavily tanned, bird-like under black hair – a hill face if ever there was one. And yes, it *was*!

'Hey,' she said as she came up. 'Hey, I know you!'

'Yes,' he said. 'You do.'

'*Puka halalah.* That was you, in the mountains!'

'Yes.'

It was him – the boy who had brought them gifts, announced by the bell on the village donkey going *tonk tonk* across the bare hillside, who had smiled, handed over gifts and spoken only gibberish. Seeing him here in the busy upper courtyard of the castle of Tuscolo was . . . strange. Very, very strange.

'What are you *doing* here?'

He pointed to his tunic. 'Learning.'

'I mean – how did you get here? How did you learn to talk?'

'Lady teach me. Lady send me to King.'

'The King's mother? That was nice of her. Why?'

'I ask her of you.'

'You . . . Oh!'

Melissa blushed. She couldn't help it. All the blood in her body seemed to rise up (*wham!*) into her cheeks.

'But – but . . .' This was crazy. He must be crazy. He

must be a simpleton. What . . . ? 'But the priests! Do they teach you? You're heathen – aren't you?'

'Hea . . . ?'

'Heathen. You don't believe in the Angels!'

He frowned. For a moment she thought she must have offended him. But then he shrugged. 'I make space for Angels in Heaven. Not hard. Plenty of room.'

'But . . .'

'Must go. Late for lesson. May be beaten – again.'

'Oh. Yes you must. Shall I see you?'

'Hope so.' He grinned, just as she remembered him grinning each time they had stood wordless on the mountain path. And he strode off towards the school.

He might be beaten. So might she, if she was late. What was it they had sent her out for? Oh, more wretched firewood. They would never burn so much if they had to cut or carry it themselves!

Nevertheless she skipped a little as she hurried across the courtyard. Something had changed, she thought. Something was different now from the ordinary trudge of the day.

She felt that something good was about to happen.

XVIII

Out of the Sea

ow say, Your Majesty,' said Padry, in the council chamber at dawn. 'Does the Angel Umbriel make use of a chamberpot?'

'A chamberpot?' repeated Ambrose, baffled. 'No, I doubt it. Not that I think it matters if he—'

'Why then,' exclaimed Padry, 'perhaps a king is more than an Angel indeed!'

Ambrose looked at him suspiciously. 'How so?'

'Thus: a king, who is only one, says not *I* but *We*. Whereas Umbriel, who has – as it is written – seven *eyes*, can have no *wee* at all!'

'All right,' grumbled Ambrose. He dropped into his chair. 'I don't suppose he leaves writing in his book for any reason. And when we look over his shoulder we will now see the word "chamberpot" added to the list of all our other sins.'

Padry sighed to see his pun go to waste. He had thought it rather a good one. Perhaps it had just been bad timing – the early hour affecting the King's mood.

But dawn starts were unavoidable if any real work was to be done before the whole pack of courtly jackals started to swarm around the King. If the boy *would* sit up late over his wine . . .

'So what have you got for me?'

'The new charter for the market of Pemini, Your Majesty. The freedom to exchange goods and money, untaxed, save for certain fixed tariffs to be paid annually to the Crown, and a share to Lord Delverdis – I fear we have to give him *something*, or he will start to make his own rules – and strict prohibitions on short weights, clipped coin and the rest . . .'

Ambrose took the scroll. His eye moved quickly down it. 'Why no unlicensed preaching?' he asked suddenly.

'That is to prevent self-named prophets taking advantage of the market crowds.'

'But why? Why can't they preach, if they've heard the Angels?'

'The Church does not permit it. Only licensed—'

'Then let them ban it, not me.'

'Your Majesty—'

The door opened. Aun of Lackmere walked in. 'At it already? Bones of the Angels! It's getting earlier each day. What has my Lord Chancellor slipped past me *this* morning?'

Ambrose dropped the scroll on the table. 'I'm to prevent prophets preaching in the market places,' he complained.

'Prophets? Damned right. String them all up by the heels. There was one down in Tuscolo quayside yesterday, I hear. If I'd known it before sundown—'

'What was he saying?'

Aun stared at his King. 'What does it matter what he was saying? Prophets are trouble, that's all.'

Ambrose slammed his hand on the table. 'I want to know what he was saying!'

The baron frowned. 'Why?'

'The Angels *matter*! When we were fighting Paigan, I heard them. I heard them twice. Now I've come away to be King in Tuscolo and I don't hear them any more. We talk about them. We even crack silly jokes about their chamberpots. But there's no *meaning* to it here. What if I've left the Path somehow, and they prefer to watch widows and orphans and prophets instead?'

'The Angels watch us all, Your Majesty,' said Padry.

'Do they? Where are they, then?'

'Damned if I know,' said Aun. 'And I'll be damned if your prophet knows either. You want to hear what he said? I'll tell you. I'll tell you without having heard it myself. He was saying, "Listen to me. The Angels have spoken to me. That makes me more important than your kings and bishops, doesn't it? I don't have to prove it to you, I'll just tell you it's true, so listen." It's the same damned stuff they all spin. Any wheelwright or landsman with a quick tongue can do it if they've a mind to. Then hayricks get burned, rents get refused, and you have to go and string men up just to put things back into place.'

'It is a question of authority, Your Majesty,' put in Padry.

'Authority!' snapped Ambrose. 'All right. I'll use

287

some now.' He took the pen and scored through the phrase that had offended him. 'You can seal it like that, or not at all!' And he rose from his place and stormed out of the room.

Padry sighed, gathered up the parchment and added it to the bottom of the pile that he carried. Perhaps, by the time they got back to it, Ambrose would see reason. If not, well, it was not a great matter. Or not yet. The Bishop of Tuscolo was elderly and his mind was tending to wander. His Grace would fuss at the King about protecting the Church, but there was no fire left in him. The next winter might well claim him. And who knew who his successor might be? Hah, who indeed? It might be anyone, might it not?

'Cub,' muttered Aun, looking out of the window.

'We are the Keepers of his Day,' ruminated Padry. 'But in the Night we cannot help him.'

Aun looked round. 'What's that supposed to mean?' he said sharply.

What did it mean? thought Padry.

What he had meant was that between them, the ruthless, pragmatic old baron and the wily chancellor, they steered their well-intentioned young King through his kingship. They were doing well, too. Laws had been given, foundations made, trade – to judge by the revenues from market and river-tolls – had risen beyond anything in Padry's experience at Tuscolo. All in less than eighteen months!

But of course there were places where neither of them could help him. The soul on the Path met many things, helpers and hinderers, but it made each step on its own. Angels, goddesses, the ancient princes who came and went from the shadows around the throne – there was nothing chancellor or baron could do for Ambrose there. That would be the blind trying to lead the half-sighted. And the stink of witchcraft was never far away. Perhaps that was why Lackmere did not like what Padry had said.

Perhaps. Or perhaps it was because Padry had said *we*. The baron, like so many of his kind, looked down on all clerks as at best a necessary evil. No matter what Padry did for his King, how often he was right, how often he said things that Lackmere actually agreed with, the baron would not permit himself to be coupled by the simple word *we*. That assumed too much.

And when I first saw you, my fine baron, when you first came crawling out of the wilderness to the Widow Develin with that half-starved boy who is now the King, your armour was stained and your hair was in tangles and your whiskers as shaggy as any peasant's. And still you look down on me. Maybe if I were made bishop in Tuscolo you will think again. It might not be long now.

He coughed and gathered his papers. He was stretching his hand for the door when he heard others approaching it from outside. They were in a hurry. He stepped back. The door burst open, revealing Ambrose again, this time with a small crowd of courtiers at his back.

'Some interesting news,' said Ambrose grimly. 'Gueronius has returned.'

* * *

'He has landed in Velis, it seems,' said Ambrose, pacing in the circle of his councillors. 'An Outlander vessel – hear this, an *Outlander* vessel – sailed into harbour and put him ashore. Just like that. I suppose his ship was wrecked and he has been sheltering somewhere in Outland all this time.' He cocked an eye at one of the councillors, who shrugged.

'We may imagine so, Your Majesty. It is said he and his companions were themselves dressed in some strange fashion that we may presume is worn in Outland. Even so, people recognized him.'

'Ah,' said Aun. 'Now, you see, we may need some of that authority.'

Ambrose glared at him. 'What am I supposed to do?'

'It depends,' said Aun. 'How many has he got with him?'

'I don't know.'

'The first question you should ask. Enemy coming? What strength has he?'

'He's not necessarily an enemy.'

'You're sitting on a throne he thinks is his.'

'And what if it *is* rightfully his?'

'Then your neck is forfeit and so is that of every man who backed you,' said Aun, looking around at the ring of faces. 'Don't think of giving it up. You can't. He'd have to knock your head off anyway, just to be sure you didn't change your mind.'

Ambrose looked at Padry. Padry opened his mouth and shut it again. His mind was still clearing from the shock of the news. A queer, tingling feeling lingered in the pit of his stomach. Gueronius was back. And he had come from Outland.

Outland? Theoretically he had known of it for years, a vague mystery, well beyond any useful horizon. But that an Outlander vessel should sail into harbour and put someone ashore – suddenly the mystery had a force that it had never had before this. How many were the Outlanders? How strong were they? He remembered an evening over wine, and the eye of Ambrose glinting in the candlelight as his finger pointed at Padry's heart. *That ship must not sail.* But it had sailed indeed. It had sailed because he had allowed it to – he, Thomas Padry, who a moment ago had been back to daydreaming about a bishop's crozier!

'What's he told them about us?' muttered a councillor. 'Gueronius, I mean.'

'And what did he promise them, to earn his passage back?' said another.

'Gueronius alone can answer that,' said Ambrose. 'So. How many men has he at this moment?' He looked at the councillor.

'A few only, we think,' said the man. 'Some were men of the Kingdom – survivors of his crew. But there were some Outlanders, too.'

'That's easy, then,' said Aun. 'Send to arrest him.'

'What for?' said the King.

'What do you mean, "What for"? Anything you like. Treason. Or if you want to be squeamish about that, for bringing Outlanders into the Kingdom. There will be laws about that, for sure.'

'I am not a tyrant,' said Ambrose. 'If he has no men, he is no threat. He'll find no friends in Velis either – that's Baldwin country. And he has a right to his lands and his liberty, according to laws that *I* have passed, Aun. If he surrenders his claim to the throne peacefully and comes to tell us what we need to know of Outland, then he may keep them. Lord Joyce can bear the message, since he was a Tuscolo man once.'

'Joyce? He's a rat. You trust too much.'

Padry winced. That, said in full council! Really . . .

'And you never trust!' exploded Ambrose. 'And you *never* forgive!'

'Forgive?' said the baron, looking hard at him. 'What has forgiving to do with it?'

'You know!'

'Do I? Tell me, then,' said the baron grimly.

'I'm talking about Raymonde, your son.'

'I thought so. My son who killed his brother. My son who lent his witchcraft to Velis. My son with all the dead of Develin and Bay around his neck – whom *you* favoured with your forgiveness without my counsel—'

'And you dispute my right to forgive?'

'I don't dispute your *right*. And I don't dispute your *right* to favour him with all those awards and offices and powers, either. Nor your *right* to try and make love to Gueronius. All I want to know is how the *hell* are we to keep you on your throne?'

'Aun, if I'm to be King, I must do it my way. Or I'll be as bad as every other king – or cut-throat – this land has had!'

292

'Cut-throat now, is it?' growled the baron.

'The Angels are watching, Aun.'

So are your councillors, thought Padry. He cleared his throat. 'Your Majesty . . .'

'. . . Watching, are they? A moment ago I thought you said they had gone off somewhere.'

'That's enough,' said Ambrose. He said it coldly and simply, and it ended the argument. 'My Lord Chancellor, you will please draft me a letter for Lord Joyce as we have discussed. Gentlemen, I thank you. You may all go. I shall now have breakfast with my Queen – if she will deign to join me.' He sat and put his hand over his eyes.

The councillors walked down the corridor in a body. Padry dropped to the back, still musing on his own reaction to the news that Gueronius had returned. Which had been, quite simply, horror. Why? He had liked the man once.

It was the association with Outland – the sinister aura of the unknown. It was the shock that someone presumed dead, mourned and mentally laid to rest, should have sprung to life again like a japing ghost. And it was the fear that everything they had done since his departure might have been done in error, and would now have to be undone. That would be unbearable – and dangerous! There must be no question of Ambrose abdicating or whatever. Lackmere had been right to scotch that quickly. The land had a king, and it was not Gueronius.

Looking back, Padry could pinpoint exactly the moment when his own loyalty had shifted decisively to the new King. It had been nothing to do with wealth or charters or good justice. Oh, all that mattered, yes. But this was a stronger reason still. *This* was why he would fight, bite, claw and spend all his wits to keep Ambrose in power.

It had been early on, before they had even got him crowned. It had been the day his mother had brought the wretched Prince Marc to him. That was when Padry had witnessed a man's sins being lifted from him and had seen that his own might somehow be forgiven, too. (Even if right at this moment they looked like coming home to roost! Outland! What had Gueronius brought with him?) But there was hope, Thomas Padry. With this King there would always be hope. That was something he could cling to. Let him only serve faithfully . . .

A touch on his arm. It was the Baron Lackmere, beside him at the back of the group, signing for him to slow his pace. Surprised, Padry obeyed. They watched the others get further ahead.

'You were right about the night, weren't you?' growled Lackmere from the corner of his mouth. 'That's what's eating him, for sure.'

Padry frowned, puzzled. 'You mean . . . ?'

'The Queen. Withholding herself, I suppose.' He jerked his chin at the councillors ahead of him. 'They'll guess now. Or soon they will.'

The Queen. Padry stopped short.

In the Night we cannot help him. A different, and far more earthy, meaning to the word 'night' than he had intended. The Queen. Maybe that was why

Ambrose was so jumpy these days. Maybe that was why the boy sat up over his wine when other things should have been calling him to his couch.

Maybe? Certainly. For sure. Thomas Padry, you think yourself a man of the world. And in some ways you are as unworldly as your own King! The baron had guessed it. Why hadn't he? After all, he knew Atti better than almost anyone in Tuscolo. And yes, he could believe it of her. Yes, he could.

Well, if that was the truth, then there was indeed nothing they could do to help. Ambrose had made his bed, so to speak. Now he must lie on it. But it was awkward. Very awkward, at a time like this. Few things would eat a king's authority faster than a rumour that he could not control his wife. This could make things much more difficult.

'Hush it as long as we can,' said the baron.

XIX

The Demon

he King's butler brought a kid into the fountain garden. It was less than a year old. Its coat was a beautiful, shining slate grey, its legs long and delicate, its eyes soft and fearful as it stared at the crowd of courtiers surrounding the Queen. The Queen's pet lynx roused itself inquisitively from its cushion. Immediately the kid skittered away to the far end of its leash, splaying its legs and pulling in vain against its collar and the strength of the butler's arm.

'His Majesty begs you will consider it,' said the butler. 'He asks me to say that he hopes it will remind you of kindness and of good things when the day wearies you.'

'I do not understand,' said the Queen, so that all her courtiers could hear. 'Does His Majesty think that I am his goatherd?'

'No, Your Majesty!' said the butler earnestly. 'He means it as a thing of beauty for you, a living jewel chosen from a thousand of its like!'

'A jewel?' said the Queen in cold surprise. 'But it is a goat!'

The crowd of courtiers tittered. The Queen turned her head away so that the man might not speak with her again.

Her hair was braided and thick with gems. Her face was like a statue's. There was powder on her skin – thick white powder to hide the marks of sleeplessness under her eyes. She sat listlessly by the fountain. The courtiers who normally jostled for her attention glanced nervously at one another. The young knight who was carefully losing to her at chess fixed his eyes on the board with a frown. No one wanted to put themselves first when she was in this mood.

The chief lady-in-waiting looked around. Her eye fell on Melissa, who had been standing holding her tray for a quarter of an hour. She signed her forward.

'What is this?' sighed Atti as Melissa held up the tray.

'Sweetmeats, Your Majesty,' said Melissa. 'You sent for them.'

'No one here is hungry,' said Atti. 'Take them away.'

Melissa lowered the tray. The sweetmeats, still warm from the oven, were arranged in an elaborate flower-pattern on the shining silver. The beautiful smells reached out to set the juices running in a score of noble mouths. Their eyes followed the tray as Melissa backed away from the Queen. But there was nothing they could do. She had said no one was hungry.

'Take that away, too.'

The butler bowed low, dragged the kid over to him

and picked it up so that its legs dangled over his arm. He and Melissa left the circle around the Queen together, each bearing their rejected offering. The butler caught Melissa's eye as they walked side by side. His brow lifted, questioning.

Melissa shrugged irritably. All right, so it hadn't worked. She hadn't promised anyone that it would, had she?

The King's people had been at their wits' end. (They must have been, to come to her, who was only a maid after all.) They had almost begged her to help them find something to please Atti. She had racked her brains and suggested the kid. But it hadn't worked. And they would blame her now. They would tell the King she had misled them. She was angry with them, and angry with Atti, too. Atti had been moody for weeks. Now there was this news that someone or other had arrived in the land by ship, and Atti had reached her very worst.

Behind them Melissa heard her say: 'It is a stupid game.'

'Your Majesty plays with skill. See – I am forced to bring out my queen.'

'It is a stupid game. No man lets a queen have such power . . .'

Atti's words were swallowed by an eerie howl. The pet lynx was straining at its collar after the disappearing kid, mewing piteously at the sight of a new toy being taken away.

That night was worse than ever.

* * *

298

Padry was asleep. In his dreams someone had come to hammer at his door.

'Lord Chancellor! Lord Chancellor!'

He rolled over in his bed, sat up and rubbed his eyes. It was dark. It must be deep night.

'Lord Chancellor!' And more knocking.

'Yes!' he groaned. 'Come!'

Light. A lamp held by his servant, Ormond, who was himself in a nightshift.

'The King has sent for you.'

'What? Now? What time is it?'

'Past midnight, sir.'

He had been deep, deep asleep. Was he going to have to get up and drag himself along the corridors of the palace?

'What for?' he croaked.

'He wants to speak with you, sir, urgently.'

'Well, I did not suppose he had sent to ask about my health, man!'

Padry glared at the fellow, who looked back at him helplessly. Obviously the message had not given a reason. So it might be anything, anything at all. It might even be that the King had got drunk enough to want to play word-games or chess or something. Ambrose had never yet dragged him from sleep on a whim, but the way things were going . . .

One thought rose through the others, like timber floating upwards from a wreck. It must be Outland. The evil that Ambrose had predicted, and that Padry had failed to prevent, had manifested itself. Whatever it was, it was here.

'Very well!' he groaned, and flung off his bedclothes. 'No, I will dress myself. But leave me that light. I will need it.'

That ship – the Outland ship that had docked – it must have brought something with it. What? What was the worst thing that he could think of? A plague. A deadly sickness, sweeping the alleys of Velis and spreading upriver into the heart of the Kingdom! What could be done about that? Isolate, fumigate . . . Guards around infected villages . . . Of course it was impossible to plan before he knew what the danger was. The just man should wait, unperturbed, until he heard the news for himself. And then he should think clearly. Padry could do neither. Not at this hour. Not with the fear that he himself might be to blame for whatever had happened.

He left his chamber and made his way through the palace. His mind was busy with disaster, and as he approached the King's chambers the air of disaster rose around him. The corridors were lit with torches. A woman was shrieking somewhere. Men were up, some dressed, some half dressed, talking excitedly in the doorways. The Baron Lackmere came striding along in the opposite direction, wearing his mail shirt and with armed esquires at his back. He was snarling instructions to his followers about horses, rations and crossbowmen. Padry found himself brushed against the wall as the men stamped past.

'. . . And this is what you get for *trusting*,' barked the baron to him, and diminished down the corridor in an angry clatter of steel.

The King was alone in the Privy Council chamber, sitting before a low fire with his head sunk onto one hand. Plainly he had not been to bed and plainly he had indeed been drinking. But that was not the trouble.

'You can guess what's happened,' he said.

In his hand there was a letter. He waved it dejectedly. And Padry could guess now.

'Is it Gueronius, Your Majesty?'

'Yes. He has defied us. Lord Joyce says he has slipped past him and has gone to his own estates.'

'Lord Joyce,' said Padry with the coldness of broken sleep, 'plays both sides, perhaps.'

As well he might. A former leader of the Tuscolo faction, with his own personal alliances among Tuscolo families: he would be careful what enemies he made at a time like this. They should have known that.

'That's what Aun thinks. He says we have to strike now, against Gueronius, before the Tuscolo faction can ask itself who it would rather have on the throne. He's gone to put together a raiding force. If he leaves at dawn he could be in Gueronius's estates by sundown the day after tomorrow.'

So it could be worse, thought Padry, dragging the last corners of his mind out of sleep. It was not plague sweeping in from mysterious Outland. It was just politics – deadly, but familiar. Politics could be dealt with. Action was already in hand. (Although even if things went well from here there would be consequences for the King's authority, and his own as chancellor, to be considered. The only winner would be . . .)

A scream burst from nearby. The voice was unrecognizable, distorted. It might even have been an animal, except that at the end it trailed away into the sound of a woman sobbing, '*No, no no!*' Padry thought a servant must be having a fit. Then he realized that there was only one person who could make a noise like that in the King's corridor.

It was Atti.

'This is the end,' groaned Ambrose.

The end? thought Padry.

'Did you hear her,' said Ambrose, 'when she came to me on the knoll? What she asked for?'

'Why – to be Queen,' said Padry, writhing inwardly at the memory and at all the other memories it brought.

'That's what I heard her say. I should have listened better. She asked for justice against Gueronius . . .'

The screams rose to a pitch that sounded like a beast being tortured. Then they collapsed again into weeping.

'Gueronius did it, you see,' said Ambrose softly. 'It was Gueronius who destroyed her house in Velis. And it was his uncle Septimus who destroyed her father's house in Tarceny when she was an infant . . .'

'My lord – it was not Gueronius she was fleeing when she came to you!'

'No. It was you. But behind you stood Gueronius. He stands behind anyone with power in her life. You, my mother, me . . . I brought her here and made her my Queen. I made her submit to me. I tried to heal her by taking power over her. And so he stands behind me, too. He *is* me, beyond the curtain in her dream. She's been fighting that. With her waking mind she's been fighting, telling herself it's a dream, telling herself she loves me. But she's been losing. Ever since we came here she's been losing. And now I've let him . . . Aun was right – I should have had him murdered!'

'*For pity's sake!*' shrieked the Queen from beyond two oak doors. '*Where is the locksmith?*'

'I've got us into such a mess,' Ambrose groaned.

'Your Majesty sent him a fair offer,' said Padry. 'All the Kingdom will know how he received it.'

'I didn't mean that. I meant coming here in the first place. Trying to do things my way when they can't be done like that. Aun says I've been weak.'

'It is not always weakness to offer peace—'

'*Hi-hi-hiiieh!*' broke the sounds from next door.

And another woman cried, '*You there! Spice-water for Her Majesty! Now, you useless slut!*'

Ambrose started up as if stung. Then he flopped back again. His eyes were screwed up in pain, squeezing little bright tears down his cheeks.

'I love her, Padry,' he whispered. 'I can't help it. I don't want to help it! But I can't help her, either. Whatever I do seems to make it worse!'

'I am sure she recognizes your devotion, Your Majesty,' said Padry.

'Oh come, my Lord Chancellor! Don't tell me you've not wondered about those ladies-in-waiting?'

'Er . . . not to any great extent, Your Majesty.'

'You must be the only man in Tuscolo who hasn't! Everyone looks at them. They're pretty. Not much use though . . .' He laughed bitterly. 'Spice-water! What good's *that* going to do? No, she likes pretty things – except when they come from me! But there's one of them who isn't. The Lady Caterine. She's fat and heavy, and not very clever either, the poor girl. Why did Atti choose her? I've heard men ask each other that. They also ask why the Queen's not pregnant yet. *I* know why. The Lady Caterine knows why, too. Because it's *her* job to sleep against the door between the Queen's bedroom and mine, in case I have it in mind to join my wife during the night. She is Atti's doorstop!'

(More shrieks, and more twittering of anxious female voices around the Queen.)

'It'll take more than a pair of fat buttocks to keep out Gueronius's knights,' said Ambrose with a sickly grin. 'She knows that much.'

'Your Majesty! At this moment Gueronius is a pauper and a fugitive. He can hardly—'

'Can't he?' said Ambrose. His face was flushed, his eyes drunken, yet his glare made Padry think again. Gueronius . . .

Gueronius was a war leader, hard, cunning and dangerous. He was the head of a faction whose members had lost power and favour under Ambrose. What would he do now?

If Lackmere's riders could catch him in the open, well and good. But there was more than one strong place in his former estates that might open the gate for him. If he shut himself in one of those, Lackmere would not be able to touch him – not with the sort of force that he could throw together in half a night. So that would mean a siege. Gueronius would call for aid. The Tuscolo faction . . . What would Seguin do? Wouldn't he jump at the chance to make trouble? There were others, too. Where was Joyce at this moment?

The devil of it was that the King's best support was in the far south, in Develin and Lackmere – much further from Tuscolo than Gueronius and his possible allies. The sands had shifted fast enough in Ambrose's favour eighteen months ago. Why should they not shift as quickly back again? If Ambrose were forced to retreat from the capital . . .

An image rose in Padry's mind of the palace corridors – these very corridors – filled with men and women on their knees, pleading one after another that they had been forced to act against their will, that they had been secretly loyal to Gueronius all along. He saw them. He saw the faces of the armed men at their backs, and the drawn swords. He could almost smell the blood and the fear.

He sucked in his cheeks. It was ugly. It could get very ugly indeed.

'I think . . . it would be advisable to raise a loan,' he said. 'A large one, since we may need to muster a force. I will approach the best sources in Tuscolo in the morning. If I can do that before the situation becomes widely known, we may save ourselves a few pennies in interest . . .'

'*No, no! Don't let him in!*' screamed Atti's voice from another room.

'I can't stand this,' muttered Ambrose. He pulled himself from his seat and crouched before the fire.

'Also I will send to money-houses in Pemini, Watermane and Velis—'

'Wait,' said Ambrose. He was staring into the embers. 'We need to remove Gueronius, don't we?' he said.

'My former pupil,' sighed Padry, 'could oblige us greatly at this moment by breaking his neck in a fall, yes. Failing that, however—'

'There's a way of doing it.'

The King bent down in the hearth and, putting his face painfully close to the embers, blew them into a soft rush of flame.

'Your Majesty?'

'I don't mean breaking his neck. But capturing him. The princes could do it. They could come on him anywhere – inside his keep, among his men . . . There's six of them now. Hergest and Galen came out of the pool this winter – did you know that? It should be enough.' With his bare hands he was taking logs from the hearth, beginning to build the fire again. 'It's the sort of thing they've done before,' he said.

Padry stared at him.

The princes. It was the sort of thing they had done before.

Slowly thought returned to his brain. But now it followed a different path. Not politics, but something deeper: the things he should never, ever forget, and too often did. Beyond the Abyss was the Lantern. Beyond the Lantern, Madness. Beyond Madness, Penitence. And then . . .

'Your Majesty,' he said carefully. 'The Demon is a lure for the rising soul. It is the power that turns things upside down.'

Ambrose barked a laugh. 'I might have known you would say that. Croscan and his Path again! Padry, I don't know whether my soul is rising or sinking. But I want to keep the peace and keep Atti safe. This way, I can do that *and* win.' He stood, and brushed ash off his doublet with his hands.

'Your Majesty! What use is it to win if by winning you lose the only thing worth having?'

'Lose what? *She's* the only thing worth having! If she's got to be the price then it's too damned high! And if I must fall, then I will fall in my own way – or jump first.'

'But your followers . . .'

'Would prefer a bloody victory won with iron and gold? I wonder! It's surprising what people will shut their eyes to, so long as the reward is success. My father took Tuscolo by witchcraft, seized the crown by witchcraft, and failed not because of what people thought of his witchcraft but because my mother betrayed him to his enemies. All right, Thomas' – he took a sip of wine from his goblet and held it before him, turning the dark liquid around and around in the bowl – 'all right. You don't have to stay. Just see that I'm not disturbed.'

Padry stared at him, shaken at the change in his King, and shaken all the more because the King had for the first time called him *Thomas*. Thomas, as if he were a brother, a friend, a fellow traveller; as if this

307

decision had been made together, as if this corruption were a thing they shared. And as he watched his King pacing and chanting and sipping at the goblet in his hand, Padry knew they shared it indeed.

I must stay, he thought, even as he backed towards the door. He must not be left alone to do this. He must be stopped if at all possible.

But – but if he *couldn't* be stopped . . .

Of course the corridor would have to be watched . . .

New flames were leaping in the hearth. Ambrose took another sip of wine and looked into his cup again.

'Come, Talifer,' he said.

'Come, Talifer, come, Rolfe, come, Lomba, come, Marc. Come, Hergest and Galen, if you can hear and understand. Come to me in Tuscolo.'

He paused. There was no sound but the soft roar of the fire.

'This may take a while,' he said.

Firelight danced on the walls and glittered on the polished metal of candlestick and cup. The air seemed darker and thicker. Padry looked at the chairs and chests. He could almost see them forming themselves into brown rocks lying in an endless, weary brown land. A faint throbbing, so low that he could barely hear it, was growing in his mind. The smell of dank water came faintly to him. He remembered it at once.

'Sire, this is insane!' he pleaded desperately. 'You will destroy yourself!'

'Shut up or get out!' snarled Ambrose. 'Or shall I

have the guards come and drag you out by the heels?'

'Your Majesty, I *beg* you—'

'You want to talk about demons again?' cried the King. The fire was in his eyes and drink was in his blood. 'Gold is a demon, Thomas! Iron is a demon! Go you to your demons and *leave me with mine*!' And, turning away, he continued, 'Come, Talifer, come, Rolfe, come, Lomba. Come, Marc, come, Hergest, come, Galen. I have need. Come to me in Tuscolo . . .'

Padry fled from the chamber.

Even as he closed the thick oak door behind him he felt that the room had changed – that if he opened it again he would see not the hearth and the tapestries and the throne but a barren, rocky landscape under a dull sky. And somewhere far across it something had begun to move.

XX

The Heir of Tuscolo

veryone was busy these days, thought Melissa. They were all busy and snappish, and tired with broken nights. It was hard for a poor honest maid to get everything done the way they thought they had told her they wanted it. And if she did it wrong she would have to do it again, either right then or later, during those bits and scraps of time when she was not doing anything and not waiting to be called either. And that made it even harder to have any time for herself, to slip away and see someone she wanted to see. Especially if that other person had a dayful of stuff that he also had to be doing.

She still called him 'Puck', from the greeting *Puka halalah* that he used to give her in the hills. She could not pronounce his real name, which was full of impossible hill sounds. (She had wondered whether the hill people were born with their tongues a different shape, but he had showed her his, and no, it seemed the same.) Puck had lessons to attend morning and afternoon, and there were also times when he was supposed to be in the library and times when he went to help in the stables. And even though his day seemed far less full than hers – as she kept telling him – he often seemed to be busy when she could get away.

But there was always the Grand Audience, held twice a week when the King was in Tuscolo, and the Queen would be dressed up and go down with her ladies to the great hall and sit on her throne beside the King, and together they would listen to person after person coming before them on important matters, and the King would tell his herald what he had decided about them, and the herald would bellow it down the hall and everyone would say how good it was. Grand Audience never took less than two hours, and in those two hours it was possible for a maid who had done everything right so far that day to slip off and find her way to the upper stables. And shortly before noon, there he would be, too.

And it was a good day. The stables were almost empty because the Baron Lackmere had ridden off before dawn with a lot of armed men and most of the horses in the castle. Half the stableboys had slipped off somewhere – to get themselves drunk, most likely. The rest seemed to be playing knucklebones in the tack room. She found Puck raking up some foul straw in one of the empty booths. He smiled at her broadly as she came in.

'Are you the only one working?' she demanded. 'Why do you put up with it?'

'Master Copley teaching me to ride horses. I work for him, he teach me.'

311

'Does he? I bet he wouldn't do that for everyone.'
But people liked Puck. It was the way he smiled, which always made you want to smile, too. Also, he was the only hillman most of them had ever seen. Hill folk were something to wonder at here, but not something to be afraid of. It was different in the March.

'Fallen off much yet?' she asked.

'Oh no. I am good at learning.'

'You're good at saying how good you are. That's for sure.'

'No, it is true! On way here, I learn to sail boat. Learn in a day. Fisherman teach me.' His arms hauled on some imaginary sail.

'Don't believe you.'

'You are wrong. He let me sail myself, at finish.'

'Oh well,' said Melissa carelessly, as if she had been sailing all her life. 'Here, I've got something for you. Come and sit down.'

She chose a pile of fresh straw, around the far side of a wooden stall. Puck threw a glance over his shoulder towards the tack room where the stableboys were roaring over their game, shrugged and followed her. They sat side by side in the thick-smelling air of the stables. She opened her little pouch. 'Sweetmeats,' she said.

'Yum,' he said, with wide eyes. 'Queen give those to you?'

'She didn't want them.'

They were the last of the tray that Atti had sent away the day before. They were old and a bit stale now. Yesterday they had been fresh. The Queen's maids had fallen on them like vultures when she had got the tray up to the royal rooms. She knew just how good they had tasted then. But he didn't.

'Yum,' he said again, and rolled his eyes. 'Long live Queen, yes! Glorious and happy.'

'I don't think she's ever been happy,' said Melissa quietly.

'No? Maybe she not starve enough.'

'What do you mean?'

'You know. You starve a bit – not get sick, just hungry. Then eat. Then – ah!' he put his hands on his belly and his head back, eyes closed. 'No worries. None at all.'

'I used to think like that.'

He looked at her, bird-like, clever. Afraid of what she had said, Melissa hurried on. 'The man who destroyed her house is back. She's frightened. She thinks he'll do it again, you see.'

He frowned.

'Maybe you don't understand,' said Melissa. 'Up in the hills and all.'

'Why not? You do that to us, too.'

'Did we?'

'Oh yes. You not love enough, your people.'

And while Melissa was puzzling over that, he added, 'Maybe Queen not love enough, either.'

Melissa shook her head. 'That's ... Do you remember that kid, in the hills? The one you brought up for our first spring, and we ate it together in the outer courtyard.'

'She cry and run into house. Oof! I don't forget that.'

'She wept and wept for it. Days afterwards, when I thought she was over it, she would start weeping again. She said, "I loved it. It was so beautiful." Even though she had barely laid eyes on the thing. But when we brought her a kid yesterday, just like that one, she wouldn't even look at it!'

It still made her angry. It hurt that it had been her idea that the King had relied on. And it had let him down.

'Maybe she loves the hurt thing, not the whole.'

'Maybe,' said Melissa.

Look after her, pleaded voices in her memory. *Help her.* Help her. But how? They might as well have asked her to 'help' a mountain. Stop the snow falling on it, maybe.

'Any more?' said Puck, leaning over her shoulder and looking interestedly into her lap.

'One. The best. I saved it for you.'

'Thanks.'

And as he put it into his mouth, she said: 'I saved this for you, too,' and she leaned back and kissed his cheek.

She had planned to do it. She had planned it more or less just like that. She had been wondering for almost three years what it would have felt like if she had stayed in the outer courtyard and kissed the boy who had brought her the kid. And the moment she did it Atti and everything else was forgotten.

His cheek was harder than she had expected, and also smooth. Hillmen did not grow hair on their chins. Close up he was rather smelly. And she felt the sudden

314

rise of blood in herself, and he looked at her, startled. And there were crumbs all over his lips, and . . .

She laughed, and jumped to her feet.

'Hey, wait!' he said.

'Not likely!' she cried. And picking up her skirts, she ran, still laughing.

He was after her. She hadn't planned this. She did not know what was going to happen. She did not know whether she was going to let him catch her, or what would happen if he did. Somewhere in the back of her mind was the thought *You've done it now*, and also another that she must not get her clothes all smelly from the stables, because the ladies would realize and she would be punished for it. But it was all washed away in the thrill of her blood at the young man hunting her around the booths and piles of straw.

She burst, laughing, into the light of the upper courtyard and stumbled to a halt before a woman in a dull gown who seemed to have come from nowhere, and who should have been hundreds of miles away.

'Melissa,' said Phaedra. 'You must get me into the Grand Audience. At once!'

The guard shrugged. He thought the chamberlain had already entered. They'd have started now. There was no going in there for two hours at least.

'But it's the King's mother!' Melissa said. 'She's waiting outside the doors! And he doesn't know, and the guards out there don't know her to let her in!'

At once, Phaedra had said. And Melissa knew that *at once* meant it was very, very important – more important than any guard or even the lord chamberlain could understand.

'More than I know either,' said the guard. 'I'll let you by, miss, and you can see if the chamberlain's there himself. But like I said, he'll have gone in by now.'

She ducked past him and into the little maze of rooms and corridors behind the back of the throne. They were empty. She could hear the burble of the court gathered in the great throne hall. She heard a trumpet call for silence. She stood, heart beating, at the bottom of the stairs that ran up to the royal living quarters. Twenty minutes earlier she could have caught the King himself on this stair. But twenty minutes ago she had barely been free of her own duties and was on her way to the stable. Oh, why did this have to happen today?

If she went up to the living quarters . . .

But there would be no one there now. Everyone useful was already in the hall. And when they were all shut away together she could not talk to any of them, except by going in there herself. Her heart beat hard at the thought.

Footsteps. An elderly clerk came hurrying along the corridor, checking over a paper as he did so.

'Please, sir,' said Melissa desperately. 'Have you seen the lord chamberlain?'

'He'll be in the hall with the chancellor and the King,' said the clerk, barely looking at her as he hurried past. 'I've got to get this to the chancellor now.'

'Could you please say to the lord chamberlain . . .'

But the clerk hurried on, waving her away with his hand.

Grimly Melissa followed him. At the rear door to the hall the man spoke in urgent whispers to the guard, who stepped aside and opened the door softly. The clerk passed in. Muttering to the guard and pointing into the hall, Melissa pressed after him. She was through before the guard thought to stop her.

She was standing at the back of the throne platform. There were people all around her, pressed back against the walls. She could not see past them. From the open space before the throne a voice was speaking in a steady tone, pitched to carry the length of the hall:

'That thou didst consort with Outlanders, and didst bring them unbidden into Our realm. That thou didst refuse Our peace, when it was offered unto thee. That thou didst conspire with several parties to raise rebellion in this Our realm, that thou didst plan violence against Our person and against any servant of Ours that we might send to you in pursuance of our will—'

'This is no law!' cried another voice. 'You cannot judge me! I am the King by right . . .'

'Silence, sir!' bellowed a herald. 'Until the charges are read!'

'. . . That I brought Outlanders unbidden?' continued the second voice. 'How were they unbidden? *I* bid them come. What do you know of Outland, any of you?'

'Gueronius, be silent,' said the King. 'You shall have

your chance to answer. But first you and all present must know why you are here.'

Melissa pushed her way forward among the court officials, still hoping for a glimpse of the lord chamberlain, or at least of someone who might know her and who might be able to interrupt the King with her message.

'I am here because of witchcraft! *Your* witchcraft. Your devils snatched me and dragged me through a netherworld to bring me here! Have you no shame, you bastard of Tarceny, that you mock me like this?'

Melissa looked down the long hall. It was just as crowded as it had been on the day when she had been up in the gallery. Now she saw the packed masses of faces down both sides of the room, all turned in her direction. She saw the guards and the banners on the walls. She saw the knots of court officials around the throne. She saw the King, and beyond him the Queen on a slightly smaller throne, both looking down on the man before them.

The man knelt at the foot of the steps. He was dressed in, of all things, a nightshift. His hair was wild and his face was covered in several months worth of beard. His arms were held behind him and guards stood at his back.

'Witch!' he cried at the King. 'Son of your father! May you be taken as he was, by the devils you sent for me!'

'Gueronius,' said the King again. 'Plead, or waste your breath. But after this chance I can give you no other. You have heard the charges. Will you not speak to them?'

'Charges? That I sought to take back what was mine? Guilty, by all the Angels! That I was denied by witchcraft? Guilty! That I am mocked, put on show, by a trickster and a consort of devils? Guilty, guilty, guilty!'

'Very well,' said the King coldly. 'Then I have another charge to add to this.' He turned to the Queen, watching pale upon her throne.

'Your Majesty will remember,' he said, pitching his voice for the hall to hear, 'when you came to me in Tarceny, and sought justice against Gueronius and his house for the wrongs they had done to you. Then I was but Lord of Tarceny and could not judge. But fate has turned. Now under Heaven there is no one who can judge this case but me. What would you have me do?'

Melissa. What would you have me do? The hilltop above the lake, and the cloaks blowing and the grass stems flattening in the wind. And the neck of the red knight as he bowed before the King, so that she could have cut his head off with a word.

Atti looked away from the King.

She looked away, and her eyes fell on Melissa, the serving maid, standing in the front rank of the King's officials.

She had seen her! Now, Melissa!

An urgent, silent gesture of her hand. And with all the room waiting for the Queen to speak, the Queen was silent. One finger beckoned Melissa forward.

With her heart flapping in her chest, her throat tight, Melissa came to the finger's command. She had to walk right out in front of everyone, before a thousand eyes, past the throne of the King (turn, bob hurriedly, walk on), before the wild-eyed prisoner, to reach the Queen where she sat with her ladies around her. The eyes of the ladies were fierce with anger. The eyes of the Queen showed nothing at all. She bent her head. She put her hand on Melissa's arm. Melissa whispered her message.

The Queen sat back and sighed as if she thought the world very stupid.

'Your Majesty,' she said at last. 'I will speak on this. But first there is another who seeks admittance. It may be that what she would say will also bear on this case.'

The King frowned. 'The Audience is begun. The charges in this case read and answered. May we not—?'

'She has come a long way. It is your mother.'

The words carried down the hall. An echo of murmurs, wondering, wary, rose from the crowd. The King hesitated. Then he spoke to the herald. The herald called. A flurry broke out at the doors as the guards down there realized that they were being asked to do something. The doors opened. Armoured men hurried out through them. There was a pause, in which the sea of murmurs rose to a roar. And then a trumpet-call crashed through the noise. Melissa jumped. She realized that she was still standing out in front of everybody at the side of the Queen. But she could not move because the Queen was still holding her wrist, hard, as if she

320

was nervous. She did not seem to realize that it was Melissa, rather than the arm of her chair, that she was holding.

Melissa watched Phaedra walk up the hall between the lines of people. Dressed in a drab and shapeless gown, she moved before all those jewelled ladies and lords. Her feet were bare, her head high, she looked neither right nor left. And a stir spread along the crowd like a slow shiver, as if something dead, some unpleasant memory, had appeared again to walk among them. The grip on Melissa's arm tightened. She winced.

'Your Majesty,' said Phaedra, bowing. 'I ask leave to speak in this case.'

'I will hear you,' said Ambrose.

Phaedra looked down at Gueronius, who was staring at her open-mouthed.

'I sue for pardon for this man.'

'I thought you would. Why should I do this?'

'I will tell you a story, if you will listen.'

The King hesitated. Then he said, 'Very well,' and gestured to his right where the heralds stood. 'Tell it so all may hear.'

Lifting her gown, Phaedra climbed up the steps to take her place by the throne. The herald came to stand beside her. She signed to him that he would not be necessary. She spoke down the hall.

'There was a woman, and she had a son.'

Her voice was softer than a herald's bellow, but still clear. Melissa could see all the faces of the court turned to her, the people at the back of the crowd with their chins high and probably on tiptoe as they strained to listen.

'Her husband made alliances that were not good. His allies brought him victory, but the price for that victory was to be the life of the son.'

There was absolute silence – an utter stillness. They were watching her. Melissa wondered if she were the only person in the room who did not know what Phaedra meant by *allies*.

'What should the woman do?' said Phaedra calmly. 'Her husband did not wish to lose their son, but he could not forgo his alliances. So every day that passed brought the child peril. At last the woman went to her husband's enemy, who was the King, and said to him: "I will let you into my husband's castle so that you may capture him. Only promise me that neither you nor your followers will harm my son."

'The King agreed.

'Moreover, for he knew that others might one day try to use the child against him, he said: "And when I am King in this land, and if your son is brought to me for treason, I shall pardon him. Once. After that I may not help him." That is a hard thing for a king to promise, Your Majesty, as you will know. But he did, and the woman remembered it.

'And for that promise she betrayed her husband.

'And although her husband is long dead, and that King is dead, and her own son now sits upon the throne, she still remembers it. The name of the King who made this promise was Septimus, of the house of Tuscolo.'

She looked around the room, while the watchers understood. Then her eyes fell on the man before the throne.

'For his sake I ask you to pardon the heir of Tuscolo who kneels before you.'

'But . . .' said Ambrose, frowning. He was leaning forward on his throne, trying to think his way through to a judgement. And Atti was leaning forward, too, hanging on his words. They all were. And the nails of the Queen were digging so hard into Melissa's wrist that she could have cried out with it.

'Oh, very *well*!' said Ambrose. He sighed heavily. 'Yes, I suppose you are right. I will—'

He got no further. With an exclamation the Queen rose from her seat and stalked out of the hall by way of the door behind the thrones. The courtiers parted for her left and right as she drove through them, and all her ladies hurried after her. Melissa was left by the throne, cradling her wrist in which the marks of the Queen's fingers were printed in angry red.

'. . . I will think on this!' shouted the King. But he was too late. The room was dissolving into uproar. He rose from his throne and glowered around him. 'Take him away!' he yelled, pointing to Gueronius. And he swung on his mother, and cried: 'Damn it, did you have to *do* that?'

'Yes, I did,' said Phaedra.

'That story has nothing to do with this!'

'Yes it has. Although perhaps it should have been for you to ask *his* pardon. You did take his throne after all.'

'I didn't want it!'

'That did not stop you. And you are treading too close in your father's footsteps for any of us to be comfortable. He, too, used the princes to eliminate a rival – Gueronius's grandfather, in fact. Had you forgotten?'

'That's not fair! I'm not like him!'

'Are you not? Would Gueronius have lived if I had not come? Will he yet?'

'I said I would think about it! But I'm not like my father! And Atti's not like you!'

Phaedra looked at him for a moment. Then, deliberately, she said: 'How did you woo your bride then?'

When the King did not answer, she went on, 'In her dreams, when she was a child. Did you think I did not know? We prise each prince from Beyah's grip, one after another. And you use them to repeat your father's sins! Including his sin against me! What do you think I feel?'

'I don't *care* what you feel,' Ambrose screamed. 'Leave Atti alone! Leave *me* alone! Go back to your damned pool, and next time come when *I* send for you!'

'Very well,' she said coldly, and left him there.

XXI

In His Cell

o, I will not undress,' said the Queen to her ladies that evening. 'You may all go. Melissa will stay and put me to bed in due time.'

The ladies shot dubious glances at one another.

'Your Majesty—'

'I said that you may go.'

They left, one after another through the door.

'Bring me a shawl, Melissa,' said the Queen. 'And make ready a lamp. We are going out again.'

Moving stiffly, Melissa searched for a square of warm cloth and arranged it around Atti's shoulders. Then she went to the Queen's reading desk. The lamp there was full. One of the other maids must have seen to it earlier. Melissa was grateful that she was not going to have to do any more rummaging in cupboards than was necessary.

Atti watched as she returned. Melissa came slowly, trying to make her step look as easy as possible, but she could not do it.

'Did they punish you, Melissa?' said the Queen.

'Yes, Your Majesty.'

'For coming into the hall today?'

'They said I had a straw on my dress, Your Majesty.'

'They are jealous. Which ladies did it?'

Melissa hesitated.

'Which of them did it, Melissa?'

'The Lady Caterine and the Lady Hermione, Your Majesty.' She had never thought that women brought up to be ladies would know how to hurt so much.

'I shall dismiss them in the morning.'

Melissa opened her mouth to say that dismissing two ladies for beating a maid would not cure anyone of jealousy. It would make it worse, not better. But she could not tell Atti she was wrong.

'From now on,' said Atti, no longer looking at her, 'you will be my personal maid. You will sleep in my room. You will always go where I go.'

(Why? thought Melissa. Why do you see me now, when you didn't before? Because I am a hurt thing, like you?)

'Did you hear me, Melissa?'

'Yes – thank you, Your Majesty.'

And she wondered how she could possibly get to see Puck after this.

'Come,' said the Queen. 'We are going to the cells. You must lead the way.'

They passed down stone corridors, making their way by the light of the lamp in Melissa's hand. Many of the household were already in bed, but the castle of Tuscolo never truly slept. There were guards at some of the doors, late walkers in the corridors, clerks in a copying room working in the glow of lit rushes. A pair of councillors, debating something in a passageway, stopped and bowed as they passed. Atti ignored them.

They left the main buildings and walked along a battlemented wall. The wind was strong that night. It moaned in the draining holes and drove thin clouds over the moon. The wall-walk ended in a low door set in a squat, square tower in the angle of the upper courtyard. Atti nodded at it. Melissa reached for the door ring. The iron felt very cold.

Clack! Loud enough to make her jump. The door opened inwards. There was a small, firelit chamber and two armoured men who looked up at them with startled eyes.

'I wish to speak to the prisoner,' said Atti.

There was the slightest shake in her voice.

They bowed and led the way down two flights of steps. At the bottom was another door. They drew the bolts and opened it for her. There was a sudden movement inside, like the flitting of a beast in a cage.

What are we doing here? thought Melissa.

Atti had stopped before the dark doorway. She put out one hand to support herself against the stone. She looked down, as if she were concentrating. (No, not concentrating. That trembling of her shoulder was not concentration. It was . . .)

Atti drew breath once, twice. Then she lifted her head. 'Remain where we can call you,' she said.

The men bowed again and left.

It was Melissa who went in first. The lamp showed her a small chamber cut out of the ground. There was no furniture in it. The floor was of beaten earth. It stank of a man's filth.

The man – the wild-eyed man who had knelt before the King that morning – was sitting up on a rough pallet on the floor. There was a blanket around his knees. He was still in the same nightshift that he had been wearing before. He stared at the girls. They looked down on him.

'The King considers your case, Gueronius,' said Atti.

The wild man did not answer.

'He has not yet pardoned you, although his mother has asked that he should. He will listen to me as he has promised. What should I say to him?'

'What should you say?' repeated the man. His voice was thick. He must have been asleep until the moment the bolts were drawn. He might even have thought they were the hangman come to carry him out to his end. But he looked up at them and the candlelight glinted in his eye.

'Say what you like, only tell me – tell me in what way I am supposed to have wronged you.'

'On your knees,' said the Queen calmly.

Slowly the man levered himself from his pallet onto his knees, watching her all the while.

'In what way have you wronged me, Gueronius?' whispered the Queen. 'You and your house have hurt me more deeply than you can possibly imagine. You have hurt me in my mind, Gueronius. You carried fire and sword into places I loved. You killed the faces I

328

remember. All those wounds are in my head still. Shall I wash them in your blood?'

'I would never have hurt you,' said the man simply, 'if I had known you.'

'What do you mean?'

He gave a helpless gesture. 'How could I hurt something so beautiful? I tell you, lady, in Outland I have seen great wonders. I have sung for my supper in courts whose wealth surpasses anything our highest kings ever knew. I have seen gardens filled with birds of fantastic plumes, learned secrets of a power that would lay low our highest defences. Yet *never* did I see anything so wonderful as when I looked up in my own throne hall and saw you there, ready to pronounce my death!'

'Do not weary me!' said Atti. She bent down to look into his eyes. 'How many times a day do you think I hear such things?' she went on. 'Men surround me like moths. Each of them swears they would die for me and they speak the truth. They look at me and see beauty. They dream dreams of beauty and want to live in them. Yet all they have seen is beautiful skin. *I* am not beautiful, not within. *I* know that. And my dreams are terrible, because you have made them so! Pronounce your death? Why should I not?'

'Why did you not?'

'I was not given the chance.'

'You were. *He* gave it to you, that tight-arsed priestling who has made you his mate. And yes, my lady, you wanted to speak on me. But you did not know what to say. So you had them let in the King's mother instead. Maybe you did want to punish me, yes, for things I did not know I had done. But something stopped you. And something has brought you here now. If you wanted to kill me you would do it in another room, with a word, and never look to see what you did. I know this. What is it that stops you? Maybe it is pity. Maybe. Maybe it is something else—'

'Don't deceive yourself!' Atti hissed. 'Why did I hesitate? Just for this, perhaps. That in you – base, mad, filthy, loud-mouthed – I saw something of myself that no one else will ever see. There. Will you stake your neck on that now?'

'*I* do not stake my neck, my lady,' he said levelly. 'I cannot, because it is not mine to stake. It is yours.'

And as she watched him, he went on, 'Let me tell you, lady. I do not fear death. I have lived cheek by jowl with death these past four years. Once I lay in fever for days from the bite of a snake. Fever burns, lady. The bite burns until you scream. Shall I tell you of my snake? It was brightly coloured, beautiful. But it crawled on its belly and bit whatever came near to it, because it knew only fear. I do not fear. I do not fear what your word can do to me, for already I burn as I look at you!'

'*Snake*, is it?' cried Atti. 'And which of us is the snake? Down on your belly!'

'As you wish,' said the man calmly, and dropped forward on his front.

'Crawl!'

'Not from fear but for you!' he said, and began to wriggle clumsily, propelling himself with his elbows

330

across the filthy floor. In the lamplight Atti's eyes were wide as she watched him. 'Crawl!' she shouted again.

The man writhed and suddenly he was closer. Alarmed, Melissa backed away. The wall stopped her. She looked at the door, wondering if she should call the guards. Atti gave a cry of disgust as he reached for her ankle and backed away, too. The space was narrow. There was no room.

'Do not fear me!' he pleaded. 'I could not harm you.' And deftly he caught Atti's foot and pulled it from the floor, so that she was forced to lean back against the wall for balance. She kicked, but he held her.

'Feel my fangs, lady,' he whispered, and kissed her foot where the line of her shoe bared the naked skin.

Atti stared at him. Melissa stared, too.

'Snakes bite in fear, but I cannot,' he said as he let her go.

Atti kicked him in the face. 'Off me!' she cried. 'Snake!'

He made no sound. He crawled from her on his hands and knees to the far corner of the room. There he crouched, watching her. She looked at him. And she laughed.

The walls bounced with the sound – the sound Atti never made. Laughter, like the peal of a trumpet. 'Gueronius,' she said, 'you are not a snake.'

He said nothing.

'I think you are a rat,' she said. 'A dirty, filthy sewer-rat.'

He watched her impassively.

331

'I will go to the King now,' she said, with a strange smile. 'And I will lie with him. *He* is a good man, after all. And afterwards we will talk together. We will talk of you. Then, maybe, I will decide.'

With that she turned and went to the door. Melissa, enormously relieved, slipped out ahead of her and began to climb the stair. She had gone three steps ahead of her before she remembered that they had left the cell door open. She hurried back down to the bottom. The man was still crouching where they had left him. In that last glimpse from her lantern, as she closed the door, she saw the bruise beginning to show on his cheek, above his matted beard.

With shaking fingers she slid the bolts into their holes. At least these ones went all the way home, she thought. *Clunk, clunk,* shutting away the man in his darkness. But they could not shut away what she had heard.

They walked back towards the living quarters. Atti said nothing, but as they hurried along the wall she laughed again and the stones rang with her triumph. They reached the royal apartments and entered the Queen's rooms. Softly Atti passed through the antechamber and the dressing chamber, and on into her bedroom.

There she stood for a moment.

In the far wall of the room, disguised among the panelling, was the through-door to the King's bed-chamber. On the other side of that Ambrose slept, with his servants in the antechamber beyond.

There was light coming from under the door.

Atti stepped quietly across the room. Her fingers drew the bolt, which the locksmiths and carpenter had fixed there during her panic of the night before. She passed through it and said something to the man who was in there.

Melissa heard Ambrose laugh, too, sudden with his surprise. The door closed behind Atti. Melissa was left in the Queen's bedchamber, with a lamp in her hand.

XXII

The Wall and the Water

o the Queen is holy now,' said Puck as they sat together on a pile of stable-straw during another Grand Audience.

'I don't know about that,' said Melissa.

'She will go to a holy place.'

'On pilgrimage,' sighed Melissa, thinking of all the hurrying and scurrying, fetching, demanding and rejecting that there was still to do before Atti would be content with her costumes, horses, trappings and escort for the long trip into the south.

'And she forgives her enemy.'

'She did,' said Melissa grimly.

But she did not think that Atti forgiving Gueronius was holy. And she was not sure that 'forgive' was the right word. Did you 'forgive' a new plaything?

Atti had intervened for him, in a carefully staged appeal before another Grand Audience. And Ambrose had granted her plea that Gueronius should be spared. The former King was banished to his estates with a warning that his life would be forfeit if he strayed outside them or assembled too many men on them. And that, everyone thought, was that. But Melissa didn't.

'I don't like the way she laughs,' she said.

'Laughing is good. More good when she has been sad.'

'That depends why she's laughing, doesn't it?'

His eyes narrowed. His words might be clumsy but his mind was as quick as anything.

'Why is she laughing, you think?'

'Don't know,' said Melissa.

Which was true. She didn't *know*. But she saw that light in Atti's eyes. She had seen it first in the cell, in the gleam of her lamp as Atti watched the man crawling before her. Something had happened there – something big, in Atti's head. Atti still laughed when she thought of it. And she wanted more.

'You kiss me now?' said Puck.

'No thank you,' said Melissa.

'Oh,' said Puck, sounding dashed. 'Right.'

'Sorry,' said Melissa. 'I'm just not sure.'

He looked so dejected that she slipped an arm round his shoulders and gave him a hug. But she made it only a short one, in case he mistook her. He did not respond.

'I'm in a bad mood,' she said. 'That's what it is.'

They sat in silence for a while, listening to the small sounds of horses fidgeting and breathing in their stalls.

'You busy?' Melissa asked.

He stirred. 'King travels. Queen travels. Much to do in stables. And I study, too.'

'The King's travelling as well?'

'He will go to the lake. See Trant castle. Meet Outland-man there.'

'You know a lot, don't you? You're very clever.'

He said nothing.

I'm *sorry*, Puck, she thought. I didn't want to hurt you. It's just that . . . Well, not yet. Not yet. I want to wait a bit and see.

'Sing me that hill song, Puck,' she said.

'What song?'

'That one you sang at our spring supper in the mountains. Like this.' And she hummed the long, slow notes that she had heard once and never forgotten, and that seemed even now to be tinged with tears.

He frowned. 'That is Lament. The World-Mother song.'

'Sing it for me, Puck. I'm in that kind of mood.'

'No. I don't sing that. That is hill stuff. Leave that behind. Why bring her here? You don't want her here.' He sounded cross.

She looked at her feet and wondered what the point of anything was. 'Well, if you're busy, Puck, I'll get out of your way, shall I?'

'See you again. And next time, maybe you be sure.'

It wasn't that she didn't like him, she thought as she made her way slowly back to the royal apartments. Of course she liked him. He was clever, funny, nice, thoughtful. He would never be handsome – it was hard to imagine a hill face that would be handsome – but he was different. He had risked his neck for her in the mountains, bringing all that food across the valley in the winters. She saw that now. And he had come all the way to Tuscolo by himself, learning a new language and new things among a strange people. That wasn't just brave or clever. That was – well, it was lots of both. And he had just about told her that he had come because of her. She might meet a richer man, but she wasn't likely to meet a better one, was she?

And yet a voice within her said: *No. Wait.*

Wait, because something else might happen. Things would not go on as they had done. She did not know why, but she felt a change was coming. And what would it bring?

Could it bring the moon within reach?

Wooden scaffold cloaked the stained and crumbling battlements. Hammers sounded faintly from within the old courtyard. Out on the huge, glittering lake the sails of fishing boats moved silently. The roofs of the hamlet by the water's edge were bright with new straw. The hillsides had been broken to fresh earth for the first time in years. A flock of goats moved peacefully under the olive trees, sounding the lazy tonk of their bells along the shore. Hearth-smoke drifted in the autumn air. And a thing done with a pen, eighteen months before in Tuscolo, had become real. Settlers had reclaimed the waste around Trant castle.

Below the walls, on the green slopes that ambled gently down to the shore, a gaily-coloured crowd had gathered. The King was there. So were his counsellors and much of the nobility of the land. Among the hundred banners that stirred in the gentle breeze were the devices of Trant and Tarceny, of Develin, Inchapter and Lackmere from the south, of Velis and the Seabord, of Herryce, Faul, Joyce and even Seguin from the heart of the Kingdom. Sunlight gleamed on gold chains, lit bright cloth and flashed from polished steel. Two thousand eyes watched the lake, and the slow progress of the three small boats that bore an ambassador from Outland to meet the King.

'We still haven't decided what we are going to decide,' fumed Ambrose as the boats crept closer in towards the quay.

'Your Majesty,' murmured Padry. 'Nothing will be *decided* today. He will make a speech of friendship and we will answer. If he makes proposals or demands, we will undertake to consider them. No more. We can hardly know what we are going to do before we know what he asks. And remember. His King is but one of many in Outland, some greater, some less than we. We do not buy from the first stall in any market – not until we have been up and down the stalls and heard what is offered and for what price.'

Padry had in fact already drafted much of the record of the meeting for the King's chronicles. It had been childish stuff, but he was pleased with it.

The Ambassadors were led before one of high bearing and rich dress, and they fell on their faces before him, saying: Surely this is Ambrose Umbriel, the great King. But those who stood by him said: Nay, this is the Lord Chancellor Padry, who is wise in the

338

King's council. And they were led to another place, where stood a lord and a lady of such nobility and splendour that again they fell down on their faces and cried: Surely here at last are Ambrose Umbriel and his Queen Astria, for the word of the Queen's beauty has travelled beyond the ocean and we see that it is true. But again those who stood around them said, Nay, these are the Baron Aun, the Wolf of Lackmere and the Lady Sophia, the Woman of Develin, who are mighty indeed but not the King. And they were led to another place . . .

All good stuff for the Kingdom to read and repeat in gossip. Put Outland in its place, that's right . . .

'Maybe we should not go to the market at all,' said Ambrose.

Padry was still wondering how he would deal with the Queen's absence in his chronicle. He took a moment to absorb what the King had said.

'There are three possibilities, Your Majesty,' he replied. 'You may return to the monopoly of Velis, or something like it. Meetings shall happen only in certain places, neither in our land nor in theirs, and only certain merchants of ours shall be permitted to traffic with the Outlanders, for which right they will pay a toll to you. Or, second, you permit Outlanders to enter our land freely, and go wherever they wish so long as they abide by our laws and pay the same tolls in our markets as our own merchants do. Or you steer a middle course—'

'You have not mentioned the fourth way,' said Ambrose. 'Which is that we forbid all contact between our people and the lands beyond the sea.'

339

In that close crowd it was difficult to avoid being overheard. Two paces away, the Lady of Develin turned and looked at them.

'It is harder to pour wine back into a bottle than it was to pour it out in the first place,' said Padry, dropping his voice further. 'Harder still when the wine is Knowledge.'

'What I know is that Wulfram brought a great evil from over the sea,' said Ambrose. 'We live with it today. What new evil will follow now?'

'There you go again,' said Aun, from the other side of the King. 'But in one matter I agree with you. This black powder the Outlanders have, which takes sudden fire and hurls metal or stone balls long distances like trebuchets – you should ban all use of this except by your own armourers, on pain of treason. If there is a weapon here that will bring down walls such as these, then the only safe course is to make sure we have it and deny it to anyone else.'

'It is not simply a matter of powder, Aun . . .'

'Your Majesty,' said Padry more firmly. 'We deceive ourselves, I think. I could write you a decree, banning meetings with the Outlanders. And you might have it published throughout the land. But so long as there is profit in it, the traffic will continue. It will slip through your fingers like water that you tried to hold in your fist. And a king must not make laws that will not be obeyed, or men will discover the habit of not obeying his law.'

The Lady of Develin was still watching them. She might not be able to hear what was said, but she was reading Padry's lips. As he finished, she nodded. Then she turned to face the lake again. They all did.

The boats were creeping closer under the gentle breeze. They were ordinary, single-masted, open-decked lake-craft from the northern end of Derewater, engaged to bring the ambassador and his party down from Watermane. It was possible to see the crewman in the bow of each, the helmsman at the stern, and the heads and shoulders of others squatting in the waist.

Just ordinary boats, crewed by the King's own men; and yet, thought Padry, they were three. Wulfram had come to land in three ships, according to *The Tale of Kings*. And in these three craft were men who had been born on the shores from which Wulfram had set sail, three hundred years ago. There was something powerful in the thought. It was more than powerful. Everyone sensed it. There was a shiver of excitement in the crowd. These would be the first Outlanders any of them had ever seen.

Outland! All their lives it had been a myth no more real than a story of the beginning of the world. A necessary curtain for the mind. Now Gueronius's return had ripped that curtain aside, letting in a light that changed the shapes of everything. Now every man and woman in the crowd around the King – yes, and every barrow-boy in every market from Watermane to Jent – knew that if a ship sailed from Velis and set course boldly across the ocean, it would come in a fortnight's sailing to a hot, savage coast, which, if followed first south and then around a cape to the north, would lead to the trading stations where

strange goods were offered by mariners from lands
that were not the Kingdom. And they knew, too, that
a ship which sailed on from there (Padry was not
exactly sure how far or in which direction, but he
fancied that it was north and say a month, or two at
most) would cross another sea and come to a great
cold land of many kingdoms where men knew the
Angels and yet also things that were not the Angels,
and spoke many different tongues, of which some
seemed close to the words of the Kingdom and
some seemed to have no words a man could understand at all.

Curiosity seized first upon the things that were most
trivial – the broad hats and great cloaks that
Outlanders wore, their habit of painting their faces,
the bizarre things they thought good to eat. A
hundred little myths were already running in the
Kingdom about the quaint customs of foreign lands.
And Padry sifted and sifted among the rumours, looking all the time for some hint of the evil that Ambrose
had predicted. For despite his brave words to his King
he was sure that it would come. It was his failure that
had allowed Gueronius to cross the sea. It would not
be like the Angels to leave him unpunished.

It might be a plague, although no plague had yet
struck. But more and more Padry suspected that it
would be an idea. It would be a heresy that would split
the Church and set the Kingdom off into a war more
bitter and deadly than any yet. Or it would be that
men, having discovered that one boundary of their
world had moved, began to question others – law,

kingship, even faith – with similar results. Or it would simply be fear. Peace rested not only on the power of the King but on the shared belief that the world would stay the same. What would men do – indeed, what would they *not* do – once fear had gripped their hearts?

The banners of the Kingdom were drawn up in a great coloured forest along the shore. They made a brave sight. The pennants of the small barons clustered around those of the greater lords and churchmen to whom they were allied: Seguin, Develin, Jent, Lackmere . . . Each gaudy device meant a following of knights and squires and footmen ready to face any strength that came against the land. The Outlanders would make their enquiries and be impressed, as Padry meant them to be.

Ah, but look again, with an eye born in the Kingdom. Read the stories that lay behind the banners – the feuds that would set the men who held them storming against each other in an instant! Fissures ran hither and thither through the host. Look at the banners around Lackmere! Eight, ten, twelve . . . Yesterday that house had been no more than a petty barony itself. Today, because of the King's favour to both father and son, it was one of the three great powers of the south. Such a rise created jealousies, weaknesses as well as strength. Look there, at Baron Seguin with his retainers and allies around him. What thoughts were trundling through that ape-like head at this instant? And the banner of Gueronius was held by hired men, because Gueronius himself was still sulking on his estates. Why wasn't he here? Pique? A genuine misunderstanding about the terms of his exile? Assume the former. There would be more trouble with him yet . . .

Bump! The first boat had scraped against the jetty. The low sound of wood on wood seemed loud along the shore. A palpable shiver ran through the host. Padry saw a fist clenching and unclenching in the crowd to his left. It was the Lady Develin's. And his own palms were sweating. His throat was dry. His stomach felt hollow, as if it sensed the arrival not of a man but of some monstrous creature like one of the princes that Ambrose had dragged from the pool of tears.

Remember, we are strong, he said to himself. We are strong enough to deal with Outland. As long as we stick together.

His eyes flicked to Seguin again.

Trumpets blared at the lakeside. Men were stepping from the boats to the jetty, some in rough sailor clothes, some in costumes so dark they seemed to be black. There were feathered hats and caps down there, also black. Padry swallowed. (Why did Outlanders wear to court colours that should only be worn at funerals?) He rubbed his palm against his robe. Lines from his record of this meeting were still running through his head, but he knew they were all lies. Perhaps *The Tale of Kings* lied, too. Perhaps the invasion of Wulfram had begun not with the heroic crunch of three great keels on the shore near Velis, but like this, quietly, with soft-tongued emissaries sent to a new land to speak of trade. He could see the Outlanders now, beginning to toil up the short slope towards them in a small group. The face of the ambassador was painted pure white under his dark cap. The shoulders of his costume were so flat and broad that he seemed almost square. He held a short white sceptre in his hand.

'Do as you wish,' he heard the Baron Lackmere grumble. 'But I do not like it that Gueronius keeps Outlanders in his castle, or that with their help he casts great tubes of iron. And if I cannot prevent him from this, then I would send for Outlanders myself to help me do the same. At least then we should be on a level with Gueronius, and with Outland, too.'

There came a moment in the evening when the chatter and the hurrying eased, when the King was in his castle and the Outlanders in their tent, and there were no more cries of 'Chancellor' from the edge of the frantic scrum. In the courtyard of Trant the sound of hammers stopped. The repair gangs called to one another, gathering and storing their tools. Wheels rolled. Voices muttered off into the distance. And then there was silence – blessed, thick silence, like cool oil in fevered ears. Padry took himself to the chamber that had been set aside for him in the round north-east tower, laid a fresh sheet of paper on his table and set a lamp beside it. Then, with relish, he dipped his pen.

Some words were more important than records or treaties. And now was the time to set them down.

He was writing out, from memory, the lost second work of Croscan: *The Path of Signs Illuminating the Ascent of the Soul.* It had been the King's suggestion, after they had despaired of recovering the looted book. It was a mighty effort for a busy chancellor to take on in his spare time when, really, he had little or no spare time at all. But somehow the full cycle had to be completed for all those thousands of souls who would come after, groping blindly along the Path. In the eyes of Heaven, perhaps, there might be no other task in the Kingdom that mattered more. And Padry knew he was almost the only person left who was capable of it; who could recall the passages that he had once learned by heart, and could write them with understanding, so that the flaws in his memory should not reduce the work of the great sage to gibberish.

He had been at it, on and off, for weeks; whenever he could snatch a half- or quarter-hour to scribble out something for his clerks to copy. But then all this business with the Outland ambassador had come along and drowned out everything else, and days had gone by without a moment for Croscan. Now, in the calm of the lakeside evening, he had a chance to catch up.

That was why the knock on the door was unwelcome.

'Your pardon,' said Lex quietly, 'but may I speak with you?'

'Yes,' sighed Padry. 'If it is important.'

It was plainly important. At least it was plainly important to Lex, judging by the uncharacteristic, hesitant way in which he seated himself opposite his master.

'The Bishop of Tuscolo . . .' began Lex.

'Yes,' said Padry, nodding sadly. 'He is leaving many stranded sheep. But he has had a long life in the service of the Angels and we should be glad that he is now approaching his reward.'

'It's not that,' said Lex. 'At least, it's not only that. It's the King.'

'Yes?' said Padry, now mystified.

'He – he has asked me to be the next bishop.'

Padry was still holding his pen over the page. A drop of ink had gathered at the nib. With great care he set it down so that there should be no blot on the page of Croscan.

'I see,' he said slowly. 'I see.'

Then he said: 'Did he say why?'

Lex shook his head in disbelief. 'It goes back to that – that experience I had in my last winter at Develin. I told you about it. What I'd forgotten was that Ambrose – Luke, as he then was – was with me at the time. He – he says an Angel spoke from me.'

'Oh,' Padry said. (Really, he was being very calm about this, he thought. He should be pleased with himself. But maybe it was because he could not quite believe it yet.) 'And did it?'

'I don't know. I don't remember it like that. But he's firm about it. He says it happened, and he will swear it before every other bishop in the land.'

'I see,' said Padry again. 'And he thinks this will make you a good bishop?'

'I suppose – yes, he does. And that's the problem. I'm not sure I will be. Being a bishop is far more than having a view, isn't it? It's . . .'

It was being one of the great lords of the land: administering territories, presiding over councils, doling out favours to others, making alliances with neighbouring landlords and holding your own against those who would encroach on your estates. It was intervening in the squabbles of the priests and monks, understanding not only the doctrinal points at issue but also the networks of power and region that underlay them. It was supporting the Crown on all matters to do with order in the Kingdom, without allowing the Crown to take the Church for granted. (Well, there should be no problem *there*, so long as Lex as bishop could turn a blind eye to Ambrose's occasional – very occasional – dealings with his shadow-world.)

Lex as bishop. There. He had thought it.

Now he knew it was going to happen.

He looked at his thumbs.

'I do not suppose,' he said, 'that you will be a worse bishop than many who have carried the crozier. Pick the right men to have around you and they will see that others feel the authority that you believe you lack. The only advice I would give you, if you wish men to remember you well in your office, is to seek nothing for yourself. The moment we look for rewards, more than we already have, we begin to twist from our true paths. We stand at the doors of Corruption, or Disappointment.'

'You wanted this,' said Lex. 'I know that. I'm sorry . . .'

'Don't trouble yourself,' said Padry with a sigh. He picked up his pen. 'I advise you to accept. All that I ask is that you find me an assistant as able as the one I am about to lose. And that you now leave me in peace. I would – I would like to be by myself for a bit.'

The moment Lex was gone he put his pen down again, and rested his head in his hands. He listened to his assistant's feet fading down the stair.

Then, abruptly, he rose.

Seven years now? Eight, in this office, shoring up the battered fabric of his masters' kingships with his wits and pen? He had not pushed himself forward. He had not competed for titles or offices. He had not taken a *single* bribe – well, none that counted. And what he had taken as a rule he had passed on in alms.

Why had he not simply gone to the King and said, *Please will you make me Bishop of Tuscolo?*

Because that was not what good servants should do! They should make their master aware of his powers in the matter, of the qualities he should look for – all that. And then they should wait for merit to be rewarded.

The pen lay on the table before him. The half-written page discussed the import of the Moon on the arc of Ascent – the trial of faith, when Truth and Untruth meet. A moment ago he had been full of it, flowing with Croscan like a fresh spring, watering the barren land. Now the water was bile, and he . . .

He left the room. He stomped down the stair with

349

his hands clutched behind him. In the passageway below was the door to the hall. Light came from within, and the sound of voices. The King was there, dealing with some matter of the new settlement that had had to wait until sunset before he had time to hear it. Padry did not go in.

Ambrose! How could a man so young be so wise, and at the same time so damned naïve? To award a bishopric for the sake of some obscure and distant revelation! *The Angels matter. Now I don't hear them any more . . . Trying to do things my way when they can't be done like that . . . I just had not realized that so much of it would be about money!* By the Angels he pined for, he wouldn't have lasted a year if Padry hadn't been there to see him right!

And what thanks did he get? Had Ambrose even thought of him? Had he seen anything in his chancellor other than a reasonably efficient spiller of ink? Had he considered whether this was a servant deserving of reward? Or had he thought . . . ?

Ah, but that word 'reward' . . .

At the end of the passage was a stout door. The bolts were rusty but they moved under his hand. It was a postern, opening out onto the ditch and to the grassy slope beyond that ran down to the lakeshore where the ambassador had landed that afternoon. It was dusk. The air was cool.

He made his way down into the ditch, splashed over the thin puddles in the bottom and climbed up the far side. His eye picked his way in the dimming light, but his mind was turning over the word *reward.*

350

Do you see how you trap yourself, Thomas Padry? You spoke true words in your jealousy just now. You told Lex – who has never sought rewards – to expect nothing for himself. Quite true. Good advice.

But have you ever taken it? You, the wise, just man who presumed to give it? You wanted that bishop's crozier for your own. You persuaded yourself it was right that you should have it. You imagined that the King would see you as the one and only possible candidate – even though you knew that he has been casting around for some mystic contact with the Angels that he feels he has now lost. (Oh, you did a good job bringing him across the lake, Thomas. Never doubt that. But did you ever ask yourself what it has cost *him?*)

And haven't you done this before? When you fixed your eyes on the child Atti and ran away from all your duties, to the ruin of the Kingdom? That beautiful little thing, whom you wanted for yourself and told yourself, oh, so many good reasons why she should be yours and no one else's? She was a reward – a flower beside the Path that you felt you could pick because of the virtue you had shown in following the Path so far. You should writhe in self-disgust, Thomas! You should weep for shame! And perhaps you should weep for Ambrose, too, who has told himself all the same beautiful things about her that you did, and has found out that they were lies.

A roosting bird flew, startled, from a branch. Padry blinked. He was standing in a grove of trees, with their dark branches whispering in the dusk. He could hear wavelets lapping close by. Where . . .

351

Oh yes. He had wandered down into the old outer works by the lakeshore.

Once Trant castle had been much bigger. Once there had been buildings out here, enclosed in another wall or palisade. All that was gone now. Only, among these trees, there were still some old stones: the remains of a square court, with broken paving. A few round columns stood like stone trunks shorn of their limbs. And there, dimly seen among the trees, the shape of a wide-bowled fountain, just as there was in Tuscolo, or Velis; or in Ferroux for that matter, or Tarceny, or that strange house he had once found in the mountains.

Trant, too, was one of the ancient houses of the Kingdom. Trant, too, had known loss and ruin and tears, tears, tears as the generations had passed. For these last twenty years it had stood empty, with no more meaning than a tombstone. The wind had sighed and the grasses waved where men and women had once been. Now the place was beginning to live again. All the Kingdom was beginning to live – at some cost to the King, and to his servants.

Ayah! Enough self-pity! If you must seek reward, Thomas, then find it in the good work you have done. Find it in Ambrose, almost the last of your pupils. You beat him and barely regarded him. But you did teach him. So did other, better men now dead. And see! Now he is King over a healing land.

Or find it in Sophia, Lady of Develin, who drove you to distraction in tutorial, and ten years later dictated the peace that put Ambrose on the throne.

Or in Lex, now – hah! – to be Bishop of Tuscolo. Oh, how the old masters at Develin would have rolled their eyes and spluttered if anyone had suggested it at the Widow's high table! Look, and say to yourself, *My pupils! I had a hand in this!* Could any schoolmaster ask for a greater reward?

And yet always beware. The reward lies at the end of the Path, in the reunion of the soul with the Godhead. It does not lie beside the way. Nor does it lie in the steps that have been trodden. A pupil may betray his teaching at any time. The foot strays easily. A philosopher must not weep. The just man keeps walking, and keeps to the Path.

He kept walking. He made his way down to the lakeshore, to the lap of the waves and the jetty, where the three small boats lay knocking at timbers that smelled freshly of the saw. At his belt his fingers found his three signs of Faithfulness: the Lantern, the Leaf and the Dragon. They were old friends. He could not remember how he had come by them, but by all the Angels they were the friends he needed now.

He walked by the lake for an hour, as his lips and hands practised his private litany. When he turned for the castle and bed, the moon was up.

It was the old moon, just past the full. The first fringes of shadow had begun to show on its face.

XXIII

The Forbidden Door

he King returned from Trant. The Queen returned from her pilgrimage. Lex, once one of the lowliest clerks in the land, took the crozier of Tuscolo before the eyes of all the bishops. New settlements were decreed in Baldwin and Tower Bay. The court heaved and clamoured and bothered.

More ambassadors came from Outland, talked of treaties, brought presents of strange incense and marvellous creatures, and left the courtiers aping their manners of dress and entertainment. Caps and headwear grew to outrageous shapes and sizes, shoulders broadened, the toes of shoes curled. Faces were painted. No edict caused Padry more grief that winter than the one in which he set out precisely how much of the face a count, lady, baron or knight might cover, and sternly forbade anyone but the royal couple to use gold.

And one mild day, shortly after the new year, the King asked the Queen to go riding with him. It had not happened for months.

Melissa could not ride and therefore could not accompany Atti beyond the stables. So for the first time since returning from the pilgrimage she was going to be free from Atti's side. She thought that if Puck were in the stable when they waved the Queen off, she would catch his eye, maybe. Then perhaps she could walk with him and speak with him, and make things better between them. He was too good a body to be sour for weeks on end, wasn't he?

But he was not there when the Queen's party reached the stable. Melissa's eyes searched among the gentlemen-of-the-horses and knights-of-the-stirrup and all the other do-nothings who trailed around wherever the crowned heads went. She saw Master Copley and the chief farrier, the master blacksmith and great numbers of stable hands, all in their best rig and looking respectful; but Puck was not among them. And only then did she remember that all the scholars would be at their studies at this hour. Puck could not have been here even if he had wanted to be. Disappointment settled on her, cold and clingy, like wet clothes after a shower of rain.

'Here, lass, hold this for a moment.'

It was a little bearded man, one of the stableboys. He pushed something into Melissa's hands as if to rid himself of it while helping one of the ladies-in-waiting into the saddle. Melissa took it without thinking. Then she realized that he did not want it back.

It was small, wrapped in a canvas rag and tied with a straw.

She looked up, surprised, into the man's face. He

winked and jerked his head just a fraction towards the school house across the courtyard. *It's from him.*

She gave him a quick smile to show she had understood. With the lady-in-waiting looking down on them it was all she could do.

The Queen rode off to her meeting with the King in the meadows below the castle. The servants, and those ladies-in-waiting who had not been chosen to accompany her, made their way back to the living quarters. Melissa went briskly into the Queen's bedchamber before anyone could think of something else for her to do. In that most private of the rooms of the palace, she opened her hand to see what Puck had sent.

It was a tiny wooden carving of a kid goat, lying with its legs curled up under it. It was pretty, and beautifully smooth. She had not known that he could shape wood, but she was not surprised because he seemed to be full of little surprises like that. She wondered what else his hands could do.

And she laughed aloud at that thought. (No, Melissa! No, be careful. First, be sure that you're sure!) But it was a nice thing. She could make a brooch of it, if she could find a brooch-pin. Then she could wear it when she chose. And sooner or later he would see her wearing it, even if there was never a chance to speak to him without anyone hearing. Meanwhile . . .

She went to the little closet where she was allowed to keep her things. She removed the little wallet in which she kept the small pile of coins which were her pay. She took from it the rag in which she kept her other treasure: the little white stone that Ambrose had left on the moonlit pavement in Tarceny, more than two years ago. She put the goat beside it on the cloth and looked at them together. Two treasures, two men. She could love two men, couldn't she? Especially when they were both, in different ways, just a little beyond her reach.

She folded the cloth up again and stowed it in the wallet. She was in the act of putting the wallet away again when a sound behind her made her start.

It was Philip, one of the King's pages, standing in the middle of the room. He had come through the door to the King's bedchamber. How had he done that? The door should have been bolted!

Unless – somehow – he had already been in here and unbolted it himself.

'You are to come with me,' Philip said. 'He wants to speak with you.'

He? The King?

But wasn't he supposed to be in the meadow, riding with the Queen?

'Quickly,' the man said. 'No questions. And you are to tell no one.'

She rose and followed him through the forbidden door.

He was waiting for her in the Privy Council chamber. He was dressed in riding gear, pacing to and fro, impatient. He must know he was late for his meeting with the Queen.

Two other men were with him. The Baron of Lackmere stood at the hearth, glowering into the cold ashes. Padry, the lord chancellor, sat on a stool against the wall. There was not even a guard at the outer door. Philip left. His footsteps faded down the passage. She was alone with the three men who between them held the reins of the Kingdom.

'Thank you for coming, Melissa,' said Ambrose. It was the first time he had spoken to her directly since they had come to Tuscolo. She curtseyed, as a good little serving maid should.

'I have to ask you some questions, Melissa. I'm sorry about this, but I must. And I have to ask you not to tell anyone that I have asked them. Not even the Queen. Do you understand me?'

'Yes, Your Majesty.'

'Thank you. You went with Her Majesty the Queen on her pilgrimage to Jent, did you not?'

'Yes, Your Majesty.' A horrible, dull feeling crept into Melissa's heart. That pilgrimage. She knew where this was going.

'Don't be afraid. You accompanied the Queen all through the journey, did you not? You know whom she met and what she did?'

Whom she met. Yes.

'Yes, Your Majesty.'

'Did she meet with anyone on the way?'

'Why yes, Your Majesty.'

'Who?'

Melissa hesitated. 'There was – there was an abbot and his followers. He was also going to Jent, and the

358

Queen let him join our party for safety. There was my Lady Faul, who—'

'Early in the journey. At the manor of Haventry.'

She looked into his eyes.

'Did she meet with anyone at Haventry?' the King insisted gently.

She could have reached out and touched his cheek, run her fingers through the short hairs of his beard, whispered to him: Don't be sad. You mustn't be sad. (*Did she meet with anyone at Haventry?*)

'No, Your Majesty,' she said, and her heart thumped once, like a knock at a hollow door.

'You spent the night there, but the lord was not present?'

'He was not, Your Majesty.'

The King sighed. 'Thank you, Melissa. You have helped me greatly. And I am glad – more glad than I can say – that it is you of all people who looks after the Queen. I haven't forgotten that I have promised you a favour, should you ever ask for it. You must not forget it either.'

'No, Your Majesty.'

'You may go.'

She curtseyed and slunk out of the chamber. She felt like a whipped dog.

He didn't want me to tell him, she said to herself. She said it over and over as she made her way down the empty corridor.

It was there in his eyes. He did not want me to tell him.

He did not want me to say what she did.

XXIV

Love's Last Stand

un, Baron of Lackmere, jerked himself away from the cold hearth.

'Well, what else was she going to say?' he growled. 'Next time, let me do the asking. Then we'll get at the truth soon enough.'

'Gueronius was not at Haventry,' said Ambrose.

'No? But he left his castle at Appleton, which is a day's journey away, a day before Her Majesty turns aside from her route with a small escort to see Haventry, which is a place of no especial interest except that it is one of the manors of Gueronius. And on her return from her pilgrimage nothing will do but that she must plan another, this time to Luckingham, which is a shrine of no great importance but lies close to another of Gueronius's manors. And I ask: Why this sudden delight in pilgrimage?'

Ambrose made a sudden, angry gesture. 'You've never understood her! You don't *want* to understand her, Aun! What do you think it's like, living with nightmares like that? Nightmares? That hardly begins to—'

'I remember being woken, up here in the castle, by

screaming from below the walls,' said Padry. 'I lay wondering who it was that was torturing an animal. In the morning I found that it had come from the convent, and that it had been her.'

'I used to be able to go to her,' Ambrose said sombrely. 'I could stand beside her and tell her to turn and face the one she feared. I'm still sure that was right. If she could only face it and speak to it, she could begin to control it. But then I brought her here, became King for her, and we made her do that act of submission. I made myself a part of the thing that is her enemy. Aun, it was I who suggested that she seek the Angels and the shrines. If I can't be a comfort to her any more, I pray that at least they can. And now I must go to her, because she is waiting in the meadows for me. I hope she never learns that I tricked her this morning in order to talk with Melissa, because that will only make it worse still—' He turned for the door.

'Stop,' said Aun. 'I haven't finished yet.'

The King halted.

'Maybe she *is* doing what you told her,' said Aun. 'Had you thought of that?'

Ambrose glared at him. 'What do you mean?'

'I mean that you had better sit down and think damned hard about this. The one thing I couldn't work out was why she would dally with Gueronius of all people. When I fear someone, I run from them. Or I work to destroy them. But that's not what you told her to do. *You* told her to take control of him. That's what she's up to – believe it. The second thing is, a husband can choose to shut his eyes to what his wife is doing. A king

361

can't. Too many of us depend on you. And if Gueronius is in it, then it's not just cuckoldry, it's treason. *And* he's still building those cannon-things of his—'

'Aun. Let me tell you I *don't* believe it.'

'Don't you? Others do. Whispers are already starting. How do you think I heard about it?'

Ambrose took a long breath. 'Padry?' he said.

'Your Majesty, I had not heard it before now,' sighed Padry. 'But – if there are rumours, then yes, we must consider it carefully.'

And objectively. And how were any of them to do that?

'I don't believe it,' muttered Ambrose.

'Then you must find out,' said Aun.

'I just have!' Ambrose waved his hand at the door through which Melissa had disappeared.

'Have you? Bring the girl back and put her on the rack and then see what she—'

'No!'

'No, I wouldn't want to do that either. Not to her. But any of the Queen's other attendants—'

'No!'

'All right then,' said the baron grimly. 'You'll shut your eyes to what she's done. You'll give her one more chance – and that girl has let you do it. But from now on you must watch to see what your Queen does next. Watch with both eyes open. Put a spy in her—'

'No, Aun!'

The two men glared at each other.

'She's my wife,' said Ambrose. 'I will not have a spy set on her.'

'She's your wife,' said Aun. 'It is your right to know what she does.'

'I'm going to trust her. That's my right, too. It's not my fault that you don't. You talk to me about what's in her head. What about yours? Why can't you trust, ever?'

'Trust, is it?' growled Aun. 'I know how this bit of the talk goes. In a moment it'll be about forgiving, too. I always know I've got you in a corner when you talk to me about forgiving.'

'I hadn't been going to,' said Ambrose coldly. 'But perhaps it's not a bad idea. And that reminds me. Padry, I think we need a marshal in the south. To watch over the southern frontiers, and organize an armed force if the wild men ever raid in strength. Why not the son of our baron here? What do you say?'

Aun scowled.

'Your Majesty will know that I do not love the man myself,' said Padry carefully. 'Although I admit that he has discharged such offices as you have already granted him with reasonable purpose and honesty . . .'

'Draft me a letter to him, laying out the necessary rights and duties. Baron, your son will be a great man. You should be proud . . .'

'I will do as you wish, Your Majesty,' said Padry. '*But*' – and he fixed the King with his eye – 'but I believe we stray from the matter in hand.'

The King looked from one adviser to the other. He turned away. He paced slowly to the hearth and faced them again. His back was to the dead fire.

'I have the right to love her,' he said. 'King or not, I love her. That is my first law. Everything else can follow in its place. I will believe in her, even if all the world doubts her.'

They looked at him and he looked back. The wind moaned in the chimney.

A year ago, thought Padry, he would have spoken three words and settled it. Not now. His confidence had been eaten away. There was a frailty in his defiance that invited contradiction. Did he know? Did he understand what had happened to him? Perhaps he did. Perhaps he knew that he was blinding himself. But he was still doing it. Still the young man would lean on his love and tell himself that she was true.

And it was Thomas Padry who must play the corrupter.

'Your Majesty,' he said. 'You may believe if the world doubts. But can you save if the world is betrayed?'

'What do you mean?'

'The world we know depends upon you. Some good it has already had from you. But for the most part it still waits. What of the children in the furrows? We were to have the Church take up their schooling, but on that we have hardly begun. What of the poor? What of Outland? If we believe, and our belief is misplaced, your rule will fall. Your people will wait in vain. More, they will suffer with us. Do we have a right to condemn them?'

'I am not condemning anybody – of treason, or any-thing else.'

'We are not advising you to condemn. We are saying

only that you should find out the truth. And that if you do *not* find out the truth – then yes, the Kingdom may indeed be condemned with you.'

The King looked at him.

'What case can be made for blindness?' Padry coaxed. 'Only look for the truth. After, if you will, you may love her as she is. Not as you wish her to be.'

(Oh, honeyed words, Thomas Padry! If treason were proved, what would be left to love? But that thought must not be spoken – not yet. A wrong word would tip the balance irrevocably.)

The King was still looking at him. There was something desperate in the young man's eye. Something there was begging him to speak again – to postpone the choice that must be made.

Padry closed his mouth and waited. The King looked down at his feet.

'All right,' he groaned at last. 'What do you want me to do?'

'Find out!' said Aun, surging into the breach that Padry had made. 'Next month, when she goes to Luckingham.'

'No spies,' said Ambrose. 'I believe she's innocent, and an innocent woman has a right to her privacy.'

'Even from her husband?'

'Well, if I go with her . . .' said Ambrose, grinning mirthlessly.

'No, don't do that. But if that's the way you want it, you could watch her on the night in question. Just have one of your princes show her to you—'

'No!'

'Why not? You're always telling me that their witch-craft is no more evil than many of the things we do.'

'I said no spies,' said Ambrose thickly. 'The fact that a spy is a prince doesn't mean that he isn't a spy. If I had the Cup it would be different, but—'

'We could get it for you.'

'Mother would not let us have it.'

'How do you know that? It was you who gave it to her. I was there by the pool on the day that Paigan died. Do you think I've forgotten?'

Ambrose looked helplessly at Padry. 'Thomas?'

Padry, too, felt helpless. Every way seemed closed. He could not see the Path.

'I would counsel any course other than witchcraft,' he said slowly. 'Every time we resort to it, we risk a scandal as bad as or worse than any cuckoldry. But scandal is not treason. If we fear treason, we *must* find out whether or not it is true. Therefore, if Your Majesty will not consent to other means . . . I think we will have to do as the baron suggests.'

'Very well,' Ambrose sighed. 'If you bring it to me, I will look. But I will look alone.'

XXV

Padry's Quest

emini was a trading town, set on an island in a long river lake a dozen leagues downstream from Tuscolo. The island was joined to the lakeside by a causeway, part natural and part man-made, and in the pool below the causeway were many rivercraft. Padry could see their masts as the barge he travelled in approached the town from the southern, upstream side. It was the sight everyone spoke of when they first came to Pemini: the 'leafless wood' clinging to the side of the island, with all the hulls out of view behind the causeway so that the masts looked like trees indeed. And you could tell the fortune of Pemini, they said, by how far the wood spread around the shore.

Padry, born a Pemini man, felt a strange mix of emotions as the boat neared the town. He wanted to swallow, even to wipe his eye, as the familiar shapes of the roofs and steeples rose from his memory. No doubt all men who had made good felt such things when they came back to the squalid places of their childhood, he thought, but it was curious all the same.

Yes, curious. There was a definite lump in his throat. And the 'wood' had spread indeed – there must have been sixty, maybe even a hundred masts in the pool. It looked, too, as though they were rebuilding the old Church of the Martyrs, which had stood ruined since the city was sacked twenty years before. And wasn't that new bronze on the roof of the guildhall? The town was enjoying good times. And so it should, after all their King and his chancellor had done for traders these past few years!

The barge passed the squat light-tower at the downstream tip of the island, and changed course to work its way back up into the pool. Now they were out of the river current and the going was slower. But the crewmen were nearing their pay and a night in port, and they sang as they pulled on the long oars.

'*South wind, sweeping the waters,*' they bellowed in a mix of voices. '*Shaking the sails above . . .*

'*South wind, sweeping the waters,*
Take me back to my love.'

And singing, they brought their cargo home.

He climbed onto the wharf and looked about him. All along the harbour front the houses of merchants showed new paint and new friezes, even busts and carvings on new porches. There was a new customs house, almost filling the eastern end of the wharf. In the crowds around it Padry glimpsed a number of men in Outland costume. Snatches of Outland talk came to his ear. A long Outland vessel lay in the harbour, with men stripped to the waist stowing bundles of skins under oiled canvas. They worked unselfconsciously, as if they already belonged there, and the down-to-earth, profit-minded Pemini folk hurried past and gave them barely a second look, for they were used to Outlanders now. Behind the harbour front the narrow alleys ran gently uphill, reeking of slop and tumbledown dwellings and ringing with the sound of raucous children. Some things had not changed at all.

In a street near the southern wharf stood the new almshouses, which the merchants of Pemini had raised by public subscription. Here Padry came with the half-dozen young squires who had escorted him from Tuscolo. He knocked at the porter's door, in the archway to the street, but there was no answer. The door was not fast, so they entered and looked around at the low houses, which were arranged in a small square with a garden of paved walkways and a circular pool in the middle. There were a few people in the doorways: the poor and infirm of Pemini who were allowed to live here. Padry caught one, an elderly woman, as she hobbled past.

'The porter who works here,' he said, 'where is he?'

The woman stared at him: a wrinkled, toothless face that was frightened because it would always be frightened. He had to repeat his question.

'Porter? 'S him,' she mumbled, pointing a skinny finger across the square.

There was a man there, dressed in rough brown. He was on his hands and knees, teasing weeds from between the paving stones with his fingers. He did not look up as Padry approached. His shoulders were broad and the back of his head and neck seemed very broad, too. Padry could see the yellow flesh gathered in folds between his skull .and spine. The head was hairless and very smooth. It gleamed in the late sun. But there was nothing now to suggest that the man before him was anything other than a man.

Padry crouched down beside him and said in a low voice, 'Highness?'

The man stopped weeding and looked at him. He frowned. 'I remember you,' he said. His voice was low and hoarse, but still a man's. 'I do not recall your name.'

'Thomas Padry, the chancellor, Your Highness. We last met in Tuscolo.'

The frown deepened. 'So. But let us not use titles. You are Thomas, I am Rolfe. You have come from – from my great-nephew, I suppose.'

'Yes.'

'What does he want this time?'

'Your help.'

'Does he ask or command?'

'He commands.'

'Very well.' Slowly the man climbed to his feet. At his full height he came to Padry's shoulder and his barrel of a body had a pronounced stoop. And still he seemed to be nothing other than a man now. 'Is it kidnap again?'

'No. It is a journey, to the mountains.'

'For what purpose?'

'You are to ask the mother of the King for the Cup

that she keeps. And you must ask it in the King's name. Then you must return with it to Tuscolo.'

The prince frowned. 'I would prefer even kidnap to this,' he said.

'Nevertheless you are to ask for it and to return with it.'

'May I say for what purpose the King requires it?'

'No.'

'And you came to me because of all my brothers I am the closest to Tuscolo?'

'Yes.'

'My misfortune. But the King has also commanded me to serve. I serve the city of Pemini, and through them I serve Pemini's poor. I may not leave my post here at a whim.'

'It is no whim but a command, and it overrides the command you have been given. Direct me to the city officer responsible and I will secure your release.'

The officer in question could not be above the rank of alderman, after all. This would be the cheapest bribe Padry had paid in years.

The ancient prince nodded and wiped his nose on his sleeve. He looked around at the court. 'She does not let me forget, you see,' he said.

The court was newly built: a square of house-fronts constructed from good stone, whitewashed and capped with orange tiles. And yet something about it teased at Padry's memory. It was not the houses themselves but the shape and scale to which the thing had been built, and the pool of water in the middle . . .

There should be columns, Padry thought suddenly.

The houses should have a colonnade along the front of them. He felt it very strongly, although it was surely unusual for separate house-fronts, even in an institution like this, to be united with a colonnade. And the pool . . . It should not be a pool, really. It should be a fountain, even though . . .

And then it would look exactly like the little fountain courts in Tuscolo, and in Velis, Tarceny, Ferroux – all the places where the first princes had made their strongholds.

He looked sharply at the man beside him.

Rolfe rubbed his face with his sleeve again.

'When I came here, the building had already begun. The alderman thought the design was his own. He was pleased with it. I was able to persuade him that at least there should be no fountain, or he must pay for an ass and a man to watch it in order to drive the pump all day. But water there had to be, and instead of the Cup I must have the Pool. She does not forget, nor does she mean me to forget, until the day she or I depart.'

'I see,' said Padry guardedly. *She* must mean the weeping goddess. Strange how easy it had been, with all the busy doings of his days, to put her out of his mind! And yet she would still be there, in that other world which was an echo of this one, weeping and weeping for a child who had been lost to a cruel hand. And because of her, and despite all the King did and all that Thomas Padry did to help him, men still dreamed dreams. They remembered, deep in themselves, what had been done. And they acted upon it.

He felt suddenly cold, as if a chilly wind had breathed upon his neck.

'How is little Melissa?' asked Rolfe suddenly. 'Is she happy?'

'As to that,' said Padry, 'I hardly see her—'

He got no further. Something whipped past his shoulder and struck the prince full in the face. Rolfe flailed and fell. There was a splash as he hit the water, and cries from the gateway behind him. The men around Padry yelled. Metal rasped from scabbards. They charged, still yelling, at the gate. There was no one there.

'This way!' cried one. 'They went down the street. Follow me!'

He vanished through the arch, yelling, '*Murder, Murder!*' Others ran after him. Padry stood frozen to the spot. The pool at his feet was discoloured. Dark liquid was mingling with the water. Could it be blood? The body of Rolfe was moving feebly where it lay just below the surface.

No, it was not moving. It was the after-currents of his fall into the pool that made the arm wander so. Padry could see the eyes. They were open, staring up at the world from under the water. Under the water, where he had lived these three hundred years. And that dark thing attached to the side of the head, where the tendrils of blood wavered like smoke, was the butt of a bolt from a crossbow.

One foot protruded from the pool, caught by the heel of its sandal on the lip of the stone paving. The wrinkled flesh, tanned above, pale below;

the stitching in the leather; the way the sole was bent almost double against the stone by the weight of the limb dragging upon it: every detail of that foot wrote itself into Padry's shocked brain.

'I didn't think they could die,' he muttered aloud.

'Plainly they do, though,' said someone beside him.

It was Taxis, one of his men: a young squire from near Develin, hand-picked by Baron Lackmere for this mission. In the gateway loitered his brother, Tamian, peering out into the street from which the sounds of a crowd in pursuit came ever more faintly to the ear.

'This is a mess, isn't it?' said Taxis, musing over the dead man in the pool.

A *mess*? How could he be so . . .? A moment ago Padry had been discharging his orders, giving his message, arming the King with the powers he needed. And now?

Now a man was dead. A man who had been more than a man, dead from the trivial little punch of an iron-tipped bolt and—

'What do we do now?' asked Taxis.

'Do?' repeated Padry. His lips were numb.

But slowly his shocked mind gathered itself. What now? A door had been slammed shut in their faces. The mountains were a week away. The nearest of the surviving princes was – well, Talifer was all the way in the south, near Lackmere. Of all of them he was the only one now whom Padry felt he could approach and reason with as though he were fully a man.

There was not time! Not if they were to be back in

Tuscolo, with the Cup, while the Queen was on pilgrimage!

Why had this happened?

From the doorways and windows of the almshouse court, faces stared at him. The place was so quiet that the clink of Tamian's armour sounded clearly as he strolled over to join them.

'Who was it?' asked Taxis.

'Crossbowman,' said Tamian. 'Maybe more than one, although only one bolt was fired. I didn't see them clearly. But Cravaine did. He was out and after them right away. The hue and cry's up. Whoever it was won't get far.'

Padry stared at the body in the pool, still wrestling with what had happened. The words of the squires persisted in his ears.

'Cravaine saw them?'

'What's the matter?'

'Just this. Why aren't we all taking cover?'

Taking cover? thought Padry.

'Because Cravaine got after them right away.'

'Yes. But how did he know there weren't others – on rooftops, behind windows . . .'

'Maybe they followed us and didn't have time—'

'Yes, but how did he *know*?'

'Well, if they catch the fellow—'

'*If* they catch him.'

'Why shouldn't they?' demanded Padry, rousing himself. 'You said your friend was on his heels!'

'Not my friend,' said Taxis. 'And that's the point. This mission we are on – it's about the Queen, isn't it?'

'What if it is?' said Padry warily.

'Just this. Cravaine's a Queen's man. Oh, he's a southerner, right enough, like Tamian and me. He came to Tuscolo at the same time as we did. No doubt that's why he was picked for this. But he became a Queen's man within a month of arriving. Just one look she gave him and that was all it took. I saw it happen.'

Tamian was nodding in agreement.

'And he was after them quick, wasn't he? So quick, in fact, that he might have been expecting this. I don't know who fired the bolt. But if it had been me, in a strange town and all, I'd have been a lot happier if I knew there was someone there to lead the pursuit in the wrong direction . . . Maybe I'm wrong. Maybe they'll be back in a moment with whoever it was by the collar. But if they aren't, then we have some thinking to do. And we'll have to do it quickly.'

Padry opened his mouth and shut it. His world had turned inside out. He had thought himself safe, guarded, secret. It had never occurred to him that there might be any danger in this mission. Now suddenly he was blind. A hidden enemy had struck without warning. He might strike again. They knew where he was. Windows, doorways – any patch of shadow might hide a knife or a crossbow. Why hadn't he taken cover? He had been standing here in the open, too stupefied even to think that there might be other attackers!

Someone had betrayed him.

Who?

He had no answer.

He looked down at Rolfe's foot. That mute, obscene limb, at once so meaningless and so pitiful! Three hundred years the man had lived – almost as long as recorded history! He had been released from a hell on earth, found himself, was starting anew – Angels alone could understand what a journey had been travelled in the man's mind! And now the mind had been smashed, the Path cut, the light denied – *for a woman's smile*!

He stood at the poolside and shook with his own anger.

'They're taking their time, aren't they?' said Tamian.

'Believe me now, do you?' said Taxis.

Padry clenched his fists. 'We're going on,' he hissed. 'We'll go the long way, under the sun.'

He would be late, probably too late. But he would get there. They would not stop him, the damned, treacherous, murdering . . . He would get the Cup, and bring it back. He would show them how *vain* and *wasteful* was the thing they had done here!

'You think we can do it?' asked Taxis.

'I know the way. I've been there before.'

'Then we had better start now.'

'I want to bury him—'

'*Now*, master. Before they find we've given them the slip.'

Atti emerged from the throne hall into the sunlight of the fountain court, and Melissa carried her train. They walked slowly, because the way was crowded with young men with brightly painted faces, in brightly coloured tunics and hose, bowing and smiling as they always did, and pushing each other with their shoulders to keep their places before the Queen even as they backed from her path.

'Your Majesty,' said one, waving a feathered blue-velvet cap before his knees, 'I beg you – have you yet thought who might be your escort to Luckingham?'

'Why, no,' said Atti. 'There is time yet, surely.'

'It is but a fortnight away, Your Majesty.'

'Time enough. Indeed I am not sure I shall go at all. Travel wearies me so.'

'I beg you, Your Majesty! Have pity on those who wait to know if they are to have the joy and honour of guarding you—'

'And reckon on those who have shown themselves most true,' broke in a gallant in red, bowing and waving even more than the one in blue.

'Why, sir,' said the Queen, 'how am I to know who is most true? Since you all say the same, act the same, dress the same, aye, and even sing the same – how am I to tell one of you from another?'

'Your Majesty jests! You know me well enough, I think.'

'What, sir,' said the Queen lightly, 'have we spoken before?'

'Most recently – of a matter in Pemini, Your Majesty,' insisted the young knight.

The Queen stopped and looked at him. Melissa could not see her face, but from her tone she thought that Atti might be frowning.

'I may recall it,' she said. 'I believe I do, indeed. What of it?'

'The matter is dealt with,' said the young man in red proudly and bowed again.

'Fully dealt with, sir?'

'The main matter, yes. A rat or two has slipped beyond our reach for the moment, but I have friends who shall see to them as swiftly as may be.'

'Let them see to it indeed. There must always be rats in our realm, I suppose. But I would that they troubled us as little as possible.'

She turned away. As she did so a pale silk handkerchief seemed to slip from her hand and flutter to the paving. Immediately three or four of the young men jumped for it. The red knight was the nearest and was the winner.

'Your Majesty,' he cried, presenting the handkerchief for her attention.

The Queen turned back, looked at it and sighed. 'Truly, I believe the gardeners should be beaten for their laziness. See how filthy it has become! No, I do not want it, Sir Cravaine. Do with it as you will.'

With a broad grin of triumph, the red knight bowed again. As the Queen moved on, Melissa glimpsed him among the crowd, tying the square of silk to his sleeve.

By the fountain a chair had been set. A group of musicians waited there to play. They were 'Lo-di-lay' singers, a new fashion from Outland. They wore black hose and doublets, and great black cloths bound around their heads, with their faces painted white and their lips painted black. They would play and sing their mournful ballads, interspersed with long choruses in which there were no words but a constant, meaningless lolling of the tongues that was now much admired. The Queen settled herself in the chair. Melissa began to arrange her train over one arm of it so that the end did not trail in the dust.

'It is a beautiful day,' said Atti, looking up at the sky.

Suddenly she smiled one of her rare smiles. 'I believe I am a faintheart and a weakling. We shall go to Luckingham after all.'

Melissa's heart sank. For a moment her hand paused as she tucked the silken folds around her mistress. She wanted to hiss at her: *Do you think that's going to make it better? What's the difference, him rather than the King? Don't you end up hating anyone close to you?*

She clenched her teeth and bit it all back. But she could not help muttering: 'You be careful now.'

Nothing changed on the Queen's face, although she must have heard. She clapped her hands for the music to begin.

Padry sat on a ridge of rocks and thorns, resting in the midday heat. There was little shade here, but he had struggled up the hillside in the wake of his two companions to look back the way they had come.

They were on the very edge of the Kingdom, in the north of the March of Tarceny. They had passed the old keep of Hayley that morning by the side of the stream. They had followed the path up from the streamside to enter a narrow, low-sided valley where the thorns grew down close to the path on both sides. Beyond the head of the valley were the first of the true mountains.

'. . . Just as the essence of the first arc,' Padry was saying, 'is the Descent of the spark of Godhead from Heaven through all the forms of Creation, so the essence of the second arc is the *Ascent*. The same spark, buried in the human soul, yearns to be free of Creation and to rejoin itself with the Godhead. In the Descent the Path begins with Fire, which is the sign of Godhead (and also of the Angels), and the Sun (which is the sign of Kingship), through various forms down to the Abyss – the lowest that it is possible for the spirit to fall. From there the second arc—'

'Stop a moment, master,' said Tamian. 'The Angels are part of this, aren't they?'

'Yes, of course. I should say that when one meets with light at any point on the Path, one has met an Angel in one form or another—'

'So as long as I believe in the Angels, will I not find the way?'

'That depends on what you mean by *belief*,' said Padry, who was enjoying being a teacher again. 'A man who believes in the Angels may yet be slave to all his own desires. Perhaps he even tells himself, as he pursues his desires, that he is doing the will of the Angels. Yet when, at his life's end, he looks over the shoulder of Umbriel and sees what the great Angel has written on his page, every deed he has done in his belief will cry against him. Whereas one who has never heard of the Angels may yet be lifted, blindly, by the spark of the Godhead in him—'

'There,' said Taxis. 'Didn't I say so?'

Padry paused, wondering in what way he could have repeated something that Taxis had said. Then he realized that Taxis had not been listening. He had been looking back the way they had come. Now he was pointing.

Padry got to his feet for a better view.

For a moment he saw nothing. The rugged woods of the March lay under the sun and hard blue sky. Barely a branch was stirring. There was a little haze above where the stream must lie . . .

No, not haze. Dust.

Dust, kicked from the track they had travelled that morning. And by more than a donkey or cart, from the look of it . . .

Sunlight flashed through the trees. Sunlight on metal.

'Didn't I say?' repeated Taxis. 'Three times we've given them the slip. Three times they've come up with us again. They *know* where we are going.'

'Damn it!' hissed Tamian. 'I'd like to twist the head off whoever told them. Do you think it was that old fellow at the hamlet?'

'No. No, I don't.'

No, thought Padry. They knew we were in Pemini. They knew, when they chased us round the head of the lake, where we were going from there. To have followed us into the empty March like this, towards the hills, they must know exactly where we mean to go, and why.

'The Queen has told them,' he said.

She had passed the sentence of death on them. She was not nineteen years old, and yet she had done this.

'Ah. And how did she know?'

She knew they were coming for the Cup. How?

Who had betrayed them?

There had been only three people in the room when that had been discussed. Himself. Lackmere. And the King. The servants had left. The guard had been placed halfway down the corridor.

Could it have been Lackmere? He was the one who had raised the whole question of the Queen's faithfulness. Could this be a ploy to get rid of the one man who was the only serious rival for the King's ear? Michael and Umbriel! He had never liked the baron, but . . .

No. This was treason against the King. Whatever Lackmere thought of Padry, he was dog-loyal. And about as talkative as flints. That left only one.

'It'll have been the King himself, won't it?' said Taxis quietly.

Padry nodded slowly.

'He will have tried to warn her,' he said. 'When they went riding, maybe. He will have dropped hints. She will have guessed the rest.'

He would have tried to warn her, knowing of her treachery and yet not wanting to believe it. And heedless of the lives he was putting into danger: Rolfe, staring up at the sky from beneath the pool, Taxis and Tamian, and poor, fat, faithful Thomas Padry, who after a week of hard travel must himself stare up at the sky on a thorny hillside with his blood spilling over the stones around him.

'Damn it!' cursed Tamian again. 'And damn all husbands!'

The thorns wavered. The hillsides did not answer.

'All right,' said Taxis. 'The situation as I see it is this. We've one good horse, one that's going lame, and one that will be spent before sunset. If we stick to the track they will catch us – unless all their mounts are about to fall over, too, which I doubt. If we go to ground, they will get ahead of us. And they know where we are going, so if they don't jump us on the way they will be waiting for us when we get there. So—' He stopped, pulling at his chin.

'My bowstring caught the damp this morning,' said Tamian.

'I've two. And if you look at this place . . .' He waved his hand at the thickly covered slopes with the narrow path threading its way up between them.

'Where they come up through the bushes above the stream . . .'

'Let two or three come out into full view . . .'

'Not more than that, or they'll be more than we can handle. And shoot for the horses first.'

'You think we can fight them?' gasped Padry.

'Not you, master. You'll take Tamian's horse and head over that hill as fast as you know how.'

Padry stared at them. They wanted him to take the good horse, and . . .

How many enemies were approaching? Twenty? Forty? As soon as the surprise of the ambush was over . . .

'You know the way, after all,' said Taxis mildly.

He knew the way. And what use would he be in a fight? A fight, however gallant, would be a failure if the mission failed. Yes, of course. But – but to *leave* them here . . .

'We had better be quick,' said Tamian. 'With any luck they will make a midday halt before they leave the stream. But we can't be sure.'

Taxis was already wading back down through the thorns to where they had left their horses.

In a daze Padry followed them. Half his mind was protesting, the other half begging him to listen – to listen to any reason that would preserve his life if only he could swallow his pride. Think what a fool you would feel if you stayed, he told himself – you, clutching some borrowed axe or sword in the thorns and waiting for the enemy to find you and cut you down. Think of the mission, the Cup, the King! Don't think of these boys, who will stake themselves out for the crows to let you get away.

'You'll need water,' said Taxis. 'Better shift the skins across.'

They unfastened the waterskins from the two unsound mounts and tied them to the saddle of the third. They kept none for themselves.

'What about—?' Padry began.

Taxis grinned at him. 'Oh, we'll cut our way down to the stream when we feel thirsty.'

'Strange place, when you look at it,' said Tamian, staring round at the hillsides. 'Nothing here. Doesn't feel right.'

As Padry, with Taxis's help, hauled himself up into the horse's saddle, he realized what Tamian meant. *Doesn't feel right to die here.*

'Someone's here before us, though,' Tamian added.

A little further along the valley, halfway up the left-hand slope where the thorns gave way to scree, there was a cairn of stones.

'Anyone under that, do you think?'

Padry stared at it. It was a low grey hummock, about three feet high at the point and long enough to hide the bones of a fallen man. Moss was growing on the sheltered side of it. Small thorns were sprouting among the apron of stones.

Distant recollections stirred.

'It may be a former pupil of mine,' he said. 'The man that the Lady Develin mourns. He was killed in these hills some years ago.'

Tamian scratched his head. 'Not much luck, these pupils of yours, have they?'

'Sometimes I think we're all cursed,' said Taxis.

Padry opened his mouth to protest. Then he shut it again.

Tamian was patting his horse, a big brown animal, easily the best of the three that they had bought hastily in the market at Pemini. 'So, my friend,' he said to it. 'You carry this man for me. Understand? Go, then.' He turned its head up the valley. Obediently the animal began to pick its way on along the stony track. The other horses whickered uncertainly.

'Now, master,' said Taxis, pacing quickly beside

him. 'It's hot, but you keep going, understand? That horse will be good for a while. If you keep him at it he will save you. Don't stop until you've shade and can see a long way behind. And if you see anything behind, do not stop at all.'

'Michael guard you,' said Padry. He could not think what else to say.

'And Raphael on your way,' said Taxis, and turned back.

As he passed below the cairn, Padry looked behind him. Tamian was coaxing the other horses into hiding by some tall thorns. Taxis, crossbow in hand, was making his way back up through the thorns towards their first vantage point. The enemy still had not appeared at the foot of the valley.

A few minutes later the track crossed a ridge. Now he could hear nothing and see nothing of what passed in the valley he had left.

The horse carried him on steadily. The path was before him, plain, and half remembered from his journey this way four years before. He looked back constantly, but nothing appeared on the path behind him. Hours passed. He did not stop until it was too dark to see.

A week later, he and his horse came to the house among the mountains. There was no one there.

XXVI

The Fall of the Leaf

n the far side of the ridge from the track, in a hollow of the mountainside, was the pool. It was almost perfectly circular, surrounded by cliffs that on the up-hill side fell nearly fifty feet to the apron of rock around the water. The cliffs were crowned by a ring of pale standing stones. But the ring was broken. Three or four of the stones lay fallen at the top of the cliff. Another had tumbled all the way down to the water's edge. All the pool and the cliffs around it were in deep shadow. The sun had long set over the ridge-top, although it still glowed in glory on the great head and shoulders of the mountain opposite. The air was cold.

Here Padry came some hours after his arrival. He was still searching for signs of Ambrose's mother. He had known that there was some such place as this, near the house and yet hidden from the eye. This was where she sat, day after day, calling the names of ancient princes over the still surface. Here, as Padry understood it, the last and eldest of them, Dieter, was still imprisoned below the water. Here, surely, she would be. But she was not.

He called: '*Phaedra! My Lady Phaedra!*' His voice bounced among the rocks. Only silence answered him.

In desperation he even called '*Dieter! Your Highness!*' over the pool, although he had no idea what he would have done if that ancient prince had somehow heard him and responded.

Nothing moved.

Bone weary, he settled himself against the great white standing stone that stood at the lowest point of the cliffs on the downhill side of the pool. The stone, he could feel, was covered with lines and whorls that must have been carved by men in some forgotten time. He had no idea if they had meaning, or if so what it might be. He had no idea what to do.

He was already too late. The Queen would have set out for Luckingham by now. She might even be there. Everything had depended upon finding the King's mother before that happened. He had not even considered the possibility that he might fail to find her at all.

If she was wandering the hills, she might return. If she returned to the house, she would find the horse, watered and resting, and she would know someone had come. And if she came here, he would be waiting.

But he could not wait for ever. His supplies, such as they were, were in the saddlebags of the horse still. And sometime, perhaps tomorrow, perhaps another day, the pursuit might finally appear and catch him here.

And what if she knew he had come, but had decided to hide herself? She was as enchanted as any of the princes. Or what if she had simply gone away? Or been killed, even? If a prince such as Rolfe could die at the hands of men, might not she?

He did not know what to do. So he wrapped his cloak around himself and rested while the shadows deepened in the valley behind him and the glow on the mountain shrank towards the peak. He let his eyes linger on it – the last source of light that he could see. They followed the curve of its shoulders, up to the round-headed summit.

From this angle, he thought, they might have been a head and shoulders indeed, a vast being, draped with some cloth or hood. Broad shoulders that slumped and a face bowed in some intolerable pain. How would a mountain weep?

The light was fading on the last snowfield. Soon it would be gone altogether. But he was tired and cold. Here was as good a place to rest as anywhere in this cheerless land.

He drifted in and out of a doze.

As he sat there with his mind asleep, yet with his body aware of the hard rocks pressing his seat and back, it seemed to him that the colours changed. The sky was dull and pale. The mountains were no longer mountains but vague swellings in the ground that might have been any height or distance. The rocks were brown.

The rocks were brown, and now he could feel – not hear, for it was too low for him to hear, but feel – the sound of the mountain weeping.

He could see her, the woman the size of a mountain, weeping for a lost child. He could feel that weeping in his heart – all the loss and pain and darkness of the world, on and on, dragging at him like weights that pulled him into deep water. And he struggled and tried to look away, and still the weeping and darkness was with him. It had been a part of him since the beginning of his life and of the world. He could feel all the betrayals, all the murder, all the misery of three hundred years, settling with the weight of a mountain on his soul. He struggled to look away and could not. He was drowning, slowly, crushed in that enormous anger and despair. *Let them eat their sons!*

Then, in his darkness, he realized that another voice was speaking.

It was not speaking to him, and he could not hear what it said. But he thought that there were words and that among the words were names. He knew there was someone else near him. It was as if he had been standing in a field at night, under all the blackness of Heaven, and had suddenly heard someone say something from not far away. And with that he felt the ground again, and distance had meaning, and the darkness was no longer supreme.

There was a woman, standing near the great weeping figure. She was speaking to it. She held one hand raised to it, as if she were asking for something. She was saying, *Please stop*, or *Please go away*, or *Please give me what you still keep* – something like that. Padry did not know how long she had been there, or for how long she had been speaking. He wondered why he had not seen her before.

And with that he shifted, half woke, and knew that he was sleeping on a mountainside and that he would be very stiff in the morning. He tried to find a better position.

Again he dreamed the dream. First, nothing but the monstrous creature, and the terrible darkness of her grief: then, as if she had always been there, the second woman speaking to her. And again he woke.

Perhaps it was the third time, or perhaps it was the thirty-third, when his bruised and weary body knew that the sky away eastwards was colouring with the dawn and his mind still watched the two figures away across that dull land, that he saw the goddess stir. He saw her head turn to the woman who addressed her. He saw half of her face, a glimpse of cold, pale beauty. And he heard her speak.

She spoke one bitter, weary sentence. Then she bowed her head again. And Padry knew that he had seen something that had never happened before.

When he opened his eyes the sun was rising before him. It was filling the bowl around the pool with light. He screwed up his face, and shifted. His limbs groaned from a night propped on rocks. The air was cold. There was a footstep on the stones beside him. He looked up into the face of Phaedra, the mother of the King.

He looked up and knew her. And yet she was so

changed that he thought it was an achievement to have recognized her. Her face was drawn, almost haggard. And although her skin was as smooth as he remembered, there was an age and dullness in her eyes that he had seen only in those who had just learned that the ones they loved were dead.

'When you see my son,' she said, 'tell him that she has said she will depart. And she has said that I will take her place.'

Painfully, he got to his feet and faced her. In her hands she held a waterskin and some dried biscuit. He recognized both. They had come from the saddlebags of his horse, on the other side of the ridge.

'I have brought your breakfast,' she said.

Tell him that I will take her place, thought Padry as he chewed carefully at the biscuit. The mountain-woman wept for her son, who had been murdered by Wulfram and his men.

Wulfram had been beyond her vengeance, dead before she could exert her power. Instead each of his sons had been trapped in the pit of her grief – in the round pool before him, circled with the great white stones. Now they were free, all but one. Her power was diminishing. She would depart.

And Phaedra would take her place. How? Why? In Phaedra's face, as she leaned over the pool, he saw the heaviness of her grief and fear. She would take that place because she, too, was to lose her child. Or so she thought.

'Dieter,' called Phaedra, softly over the pool.

And she might. There was treason in the air. A King who was blind to treason would pay with his life and the lives of many followers. Padry knew he must hurry.

He had now what he had come for. Against his knee rested the roughly cut stone cup that he had seen once before in her hands. He had tried it for weight, thinking of the long journey back to Tuscolo. And he had seen, as he held it in his hand, that in its stone and shape it was an echo of the fountains in the courts of the great houses of the Kingdom. And they in turn were echoes of that first cup from which Wulfram had made the woman of the Artaxalings drink her son's blood. The Cup was an echo, too, of the pit and pool by which they now waited, and of that land of brown rocks, surrounded by high mountains, which in turn was a dream of the world.

'Dieter,' said Phaedra.

He must hurry. And that meant that Phaedra must hurry. Dieter must hurry. Because, Angels willing, the last prince in the pool would be his guide back to Tuscolo. He would walk a long, dark day in the land of the brown rocks, and by nightfall, or shortly after, he would be in the King's castle with the Cup in his hands. Two weeks and three deaths coming. To return, just one dark passage for the soul.

'Dieter,' said Phaedra.

Nothing stirred. The sun had risen far enough to fall on the pool itself. The rocks of the cliff opposite danced with the reflections of light from its surface.

'Should I call him, too?' said Padry.

'You may try,' said Phaedra. 'She has released him

and he knows it. He should hear any voice that calls him now.'

'Dieter,' called Padry experimentally.

The light wavered on the rocks and made no sound.

'Dieter,' called Phaedra.

'Dieter,' called Padry again. And there tumbled into his mind a memory – a memory of calling a name, over and over, with a woman standing beside him and calling, too. And the smoke had hung thickly in the air, and light had flashed upon the shafts of arrows that tumbled from the sky. And across the court the child had heard them and had come walking towards them as the spent arrows fell around her.

'Dieter,' called Phaedra.

And Padry cried, 'Aha!'

Something was moving in the water. It had not troubled the surface yet, but there, where the water darkened and went deep – surely something had moved? There seemed to be a wavering shadow there, like a shapeless blanket or sheet floating below the surface. A long limb – or was it a tentacle? – showed dark against the pale rocks in the shallows. Bubbles rose.

'There he is,' said Phaedra. 'The last of them. He will lead you to Tuscolo. I will not follow you. But I will be watching. And when my son looks into the Cup, I will be as close as I can.'

Padry rose to his feet. He picked up the Cup and cradled it in his left arm. With his right he beckoned to the water.

'Dieter!' he commanded.

And the first son of Wulfram, monstrous, rose
bellowing from the pool.

'Leave us,' said Gueronius to his servants, once the
wine was poured.

They bowed, cleared the remains of the meal and
left the hall. Only three people remained: Gueronius,
at one end of the short trestle table; Atti at the other;
and Melissa, standing behind Atti's chair. The hall was
lit with many candles and the floor covered in fresh
rushes. On the walls and tables, and on all the
surfaces, were the blooms of many, many cut flowers,
swimming in bowls of water. The brightness of the
flowers had faded with the light beyond the windows
but their scents still hung in the air, mingling with the
flavours of meat and wine and the smouldering
hearth.

Gueronius wore blue and yellow, the colours of his
house. His face was painted Outland fashion in blue
and yellow, his hair was curled and oiled, and his dark
beard curled at the tips, too. The candlelight flashed
from the rings on his fingers and gleamed from his
eyes as he watched the woman at the far end of the
table.

Atti sat poised in her place. Her back did not touch
the wood of the chair and her lips did not touch the
goblet that she held before her. She wore pale silks –
so pale that they might almost have been pure white,
except for the faintest hint of green. She wore powder
but no paint. Her hair was tightly braided and decked
with jewels. Melissa had worked for hours on it that

morning, before the two of them, and a small escort, had made the short ride from their roadside quarters over to Gueronius's manor.

Gueronius let his eyes rest on Melissa.

'Your numbers are always few, Your Majesty,' he said. 'And yet I warrant they would guard you well, if you wished it.'

'There are those who are devoted to me,' said Atti simply. 'I am grateful for it.'

'Aye, and so am I! I would have none but the very best guards around you wherever you went – so long as you wished it.'

You want her to make me go, thought Melissa. *I know that. She knows it, too.* From beyond the hall door came the clink of armour as a guard paced by on his watch.

'The devotion of others is a great gift,' said Gueronius. 'And you are rich in it. I wonder if Your Majesty understands how rich you are. With enough of it, anything becomes possible.'

'Why, sir, how so?'

'Why? It is plain. Before there is law there must be power, and all laws bend to it. I have been King, Your Majesty. I know this. But devotion – let us call it love – is a power, too . . .'

'So it was once said to me,' murmured Atti.

'. . . It lives in all our songs and stories, and contests against wrong as though it were the most gallant knight of all. When we tell of its victory, we see that the truth of it is rewarded. Even when we tell of its defeat – for love may end in death, it is true – we say that it is justified, for no right is held greater than the power of love. We sing these songs and tell these stories because this is what our hearts tell us – even as the ink-stained finger writes another law for us lovelessly to obey.'

Atti, Atti, begged Melissa. *He only says it because he wants you. That's all his pretty words mean. You see it, don't you?*

'Is it not the one who wins the victory that afterwards sings the songs?' said Atti coolly.

Gueronius shook his head. 'Not always. Oh, I grant you, *The Tale of Kings* is a tissue of lies. I have been King, have I not? And so are many songs like it. But when we see a love that is true, that we all know in our hearts, then we will sing of it from our hearts and let the false victor eat the ashes of his victory.

'And,' he added, glancing at the fire, 'when men see a love that is true, and there is still the time and chance to take up iron for it – why should not Love be the victor? Why should not the law be rewritten, so that Love – which is the true King – be placed once more upon its throne? This is what I believe, and I believe it with all the fire of my soul. Yes. Love is more than law, more than iron, more than fire. Love is from Heaven itself, and so let us thank Heaven for it.'

Very slowly, Atti sipped at her wine. She looked down at the dark surface in her goblet and did not raise her eyes to the man opposite her.

Let him crawl, pleaded Melissa in her heart. *You like that. That's what you're here for, isn't it? But don't let him have what he wants.*

Play your games if you must. Make him wriggle on his belly for you. He'll do it. He'll crawl all round the floor and cover his hair with ash if you tell him to.

But don't, don't, don't give him what he wants. Not this time!

'Is Love more than law?' said Atti coolly.

'It must be!' cried Gueronius, and his fist hit the table. 'What is law but tyranny, if it is not given with Love? My lady, did one love me, I should set them in judgement over all I did. Yes, even if I were King again, and fount of all the law, I would set that one above me in judgement in my courts and over all my subjects. And I would have no fear, because the one that loves me could do me no harm.'

Again Atti sipped the wine. *In judgement in my courts.* She would like that. He had known she would like it and she knew that, too. Her eyelids were lowered, masking her face. The whisper of the fire, the clink of mail beyond the door, were like the voices of little devils in the quiet of the room.

'So thank Heaven that you are loved, Your Majesty,' said Gueronius. 'Thank Heaven for it, when you are on your knees before your shrine. And also ask, maybe, that Heaven guide you. For some choices that it sets before us we may make any day or every day of our lives. But some we must make once, and at once, or they may even be gone before we are aware of them.'

Melissa waited, helpless. Even to the last second she could not guess what Atti was going to do.

'Melissa,' said Atti, without taking her eyes from her cup. 'You may leave us now.'

Into the antechamber of the King Padry stumbled with the Cup in his hand. He swayed and might have

399

fallen if the King himself had not jumped up from his place to catch him by the arm. Padry's mind swam with visions of the brown rocks from which he had emerged. If he closed his eyes he could still see them, all around him, with the great wall of mountains rising in the distance and the two fires burning on the peaks where the dragon lay along the rim of the world. He could still see the loping, misshapen figure of the prince who had guided him, now beginning to shamble away across the dead landscape back to the hills where it might begin to learn to be a man. He could see them and at the same time he could see the face of the King before him, pale and alarmed, holding him in case he fell.

'Your Majesty,' he gasped.

He saw other things. The guards and servants, aghast at his sudden appearance. The Baron Lackmere, glaring up at him from where he sat; a small table with a board of chess pieces set upon it; a torch on the wall, flaring and sputtering by a black slit window that showed the night outside.

He lifted the Cup in both hands and pushed it towards the King.

'Your Majesty,' he said again.

The King stared down at it. 'Take it away,' he said hoarsely.

Padry shook his head and held it out to him again.

'Take it away,' said Ambrose. 'I don't want it.'

'Your Majesty, I beg you.'

He did not add: *You betrayed me.*

He did not say: *The Prince Rolfe has died to bring you this. Two good men have died. I have walked a day of darkness and nearly died myself.*

He only repeated: 'I beg you.'

Beyond the King the Baron Lackmere rose to his feet. He was watching Ambrose.

Slowly the King lifted his hands and took the Cup from Padry.

'Very well,' he said heavily. He drew breath. 'And I suppose . . . I suppose now is the time to look in it, if ever.'

'There are also messages from your mother.'

'Later,' said the King. He looked at both of them. 'Neither of you may follow me.'

He left them, passing into his own bedchamber. Padry heard the door bang shut behind them. He sank onto the nearest seat – the King's own stool. Across the room he heard the splash of liquid. Someone – a servant – was pouring something. Still the world of the brown rocks clung in his brain. He could lift his head and see, beyond the walls of the chamber, that dreary landscape stretching away in all directions, and the shape of the monstrous prince moving distantly among them.

'Here,' said the Baron Lackmere, putting some-thing down on the small table beside him. 'Wine. You need it.'

He will not want to look, thought Padry. He will think that he will not look into the Cup. He will decide that he prefers to trust her and that he will simply come out and tell us she is innocent. He will think that we will believe he has looked and seen that all is well.

He betrayed me. And yet – what do I feel? Not much. Just pity, perhaps. He is trapped now.

Padry bowed his head. The wine was at his elbow but he did not touch it. His eyes rested on the chessboard. They must have been playing, the two of them. The Baron and the King had been playing together while they waited for news. The King had been white. He had more pieces on the board. But black had taken the centre squares. His knights and rooks were dangerous.

Padry frowned at the board, trying to clear his head. Wispy images of the brown rocks still circled in his mind. He did not like this position. What could be done to strengthen it?

He will think that he will not look, Padry thought again. He will sit and wait, counting, perhaps reciting something to pass the time. He will watch the Cup sitting before him, waiting until enough time has passed and he can plausibly emerge to announce the Queen's innocence.

And his eye will rest on the Cup. And then he will think: Why not look, after all? He is a man. She is his wife. Why *not* look – not because his servants demand it, but because he *can*?

And then . . .

There was no way out of this position. The white pieces pointed aimlessly. The power of black was concentrating against the King. There would have to be a sacrifice to gain time. The Queen? Only as a last resort. But perhaps it was coming to the last resort.

There had to be a sacrifice. There must always be a sacrifice, if Heaven were to be appeased. And now . . .

A cry shook the next room. A cry of rage and despair from beyond the door. And a crash of stone breaking!

Padry gasped and clutched the table. The pieces scattered and spilled. For a moment it had seemed to him that the whole world had shaken. He had seen it – the brown rocks, rolling and tumbling. He had seen the monster-prince fall to the ground as if stunned by a giant blow. He had felt the earth groan in his very bowels. He could still feel it – a long roar of rocks lifting, and a noise like a thousand far-off thunders as the dragon of the world took the strain.

He blinked. He was in the chamber. Nothing had changed. The chessboard was upset but he had done that himself. The torches burned steadily in the brackets. Their flames had not even flickered. There was no sign in this world of what had happened in the other.

Across the room the baron was staring at him.

'That was him,' he said. 'The King!'

Padry scrambled to his feet. Together they strode across the room and flung open the door to the King's chamber.

The King was standing at the window with his back to them. His hands were clutched together behind him. On the floor were the broken shards of the Cup, brown and scattered. The whitewash of the wall was marked where the King had flung it in his rage. The heavy stem lay within a yard of Padry's toe.

In the corridor they could hear people asking questions. Footsteps were approaching. A guard was knocking at the antechamber door. And above the others rose the voice of a woman.

'Ambrose!' she cried. 'Ambrose!'

'Your Majesty . . . ?' Padry began.

'Very well,' said Ambrose at last, in a hoarse, dry voice that was barely his own. 'Very well. When she returns, you may arrest her at the gate. I do not want to see her.'

Neither of them spoke. The voice of the woman came again, nearer now, speaking it seemed out of the air. 'Ambrose! What have you done? Ambrose!'

Padry knew it. It was Phaedra.

When he looks, I shall be as close as I can, she had said.

With a snarl like a beast the King fled from the room. And crying '*Ambrose! Ambrose!*' the voice pursued him down the corridors of his palace.

PART III

THE DRAGON

XXVII

The Raising of the Sun

 here were no more ladies-in-waiting, no garlands or musicians, no more silk-clad young knights to greet the Queen. Hard-faced men in steel surrounded her on her return to Tuscolo. She was escorted to a high-ceilinged room above the middle gatehouse. The room was furnished, with a hearth, but it was dark. There was just one long window looking inwards over the middle bailey. There she was held, alone, with the door locked and guards on the stair. The King did not come to see her. No date was set for her trial.

Columns of armed riders clattered through the gate-tunnel under her room. The first, mounted on the day of her arrest, headed for Appleton to demand the surrender of Gueronius. The second, which issued a few days later, took the road for Luckingham, because news had come that Gueronius had remained at his manor there after the Queen had passed. But he was not at Luckingham, and he was not at Appleton, and although riders hunted for him across the Kingdom no word of his capture came to Tuscolo.

It was a miserable time for Melissa. She was allowed to stay in the Queen's rooms in the keep, which were now empty except for her. But otherwise the castle treated her as if she might be in league with its enemies. Three times a day she went to the gatehouse to attend the Queen. If she carried anything – a basket of sweetmeats, a shawl, a spare blanket – the guards examined it carefully before she was allowed in. They did not search her body but they let her know that they might. And the first time she left the Queen in her prison, a sergeant led her straight to the castle dungeons. There, behind a low, iron-studded door, was a chamber with strange and cruel machines, winches and iron spikes, and a small man with a head like an egg who explained to her, in a wheezy, kindly manner, what the machines did, and what they would do to her if she were ever suspected of carrying a message, pen or paper, a tool, or any other forbidden thing in to the Queen.

Few people spoke with her. No one else seemed to trust her. She seemed to be watched wherever she went. Even when she was with Puck she was tongue-tied and depressed. She knew that eyes were following them as they walked aimlessly around the courtyard together. Those steel-clad men were adding Puck to their list of suspects. Perhaps he, too, would be called down to the dungeon room for a talk with the friendly, egg-headed man about his machines.

When Puck enquired about the Queen, she asked him sharply why.

He shrugged. 'Sorry for her,' he answered.

'You're a good person, Puck,' she said. And she wanted to ask if he was not sorry for her, too. But she did not, because she feared he might not be.

'Don't bother with the bed, Melissa,' said Atti in the dark gatehouse room at dusk. 'And I don't want you to wait on me. Just make up the fire and talk to me.'

Melissa put the warming pan in the bed anyway. (There was no point in letting it go cold, was there?) Then she crouched by the fire, laid some logs and blew the embers back to life. When she looked up she found that Atti had brought the supper tray over to the hearth herself.

'We'll share it,' she said. 'One plate between us, just as we did in the mountains. Were you sorry to leave the mountains, Melissa?'

'Not at the time, Your Majesty.'

Atti sighed. 'Neither was I. And don't call me "Your Majesty", Melissa. I should never have let you do that. How silly I was. We would have been much happier if we had just stayed up there – all of us would have been. I wish I could see the peaks again. Here – you must eat those, because I don't like them . . .'

'Those' were a small pile of honey-cakes, which the ladies-in-waiting would always squabble over and which Melissa almost never tasted fresh.

'What did you like best about the mountains, Melissa?'

'No other people,' said Melissa promptly. 'No trouble. And when you did meet them, they said what they meant so you didn't have to guess.'

'Of course we miss that now,' said Atti. 'Although if you had asked me at the time I should have said that was what I liked least. For me, I suppose . . .' She put her head on one side. 'Oh, those gulfs of air, and the hillside dropping away beneath your feet so that your stomach turned just a little with the thought of it! I feel that I have lived my life on the edge of a fall. But at least I could see it then.' She paused. 'And the mountain waters. Do you remember how they turned that grey-blue colour when the snows melted? So cold and so beautiful! I've never seen that anywhere else. Oh – and do you remember that kid – the one the hill boy killed?'

'Yes, Your M— Yes, I do.'

'I know he was trying to be kind to us but . . . Do you suppose if we had stopped him, he would have let us keep it? I often wonder.'

'Maybe. But when it grew there'd have been trouble with the other billy. One of them would have driven the other out. Then it'd have had to live out on the hillsides with no dams. Not much of a life. A wolf or lynx would have got it in the end.'

Sometimes there was just no place for a thing, even if it was beautiful.

'I still cry for it, you know.' Atti brushed her cheek as if tears had already gathered there.

'Tell you something,' said Melissa, who had now had time to stop being a queen's servant and go all the way back to being a girl's companion. 'That hill boy. Couldn't talk a word then, could he? Well, he's here in

Tuscolo. He's a scholar now. He talks and writes as well as the rest of them.'

Atti's eyes opened wide with astonishment. 'Truly, Melissa? You've seen him?'

'Plenty of times.'

And Atti looked at her, and the corners of her mouth turned in that rare smile.

'And – do you like him?'

Melissa stopped, with her mouth open.

How did she know?

How could Atti, who paid so little attention to others, guess at all the silly thoughts that chased through her head about Puck? How did she do it?

It must have shown in her face, for Atti laughed – a sudden, delighted sound, light and sweet and free of any triumph or fear. And Melissa had to laugh with her. Her chest forced it up through her in great gulps. And they went on laughing until both of them wept indeed.

'Will you marry him?'

'Might do,' said Melissa carefully. 'I don't know. All sorts of things to think about, aren't there?'

'Oh, but you should, Melissa! And he'll be good and honest to you and you will have a lovely life together. You should have told me! I would have ordered him to marry you. And I'd have given him a farm, in Baldwin, where the soil is good, and he would look after you and see that you do not starve. Maybe you should ask it of the King. He did say that he owed you a favour. Maybe you should. But perhaps it should not be in Baldwin after all. You should

411

go far away, back to the hills, where none of us can trouble you.'

'And gut fish, day in, day out?' said Melissa dryly. 'I can't wait.'

Atti laughed again. 'I hated that – even though they were dead. And I remember you were so good at it. And the corn – I could not understand how you made it come so quickly. I tried and I tried!' And she looked down at her hands as if she expected to see there the same calluses that they had both had from scraping their living in that house in the hills.

She looked at her long white fingers, pale in the darkening room. And Melissa saw her face change. She saw Atti remember, as she seemed to have forgotten, that the hills were far away in time as well as distance. And time had wiped the marks of them from her hands, just as it had twisted the paths of her life to lead her to her palace, and to her prison. And for all she knew there would soon be a court, and a sentence to an early, horrible death, or to a life spent lingering behind lock and bar.

Atti's face composed itself, deliberately, with a quiet effort of will. Suddenly Melissa knew that for Atti waiting here and not knowing what would happen must be the most terrible thing of all. It must mean all her nightmares were with her now, in the waking world. The curtain was drawn, the destroyer was in the room. On an impulse Melissa put her arms around her and hugged her, as sometimes she had hugged her under their blankets in the nights of the hills. 'You poor thing,' she said.

She felt Atti's surprise at her touch – the sudden hardness of the shoulders within her arms. And then she felt them unlock, as if at an unaccustomed jolt from Atti's brain. She felt Atti pat her clumsily on the shoulder, accepting the embrace. Neither of them spoke.

Then the guard thumped upon the door and told Melissa it was time to leave.

Slowly she walked back along the wall with the image of Atti's face before her. In her mind she wailed: *But what could I do? I tried to stop her, really I did!* And her thoughts answered: *You did not try hard enough.*

Did you stand in her way? Did you block her door? Did you run out and cry 'Rape!' when they were together? You wanted her to betray the King, didn't you?

No, no! Why would I want a thing like that?

You know why.

In a kind of dream she reached the inner courtyard and the living quarters, bustling with the lights and music of evening. She made her way along the passages, meaning to climb the stairs to the Queen's empty chamber and hide herself there. There was a stir in the corridor ahead. A voice was calling, 'Way there!' People were pressing themselves against the wall. And as she watched she saw the furthest ones sink into bows and curtseys.

The King was coming.

He came, with a torchbearer ahead of him and the Baron Lackmere at his shoulder. He was dressed in a tunic of green, rich with gold. His hair was long and

413

his beard trimmed and both were oiled and curled. He was frowning.

'Way there! Way for the King!'

So much she saw, before it was her turn to sink into a curtsey. She lowered her eyes and watched his feet pass on the flagstones. And then she felt him hesitate.

When she straightened, he was looking back at her over his shoulder. Their eyes met. She saw that he knew where she had just been. And he wanted to talk with her. He wanted to hear how it was with the woman down in the gatehouse. Only Melissa could tell him.

She remembered him as he had been in the mountains, laughing and waving his thorn branch over the heads of the goats in the sun. '*Ho, knights, to the Dark Tower . . .*' Or crossing the muddy court at Tarceny with firewood in his arms. There had never been a shadow in his eye, then.

The Baron Lackmere checked his stride. He looked back and saw her. He looked at the King. Then he muttered something. The King hung his head and walked on. The wave of people bowing and curtseying swallowed them, and they were gone. And the murmur of voices, ordinary voices gossiping and complaining, the scrapes of shoe-leather, the sound of a door banging, filled the corridor again. Melissa made her way upstairs to the Queen's chambers. It was dark, and she had no light because maids did not get candles or rushes. She felt her way to the bedchamber and then across to the forbidden door.

She drew back the bolt softly. The door would open.

Without a light, she undressed and put on her nightshift. She went to the little closet where she kept her things. In the darkness her fingers found her two treasures: the wooden goat and the pale stone. She took the stone from where it lay. Then she wrapped a blanket around herself and sat with her back to the post of the King's door, holding the pebble in her hand.

She waited for hours. Slowly the noises of the house around her died away.

Of course it was never completely quiet, even in the middle of the night. There were guards on the roofs, and on some of the doors, and somewhere men might be drinking in a watchroom or working late on some writing for the lord chancellor. And by the time they stumbled to their beds the monks might be rising for the midnight prayers, and soon after that the first scullions might be crawling wearily from their blankets to rekindle the oven fires so that there would be fresh bread on the King's table in the morning. She sat and listened to the different noises, to the clink of an armoured watchman pacing away the night, to the laugh of a drunk in the courtyard, and waited for the footsteps beyond the door at her back.

Atti had always slept with ladies in her room. The King slept alone.

The King slept alone so that Atti, if she ever chose, might come to him in the night without having to trip over an inconvenient body on the floor of the room.

Now she was held in a prison and the King slept alone still.

Melissa heard them – the King and his torchbearer, coming along the corridor. She heard the King speak to the guard at his door. (He always had a word for guards and servants when he was allowed.) She heard his body-servants in the outer chamber rising to their feet to attend him. She listened to the short night ritual as they removed his fine clothes and dressed him in his bed robe. Then the goodnights, the lights being doused, the door closing.

And wait, and wait, and wait. At least one servant would be bedding down in the outer chamber. If he had had a hard day he might be asleep quickly. There was also the guard in the corridor, but two doors stood between him and where the King lay. If there was little noise he might hear nothing at all.

The King might sleep, too, of course. But from the way he had looked in the corridor Melissa did not think that he would.

Everything was quiet – as quiet as it ever was. Softly Melissa got to her feet. She clutched the pebble in one hand. She put her other hand on the door-ring. Her heart was beating hard. Her blood was tingling in her throat. She had never, never thought of doing this before. It had never been possible. And now it was so easy.

The handle clacked loudly in her hand, sending a jolt through her whole body. She stood in the open doorway. The room beyond was black as pitch.

'Who's there?' said his voice hoarsely.

'It's Melissa, Your Majesty.' Hesitantly, in the utter dark, she took a step towards the bed. She did not know this room nearly as well as the Queen's.

She heard him roll in his blankets.

'Melissa?'

'I've got something for you, Your Majesty.'

I've got something for you. But it was not a flower this time. Her left hand, fumbling, found the unseen bedpost.

'For me? From the Queen?'

Of course he would think that.

'Something you lost a long time ago. Rolfe saw it. He said it was important.' She was thinking: *Don't send me away. Please don't. Just because it's from me, and not from her . . .*

'Rolfe? But he's dead.'

She had not known that.

'He saw you lose it. He told me it was important. I've been keeping it. Now I thought you might want it again.'

'What is it?' She heard the edge in his voice. She understood it. Here was someone approaching him in the darkness – someone whom he thought he trusted, but who was also one of the Queen's people. What if she had a knife?

Who knew what Melissa, harmless little Melissa, was really thinking behind those eyes of hers?

Who indeed?

He was about to call the guard.

'It's – he said it was a dragon's tooth.'

'The dragon!'

417

She heard him sit up. The noise guided her. She reached, and found his shoulder. She fumbled for his wrist, held it and placed the stone in his hand. Still holding his wrist (oh, for as long, for as long as she could!), she felt him turn it in his fingers. She heard him sigh.

'I thought it was gone,' he said. 'It was the last one, and I had kept it for so long. I never dared tell Mother that I no longer had it. But I suppose she knew. Where did I lose it?'

'In the fountain court at Tarceny, when . . .'

'Yes. I remember.'

He said nothing. Melissa stood before him and neither could see the other.

'How is . . .?' he began. Then he stopped himself. 'Aun says I must not ask about her,' he said. 'No one wants me to ask about her.'

No, we don't, thought Melissa. And still you are asking. And I'm not going to tell you about her. That's not why I came.

After a moment she opened her mouth and said, 'Is there anything else, Your Majesty?'

On the tongue of a servant there is just the slightest difference between 'Is there anything else?' meaning, *Please dismiss me now*, and 'Is there anything else?' meaning, *There is something else, and I would like to do it for you*.

It is slight, and it is unmistakable.

'I think . . .' said the King in the darkness.

And then he said: 'Yes, Melissa. Please stay.'

She sat down on the bed beside him, and slipped

an arm around his waist to claim him for hers. With her other hand she reached across for his, still wrapped around the stone. She could feel the warm press of his thigh against hers, the hardness of his arm and elbow, pinned against her ribs. She could feel her breath catching in her throat and her heart going *thump, thump, thump* inside her. She was aching for him and she wanted him to know it. She knew that he was still hesitating. His brain was fighting a losing battle with his body. She wanted to say to him: *Why? What for? No one knows. Here in the darkness no one sees. You are not the King. I'm not a maid. There's no past and no future. We're just two bodies that mustn't be alone any more.*

And anyway, she thought as she lowered her head onto his shoulder and began to rock him gently to and fro as they sat together. Anyway, don't lords take maids to their beds? I bet they do. I bet they all do. And who complains? Who cares? I don't care. I don't care even – even if you're thinking of *her* as you put your arms round me. I'll make you think of me soon enough. I will. Feel my heart, *thump, thump, thump* under this breast. Put your hand up to feel it. Here. Please. Or cover my face with kisses, or run your fingers like spiders up my thigh. It's only a nightshift, see. I've thought of everything . . .

'Melissa,' he breathed, turning towards her. And his breath was warm on her brow.

And then he stopped.

For a moment she clung to him, willing him on. Then she heard it, too. Faint in the night, borne by a

419

low wind from the gatehouse, the sound of a woman screaming.

Oh, no, thought Melissa wearily.

And: *Oh, you bitch! You don't even love him!*

The King loosed hold of her shoulders. He pulled himself from her slackening arms. She heard him feel his way to the window. She heard the shutters rattle. She saw the pale square of the night sky as he pulled them open, and the darkness of his shape, his hair shaggy around his head as he stood there and listened.

Another scream. And another. And then a pause. And then yet another.

A longer pause.

And more screams.

They were like cold fingers, those faint sounds. They chilled her. They chased the blood away. They were like the noise of a mosquito in the room, which she could never see or catch but would not let her be. Even after the noise was gone, she was still listening for it. They both were.

At last the King straightened and turned to face her. He was a flat black shadow against the window. But perhaps he could see her peering back at him.

'Melissa . . .'

'We should *never* have come here!' Tears were already starting in her eyes.

'No,' he said. 'We shouldn't.'

'Wouldn't have made any difference,' she choked. 'Wouldn't have made any difference. You'd still have chosen *her*!'

420

No answer. No answer meant yes, he would have done.

'I'll go,' she said.

'Melissa . . .' he said. 'Thank you. Thank you twice, and many times.'

Perhaps he could see her, perhaps not. But he must know, surely, as she rose and felt her way from the room, that she was weeping tears of rage.

'Is there anything else, Your Majesty?' asked Melissa in the gatehouse.

She had made the fire. She had made the bed. She had cleared the stinking chamberpot and replaced the jug of water. She had not helped Atti to dress, because Atti had already dressed herself even before Melissa had entered. And all the while that Melissa had worked about the room Atti had sat wordless, looking out of the window at the middle bailey: at the first comings and goings there in the greyness of dawn.

She sat pale and still like a statue. Her night must have been torment but there was no sign of it now. She had even done her own hair, plaiting and pinning the long tresses as carefully into place as any of her servants could have done. Her small, straight figure despised the world around it. Looking at her, Melissa could have believed that the Queen knew exactly what her maid had been doing last night when her cries had torn the air.

'Is there anything else, Your Majesty?' Melissa repeated.

'No,' said Atti at last. She did not look round.

Tight-lipped, Melissa closed the door. She muttered something to the guard. Then she left the gatehouse and began to make her way back along the curtain wall. She did not look back to see if Atti were still at her window.

Beneath Atti's room, the middle bailey gates were admitting the first of the morning's traffic. There were carts piled with straw for the stables and others with timber for the roof repairs or wine butts for the cellars. There were men on foot, too. Mainly these were scholars, wearing the monk-like hooded habit that all the King's scholars wore. Most if not all of them seemed to be full-grown men. Melissa could not see any boys among them this morning. She wondered idly if the younger scholars had been getting drunk in their lodgings last night, to be so slow out of bed today. She supposed they would all be beaten. She hoped Puck was not among the offenders. He might well not be. Most nights he finished work in the stable so late that they allowed him to sleep there.

Puck. She felt bad even thinking about him. But she also felt angry. Everything wanted to turn her his way. Not Ambrose. It had to be Puck. He was the little warmth on the end of the stick when the moon was out of reach. Mam would have said so. Atti had said so, in her moment yesterday when she was being human. Even the King would say so if she asked him. And he would give them a farm if she asked for that, too. He didn't forget his promises.

After last night, maybe he'd even be glad to be rid of her.

And everything here was wrong. They were all betraying each other and being terrible to each other. Somehow Atti was going to have to be punished, and what would Melissa's place be after that? She couldn't help any of them. Why should she stay?

But she did not want to go. Hopes and dreams – they were what made life worth living. She was so close to him still. Even after last night he was still close. There was only a door between them – a door that she could open. And a door in his mind that he could. And maybe, yes, a time would come when she would go, and choose Puck, and a farm. But not yet. Like a stubborn she-goat cheated of pasture, she did not want to be herded by the world.

She was approaching the inner bailey. Ahead of her was the Gryphon Tower, where the short, high wall of the inner courtyard joined to the curtain wall of the castle. The door into it stood open. There should have been a guard on it. There certainly had been when she had left the inner courtyard in the dawn. There was none now. Melissa looked up at the battlements of the inner bailey. There were one or two men up there that she could see. Perhaps the guard had just been changed. The night watch had trooped off and the day watch was still sorting itself out. She could see the head and shoulders of one armoured man, looking down into the middle courtyard. Just beyond him she could glimpse another, busy at the flagstaff. She saw the early light flash upon his helmet. She heard the squeak of the little pulleys at the staffhead as the royal banner rose foot by foot towards the peak. As it rose, the morning wind caught it, flicked it out and dropped it again.

Melissa stopped, puzzled. What she had seen was . . .

It rose. It flew. It was not the King's standard.

There, on a blue field, was a great yellow sun, with many rays shaking outwards from it across the cloth. And Melissa knew it. She had seen it before.

It was the banner of Gueronius.

The students had started to run. They were all running in a body like men in a race. They were running not towards the school but to the upper gate. They were carrying things in their hands – weapons! The gate was open to meet them.

And men were jumping from a wagon, where there had not seemed to be men before. They were coming out from under the straw, shaking the golden strands from their heads and limbs. They, too, were armed. And all around the courtyard men were shouting – cries of anger, cries of alarm. There was a scraping, tinkling sound from the middle gatehouse behind her. She knew what it was. She had seen the men-at-arms practising many times, in armour and with blunted weapons. Men were fighting in the gate-tunnel, under Atti's floor. She saw the jerking, swirling movements in the shadows there. Their weapons were not blunted now. An armoured man was lying still on the ground, just inside the middle gate.

The first of the false scholars had reached the upper gate. The gate was still open for them. The guard there was waving them on, slapping one on his arm as he passed. They were Gueronius's men. And Gueronius's men held the upper gatehouse already! How had that happened? Traitors! And what would happen now?

Something whispered in the air – a pale flash that passed in an instant – an arrow!

It had not come near her. But it jerked her back to the day she had fled from the red knight in the woods, with his arrows hissing close through the trees as she ran. Gulping, she ducked into the open doorway of the Gryphon Tower. There was no one in the chamber inside. There should have been. But whoever it was must either be dead or a traitor.

They might kill her if they found her. They might kill everyone.

How could this be happening? To a house like Tuscolo!

The chamber was lit only by the doorway behind her onto the curtain wall, and the doorway ahead to the wall of the upper courtyard. No one could see her from outside. If someone came into the chamber, down or up the stair, or along one of the walls, she could run out along the other wall. She must have somewhere to run. If she got trapped they could kill her.

A flurry of shouts from somewhere in the inner courtyard. Metal clashing. A bellow of pain. They had caught someone. (Who?) They were killing him now. Footsteps paced above her on the roof of the tower. That would be one of the traitors. If he knew she was down here, what would he do? She heard him laugh.

How long would this last? And what would happen when it was over?

More calls. Hoofbeats. What was happening? She must not go to look. She must stay here in the shadows, watching both doors for the first sign that she must run.

And then a new voice, ringing out across the inner courtyard. 'Ho, there! Treachery! Help to the King!'

She knew it. It was the Baron Lackmere. And without thinking she was in the doorway to the upper wall.

'Ho, there! Help! Help to the King!'

She looked for the baron and saw him. His head and shoulders were leaning from an upper window in the living quarters. From the council-chamber window. His hand gripped the sill and he looked down into the courtyard.

'Up here! Help!'

Iron-shod feet clattered on the battlement above Melissa's head. 'He's there!' someone cried. 'In the living quarters!'

'Hey, Tuscolo!' called another voice. 'Hey, Gueronius! The usurper's in the council chamber. Get him! Get him!'

Melissa hesitated a moment longer. Then, as if someone had shoved her between the shoulder-blades, she ran out into the deadly light.

She flew along the short wall. Ahead of her was the great rectangular keep. The wall door was open. Shouts and clashes sounded from inside. As she darted through the doorway, men in student's gowns with swords in their hands were climbing up the spiral stairway. The sounds of fighting were above. There were King's men up there, defending the upper storeys. They could not help him. She barged straight in among the armed men and squirmed between them. One cursed and another struck at her with his hilt, but there was no room for them to swing. She was through. And behind her the men were still climbing upwards, knowing nothing but their own little corner of the fight where their deaths danced on the battlements above them.

She reached the door to the living-quarter corridor. And she was too late.

A crowd of armed men were gathered at the far end, at the door to the Privy Council chamber. Some were throwing themselves against it – *crash! crash!* Others stood about with swords drawn, waiting for it to give. And it would. It would give. *Crash!* It had gone.

In they went, swords up. Bellows and clashes sounded from inside. Unheard in the din, Melissa screamed. Then she charged down the corridor.

She ran to fight, with her fists curled. But halfway she swerved and ducked through the door to the Queen's antechamber. She raced through the Queen's bedroom, flung open the door to the King's chambers and hurried on.

The King's bedroom was empty. The antechamber was empty. There were men in the Privy Council chamber beyond – men, but no sounds of fighting now. As she reached the council door it was flung open from inside. A wild-eyed man stood there, sword in hand, lips drawn in a snarl.

'Find him!' cried a voice from beyond. 'Search the rooms. Under the beds. The chimneys! The garderobe! Pull him out!'

The man had half lifted his sword at the sight of Melissa. Now he lowered it and shoved her aside. Others followed him, lumbering through the private rooms of the King, opening his chests, spilling his robes, prodding at his hangings with the points of bloody swords.

'He was never here, I guess,' said another, calmer voice. 'We've been drawn to the wrong point.'

The first voice swore. And Melissa knew it. It was Gueronius.

She looked in. He was there. Not, as she had last seen him, in fine silks with his hair trimmed and scented, but a wild figure in a ragged cloak, from under which peeped the gleam of mail.

On the floor at his feet lay the Baron of Lackmere, still gripping the hilt of a long sword with one hand. The other was pressed to his stomach and was covered in blood. Blood was swimming out from his wound, soaking into the rich carpet and the brightly coloured tunic that he wore. His face was very pale.

A man was kneeling by him. It was one of the Queen's knights, whom she had not seen since her arrest. He was wearing a rough leather jacket. Wisps of straw were still stuck in his buckles and collar.

'A clever ruse, my lord,' he said to the baron. 'Although I think it has cost you dear.'

428

Gueronius cursed again. 'Come on,' he said. 'The day is not yet won.'

Thoughtfully the young knight prised the sword from the baron's grip. He looked at it for a second. There was no blood on it. Then he rose and the two men stalked into the King's chambers. Their eyes fell on Melissa as they passed. They regarded her no more than if she had been furniture.

She was alone in the chamber with the fallen baron.

After a moment she pushed herself from the wall and knelt by the wounded man. The hand on his stomach was red from fingertip to wrist, and still the blood was coming. It was coming slowly but with a horrible purpose that did not mean to stop. She gathered up the corner of his tunic and pressed it to the place. At once her hand was bloody and the cloth she held was bloody, and none of it seemed to do any good. The baron's face was white and drawn with pain. His eyes were closed. She wondered if he was even breathing.

Outside voices were calling. But they were not the cries of combat now. They were instructions. *Come here, Look there, Search among the bodies.* The fight was over but they were still hunting for the King.

Someone came into the room behind her. It was the royal page, Philip. He was looking dazed.

'Where's the King?' he said hoarsely.

'He got away,' she said. 'The baron distracted them.'

Philip put his hand to his head. There was a large bruise there. 'The courtyard is taken,' he mumbled. 'And the keep.'

'They were taking the middle gatehouse, too,' she said.

So Atti would be free now. Soon she would be demanding her maid. Melissa did not think she wanted to go to her.

And the King . . . He might have got away for the moment. But he must still be in the castle somewhere.

'Help me,' she said to Philip.

Philip looked down at the baron as though wondering how either of them could help him now.

'Help me lift him,' she said.

The baron gasped once with pain. Together they struggled to carry his limp weight through the antechamber to the King's bed and laid him there. They laid him, bleeding, on the very blankets where she and Ambrose had embraced the night before. And when she straightened, trembling from the effort, there was blood on her clothes and blood on Philip, and a bloody trail led back through the antechamber door. A faint, foul smell was stealing into the air. She thought it came from the wounded man. She wondered if it meant his gut had been pierced. And she did not know what to do next.

'See if you can find the surgeon,' she said. 'Or anyone who can help.'

Philip nodded, still dazed, and shambled out along the bloody trail. Melissa supposed that he would not be able to find the surgeon. Or that if he did, the surgeon would be dead. Or that even if the man were alive, he would not come soon enough for the baron.

Quiet descended on the King's chambers. The

430

searchers had gone. The rooms lay in chaos. All the contents of the chests were spilled on the floors. The hangings were torn from the walls and lay in heaps. Dust motes turned thickly in the beams of the strengthening sun. Melissa sat trembling upon the bed.

A hand stole over her own. She jumped and looked down.

It was the baron. His face was white. His head had barely moved, but his eye glared up at her with a desperate fierceness. His hand gripped her wrist, hard and cold.

'You are of the King's party?' His voice was a whisper.

She stared at him, horrified. If he had not held her fast she might have jumped away.

'Choose, girl. King or Queen. No – hiding now!'

'King, my lord,' she mumbled.

'Find me – one who can use a pen.'

Still she stared at him.

'Quickly!' he hissed.

She ran from the room.

XXVIII

Weapons of Paper

rom the passageways behind the great hall there was a door to a little court-yard where a stunted olive tree grew. From here a ramp climbed towards the main upper courtyard. Halfway up the ramp was another door, which led to the crypt of the royal chapel. Normally this door was locked, but over the past year Padry had had it left open so that he could slip quietly out of the Grand Audience for a few moments when he was not needed, pass through the chapel, and take a walk by himself in the King's cloisters to refresh himself between each smothering hour in the great, packed chamber.

And from the far corner of the King's cloisters it was possible to enter the Eagle Tower, to gain the townside wall of the middle courtyard, and so come to the school building without passing through the upper gatehouse, now watched by armed men under the banner of Gueronius.

Padry tried the door that led into the upper floors of the school. It was open. Thank the Angels!

'In here,' he hissed. 'Follow me.'

He took Ambrose by the arm and dragged him into the building.

They were in the long schoolroom that occupied the whole of the upper floor. Rows of empty benches faced them. Windows gave onto the courtyard on their right. Above them were bare rafters and the flat roof. Something scuttled up there – a rat or mouse. Padry could hear no other sound but his own gasping and that of Ambrose beside him.

His lungs heaved and his throat was sore. They had been running since the moment that Lackmere had caught them both in the council chamber. '*It's treachery! Get him out of here – Get him out!*' They had run like animals. Sometimes they had run bent double. Padry's limbs were shaking.

Still nothing moved inside the building. The school seemed to be empty. Most masters and all the scholars must still be in their quarters in the town – held perhaps by allies of Gueronius, who had taken their robes to aid their attack on the castle. Cautiously Padry made his way to a window into the long middle courtyard.

There were not many people in view. The castle folk would be hiding. Most of the attackers would be in the upper courtyard, subduing what was left of the resistance. But there were men on both gatehouses. *Both* gatehouses. And now, above both gates, flew the sun on the blue field.

There was movement on the other side of the middle bailey. Armed men had begun to search the stable and the other buildings there. In half an hour, an hour at most, they would have worked their way round to the school.

Get out! rang the voice of the baron in his ears. *Get OUT!*

Padry cursed softly.

Both gatehouses taken, and probably the living quarters and the keep, too, by now.

How had it been *possible?*

He knew how it had been possible. He could see now how the risks they had taken, which had seemed such little risks at the time, had been disastrous. Of course the court had been riven by the arrest of the Queen. No one who was so much adored would lack for allies. They had known that. They had known, too, that it would be said that the King had used witchcraft to find her out. So they had banished the knights of her party. And when they had begun the search for Gueronius they had sent their trusted men and kept those they were not sure of behind. Of course they had.

And among those they had been unsure of, there had been some willing to betray them. Of course there had been.

And Gueronius – for all his faults, he was a fighting man. He knew how to elude a blow and how to strike for the open throat. They had left themselves open. And he had struck.

The sun of the house of Tuscolo flew over the gatehouses and over the keep, too. Angels alone knew what had happened in the lower courtyard. And at his back was the castle wall and a hundred-foot drop to the roofs of the town. Rope? There wasn't much he could make rope from in the school. There wasn't the time to make it. And the thought of swinging himself out over that horrible drop, trusting to whatever blankets and cords he had managed to fashion together, made him shiver. He knew how *that* would end.

'Your Majesty?' he said softly.

There was no answer. Padry looked round.

Ambrose was sitting slumped against the wall with his head in his hands. Padry bent over him, and shook him lightly by the arm.

'Your Majesty – you must call the princes.'

There was no response.

'Your Majesty,' said Padry, shaking harder.

Ambrose looked up. His eyes were dazed. Shock, of course. One moment you are King, the next you are on the run. The young man could hardly understand what was happening.

'You must call the princes. We need them to get us out. It is the only way.'

Ambrose stared at him.

'They are searching for us, Your Majesty. They will find us here.'

Ambrose shook his head, and hid his face in his knees.

'Your Majesty!'

'I broke it,' said Ambrose, and sobbed.

Padry drew breath to urge him again. Then he let it out. Slowly he straightened.

Look at him, Thomas Padry. Look at your King.

Do you remember the boy you found, with the lantern in his hand? *That* had been a king indeed. And you took him, and transplanted him here. Now see what has become of him! Look what you have done. Majesty? Where was the Majesty in this dazed, sighing creature, betrayed by his wife and by his guards?

How long would it take to shake him from his stupor? How long after that to call the princes? There might not be time. There would not be time. Damn it!

The castle was lost. The world was turned upside down. It was stupefying. He felt the shock of it himself, clogging his mind and distracting him with irrelevant thoughts. Lackmere had not felt it. Lackmere had looked from the council-chamber window and seen at once what was happening. *Get him out!*

How?

Think, Thomas Padry. Think. You've been here before – in a house in sack. You got out then. Why not now? And this was not a sack. The enemy was being slower about his search – slower but more deliberate. Hiding was no good. They needed help. And if there was no help . . .

He peered out of the window again, searching for some way of escape.

Outside the school was a cart. A mule still stood in its traces, waiting patiently for whoever had brought it here to show it what it was to do next. The cart was half full of straw. Piles of straw lay all around it as if some demented stable hand had taken a fork and started to unload it in all directions.

That was no way to treat one's load, thought a habit-driven corner of Padry's brain. Even straw cost money.

But of course the load had not been straw. Not this morning. This morning it must have been armed men. The straw had only been there to hide them from view.

He looked at the cart and decided that it was hopeless. But he couldn't think of anything else. And there was something sweet, some little revenge, in using the enemy's device against him.

If it could be made to work a second time . . .

The stables were busy. There were guards outside it – Gueronius's men. Melissa approached warily. As she came up she saw the stable hands emerging, one after another, leading the horses out into the open. Some led two horses. Some led three. They were emptying the stables. Among them was Puck.

He was there! Praise everything, he was there, and unhurt! He must have spent the night in the stables and had somehow been out of the way when the fighting started. Now he was holding the halter of a big brown horse that looked about twenty times his size. She sidled up to him through the crowd. He jumped when she touched his arm. Then he grinned. The sight of his smile was like a warm beam of sun in that terrible morning.

'Good to see you safe,' he said. 'Hurt at all?'

'Not me,' she said. 'What's going on?'

He shrugged. 'They search stables. They want

437

horses out so they can do that.' He pulled a face. 'No school anyway this morning, so I help.'

Melissa glanced at the stable door. Yes, there were men in there. She glimpsed one poking through a pile of hay with a long pole-arm. She knew who they were looking for.

There was an armed man standing only ten feet away from them.

'I need you to come with me,' she murmured.

Puck looked at her, surprised.

'*Puka halalah*,' she said.

Puka halalah. For the King.

He lifted an eyebrow and said nothing. But he tapped another stable hand on the shoulder and gave him the halter of the beast he was holding. Then he followed her, back towards the gate to the upper courtyard.

There were armed men everywhere, watching them. She felt surrounded by a cloud of eyes and steel. Firmly she took his hand in hers as she walked. Let them think she had called him away for a cuddle while all the fine folk were distracted. She needed the comfort, anyway. She'd have liked nothing better just then than to sneak off with him to some quiet corner where they would both be safe and hold him, hold him, hold him until all these awful things were over.

But she was of the King's party. So was Puck. Puck could use a pen. There would be pen and ink in the council chamber. And paper. Stacks of it.

* * *

438

From the corner of the school to the middle gateway was a little over a hundred yards. It was the most horrible journey of Padry's life. The mule did not seem to understand what he wanted. The cart bumped and jolted, and with each bump and jolt it shook the piles of books and papers, chests, hangings and other things that Padry had loaded it with, and he thought that the piles must subside and reveal the secret he carried towards the gate. He did not dare to look behind him.

I'm a schoolmaster, he thought. That's all. A frightened scholar, making for safety with as much of the King's library as he thinks he can get away with. Gueronius and his cut-throats had no time for books or scholars. They would only sneer and let him through. Believe it, Thomas Padry. If you believe it you can act it. If you don't, you are for the scaffold and so is he.

Bump. Bump. Shake. He was obsessed with the thought that the guards were watching him as he rode high in his cart, and with the fear that any jolt might disturb the precarious piles of books and scrolls that he had built to conceal the cart's passenger. He wanted to have these last moments, to drag them out, because as soon as he reached the gate he would be the plaything of death. The seconds seemed to stretch hugely as he looked and looked at the distant gate-house, listened for the shouts, tensed for some flying arrow. The mule's hooves plodded across the packed earth of the middle courtyard and its head nodded up and down as it walked, and the gatehouse seemed no nearer.

And then suddenly it was very near. His moments were pouring away like water from a jug. The guards were busy with something. They were bending over something on the ground to one side of the gate-way – yes, a dead man. They were removing his armour – stripping him of anything of value as crows strip the flesh from carrion in the fields. Nearer, nearer. This was madness. They would never let him through. Of course they would check the cart. Why in the name of the Angels hadn't carts been checked that morning? But the men who should have checked them were dead now. They had not been suspicious. It had been just another day for them. A day on which they had died. And on which Padry, too, would die, trying valiantly, stupidly . . . It was too late to go back and hide.

They had not looked up. One of them was laughing. Oh, they had stripped the groin. Of course they had. And the coarse, sick jokes that pillaging soldiers always make . . .

You keep at it, my children. You cut up his manhood with your little knives if that's what pleases you. He won't mind. And meanwhile I will just drive quietly through.

'Halt.'

Padry had not even seen the man in the shadow of the gate-tunnel.

Man? Men – several of them. Again, with maddening irrelevance, his mind dithered off to wonder whether those long pole-arms could possibly have been smuggled into the castle that morning, or

440

whether they had been taken from the hands of the dead. The men around the corpse had paused and were looking his way.

'So where do you think you're off to?' said a lazy voice in the gate-tunnel.

'Pemini,' said Padry, and his voice was a whisper. He cleared his throat. 'Pemini,' he tried again. 'It's my home,' he added.

'Pemini, is it? Well, *Pemini*, no one's going anywhere from the castle this morning. What have you got there?'

'Books,' said Padry. 'They're mine. I brought them here.'

Men were walking round the cart – armed men. They wore padded jackets. Their helmets would not have been their own.

'I have to go this morning,' he said. 'It's urgent.'

'Books,' repeated the voice. Padry could see the speaker now. It was a tall, grinning young man, bare-headed, leaning lazily against the wall by the gatehouse door. 'Books, is it?'

'A heap of them,' said one of the guards, peering in over the cart tail.

'A heap. Why does a man go travelling with a heap of books, do you think?'

'Soon see,' said the guard. And he clambered up into the cart.

Padry watched, frozen. He saw the hairs on the man's hand as it clutched the cart rail. He saw the dark stains on his knuckles, the little frown of effort on his face as he hauled his big body up onto the boards – the lips, the fat cheeks, the beard. This is a man, Padry thought. A man like me. I could like him. I could joke or drink with him. And he's going to poke with that sword – that short, bloody sword – among the scrolls and papers. He's going to find the King. And then . . .

His body took command. His knees straightened. He stood up on the cart seat and faced the searcher.

'They're valuable!' he said, choking. 'You must not damage them!'

'Soon see,' said the man grimly. And he jabbed his sword hard into a pile of scrolls.

'No!' cried Padry.

Jab, jab! Padry stepped into the back of the cart. He stood up to his ankles in scrolls, astride the spot where Ambrose lay under a rug he had taken from a master's sleeping room.

'No!' he screamed. The soldier ignored him. The point struck a book, piercing the cover and pulling it open as the man freed it. He lunged again, straight into the pile between Padry's legs.

'No!' Padry screamed, and pushed the man with both hands.

The man stumbled. But he did not fall. He crouched, eyes blazing, and lifted his blade. It hovered before Padry's throat. Instinctively Padry snatched at the point with his bare hand and howled as it twisted in his grip. He stepped back. Blood was flowing from his palm. He held his hands up.

Let them see it, he thought wildly. Let them see that I'm bleeding.

Let them think the blood on his point is mine.

Men were shouting. They were climbing up into the cart. Still the point of the sword hovered before his eyes. He saw the fresh red stain on it. And his raw hand screamed with the pain.

'What is happening down there?'

A woman's voice. *Her* voice, from above them. He looked up. They all did. She was watching from the battlements of the gatehouse with the banner of Gueronius flying over her head. There were others up there with her – bowmen, Padry thought. The gate-house had been her prison. Now they had taken it and made it her stronghold until the castle was secure.

'We have a rat by the tail, Your Majesty,' said the tall young man, standing by the mule's head. 'It is squeaking a little.'

Padry looked up into her eyes. He looked for her loathing. He looked for her contempt. He saw them.

Oh, she was beautiful there, framed by the blunt teeth of the battlements. She was a cold angel, casting her eyes down from Heaven upon the corrupt and unworthy world beneath. And everything he had done was wrong. All his best and most noble efforts had been vile. He had betrayed her. He had betrayed her every day of his life since he had taken her by the hand in the garden. That was what he saw in her eyes. Death must look like that, he thought. Like the beauty and thrill of steel plunged into warm flesh.

And he thought, too, that she knew what he was doing, blustering here at the gate. She knew who it was who lay in the cart beneath his feet.

'Let him go,' she said coldly.

'But Your Majesty—'

'He is of no account. Have you found the King yet?'

'No, Your Majesty. But—'

'Send to my Lord Gueronius to search the chapel. He will try to seek sanctuary. And until it has been searched, do you set a watch upon it yourselves, to be sure that none can leave it.'

'Yes, Your Majesty—'

'*Now*, sir.'

They climbed off the cart. They stood aside in silence while he took up the reins and urged the stupid, damned mule down the gate-tunnel and into the outer bailey of the courtyard. And all the while she looked down on them to be sure that it was done. And as he drove across the wide space beyond the middle gate, the wheels of the cart echoed the words she had spoken, again and again in his ears.

Let him go.

Let him go.

Let him go.

And he would never, never know whom she had meant by *him*.

He made for the River Gate, which led out not into the city but to the meadows beyond the walls. The gate was open. The guard were men of the castle, still with the tabards of the Moon and the Oak Leaf, quartered with the Eagle of Baldwin. The gate sergeant was a man he knew slightly.

'Are you for the King?' Padry asked them.

The gate-sergeant eyed him warily. 'Which King would that be?' he asked in reply.

Padry cursed him and drove out of the castle.

At last, in the cover of some willows, he was able to halt the wagon. He climbed once more into the back and raked through the flimsy piles of paper. Here was the rug. He did not stop to see whether it was pierced, or whether it was soaked with blood. He tore it aside to reveal the man underneath.

Ambrose's eyes were closed. His face was drawn with pain. His leggings were bloody. There was a wound in his upper thigh where the sword had ripped through the hanging. Padry peered at it. It was not big, not deep. Blood was still coming, but not fast. It must be cleaned and dressed. There would be threads of fabric driven into the flesh. They would have to be picked out. He could do none of that himself. Not one-handed. And he could do none of it here. At any moment riders might issue from the castle to pursue him. It was a miracle that he had been allowed to pass through the gate. A miracle, too, that Ambrose had not cried out, and that any movement he had made had been covered by the scuffle in the cart.

Ambrose's hand was thrust inside his tunic. Fearing another wound, Padry drew it out. But there was no more blood. Instead he found the King's fingers curled around a small leather purse that was slung from his neck. Inside the purse was not money but a small white stone, covered with curved lines cut into its surface.

Ambrose convulsed. He clutched at the stone and held it. His eyes opened, burning with pain. But the stupor was broken. The man was back. The wound had woken him at last.

His voice was a fierce whisper. 'Where?'

'We are away, Your Majesty.'

'Help,' hissed the King. 'Get help!'

'As soon as we can find it, Your Majesty.'

Ambrose closed his eyes again.

There was nothing to do but drive. And so Padry drove. At a crossroads near Parter's Bridge they came upon loyal riders, who were part of a column returning from the fruitless hunt for Gueronius.

'My lord,' whispered Melissa. 'My lord!'

Beside her Puck crouched at the bedside, looking grimmer than she had ever seen him.

'My lord – we have paper and pen.'

The baron's eye flickered. At first Melissa thought that he must no longer be able to speak. But then his lips moved.

'It's dark,' he complained. 'Can you see to write, boy?'

It was bright day outside. Warm beams shot into the King's chamber and fell upon the baron's legs. Melissa was surprised that he couldn't feel them. He lay as she had left him, with one hand still pressed to his stomach and all the bedclothes soaked in blood. The surgeon had not come. Or if he had come, he had only looked at the fallen man and then had stolen away again. And that foul smell had thickened in the air.

'I can write, sir,' said Puck solemnly. The pen, long, white-feathered and silver-nibbed, rested in his hand. An ink bottle of beautiful glass was on the floor beside him. On his knee were documents he had lifted from a chest in the Privy council chamber, closely written with words that Melissa could not read but must mean many important things about land, wealth, property and the Kingdom. Puck had folded the top one so that only the blank space at the bottom of the document showed.

'Write – what I say.'

Puck nodded and waited. Somewhere close, armed footsteps hurried down a flight of stairs. Melissa glanced at the door, afraid that they might be discovered. But Puck ignored them. His bright, capable eyes never left the man on the bed.

'To my Lady Develin, in Develin. Greetings,' whispered the baron.

Scratch-scratch went the pen in the warm air. Melissa watched the lines forming on the blank paper and wondered that Puck – *her* Puck – could do something so marvellous, and do it so calmly while men hunted through the castle with iron in their hands.

'The King is betrayed,' muttered the baron. 'Haste you to him. Or the years will bite their tail.'

Scratch, scratch-scratch. Puck looked up.

'Sign that it is dictated by me,' said the baron.

Puck lifted an eyebrow as he wrote. He was surprised that the letter was so short.

'Damn her,' groaned the baron. 'Queen? Adulterous, treacherous bitch of a—' His voice broke into a hiss of pain. 'Another!' he muttered. 'Quickly!'

Puck shuffled his paper until he found another blank space.

'Is the pen sharp, boy?' said the baron. 'Will it write for me?'

'It will write, my lord.'

'Write, then. To my – my worthy and well-beloved son Raymonde. Raymonde diLackmere, in Lackmere. Greeting.'

Melissa gasped. The baron hated his son. Everyone knew that.

'Raymonde,' whispered the baron. 'I would that you know you are the heir of my body, my lands and my spirit. There is no other. I hold you worthy of it. All the things that should be forgotten, I have forgotten. All that was wrongly done I – I forgive.'

He lay, face half sunk in the bedclothes, eye fixed upon nothing. Only his mouth moved. His words seemed to come from far away.

'Is it sharp, boy?' he whispered again. 'Is it sharp?'

'Yes, my lord.'

'Write then. Write that he has my blessing.'

As the pen moved, Melissa stared at the dying, angry man, and wondered if his words were true.

'There is more, boy.'

'I am ready, sir.'

'Raymonde, know you that I am this day foully and by treachery stricken. I am but an hour, I judge, from my meeting with the Angels. Therefore I bid you come find such tomb as they may lay me in, and there have flames lit and prayers said for my soul, for I know that I have been over-sparing of prayer in my life . . .'

His voice had sunk to a mutter. He paused.

'Is it sharp?'

'Yes, my lord.'

The baron's free hand curled into a fist upon the sheets. Hoarsely he continued, 'Yet first and above all I lay this on you. That you make no delay, but come with all the force that you can. For our lord the King is betrayed. Bring to him, therefore, every . . . every horse and spear and man in the lands of Lackmere. And if by ill chance you should come . . . too late to save him, then I lay this on you also. That you shall make war . . . unceasing against his enemies. That you spare none who had a hand in the making of this day. So I charge you, as . . . as you are a vassal, and a knight . . . and as you are my son.

'I have finished, boy,' he gasped. 'Write that he has my blessing.'

'I have written it already, my lord, as you said.'

'So. Then . . . give it.'

Puck laid the paper on the bed, a few inches from the baron's eyes. Slowly the baron drew his bloodied hand from his stomach. The forefinger, dark and sticky, hovered over it for a second. It pressed upon the page. When it withdrew, a red-brown fingermark was left below the words that Puck had written.

'Now go, boy. Ride . . . into the south. Bring me my revenge.'

Puck nodded. 'I will go,' he said simply.

'Puck!' cried Melissa.

She stared at him. Into the south? *Where* into the south? Where were these places? Puck could have no more idea than she had. How would he get there?

449

'Ride', the baron had said. Where was Puck to get a horse? He'd not get one of the King's out of the stables!

He smiled at her wryly. '*Puka halalah,*' he said.

'*Puck!*' she wailed. 'Don't be stupid!'

The stupid, simple, childish . . . Why did he think he could do this?

'Do not worry,' he said. 'I am a small one. They do not look for small ones. Only the big. I wait a bit – go when gates open. It will be fine.'

When she did not answer, he touched her arm. 'We do a good thing now.'

He pulled his scholar's habit off over his head and lifted his long undershirt. She saw the lean ripple of his ribs under his brown skin. There was a thoughtful expression on his face as he tucked his two papers into the back of his loincloth and dropped his shirt again. Then he pulled his habit back on and twisted round to see.

'Nothing shows?' he said.

And there he stood, the clever, funny boy who had come all the way from the hills because of her; whom she had kissed in the stables and who had been so put down when she hadn't wanted to do it again; who had carried food up and down the mountain valley for her in another life, years ago. He was as lithe and as quick and as brown as her own father had been. And now he was going to go away, by roads he did not know, with bloody-handed armed men all over the place who would kill him at once if they knew what he carried!

And she could not stop him. He was of the King's party. So was she.

'You'll need money,' she said grimly. 'I don't suppose you've got any, have you?'

He shrugged, helpless. (He hadn't even thought of it! How like him! How – *simple*!)

She looked around the ransacked room. 'I don't suppose I have either any more,' she said.

But the searchers had been looking for a man, not loot. They had opened her closet, spilled and poked among her things, but they had not got down and rummaged with their hands. Her purse was still there. So was the carved kid.

She took the purse and put it in his hand.

'Buy yourself a horse,' she said. 'Or a mule, or whatever you can get. I'd come with you, but it won't stretch to two. And I can't ride, anyway.'

'How!' he said, weighing the purse. 'You are rich!'

'Not any more.'

'When I come back, I give it again to you. Marry you, too, maybe.'

'Anything you say,' she said shortly.

She hugged him once, and he was gone.

The baron lay, still as a dead thing, on the King's bed. His face was white and his right hand was white on the bedclothes, and his left was black with old blood. He breathed in gasps so faint she could barely hear them, and with each breath a fresh trickle of red blood oozed between his fingers. His eyes were open but they did not follow her when she moved.

451

'Damn her,' he muttered. 'She's sunk us. The lying . . .'

His head moved a little. He was trying to lift it. He could not.

'Dark,' he whispered.

Melissa sat in the sunlight and looked at the gleaming window.

'There's a storm coming, my lord,' she said.

She had never liked him. She had not liked him the first day she had seen him, on the knoll above Aclete, standing with the King. And he had not liked her. Now she thought that she should hate him. She should hate him because he had sent Puck away. She should hate him because he had made her help him do it. She should hate him, above all, because she must sit with him when there was nothing she could do.

It was too much effort. So much had happened in the last few hours that she did not think she could feel anything any more. *When I come back, I give it again to you. Marry you, too, maybe.* But Puck would not come back. He had gone where the baron was going. And he had gone with a smile.

'Is it sharp?' murmured the baron. 'Is it sharp?'

'The letter is written, my lord. It has gone.'

'Spare none,' the man whispered. 'As you are my son.'

After a little she took his right hand and held it. It was lifeless. Maybe he could not even feel her touch at all any more. Still she held it as time slipped past, and men moved and called in the building, and no one came near. She held it as she had held the hand of the dying hillwoman, years ago in Aclete. *Look after her.* That was what it had been then. Now it was *Spare none.* Why did the dying cast such loads on the living? Wasn't being alive hard enough already?

Look after her. The adulterous, treacherous . . .

Spare none. Not even Puck.

Suddenly something huge had been lost – something she had barely known she had. She hadn't known it because she had always been so sure he would be around that she had spent her time dreaming about other things. Why did she only see this now? And when these armoured men were done killing each other, they would find Puck somewhere. Confident, capable Puck. Simple, brave, childish Puck. And then they would kill him, too.

'Sharp?' whispered the baron.

'Yes, sir. I think it is.'

He did not speak again.

XXIX

Signs at Bay

 month later Ambrose's host was camped at Tower Bay on the shores of Derewater. It was a grey afternoon with low clouds and a low, steady southwind teasing the banners and rippling the surface of the lake. The light was poor. Across the lake the hills of Tarceny showed like clouds, dull shapes with no detail to be seen. To north and south the water reached away and melded colourlessly with the sky.

In a field outside the castle, before a line of willows, Ambrose was sitting in the open. He wore a long, loose robe which fell to his ankles. The crown on his head was new. It had been fashioned hurriedly for him from the coronet of a loyal baron, because the crown of Tuscolo had been lost to Gueronius along with everything else in the King's treasury. He was reading from a scroll that he held in one hand. His attendants stood at a respectful distance.

Padry limped towards him across the grass. He had been away for three weeks and had spent the last three days of it foot-marching. It had left him very sore. All

454

the horses had gone either to knights and squires or to the carters. Everyone else was using the legs they had been born with.

'Greetings, Your Majesty,' he said, bowing. 'I bring you fifteen hundred men from Pemini and the river, and promises of more.'

Ambrose looked up. He showed no sign of surprise or joy at Padry's return. His face was composed. But it was gaunt – very gaunt, as if he had eaten very little for a long season.

'Fifteen hundred?' he murmured. 'You said—'

'Eight hundred I pledged to you. Twelve hundred I hoped for. But Pemini has prospered and knows to whom it owes its prosperity.'

'Those who have profited from my kingship take my side,' sighed the King. 'Those who think they have not, take the other. Fifteen hundred. I suppose it is good. And my Lady Develin brings us six more.'

'Six? Six thousand, Sire?'

'Six hundred, but they are all knights and men-at-arms. She has marched them to the lake and put them in boats. We expect to see her sails this evening. The main part of her host is still assembling under Inchapter and Lackmere.'

'Good!' said Padry. 'So Gueronius may hold Tuscolo but he has lost Baldwin and he is cut from the Queen's lands in the Seabord. With our force to the north of him, and Inchapter and Lackmere to the south of him, we have him in a vice.'

'So they say to me. Yet they say also that Gueronius hauls his cannon to Trant. If Trant falls, then we are cut from the south just as he is cut from the Seabord.'

'But our strength is greater, if we are given the time.'

'Have we time?'

There was something sharp in the King's tone.

'He that has iron has strength, but he that has gold has time,' said Padry. 'I have brought not only pikes but loans. Ten thousand crowns, from the counting houses of Pemini! And more from Watermane, which reached me on the road. I have secured them against the Queen's estates in Baldwin and other interests and promises it seemed good to me to make. In truth' – he chuckled – 'ten thousand may be gone in less than a month. But our soldiers and suppliers – they will not know how fast it goes. They will accept my promises for a full season now, expecting that they will be paid in the end. And they will be, if the Angels permit it.'

'I have lost count of my debts.'

Padry tapped his head. 'I have them all here. All your great debts and many of your little ones. I am your conscience, Your Majesty. The carrier of all your sins. And if I am slain before I can write them all down – why, your conscience will be wiped clean, as if the Angels themselves had forgiven you.'

'Not all debts can be measured in gold.'

The King's brow was pale. Little beads of sweat had formed upon it. Padry saw how shrunk indeed the flesh of his face had become. He could almost imagine the outlines of the skull beneath it. The hand that held the scroll lay in his lap. The other was turning something small in his fingers.

'Your wound,' said the King suddenly. 'How is it?'

Padry glanced down at his own hand. A big white scar covered the palm, surrounded by little clouds of red beneath the skin.

'I am healing, although not as quickly as a young man would. If we must fight this month I shall strike my blow for you one-handed. But perhaps it will not come to that. Your Majesty, I have counsel for you, if you will hear it.'

The King nodded slowly.

'It is that we send an embassy to Gueronius, with terms for peace.'

He expected a protest. None came. The King watched him with dark eyes.

'We will propose a division of the Kingdom,' said Padry quietly. 'The Seabord, the March and the south shall be yours, the lands around Tuscolo his. We shall exchange Baldwin for Trant, keeping Pemini and Bay. We shall say that it is better for all if we part in peace rather than fight in war. If we fight among ourselves, Outland shall surely learn of it. And that might destroy us.'

The King frowned.

'Gueronius may accept it, Your Majesty. A fortnight ago he would not have done, but he knows now that the scales tilt against him. Part of a kingdom is better than nothing.'

'You would divide the Kingdom?'

'To spare the lives and goods of many thousands of your subjects, yes. To preserve your rule across the greater part of your land, Sire, yes. And who is to say what the future will bring? A division need not last for ever.'

Indeed Padry had started to wonder how long Gueronius could keep the loyalty of his followers after such a peace. They would wake from their hangovers and find that Ambrose was controlling all the wealth-routes from the lake and the sea. And at Ambrose's side would be cunning old Thomas Padry, wielding his pen, ready to make this deal, that promise, send a letter or two . . . And there would always be the chance of some monumental act of caprice from Atti or Gueronius to hurry things along. Why, Gueronius might find his supporters leaching from him like sand-grains in the tide!

'My rule is no matter,' said the King.

'Forgive me, Your Majesty,' said Padry urgently, 'but it is. It is! You did not take the crown to break heads but to build schools. Not to slay lords, but to give law. I say this not in flattery, my lord, but because in my heart I know it is true. In this you have been the greatest King of all the sons of Wulfram. For the sake of your people—'

'Thomas,' said the King, smiling grimly.

Padry stopped. The eyes of the King had fallen to his belt.

'You still carry the dragon.'

'Why . . . Why, yes, Your Majesty.'

'Tell me then. Why does he bite his tail?'

Padry frowned. He could not see where the question was leading.

'In the lore of the Kingdom,' he said, 'a dragon is a

symbol of Eternity. He bites his tail to signify that the end is only a new beginning. In the lore of the hills . . . I suppose he takes his tail between his teeth for a better grip, or else the world he holds would fly apart with the folly of all that are in it.'

The King's skin was pale. The sweat was running off it and into his beard. But his eyes were bright. They were eyes that had seen all hope and love turn to ash. They had seen the future diminish to a tunnel of shadow. They looked steadily into Padry's face.

'Both answers are right,' the King said. 'Listen, Thomas. The lamp is out and the leaf has fallen, but the dragon does not loose his hold. He binds the world together. Why? Because all that suffers in the world will also be renewed. Every end is also a beginning. So our work, too, will be renewed. It will be renewed, but not by us, Thomas. The child in the furrows, the lord on his throne – they must wait for a little. Only a little. We must leave them for those who come after us . . .'

He frowned again, as if feeling some pain. His hand was open. In his palm lay the little white stone that he had been holding in the cart the day he had received his wound.

That long robe he was wearing, thought Padry suddenly – long and loose, falling all the way to the ground. He had rarely worn such a gown in Tuscolo. Why now? It concealed his shape. In particular it concealed the wounded thigh and the dressing that he probably still wore on it. And . . . Padry breathed in. Even in that open air he could smell the sweet scents that Ambrose was wearing. In a closed space they would be strong indeed. If he was wearing them to hide the smell of a bad wound . . .

Who was tending the King's wound? He must find out, and find out how bad it was. And yes, if it was bad, then certainly it must be kept a secret. If the counting houses had known of it, he would never have secured as much as ten thousand from them. If the army knew it, men would start to slip away.

Have we time? the King had asked.

But there *had* to be time!

'I have dreamed, Thomas,' said the King. 'I dreamed of Beyah, and her face was the face of my Queen. She is no longer weeping. She stopped weeping when I broke the Cup and her world shook around her. Now she is listening. She is waiting for something. Once I heard her cry, "Let them eat their sons." And I dreamed of Paigan, my uncle across nine generations, who was Prince Under the Sky before me. He told me that the Angels lie. I have not felt the Angels in years. The Angels lie, and I must die. Last night I saw myself dead. And dead, I led an army into a fight. And when the fight was won I gathered the other dead to me and led them from the field.'

'Your Majesty!' gasped Padry. 'I beg that you do not say such things!' (Dear Angels – one rumour of a dream like this around the camp would do more harm than a volley of arrows! Surely he could see that?)

The King shook his head. 'There is just one thing for us to do, Thomas. Just one. I do not know how it

will come to us. But we will meet it at Trant, I think.'
He closed his eyes. His fingers curled around the
stone.

'Is it well with you, Your Majesty?' said Padry, now
thoroughly alarmed.

The King did not answer. Padry fumbled for his
wrist. The skin was cold, the pulse weak. He turned to
wave the King's attendants over. 'Your Majesty knows
my signs well,' he said, keeping his voice level. 'Later,
perhaps we shall debate them, and – and my plan, too.
But I feel now that it is rest that you need . . .'

'I gave them to you,' murmured the King.

'Did you, my lord? I do not—'

'In the library at Develin.'

Padry frowned. He could remember a voice, years
ago – yes, perhaps it had been a child's voice – speaking to him of three signs: the lantern, the leaf and the
dragon. It had been the first time that he had
considered them together. But . . .

It had been a child's voice. One of the Widow's
scholars. So why should it not have been Ambrose
himself? The leaf, after all, was the badge of Ambrose's
mother's house. It *must* have been Ambrose. He had
never seen that before now.

And yet the voice had been so firm, so clear! Its
words had been almost a vision to him. The man
before him now was worn, wounded and betrayed. His
face was a mask of pain. How could the three signs
have come from him?

'Don't you remember? In Develin,' said the King.

The voice of the grown man was a whisper, all but

461

lost in the bustle of attendants as they supported him, threw his cloak around his shoulders, brought him wine . . .

'Develin,' repeated Padry. 'Yes, it was. But . . .'

In Develin, where he had first looked into the Abyss. In Develin, where a dark-haired, unregarded thirteen-year-old had turned to him and answered his questions with light.

Slowly a smile spread upon his face. 'Yes, it was. Yes, I remember.'

'Develin!' cried a voice across the meadow.

A man in the King's colours was running towards them from the castle. As he ran, he pointed out across the lake.

'Your Majesty! Develin!'

From the keep of Bay a trumpet sounded. Men were shouting on the walls, pointing southwards.

The flat grey surface of the lake had changed. Streaks of bright silver-gold lay upon the water where the sun broke through rifts in the clouds. Shapes had sprung into view there, where before there had only been emptiness. Where the water was bright they were dark, like small black-grey insects creeping on a sheet of glass. And where it was shadowed they were pale, thin and curved like the crests of waves frozen in the act of breaking. They were sails. From the shore they spread out to almost half the width of the lake, and from the first, a gentle mile away, they seemed to stretch back to the very edge of sight. A great fleet of the small lake-ships was riding up from the south under the breath of the wind.

'You see, Thomas,' said the King. 'Develin, too, was renewed.'

The south wind brought them – the warm south wind, loved by the lake-sailor, which was now a means of war. On it carried them, with a power that no iron or man could prevent, and their sails swelled and their hulls crept into sight beneath them, and the water broke white under their bows and the red-and-white-chequered pennants flew from the wide forest of their masts.

So the Woman of Develin came to Bay, with six hundred spears for her King.

XXX

Dreams and Tidings

elissa lay among the other servants on a blanket spread over cold earth. The air around her was shaped with the soft ripplings of canvas. She was in the tent of Gueronius, in his camp before the walls of Trant castle.

She was more used to sleeping in a tent now than she had been when they had first set out from Tuscolo. Hard ground was nothing new for her bones. And she had become accustomed to the sense of men lying close by, and others, many others, standing to guard with weapons and lit torches beyond the thin canvas.

She was even used to the cannon now.

There were six of them, sited further along the ridge at a point a few hundred paces from the castle walls. Each of them fired roughly four times in an hour, night or day, and kept firing so long as they had powder and the balls of iron or stone that they could fling against the castle. They fired with a horrid loud bark, which Melissa thought was hard in the middle but blurred at the edges. They made her head ache and her ears ring. If the wind was in the right direction she could smell the smoke from them, faint and sweet as it trailed through the camp. And by night, if she peered under the taut canvas wall of the tent, she could see the white flash they made, flattening the shapes of the tents into clear black shadows in the instant before the sound came.

She hated them, and she hated the bearded, chuckling Outlanders of Gueronius who walked among them, peering along each barrel before they fired. But it was not they that kept her from sleep tonight.

As she lay there, just below the surface of a doze, she knew that she was waiting for something. She had forgotten what it was but she knew that it would come and that it might be tonight. She could not have said how she knew – whether there had been some little sign that had shown itself in the day (a glance, a drawn breath, a hesitation?), to be noticed and forgotten at once, leaving only its warning behind. She only knew that she was waiting.

Then Atti screamed in the inner tent, and Melissa remembered what she had been waiting for.

She sat up, wide awake. Other people were rousing sleepily around her – guards and servants of Gueronius, jerked from their slumbers. She could hear Gueronius cursing.

Atti screamed again.

'What is it?' mumbled Gueronius's voice. 'What's the matter?'

'No!' shrieked Atti. And: 'Get away from me!'

465

'Angels' Blood! What . . . ?'

'*Get away!*'

Melissa was on her feet, groping for the flap to the inner tent. In the gloom she collided with Gueronius, who stumbled out of it cursing. She saw the paleness of his chest and shoulder and knew that he was naked except for a robe or cloak that he had thrown around his waist.

'She's having a nightmare,' he snarled. 'Get me dressed. Get me some wine!'

Melissa ignored him and slipped into the darkness of the inner tent.

She found Atti by the sound of her breathing, loud and shaking in the night. She took her gently by the shoulders and held her, rocking her and at the same time murmuring to her to bring her into wakefulness. A few feet away, beyond the flap, Gueronius was being surrounded by his attendants. She heard cloth rustle and wine being poured. Gueronius was still cursing softly under his breath.

First time it's happened to you, isn't it? she thought. *Knew it would.*

'Atti,' she whispered, still rocking the tense body that she held. 'Atti. You hear me?'

'Yes,' sobbed Atti softly.

'It was the dream again, wasn't it? It's back, isn't it?'

'Yes.'

She dropped her voice even lower. 'Was it . . . *him?*'

Him. Gueronius. The one behind the curtain. The man who had once really destroyed her house. The man with whom she had been lying skin to skin.

466

Atti sobbed again. The outer tent was in uproar. Gueronius kept an armed guard close at all times for fear that Ambrose might send the demon-princes to seize him again. Now they had come barging in through the flaps, weapons out, searching for the sudden enemy. Gueronius was cursing everyone for their stupidity. Outside, voices were calling, more armoured footsteps running. Men inside the tent were shouting, '*All's well, all's well*,' and others were saying, '*Nightmare*,' and '*It's the Queen.*'

But all was not well. She could tell from their voices. A nightmare? To the Queen? What did it portend?

She took Atti by the shoulders and shook her gently. 'It was him, wasn't it?' she said.

Atti went very still.

'That's who it's been all along,' Melissa insisted softly. 'He's the one who did it, after all. Don't you see?'

Atti shook her head. 'No,' she whispered. 'No.'

'It's got to be him! Don't you see?' Melissa shook her gently by the shoulders. 'Think! If it had been Ambrose he'd have done whatever he was going to do to you when he had you in prison. But he didn't. And whoever-it-is is still after you. Who else could it be?'

'Melissa . . . I *need* it to be him! He's crawled to me! If it was him I'd know what to do. But it's not! It's not!'

Melissa looked at the shape of her head in the darkness. 'That's why you love him, is it?' she said brutally. 'Him, and not Ambrose?'

'I don't love him,' said Atti in despair. 'It was

just – knowing it was him. Knowing I could . . . That's what I need!'

More feet, running in the night outside the tent. The jingle of armour. A man's voice calling: 'Your Majesty! Your Majesty!'

'Who wants me?' said Gueronius.

'It's *someone else!*' whispered Atti.

'Your Majesty . . .' The newcomer, whoever he was, was breathing hard. 'Your embassy to Inchapter and Lackmere—'

'Returned?' said Gueronius eagerly. 'What did they reply? Is it peace?'

'My lord . . . Raymonde diLackmere—'

'Damn it, man! What's got your tongue? What was his answer?'

'My lord,' said the man, fighting for control of his voice. 'He has sent you . . . He has sent the head of your emissary Cravaine!'

Melissa felt Atti's shoulders shrink under her arm. And she held her hard, tense because they were both tense, and Melissa's rocking became awkward and less gentle. She was thinking not of Atti beside her but of the bird-like face of a boy, suddenly solemn as she had never seen him before in the chamber of his King.

So Puck had got through. He had got all the way. That was something, Melissa thought. That was something, in all this mess. He was alive still. Maybe they would see each other again after all. Although just at the moment she could not think how.

'My emissary?' Gueronius was repeating. 'He killed my *emissary?*'

468

'Yes, my lord.'

Yes, thought Melissa. Because mine got there first. Puck got to him first, with the letter and the mark of the father's blood.

Puka halalah. Mister Gueronius, I think we've done for you now. And if anything happens to Puck I swear I'll push the knife into you myself.

'So,' said Gueronius at length. 'So. No quarter. No peace. I can send him no other until one of us is dead.'

'My lord.'

'Damn it! Why? I offered him half the south! *Why?*'

'I suppose . . . His father, my lord.'

'But that was fortune of war! And they were sworn enemies!'

'Even so, Your Majesty . . .'

'All right,' said Gueronius, pacing. 'All right. There's no use weeping about this. But if Lackmere and Inchapter are out against us as well, we must press hard. Bring me my commanders – now! Drag them from their tents if you have to. And bring me the captain of the guns. That wall *must* come down before the week is out . . .'

His voice was fading. He was marching out into the open with his men around him. The two women were alone in the tent. Melissa still had her arm around Atti's shoulders. Atti was weeping gently.

'Ambrose,' she whispered. 'I could have loved him. I tried. I tried. But everything was already ruined.'

She could not love anyone. She never could have done, because she knew someone was going to destroy

469

her again – someone close, who would bring her house and life crashing down upon her.

It could even be me, thought Melissa suddenly.

Me. I chose the King and not her. I was the one who sent Puck into the south.

And now the house was falling.

The south wind brought another sail up the lake – a fish-boat from Trant, crewed by men of the garrison. They came to Ambrose's tent and spoke to his captains there. They told of the demonic battering of the cannon, day and night, and of the way the old walls were crumbling under this witchcraft from Outland.

'First we feared it, lord,' said their leader, a grizzled knight who held one of the new manors that Ambrose had caused to be settled around his mother's child-hood home. 'Then we laughed when we saw how little each ball did. But day and night, one after another, without ceasing – the stoutest hearts cannot bear it for ever. I have seen our men weep, lord. And the stones crumble. The north-east tower will fall soon. Twice now Gueronius has called upon us to surrender and twice we have refused him. Now he swears he will kill all inside the walls. And we are loyal, my lord, but we are not many. We have families. There are women and children with us, whom we brought to your lands at your call. If Gueronius is not stayed they will suffer. And you shall have lost Trant.'

Ambrose looked around the ring of faces.

'Before all else, we must join with Lackmere and Inchapter,' said Caw, the flint-faced marshal of

Develin. 'We cannot do that at Trant, with Gueronius standing between us.'

'Why not?'

'Because it would be foolish!' said Caw harshly. 'It is what Gueronius wants. He is a war-fox, that one. He does nothing without purpose. If we come within his reach, he may overwhelm us before the southern columns can help us!'

'His strength is not much more than ours,' said Lord Herryce, who spoke for the northern knights. 'Who is to say he will win?'

'Who is to say *we* will? It is more sure to wait. With Lackmere and Inchapter we shall be two to three times his number.'

'And yet still we must find a way past Gueronius, or they must. Why not find it at Trant?'

'We do not need Trant. We need time.'

'We do not have time,' said Ambrose.

'Why not?'

'Because . . .' said Ambrose, pale-faced. 'Because Trant will fall.'

'But—'

'Lackmere will be told to hurry,' said Ambrose. 'It can be done quickly. You know that.'

In that ring of eyes they met each other's look: the grey-faced Marshal of Trant and the young, wasting King with the sweat glistening on his brow.

Caw drew a deep breath. He glanced to his mistress, Sophia of Develin, who sat in her black gown among the commanders. But she said nothing.

'Yes, Your Majesty,' said Caw at last.

XXXI

Campfires

ow the King drew upon his men-of-war. They surrounded him in a bright glitter of arms and the gay cloths of their tabards and pennants: Caw and Hob, the Marshal and Steward of Develin; Lord Herryce; the brothers of Saltar and other loyal knights of Tuscolo and the north; and the captains of Pemini and Watermane. Padry found himself more and more an observer. He put on a padded jacket and a coat of mail but they only made him feel ridiculous. He said little. When the King told him that such and such must be paid, or agreed, he shrugged his shoulders and wrote the papers with the necessary promises. There was no room for argument. Later, perhaps, he – or someone else – would count the cost.

He found himself more and more in the company of Sophia of Develin. She, too, walked and sat with the fighting men but spoke little. Sometimes in the debates they would catch one another's eye and a flicker of understanding would pass between them. The two of them were creatures of peace: of justice, judgements, politics and taxes. They had racked their brains and spent their purses to bring these men together. Now they must watch the dance of war.

'I do not like this press for battle,' Padry grumbled to her as they walked in the evening by the lakeshore. 'All reason still begs that we try for peace. Yet inexorably, it seems, we slip towards the other.'

'If we could be sure of a quick victory . . .'

'But we cannot be sure. And if we make a false move we shall rue it. A long struggle . . . What if Outland heard of it? We should see worse than traders then, I think.'

'You think that is her plan?' she murmured, looking out across the darkness of the water. 'That we should be buried beneath a new invasion, as the hillmen were buried by Wulfram?'

'I doubt it,' said Padry. 'I think she saw no further than her own desires, until Gueronius plucked her from prison in Tuscolo.'

In the moonlight the lady looked at him. 'I did not mean *her*, Thomas. I meant the one who weeps.'

'Her? You know of – of that one, my lady? I did not realize!'

'I saw her once. I have never forgotten it. Let me tell you, Thomas. It is not Outland I fear. Outland has put a tool into Gueronius's hand, yes. And in time these cannon may change many things. But you were right – we cannot pour that wine back into its bottle. The real weakness is here, in us. It is in our iron and in her tears. We are cursed – cursed because of that one hill child whom Wulfram killed at the very

473

beginning of our time! What can we do? If at every turn those tears bring us to—'

Noises behind them made her break off. They looked round. A gaggle of armoured men were emerging from the King's tent and clinking away into the dusk. A light glowed from within, diffused with the canvas.

'Has he dismissed them already?' she said, puzzled.

'Maybe there is a private audience.'

'With whom?'

The first rule of survival at court: know who is talking to the King. Even now, in all the mud and iron and canvas, that was still true. Together they hurried towards the King's tent.

'Who's in there?' Padry demanded of the guard.

'The King, sir,' said the man stupidly.

'And who else?'

'Why, no one . . .'

They could all hear the murmur of voices from inside.

'Drink, Amba, please!' a woman was saying. 'Don't you care for me?'

'No,' croaked the King.

'Ambrose – you *can't* take yourself away from me! Drink it – please!'

Padry blinked in surprise. He knew the voice. It was Phaedra.

The Lady Phaedra, here? When had she arrived?

'It is a life of a kind,' she begged. 'I live it. You can, too.'

Abruptly Sophia pushed past him and through the tent flap. Padry made to follow, but the heavy canvas dropped in his face behind her and he fought with it. It was moments before he was through.

The inner tent was lit by a single lantern, its flame wavering wildly around its chamber in the night breeze. The King was in his chair, armoured, with his head bowed. Sophia was on her knees before him, looking up into his eyes.

There was no sign of anyone else in the room.

Ambrose's eyes focused on Sophia's face. Padry saw him recognize her. He saw the King's arm grip hers with sudden urgency.

'My horse,' he hissed. 'My horse, quickly!'

The night air was alive. The lake breeze flapped the canvases and banners. It sang among the tent ropes and sent the little lake waves rushing over the sandy shore. Overhead the sky was marbled with the clouds, black and smoky silver, pouring across the face of the moon. Lanterns flickered behind the tent of the King where the royal squires led his horse to a mounting block.

'Leave us!' snarled Padry at them. 'Summon the leaders!'

They bowed and hurried away. The great beast was left standing there, towering over Padry and his master the King.

'Help me,' muttered Ambrose.

He lifted one foot and placed it gingerly on the mounting block. Padry took his arm. The lantern light played on the face of the King, frowning as he looked at the task before him, and on the face of Sophia, watching.

'You must delay them until he's up, my lady,' said Padry unnecessarily.

She nodded. But she did not turn away. She stayed, biting her lip as Ambrose put his weight on the mounting block and reached for the saddle. The King's foot fumbled for the stirrup. Padry caught it by the heel and guided it into place.

'Now,' said the King, drawing the word out into a long hiss as his knees heaved at his weight. Awkwardly Padry shoved upwards at his elbow. He heard the gasp of the King's breath in his ear. In the distance the squires were rousing the camp. '*The King! To the King's tent, all!*'

'Help me!' cursed the King.

His knees had given way. He could not mount by himself. Padry struggled to push him upwards. But the King was just weight, dead weight in his arms, and he lost his footing and fell heavily in the mud with Ambrose sprawling on top of him and the horse stepping away from them, unhappy with the fuss at its side. Sophia caught it by the bridle.

'They are coming,' she said. 'Quickly!'

'Get me up,' said the King between clenched teeth.

Padry struggled to his feet and helped him back to the mounting block. He was cursing himself for a fool – for responding without thinking to the King's commands. First see if he *can* mount his horse. *Then* send for the host! In the windy dark he could think of nothing worse than that the King's soldiers and lieutenants should be summoned suddenly in the middle of the night, only to see their liege, a

476

sick and wounded man, falling on his face in the mud!

'Come *on*!' begged someone. It might have been the King. It might have been himself.

The mounting block. The stirrup. The high, impossible side of the horse. The weight of the wounded man on his arm. And someone else was standing beside them. Padry opened his mouth to curse whoever it was and send them away.

The long face of Prince Talifer frowned in the torchlight.

'Your Highness – help him!' Padry begged.

He thought that with two of them, one on either side of the King, and Sophia at the horse's head, they might do it. They might still do it, even though he could hear the clatter and calls of a crowd approaching. If they were quick.

'Help us!' Padry said again. 'Take his arm!'

'Let him go,' said Talifer. His voice was cold. Dumbly, Padry obeyed. Ambrose was left with one foot on the mounting block and one in the stirrup, clinging to the saddle as if it were a spar in the sea.

Talifer turned away. He walked round to the other side of the horse. He was so tall that he looked across the saddle into the eyes of the King.

'Did you forgive my deeds, grandson?' he asked.

The King clenched his teeth and did not answer.

'Fourteen score years I was held in the pit, and my sins weighed me down like stones! Did *you* forgive them – pewling babe?'

His voice was passionless. His face was set. The eyes of the two men locked over the saddle. Sweat glistened

477

on the King's forehead. Beyond the tent the clatter of iron and calling drew closer.

'Who gave you the strength to take my deeds – *my* deeds – on your back?'

The King leaned forward. The leg in the stirrup was straining – shaking. Padry jumped to steady him, cursing the sick man, cursing the ancient prince and begging all the Angels that this time the wretched animal would just stay where it was!

'Who will not loose his hold, lest all the world should die?'

'*Aa-ahh!*' With a cry Ambrose jerked upwards, upwards and forwards over the horse's back. Padry caught his right foot as it flailed in the air and dragged it round the hindquarters of the animal, ready to risk any flying hoof if only he could get his King mounted before the soldiers saw him. No blow came. Talifer stepped back to give them room, looking up at the man who now towered over them, swaying in his seat.

Ambrose drew himself upright. 'A light,' he croaked. 'A light!'

Padry grabbed the lantern and lifted it as high as he could. Sophia started to lead the horse forward.

'Leave it!' said Ambrose, his voice strengthening. 'Let me ride.'

'The King!' called Padry as he came round the side of the tent. 'The King!'

There were men there, waiting. They had torches and weapons. Light glinted on armour and keen eyes. 'The King!' they cried when they saw him. 'The King!' Spears and swords rose like the surf of an iron wave.

'Soldiers!' called Ambrose across their heads. 'Make ready! Tomorrow we march. To Trant and battle!'

'Hurrah!' roared the crowd.

What's he doing? thought Padry. Battle? Why not peace?

'*Hurrah for the King!*' And there were more soldiers, more and more of them all the time, hurrying from the lines of tents. Lights danced in the distance, coming closer.

'Make ready!' bellowed Ambrose above the noise. 'We march!' He steered his horse in among them. They parted for him and thronged around him, reaching up, waving their weapons and their lanterns. Padry yelled for room and pressed forward with his light, but already the crowd was thick around the horse and he could not get close. He was pushed and shoved from all directions, and as he stumbled on the gentle slope he thought, *Why is he doing this?*

'The King! The King!'

'To Trant and battle!'

The crowd rolled down towards the main camp, surrounding and trailing the horseman like a comet's tail. All the dark fields were alive with voices. Padry was falling further and further behind. Try as he might he could not get closer. There were always other people in his way, other men, other lanterns. Still he toiled in the wake of his King, down among the tents where the soldiers came pouring from every side. His lantern was useless, his counsel discarded, but still he followed. They all did, because the rider was their King.

And in the crowd Padry saw her again, Phaedra the

mother, caught in the flare of a brazier as she watched the procession pass. He saw her with the clearness of a dream, by a tent marked with a crow's head. And yet just as in a dream she seemed to Padry to be standing in a world other than this, where there were no tents, no soldiers and no noise. There was only her son riding along the path to war. In the light of the flames Padry saw the tears like jewels upon her face.

At dawn the King struck camp and marched south along the lake. His banner led, with the loyal knights of the north around him. Then came the knights and men-at-arms of Develin, a small battle, but well armed and mounted. Next came the men of Pemini and the river, mostly pikemen in mail and crossbowmen in leather, and last a mixed force drawn from Watermane and some loyal territories of the Seabord. In all they numbered rather over four thousand fighting men with a long straggle of carters and camp followers accompanying them. They cut up the tracks and turned the fords to mud. They spread over the broad green hills and queued in the narrow places. And each man trod the world away beneath him, grunting and sweating, carrying the weight of his arms and pack, and watching all the while the earth beneath his feet and the back of the man ahead.

That night there were more disputes in the King's council. Lackmere's and Inchapter's columns had joined south of Trant but they had a long march to make up the distance. It was too far, the Develin leaders said. And even if they made it, their men and horses would not be fresh to fight. It would be best to halt for a day. Pressing on would play into the hands of Gueronius. The knight from Trant spoke again and again about the state of the north-east tower as he had last seen it, and the northern knights, who were quite ready to fight without Lackmere or Inchapter and knew well enough that they would be in the minority in the King's council if the southerners did arrive, made sly comments about the courage of the Develin men. The King listened with the air of a man distracted by other thoughts and burdens. Then he ended it with three words:

'We will march,' he said.

Why? thought Padry. And *Why now?* asked the faces of Develin. But no one spoke.

They marched again, a long day with the lake on their right and the hills of distant Tarceny like a rank of gloomy spectators. In the morning they filed slowly past the ruins of Sevel manor, one of the northernmost holdings of Trant, which had been looted and burned by Gueronius's men. After that they began to see signs of war every hour – barns broken for firewood, a deserted hamlet, a man left dead days ago, lying by the side of the road. Rumours flew up and down the force: Gueronius had retreated. Lackmere stood before the walls of Trant. No, it was Gueronius who was still before the walls. The castle would surrender that night if the King did not arrive. There was no sign of the southerners, although the men around the King still said that they were coming.

The foot soldiers shrugged and kept walking, because that was what everyone else was doing.

The light failed again. The lines of marching men and riders blended into one loose, dark mass, rippling with pikes and banners like a vast, hairy worm creeping over the hills. The sky was overcast and the setting sun was hidden in a mass of clouds over the far mountains. But to the south, low on the horizon, a strange light came and went, throwing hills and trees into black relief. The men pointed to it, wondering what kind of omen it might be.

'It's not lightning,' they said. 'Too small. Too near.'

The wind brought a soft, low *thump!* up the lake to them.

'Witchcraft,' the men growled to one another. But they kept marching, because the men ahead of them were still marching. The King was leading them.

Ambrose halted on a low ridge above the lake. From the southern end it was possible to look out and see the dark mass of Trant castle hulking on the next skyline. But it was not possible to press further. Down in the dip at their feet ran a stream, and along the stream were the lights of many fires. They had reached the northern end of Gueronius's siege lines, and Gueronius's men were ready for them.

The King held his last council beneath a great oak tree within sight of Trant's walls. Afterwards, Padry caught up with the Pemini leaders, walking back along the ridge to where their men were pitching camp.

'I will take my place with you in the morning, gentlemen, if I may,' he said.

They looked at him – a young knight of the Delverdis clan and a fat mercenary captain called Hawskill, who had been hired by the town to lead its bands to war.

'Oho! His Majesty wants to keep an eye on us, does he?' said Hawskill cheerfully.

Padry shook his head. 'I can be of little use to His Majesty tomorrow. But I was born in Pemini and I have walked with you on your way here. Give me leave to be one of you.'

He was, he felt, no more than a simple foot soldier now. Since all he could do was strike a foot soldier's blow for his King, it did not matter much where he did it. And over the past weeks, in Pemini and walking with the Pemini men, he had found himself at last growing fond of the town he had left behind him so long ago.

'Have you a pike?'

'I am one-handed, master, from a little wound I have. But I have found myself a knocking stick.' He showed them the cruel-headed mace he carried, which was as long as a man's arm.

Hawskill looked at it thoughtfully. 'Oho! You may stand beside me tomorrow, master. But I should be glad if you did not use that without you can see what you are hitting.'

A faint white flare flickered across his face. Long

seconds later came the *thump* of the cannon.

'Gueronius keeps to his lines, it seems,' said the young knight tightly.

'If he retreats now, he must leave those things behind him,' said Hawskill.

'He will not do that,' said Padry. (Gueronius, abandon a new weapon of war that no one else had? He would love those things more than any children!)

'I hope we shall see Lackmere's banners tomorrow,' said Delverdis as they resumed their walk along the ridge.

'He presses hard,' said Padry. 'They say he drives his men like a madman. He has swept the land for horses to mount his foot and will march them through the night.'

'So the King tells us. How he is so sure what happens ten leagues from hence I know not.'

Padry smiled. From the corner of his eye he could see another figure walking off into the darkness, long-limbed and moving in jerky steps like a crane. Prince Talifer had received his instructions. Now he would slip into the shadows, and in an hour or two he would walk out of the shadows ten leagues to the south, and speak with the son of Lackmere where he stood raging by the night roads.

Gueronius had his weapons. But against him Ambrose had a power that Gueronius could not dream of.

'No force will cover ten leagues in a few hours' march,' grumbled Hawskill. 'Not the half of it. We shall not see him in the morning, and we may not by the night.'

'He will come,' said Padry.

'I like it that you are so sure. Oho! Here we are, Master Chancellor. My lads have made a fire and I have a flask of wine yet that I need someone to share with me. Will you do me the honour?'

'Gladly,' said Padry.

'I must pray,' said the knight shortly. 'And then I will sleep.' He stalked off into a tall, circular tent that stood in the darkness nearby. Hawskill and Padry seated themselves on saddles by the Pemini watchfire.

'First time for him,' said Hawskill, grinning. 'His old man heard there was to be a fight and sent him off to strike a blow for the King. I'm supposed to keep him alive. Although the Angels may know how I'm going to! Mind of his own, that one. Not a good thing at a time like this. He'll be in the King's battle anyway. All the knights will. Here, I've a spare bowl that will do for you. Your health, Master Chancellor!'

'And yours,' said Padry. 'You've seen all this before, I suppose?'

'Oh, a few times. Tell you the truth, I never sleep so well before a fight. Show me the fellow that can and I'll tell you he's a better man than me, oh yes. No use tossing and turning and worrying about the sleep you're not getting. Better to sit up with a bottle and a bit of company to take your mind off things. And if our heads ache tomorrow – why there's always the chance that some kind fellow will pass by to take the problem from us!'

He chortled to himself, a sound like 'Hoh-hoh-hoh', and began to tell a story of a captain he had known who had been so drunk on the morning of a skirmish that he had led his men from one disaster to another. It was a stupid, sad tale, but they both laughed over the black humour of it and repeated the worst bits of it to one another as they refilled their bowls by the fire.

A white flash lit the distant hill lines. Some seconds later there was a muffled *thump*. In the light of the flames Padry saw Hawskill's face, listening, with a wry grin upon his lips.

'Here's to those fellows over there,' the mercenary said. 'May they drink bad water and have the flux by tomorrow.'

'Amen!' said Padry fervently and took refuge in the wine.

He felt curiously at ease with himself. Nagging voices in his head told him that perhaps he should be with the King, at prayer, or walking among the soldiers, encouraging them in the King's name. Perhaps there were around him men who even now would profit from a few words about the Angels. Perhaps his own soul would benefit from a short period of quiet meditation. But these thoughts only made him the more comfortable. He found that he rather enjoyed the wickedness of it – squandering these last hours in the company of a man who knew nothing of the Path, but whose ease and humour were a blessing in this long and horrible night when one could do nothing but wait for sleep that would not come, and for the distant dawn.

'There used to be an inn in this country,' said Hawskill. 'No, I tell a lie. It was between here and Tuscolo – a day or more from here, where road forks south for Jent—'

'I know it. They have rebuilt it.'

'Have they? I must go and look. But if the landlord is the same I will not touch his wine no matter how cheap he sells it. I swear the damned stuff smoked when he uncorked the bung. And in one mouthful I had so much grit I must take another to spit the first out with! If the trade of the landlord is to cheat his guest blind, that fellow was the master of it . . .'

And so the hours passed, in story after story. Padry told a few of his own. Hawskill listened. And at the end of each one, or maybe even before, he would nod and say, 'Aye, that puts me in mind of . . .' and off he would go on another, yet more gross or obscene than his last, and chortling 'Hoh-hoh-hoh' as he drew breath. Around them the night deepened and the murmur of the camp diminished. Horses called shrilly to one another. But even these sounds grew fewer. Every now and then there came the flash and thump of Gueronius's cannon, still battering at the walls of Trant. No one remarked on it now. Men were lying all around them, low shapes wrapped in blankets, faceless, but for now still breathing under the stars.

Around midnight, or perhaps some time after, a loud groan sounded from nearby. It was a pitiful, anguished sound, of a soul that could not sleep and could not tear itself from the thought of tomorrow. Padry looked up, wondering who it had been. Hawskill checked in the middle of another story and lifted his head to listen.

'That's the grief of the young, you see,' he said. 'They expect too much of themselves.'

Padry followed the jerk of his chin towards the tent of the knight Delverdis. There, in those coloured folds, a man lay with his mind consumed with horrors. Padry could feel sorry for him. Very probably the lad had never seen a fight before. Now he was waiting for the moment for which he had been raised and was feeling unequal to it. Padry wondered what the King was doing: whether he was asleep or awake; calm, or fevered with guilt and the burning caress of his wound.

'How do you think it will go tomorrow?' he said softly.

Hawskill pulled a face. 'Sometimes you can tell before it starts. Sometimes you can't. The King's got to break through to Trant. That'll be hard – across the stream with the other bank held against us. If you fall in that, you'll drown. And it's easy to fall in the mud and the press. If you're attacking you can't hold your formation. If you're defending you can. If we don't break through . . .' Hawskill frowned. 'What's Gueronius going to do? He's still banging away at Trant. So he must reckon that the wall's about to go. If it does go, maybe he can take the castle before we can get to it. Even then he must deal with us. He'll have to come to us then, so the boot will be on the other foot.

And at the same time he must block Lackmere if he can't bribe the man to stay away. All in all, I'd rather be where we are than where Gueronius is. By a whisker, perhaps.

'Of course,' he added, 'if just one of us gets close enough to Gueronius to knock him on the head, it'll all be over in a trice.'

Padry nodded. It was a cheering thought, up to a point. Gueronius would certainly be in the thick of it, wherever that might be. Angels above! It might even be that he, Thomas Padry, would have the chance to bash out the brains of his former pupil – brains he had once tried to fill with matters other than war. He did not relish the idea. Mainly he did not relish it because he knew that if the two of them came face to face it would, saving a miracle, be Padry's brains that would be left leaking from his skull.

'And the same if Ambrose is killed, I suppose,' he said. Then he wished he had not.

'Oh, certainly.' Hawskill looked into his bowl. He seemed to have finished it. He picked up the wine bottle and weighed it. There must have been some left, but not much. 'All things come to an end, I suppose,' he sighed. 'Enough talk. I thank you for your company, Master Chancellor. But let me be by myself now.'

XXXII

The Son-eating

adry woke in a grey, chilly dawn. The air was misty, the ground he was lying on hard and cold.

He sat up. He thought no profound thoughts. He found that he had slept in his cloak on the bare grass. He was still wearing his mail shirt and under it his padded leather jacket. His skin was clammy with cold sweat. His boots were on his feet. His bladder was full and his head throbbed.

All around him men were stirring, picking themselves up, shaking off the night. Bread was being broken and passed hurriedly around. Things were being crammed into knapsacks, horses led past. Calls sounded here and there on the hilltop. The campfire had burned to cold ash.

He needed water. But first he needed to get rid of it. There was no privacy on this crowded campsite, but who needed privacy today? The eyes that saw him might soon be staring sightless at the sky. He got to his feet, found his round iron helmet and put it on his head. He picked up his great mace and blundered down the hill a little way so that the greyness might make him more anonymous. From the sights and sounds around him he was not the only one. Of course not. Men were men, food-gobblers and piss-squirters all, until they stopped breathing.

He hitched his mail shirt up, got his hose down and did what he had to do. Then he reassembled himself. Thirsty but complete, he climbed back up the hill.

He could not see far in that light. The sun might or might not have been up – there was no telling. Low clouds had rolled in during the later part of the night. The lake was veiled. So was the bottom of the valley on the inland side and the rise of the far ground. Looking along the ridge, Padry could just make out the stand of oaks where the King had his tent. It loomed like a little low cloud in the greyness. The castle of Trant was hidden. So were all signs of the enemy. Padry could not remember when he had last heard the cannon. The army might have been all alone on its hillside.

Hawskill was standing by the blackened circle of the campfire, calling for the Pemini men to assemble.

'Water, Master Chancellor?' he said, holding out a flask. 'Drink well, for it will be a long day.'

'My thanks,' said Padry. He gulped at it, made to pass it back, and then remembered what Hawskill had just said. He drank some more.

A lump of bread was put into his hand. He looked at it and saw how filthy were the fingers in which he held it. Then he bit into it anyway. A few yards away the young knight Delverdis was standing, wooden-faced, while his attendants fastened bits of

491

plate armour over his mail. He saw Padry looking at him and turned his head to stare out across the lake.

'Here, Pemini!' Hawskill bellowed. 'Let's have you now!' Men were shouldering into a loose body around them. The air creaked with leather and rattled with pikes and helmets and spiked or flanged maces like Padry's own. Twenty paces away a band of men in lighter armour, carrying crossbows, had begun to assemble.

'One of Trant's towers fell last night,' muttered Hawskill.

'Oh! Which?'

Hawskill shrugged.

'Has Gueronius stormed it?'

'Not yet. But the King will attack early in the hope that we can prevent him.'

'Michael guard him – and us.'

'Amen to that.' And: '*Come on, you lazy pigherds! Where are you?*'

Hooves churned on mud. A huge warhorse was being led up, with drapes of white and yellow and metal plates strapped to its head and chest. They were helping the knight Delverdis into the high saddle. A lance was being held up. The knight groped for it, half blinded by his helmet. His mailed fist closed around it. The horse blew and carried him ponderously forward, towards the grove of oaks which was now showing a little more clearly at the end of the ridge. Other knights of the north passed, coming up from their tents and campsites to gather around the King. Hawskill watched them go, frowning.

'They'd do better on foot, maybe,' he muttered. 'Depending on what's waiting at the stream.'

'A horse can ford where a man cannot,' said Padry hopefully.

'That's true. All the same . . .'

Peering ahead, Padry could see another mass of men and horses forming between him and the stand of oaks. That was Develin's men-at-arms. He could see the chequered banner of the lady, the red squares just dark and colourless in this wretched light. They, too, were mounting. He wondered where the lady herself was. The lady, and the King, and somewhere away in the mist, Gueronius, too. All old pupils of his. *Not much luck, these pupils of yours, have they?* And a kingdom in play between them.

Hawskill, too, was looking ahead of him, eyeing the gap between Pemini and Develin.

'We'll have to close up,' he said. 'Forward, Pemini.'

And 'Steady there!' as the armed townsmen began to surge forward like eager hounds. 'Keep formation, damn it!'

In two great masses, bristling with pikes, they began to trudge along the ridge. The crossbowmen accompanied them, scattered left and right in no order at all.

'Where's Watermane?' asked Padry.

'Oh, they'll come along in their own good time,' said Hawskill.

There must be some instinct that forbade a commander from looking behind him, thought Padry. Look round and all your men will look over their shoulders, too. And once they do that, they'll be a moment away from running themselves. But he could not stop himself from glancing back. Others were doing so as well.

'They're coming,' said someone.

Beyond the heads and pikes of the second Pemini company, another mass of figures was moving towards them along the ridge. Distrustfully Padry kept looking until he could make sure of the banner of the Leaping Fish, Watermane's emblem, wavering over the men behind. Then he fixed his eyes forward.

It was as good as it could be, he told himself. There were two well-armoured battles ahead, between him and the enemy. And there were two more packs of stout lads behind, in case Gueronius suddenly came charging out of the mist and fell on their rear. The lake lay to his right, guarding him from that direction. He had mail on his back, a helmet on his head and a mace in his hand. Now, come all or come nothing, he must make himself ready.

'Halt,' called Hawskill. 'Crossbows, to the *left* of the battle, there.'

'What's the delay?' said a voice.

What was the delay? Twice in the next hour the column ahead – the knights of Develin – started forward, and twice they halted. Thinly through the mist the Pemini men heard the voices of hundreds of men and horses, crying aloud. They could see nothing. They could not hear the clash of steel or the splash of mud and water as the knights of the north fought to cross the stream. They could only hear the shouting, on and on, as though some giant cock-fighting pit had opened down in that dip below the grove of oaks.

It faded.

Later, after another march of fifty yards, it began again. They strained their ears, listening, trying to guess from the sounds whether the King's battle was surging up the far slope towards the castle walls or was still struggling in the mud and drowning in the shallow water before the unbroken spears of their enemies. Padry thought of the King, and also of the young knight of Delverdis. He muttered a prayer for both of them. He wondered if it would be in time for either.

'What's that?' said someone.

'Something's happening. They're dismounting, look.'

Ahead of them, on the end of the ridge, the mass of Develin men-at-arms was changing shape. Men and horses were milling. Attendants were leading horses away. The men-at-arms were gathering into a tight, well-armoured battle under a small forest of spears.

'They're going to fight on foot,' grunted Hawskill. 'So. Either the King's calling them forward, or—'

'Captain!'

To the left, and slightly downhill, the crossbowmen of Pemini were calling, pointing away into the mist. A dozen voices broke out at once.

'Quiet! Quiet all!'

Padry held his breath, listening. Ahead, the sounds of the fighting had died again. (What had happened down there?) The battle of Develin was facing left now. And from the left . . .

'Did you hear that?'

'Quiet, damn it!'

A clinking noise, as of many little pieces of metal stirred by the wind. Unmistakable. A column of armed men was moving to the left of them. Padry could not tell if it was approaching or marching parallel to the line of the King's army. He waited for it to become clearer. Long moments passed and it did not. He swore under his breath.

They must be enemy. They could only be Gueronius's men. Padry felt a sudden hollowness in his stomach. He gulped.

'Face to the left, Pemini,' called Hawskill. 'Pikes to the fore!'

For a moment all was chaos. Padry stood still, not knowing what was required of him. Men scurried and shoved past him. The pikemen, who had massed at the head of the column, hurried round to the left flank and spread themselves along the face of the reordered battle. Hawskill yelled and yelled at his men, pushing the crossbowmen off to left and right of the main body. Armoured figures clutched their maces and axes nervously, staring down the long green slope into the mist. And . . .

'There!'

A stir among the ranks, as though of a vast beast hackling up at the sight of a challenger. Down in the valley bottom, men were moving. They were spread thinly, almost like a party of landsmen innocently

496

gathering wood. But those things in their hands were crossbows, not sticks. And beyond them a denser mass was coming into view: a column of armed men under pikes and banners. Further off were horsemen – knights, from the size and weight of the shadows in that mist. And appearing to Padry's right was another body of foot, pressing down the line of the stream to find the King's flank as he contested the crossings.

Padry pulled at Hawskill's arm. Inspiration had seized him. For a moment he, Thomas Padry, was master of the day.

'There will be a gap,' he gabbled. 'If they keep to those lines of march, a gap will open for us in the middle! We could—'

'They won't,' said Hawskill.

Even as he said it the column below them halted. They had seen the King's army on the ridge. The crossbowmen swung towards them, some running to space themselves out to the best advantage. Beyond them the main column struggled to order itself. Hawskill eyed it coolly.

'Green, I'd say,' he said. 'Green, but eager. We'll see.'

The enemy mass was still ordering itself, seething and wobbling as it stretched to match the line of Pemini. Padry tried to guess their numbers. Fifteen hundred? Two thousand? He gave up. He tried to pick out the banners but they were obscure in the mist. He set his teeth and shivered, cursing the enemy for being so slow.

He badly wanted to empty his bladder again.

They were coming at last. It was most obvious with the crossbowmen, because he could see them singly. The massed column behind them seemed only to shiver at its edges with the movement of many legs. But it, too, was creeping forward across the short flat ground at the bottom of the valley. It was beginning to climb.

Thunk! went a crossbow a few paces to his left. And then *thunk-thunk-thunk!* as other Pemini bows tried the range. It was just like the first few drops of rain, heavy and threatening before the deluge. His eye could not follow the bolts. They flitted darkly and were lost in the mist. Was that a man down already? Or had he only slipped? The enemy bowmen were still coming on. They could not reply yet – the slope was against them. But very soon they would. Behind them the main enemy battle was crawling closer. How long now? Only a few minutes. Yet it already seemed an age that he had been standing here, watching them come. Why couldn't they be quicker?

Another man had fallen. That was good shooting. The enemy were raising their bows now . . .

'Heads down, boys,' said Hawskill.

And now there was nothing for it but to look at his feet, hunch his shoulders, point his helmet to the bitter sky. Now the bolts were falling among the Pemini men. The air hissed. He heard the rattle of points on metal. Green the enemy might be, but those crossbowmen knew their job. With the Pemini bowmen picking them off one by one, they still aimed their shafts into the mass of pikemen on the ridge, trying to loosen it, unsettle in, goad it into movement, so that it would be soft and disordered when their own pikemen charged into it. And Padry could do nothing but lean into the flight of arrows, one foot forward, staring at the ground and trying to make himself as small as possible under his helmet. Something clanged off a man to his right and bounced against his mailed elbow. Both men swore. A bolt should not pierce iron. But an exposed face, a shoulder-joint or foot . . . Leather was no help at close range. And the range was closing. The bolts were coming in more levelly. Someone barked with pain.

'Steady, Pemini,' called Hawskill. 'Wait for it.'

'Pemini for the King!' cried Padry, still hunching his shoulders. 'Give a cheer, boys, for the King!'

'The King! The King!' they roared. He could feel them stirring around him like hounds on a leash. Instinct screamed at them to hurl themselves down the slope. Training demanded that they lock in their places until the last moment. Away to the right there was a sudden surge of shouting as the battle of Develin closed with its enemies.

'The King! The King!' bellowed Padry.

He was looking up now. He could not help it. Over the shoulders of the front rank he saw the crossbowmen firing their bolts at one another at close range. Beyond were the real enemy, the massed pikemen and axemen under their banners – he saw the lion of Seguin waving over their heads, and other banners he knew from the lands around Tuscolo. He could see the faces, the eyes and bared teeth under their iron caps. And as they came on, they too cried: 'The King! Gueronius! The King!'

The voices blended into a roar. The enemy pikemen had picked up their pace. They were running forward. The crossbowmen, friend and foe, were scattering before them. The banners waved wildly over their heads.

'Steady, Pemini!' shouted Hawskill. 'Stand fast!'

On they came, bellowing like animals, the front rank beginning to scatter with the rush. Surely, thought Padry, now we must charge. He hefted his mace.

'*Stand, Pemini!*'

The tossing faces, mad-eyed, coming at him. It would be *that* one there, with the blond hair escaping under his helmet and his mouth so wide that Padry could see his tongue. He had a pike. It was feet away!

'*Haah!*' roared Hawskill.

'*Ha-argh!*' screamed the men around him, surging forward to the impact. And then it was chaos. Padry lost sight at once of the man he had marked. He beat wildly at a pike that came lancing past the man in front of him, stumbled, found his feet. He marked another man but the fellow went down at once, smashed by a mace that had come from somewhere. Michael – how little he could see! It was all tossing limbs and helmets and weapons, and he could only tell friend from enemy by the way they were facing. He seemed to be dancing on the spot, trying to keep his feet while the men around him jostled and stumbled in the fight. Someone was down. But he still had room to move and swing. There! He reached over the shoulder of the man ahead of him and rammed his mace like a lance at the face of an armoured figure. He felt the impact. His enemy stumbled into both of them and they tottered all three together, but another mace came from somewhere and smashed the fellow down. Padry jumped clumsily over him.

Forward now. Two paces. There were half a dozen Pemini around him but he still had space. He saw another man fall. He beat at a hand holding a sword and at a face masked by a helm and nose-piece. He stumbled and struck in a panic at an enemy which broke through the ring around him. The man slipped and fell. Padry smashed again and again at his head and neck as he lay on the ground. Each blow jarred his arms and elbows and yet seemed to do no good, for the metal clanged uselessly on the helm and neckpiece and the man seemed to notice it no more than he might notice raindrops as he climbed painfully to his knees in the mud. Still Padry beat at him, gasping with rage and terror, and still the man struggled to rise. And then another man was kneeling beyond him, knife in hand, waving Padry back. As Padry checked his stroke the knifeman jabbed in under the rim of the enemy's helmet, and the fellow buckled all at once. Not yet satisfied, the knifeman deliberately slid his bloodied point under the fallen man's chin and drew the blade across the throat. Blood soaked his hilt and gauntlet and wrist.

'That's how you do it, fatty,' said the knifeman, getting to his feet.

Padry nodded, gasping. His head rang with the cheers and jeers of the Pemini men, waving their weapons and hooting as Seguin's landsmen drew off from them down the slope. He could hear Hawskill, some way off to his left, yelling for his men to re-form. And yet more clearly than either, it seemed, he could hear still the cry of the dead man as he lay helpless and the knife had slipped into his throat. The man had cried for his mother.

There were other bodies lying scattered around them. Some were still living. He saw Pemini men bending over them with knives. He looked away. Someone screamed.

How many sons? he thought. How many here, and how many more at the streamside?

'Re-form,' Hawskill was saying. 'Back up on the ridge. Let's get ourselves clear of this lot.'

'But – should we not pursue them?' said Padry.

Hawskill looked at him. 'You think it's over, do you?' he puffed. 'It isn't. That – was just eagerness. They'll come at us harder next. And when they get up here they'll mean it.'

With a heavy, sinking feeling Padry looked around. Down in the valley below, Seguin's battle was re-forming. They were a milling, uncertain mob. If Pemini advanced now, they might yet take to their heels. But . . .

To the left, the mounted knights facing Watermane had drawn off. They had left dead men and horses under Watermane's spears but still moved as a body. To his right the enemy had also disengaged from

Develin and had fallen back down the slope. They were in good order, with crossbowmen coming forward to cover them. It was not over yet.

'Re-form, lads.'

With a weary clatter the Pemini men turned and clambered free of the strewn bodies. Here and there men stooped to snatch a weapon or a dead man's helmet. They gained the ridge-top and ordered themselves along it. Padry wondered how many fewer they were than they had been an hour before.

'The castle!' another voice exclaimed. 'Look!'

The mists had lifted. There, away to the right, was the castle: hulking, brown-walled, its black slits brooding on the scene like narrow eyes. It had changed shape. The north-east tower lay in a pile of rubble at the foot of the walls. There were people on the battlements. Padry could see their heads like black dots, tiny with the distance. And above them was the flag – the flag that the new wind teased out for the eye to see – blue and gold with the Sun of Tuscolo. The banner of Gueronius. He saw it at last, high on the ruined walls.

Trant had fallen.

'Will Your Majesty take wine?' asked an attendant.

'I shall have fruits,' said Atti. 'And clean water.'

They had set a chair for her at the edge of a grove of olives, under an awning of pale canvas. Servants and ladies surrounded her, together with a small bodyguard of armed knights. Nearby the bright yellow banner of Baldwin stirred in the breeze.

On the far side of the broad valley the armies were

gathered. One lined the far ridge, facing them. The other clumped and straggled in long masses of men and horses at the bottom. Scattered like fallen leaves between them were the dead. A distant sea of voices, clinking armour, drums and horns rose to the ear.

'We have him, Your Majesty!' one of the young knights was saying. 'His back is to the lake. And Your Majesty's own knights' – he pointed to his right – 'have gained the far end of the ridge. His retreat is cut!'

'He has the high ground still,' said another, older man. 'It will be hard.'

'I see,' said Atti.

That's your husband over there, thought Melissa, who stood at her elbow. *Surrounded by his enemies. And you could stop them, Atti. You could send to Gueronius even now. You could stop them killing him.*

A servant came forward with the juice of a squeezed orange. Atti sipped it. Melissa brought her the jug of water. She went down on one knee and poured the water into a bowl. And she looked up into Atti's face.

You could stop them, she thought. *If you ever loved him, you could try.*

Did you? I do.

Atti looked at her. Just for a second she looked into Melissa's eyes.

Then her gaze fell to the water. 'It is not clean,' she said.

It had been the cleanest Melissa could find, and she had searched for hours. Maybe, she thought savagely, maybe Atti should have seen what the

504

soldiers were drinking! But she bobbed silently and withdrew.

'How long will this take?' sighed Atti.

The crowd of Pemini men ordered itself on the ridge-top, pikes to the front and flanks and everyone else jostling in behind them. There was little space to swing. Padry felt exhausted and thirsty. His skin seemed to be covered in a layer of sticky sweat. He longed to go and empty his bladder somewhere on the reverse slope of the hill. But he knew that if he did, others would, too, and the ranks must stay ordered. The enemy attack might be only moments away. He wished he were not where he was. He wished that he were anywhere else in the world. Just let him live out this day, he thought, and he would never take up a weapon again. He would never serve a king or even a lord again. He would go away somewhere quiet, with a few books and enough to eat and drink, and live out his life where no one could trouble him. Perhaps he would even finish that wretched second volume of the Path.

The man next to him was testing his shoulder as though it hurt.

'Are you wounded?' Padry asked.

The man shook his head. In the cage of his helmet his face was pale.

'Sprained, I think,' was the reply.

'You had better take yourself off then,' said Padry.

The man glanced around. To the rear of the battle the slope ran gently down to the lakeshore. Winking in the new sun, the waters stretched left and right as far as the eye could see.

'Nowhere to go, is there?'

Hawskill overheard them. 'That's the truth,' he said. He lifted his voice. 'Now, lads. Take a moment to look behind you. That's the lake there – see it? You can't swim it and you can't hide in it. Don't think of trying . . .'

Padry was still staring at his neighbour, who must have felt his look. He glanced once at Padry and dropped his eyes. Then he muttered something, and sidled a little away in the crowd.

'We all want out of here,' Hawskill was saying. 'But the only way out is to *stay where we are*. Stand fast, pack tight, look after one another . . .'

Padry's eyes had not left the injured man. Because he knew from the voice that it was not a man. It was a woman. A woman, all dressed up in iron, so that neither friend nor foe would know the difference.

Someone's wife, or sweetheart, following in the ranks? Maybe even someone's daughter? Such things did happen.

And if there was one, he thought, how many others would there be, concealed among the men around him?

He looked around, but they were only armoured figures. The faces were shrouded in iron. The shapes of their helms, the crude, cruel axes and maces that they held in their hands were the only things that distinguished them now. And the woman, who-ever she was, had slipped in among them. When he looked for her again he could no longer pick her out in the crowd.

'. . . And some time today something's going to happen, something we didn't expect, and I dare say it'll all be looking bad. But we *stay where we are.* If we don't, they'll be burying us all along that lakeshore. This turf . . .' Hawskill stamped his foot on the thin grass. 'This turf *here* is the road home.'

Padry's bladder was aching. What would Croscan say about that? What could Thomas Padry, with his three clever little signs, say? The dragon does not loose his hold for pain. Hah. Wrap it round your bladder, Thomas, and hang on. Just as the men – and women – of Pemini must hang onto this ground. The army was a dragon, too. A great, thin worm, stretched along the top of the ridge. The Dragon does not loose his hold. But . . .

But down in the valley there was another dragon, and it had begun to move.

To the right, to the left and down there before him, one after another, the enemy battles had lurched from their places and begun to creep forward up the trampled and corpse-littered slope.

'Now for it, boys,' said Hawskill. 'Steady.' And he bellowed across to the second Pemini company, massed to the left, 'Master Knowlright, I'll thank you to keep your eyes on Watermane for me. They have the hard end of this.'

Padry watched the enemy pikemen, creeping up the slope under the banners of the Sun. He thought of all the things he had seen in his life – sack and

507

execution, monsters and a weeping goddess. None of
them had ever been more terrible, more chilling, than
these lines upon lines of men with iron, walking
steadily towards him. And now he knew what was
coming.

Thunk-thunk, went the first crossbows. *Thunk-thunk!*

Padry, with his eyes on his enemies, deliberately
pissed himself.

He pissed himself because there was no help for it.
There was no honour. There was no dignity. There was
no courage and there never had been. Either he did it
when he chose, or he would do it as soon as he lost
control. And he would fight with it warm and wet
down his legs, and if later he felt warm and wet he
would not know if it were his blood or just the urine
that he was shedding now.

It went on and on. The smell of it reached his nose.
Someone near to him swore. Maybe that had been her
– the woman with the shoulder. But he must forget
her now. Forget everything, but be ready.

'Heads down, boys.'

Head down. The rattle of the bolts, falling among
them. Were there more this time? Did crossbowmen
ever run out of shafts? Dear Angels, what if the enemy
just stood off and loosed at close range? Surely they
would have to charge! And then?

'Pemini!' called someone.

'Hah, Pemini!' cried others.

The man in front of Padry began to sway, lifting first
one foot and then the other as he bellowed, '*Hah,
Pemini, hah!*' Others were doing it, too. They were all

doing it: they were all one mass of armoured men, swaying and chanting as their enemies climbed towards them. Eyes on his knees, Padry joined in. He shouted with them. Over the chant he could hear other voices shouting other things, drawing closer. A bolt glanced off his helmet and another punched him in the shoulder but did not break the mail.

'*Hah-Pemini-hah! Hah-Pemini-hah!*'

His voice was hoarse and his limbs trembled. Still he shouted, rocking foot to foot with the men around him. He was not shouting for the King. (What were kings, after all?) He was shouting for his town – the town where he had been born, and which he had left while still a boy. He was shouting for the fighters beside him, born later but under the same roofs, the same stinking little streets, who had walked together to this little patch of ground by the lakeshore.

'Steady, boys!' cried Hawskill as the tumult rose.

'*Ha-aargh!*'

'Look! Your Majesty, look!' cried the excitable knight. 'His wing is going!'

On the far side of the valley the seething crowds had changed shape. They were bunching in from the right. Over there men were running, more and more of them, peeling away from the battle. The gap between right and centre was closing as the struggle on the flank was pushed inwards. The note of shouting rose, growing sharper, as if all the thousands of voices over there knew that a crisis was coming. And still more and more men were running, and now there were horsemen among them and the flash of swords.

'Who was that?'

'That went? Watermane, I think.'

'Now for the centre. Either they'll give at a rush, or . . .'

'Or they won't.'

No one spoke. Opposite them, the gap closed. The centre was one heaving mass of armed men, crowding together. Where the battle on the right had been there were now only littered figures, lying thickly, and the lazy swoop of black birds coming in to see what they could find.

'Go, damn you, go,' said one of the men softly.

They watched. Everyone – the Queen, the ladies, the knights and attendants, the servants and musicians – was fixed on the far hill, waiting for something more to happen.

Someone licked their lips. 'Stubborn, aren't they?'

'We just have to wear them down . . .'

'Look! Those knights!'

'Develin!'

A group of mounted knights riding along the very crest of the ridge. A chequered banner, square at their head . . .

'Damn it! Stand, stand, stand!'

'They won't see them!'

They waited.

'*Damn!* Are they all farmers, Seguin's men?'

The patterns on the ridge were changing again.

Slowly the fighting clumps seemed to peel themselves apart. Men were running the other way now, away from the struggle for the centre. A great crowd of them were running.

'Damn it!' exclaimed one knight. 'Damn it, damn it, damn it! Just because Develin had a couple of score men to put in the saddle! What do they think they're *doing* over there?'

Atti sighed and beckoned to Melissa, who bent to let her whisper in her ear.

'Well,' said another knight. 'That was that chance gone. Now what?'

'There goes Seguin, look,' said a third. 'He'll have them back together.'

The excitable knight was still stamping and cursing.

'He damned well better! Or I'll name every living man in his lands a coward tonight!'

'Sirs,' said Melissa, coming up to them. 'The Queen has a headache. She prays that those of you who can, be silent. And that those of you who cannot shall move a little further from her.'

My axe is dented, thought Padry.

Axe? he thought as he swayed with exhaustion. How is it an axe? It was a mace when this started. When did I pick up an axe?

He could not remember. He had been fighting, that was all. He had been pinned in a mass of men so tightly that he could not lift his arm. He had felt his feet lifted from the ground in the press. He had felt his own teeth snap together inside his helmet as he had tried to bite a man who had cannoned into him. That was what he remembered.

I am soaked.

I am soaked in someone's blood. Is some of it mine? In my sweat and piss. I could drink the lake if I could drag myself down there.

'Who has command?' cried a rough voice from the sky.

Padry looked up. A knight towered over him, high on a huge horse. Both beast and rider wore the chequered red and white of Develin, and the man's face was hidden in a great closed helm. The iron mask looked down on the Pemini men and showed them no pity.

'Who has command here?' demanded the Develin knight.

Some distant part of Padry's brain, where the memories that made him a man had locked themselves for safekeeping, recognized the voice. It was Caw, the lady's marshal.

'Damn all the Angels!' swore the marshal. 'Is no one in command of you?'

The Pemini men looked at one another. They were so many fewer than they had been. And many were cradling wounds, or had sunk to the ground. Where was Hawskill? Nowhere to be seen.

'Damn it! Who—?'

Hesitantly, reluctantly, Padry lifted his hand.

'Get your men together! And pick up every pike you can, because they'll come at you with horse. And don't you *dare* give ground. You hear me? You damned well stay and *die* here!'

The marshal had not recognized him. Very probably Padry would not have recognized himself. He felt his lips move.

'What of the King?'

His voice was a croak. His throat was parched. He needed water.

'The King is unhurt,' said Caw curtly, and rode on.

Unhurt. Padry knew that was a lie. It had been a lie even before the day began.

'Get together, boys,' he heard himself say. And: 'The King is unhurt.'

There was a pike by his foot. He picked it up. The head was gone. He found another. Then he realized he could not use it because of the old wound in his hand.

Shakily, the men of Pemini drew themselves into a tight knot on the ridge-top, facing all ways, pikes lowered like the spines of a sea-plant in the bay of Velis. Padry tried to count how many fewer they were than they had been. A third? A half? And Hawskill, too, was gone. Many of those still with him were dazed, bloodied, one-handed or limping. The slopes were covered with still bodies. Someone out there was keening, on and on – a witless sound. Crows and kites were beginning to hop and pick at those furthest from the standing men. (Think of lying there, shocked, bleeding, helpless. And the flutter and light scratching of the thing landing on your shoulder. The black shape of it might be the last thing you would see as its beak lunged in towards your eye . . .)

More horses' hooves. More red-and-white-chequered

knights came riding up to the rough clump of Pemini spears. Among them was the lady herself, Sophia of Develin. She wore a brown riding cloak and the black of her robes showed beneath it. Her face was calm.

'Well stood, Pemini,' she said. 'You are brave men. All the world knows it.'

The men looked up at her. Padry realized he must say something. 'A cheer, you fellows. Hurrah!'

They did cheer, for what it was worth. The lady nodded calmly and looked north along the ridge as though she was a little surprised to see enemy where she had expected to find more of the King's men.

'Are there none of Watermane left?' Padry heard her ask.

'There's that rabble down by the lakeside, my lady,' said Hob, her chamberlain. 'But I doubt there's any more fight in them.'

'Let us go and see,' she said. And they turned their mounts and disappeared down the lakeside slope.

A group of crows were squabbling over a body thirty yards away. Their harsh cawing mocked Padry's brain as he tried to think what more might be done.

'Where are our bowmen?' he asked the man beside him.

The man shrugged. He did not know.

'Flat, mostly,' said another voice.

'Stand fast, boys,' Padry said.

There was nothing else to say. Stand fast. (The dragon. The dragon.)

'They're coming,' someone said.

The enemy were coming.

How could they? Padry thought. How could they still want more? But they were coming indeed. The mass of Seguin's men, backed by mounted knights, was inching towards them along the ridge. And down in the valley pikemen were rallying again under the banners of the Sun. Soon they would be climbing back up the slope, aiming to take him in the flank as he fought Seguin on the ridge. Damn them! Damn them! There was nothing he could do.

And now, once again, that hateful hiss and rattle of falling bolts, and a man crying with sudden pain.

'Heads down,' he called unnecessarily.

He looked as his feet and thought: The dragon, the dragon.

More bolts. He had almost no bowmen of his own. The enemy could stand off and shoot at leisure. They could wait until the pikemen climbed the slope and then hit him from both sides at once. He was fainting from thirst and his limbs were shaking. What could he do? Nothing.

'Stand fast. Steady, boys.' The dragon. The dragon.

More bolts, and one slamming into his helmet with a force that made him reel. He could hear the enemy now, yelling their war-cries, jeering at him, coming in to kill.

'You bastards!' he sobbed. '*You bastards!*'

Then it began again.

Melissa watched in despair. Across the valley, the army of Gueronius was closing once again on the men who held the ridge. They were coming from the right, the left and the front, like a big loose fist. She saw the black flecks that were crows leave off picking at the dead and fly in lazy, low arcs off to a safe distance from the advancing soldiers. She could hear the shouting as the lines approached on another. And when they closed she heard again that curious, surging rattle which seemed to hide rather than reveal what was really happening among the armoured men. She watched it sullenly, hating it. She only wanted it to be over. And it seemed that it never would.

'No man should treat an animal like that,' said the Queen.

Atti was not watching the fight. Her eyes were on a mounted knight who had emerged from the olive trees forty yards away. The knight was standing in his stirrups, looking around him, looking at the armies across the valley. And yes, Melissa could see that his horse had been ridden hard. Both it and the rider were caked with mud. Its drapes, blue and white, were rent as if it had pushed through bushes. Its hide, where she could see it, had lost its sheen and was caked with pale, dried sweat. Its flanks were marked from the spurs. There was something strange about the line of muscles under the belly.

With the Kingdom tearing itself to pieces in the field, the Queen looked at the hard-ridden horse and frowned.

'Bring that man to me,' she said firmly. 'I want to speak with him.'

As if he had heard her, the mounted man turned

his horse's head and walked it along the slope towards them. A wolf-head leered on his blue-and-white surplice. Behind him more horsemen were emerging from the trees.

One of the Queen's guards strolled towards the oncoming knight and lifted a hand in greeting. The rider let his horse amble up to him and also lifted his hand. It held a small axe.

Melissa saw the blade fall. It seemed to move very slowly as she stood still and the guard stood still to take the blow. It caught him on the side of the head below the helmet. He fell at once and blood spurted like an obscene fountain into the air.

Hooves and screams! Horsemen, riding at them! Melissa gripped the back of the Queen's chair. The knights around her shouted in alarm. Some drew their weapons. The horsemen were on them, huge and black on their mounts. Melissa shrieked. Iron clashed. Soldiers were reeling. There was blood wherever she looked. An unarmed servant ran screaming between the horses and a sword came down to drop him bubbling at her feet. Then she and Atti were surrounded by the riders, and there was no one else left.

Atti rose, pushing Melissa gently aside as she clutched at her. Her face was pale. She said nothing.

'You are my prisoner, lady,' said the wolf-knight harshly.

'I do not doubt it,' said the Queen.

The knight turned his horse. All the slope seemed to be covered with armoured horsemen. More horses were coming out of the olive grove all the time.

'Sandes, wait you here and assemble the foot. Then take them to the left and down the stream to aid the King.'

'To the King. Yes, my lord.'

'Knights!' roared the ragged leader. 'Squires! Follow me!'

He set his great tired mount off at a walk down the slope. With a clattering and churning of hooves his knights drew around him. There seemed to be very many of them, following in an armoured cloud after the pikemen in the valley, who were still moving away up the far slope.

'And howl, my cubs! Howl! Let them know who's on them!'

A ghastly wailing broke from five hundred iron helms. *'Ahoo! Lackmere! Ahoo!'* At a slow trot they lumbered down into the valley. Ahead of them Gueronius's pikemen were still moving away up the far slope to join the fight on the ridge. They had not seen what was coming. The horsemen reached the bottom of the valley. Their pace checked with the far slope. Now they climbed it slowly, almost as slowly, it seemed, as the men they were following. And yet the gap between them was narrowing. Surely the pikemen must have heard them now. Melissa thought some in the rear rank were turning, looking behind them. The pikemen wavered, and halted.

The horsemen rode straight in among them. And the mass of pikemen seemed to burst like the slow explosion of thistledown under a breath of wind. Left and right men fled, dropping their weapons, running, with horsemen after them, murdering them as they ran.

'You keep your eye on these women,' an armoured knight was saying near her. 'Keep them close and out of trouble. I want to find them unharmed at evening.'

'And after that?' said one of his soldiers.

'That's not for you or me to say.'

And all the while more horses were coming out of the olive groves. These were smaller animals, with no drapes or armour but covered in mud and sweat. Their riders wore leather or mail and carried pikes and crossbows. They dropped from their saddles and waddled stiffly into the fast-growing mass of footmen assembling on the slope. Their banners were blue and white and the head of a wolf was stitched crudely on each.

'This way!' called their leader. 'March! And give tongue there. Give tongue!'

Again that eerie howling, as if a multitude of demons had possessed the souls of the men before her. It seemed like a dream – like a nightmare as they passed. And just as in a nightmare, Melissa saw Puck among them.

She saw his face, framed in a leather cap that was not his, passing her with the other men. His eyes were half shut and his lips pursed in the long, trailing cry that rose from a thousand throats.

'*Ahoo! Lackmere! Ahoo!*'

In the dusk of that day Padry was at the stream below the stand of oaks. Above him the tumbled shape of Trant castle was black against the sky. Behind him,

519

arranged along the banks, a company of Lackmere's men were pitching camp. Some of them were lighting fires. Others stood to arms watching the castle, for Gueronius and the knights who had fought alongside him all day were still up there. There he had sought to rally his men after their collapse at Lackmere's assault, and there he had been caught by the arrival at last of Inchapter's columns from the south. Now he was ringed in the stronghold he had broken, by a force far greater than the remnants left to him. And the end would come to him in the morning through the breach his own cannon had made.

Padry sat on the turf watching a half-dozen Pemini men wading in the water. They were feeling with their toes for bodies lying on the bed of the stream. All up and down the banks others were doing the same. Now and again a cry would go up, men would gather round and another heavily armoured corpse would be dragged clear of the mud. The men splashed to and fro, moving stiffly. One of them was singing in a low grumble the old lake-sailor's tune, 'South Wind'. He made it sound like a dirge. Padry wished he would stop.

As he sat on the cool bank and watched the searchers in the water, the past day seemed like a dream from which he had just woken. Then, as in a dream, he had been someone else – a madman, smashing and yelling and all the time waiting for the fatal blow to come on him from somewhere unseen. Now he was Thomas Padry again, teacher, philosopher and King's scribe. He found it hard to remember how he had gone from one to the other. Yet plainly he had. And nothing felt more likely than that the nightmare would come on him again, suddenly, and that he would find himself thrashing around once more in the iron and blood, in a dream that would never end.

'*South wind, sweeping the waters . . .*' droned the man in the stream.

Oh, shut up, thought Padry.

'*Take me back to my*— Here!' He broke off. 'This is him, isn't it?'

Shivering, others splashed over.

'There. That's his arm. Hold it . . . Get his legs . . . Lift . . .'

An armoured head broke the surface of the water. A plume of drenched and broken yellow feathers. A surplice of yellow that was smeared black with the mud of the stream-bed. The dead man was held in a sitting position as though he were having a bath.

'Lift . . .'

'It's him all right.'

Dripping and filthy, the corpse of young Hugo Delverdis was drawn from the stream. They gathered round him. In the half-light Padry could see no obvious wound. Perhaps the poor fellow had just been thrown from his horse and drowned. What difference that might make to the elderly father who had sent him here, Padry could not guess.

He was kneeling by the body, offering a short prayer, when light fell about him – the weak, warm glow of a lantern. He looked up. A woman in a dull habit stood over him with a light in her hand.

'My lady,' he said.

'My poor Thomas,' said Phaedra. 'Is it well with you?'

'It is better with me than with many, my lady.' He climbed wearily to his feet. 'I did not know you were here.'

'I followed you down the lake,' she said. 'I came by my ways and was not in danger. I thought perhaps I might snatch my son to safety if all went badly. And very nearly I did. But in the end it was not necessary.'

'No,' he said.

They looked together at the dead man before them.

'Delverdis,' she said, looking at the arms on the surplice. 'I had a friend in that house once. But they have not been lucky.'

'And the King – is it well with him?'

'He took no hurt today. But no, it is not well.'

'Where is he?'

'They have brought him to Manor Gowden.' She sighed. 'There is a council. He sent me to find you.'

'What is the matter?'

'The Queen has been taken. They will judge her.'

Padry looked at his feet. 'Must I be part of it?'

He did not want to judge Atti. What could the sentence be? Death, most likely. Why must he have a hand in that?

'I do not know where it is,' he said plaintively.

'These were my father's manors at one time. I will take you there.'

So he left the stream side and followed her. He

moved slowly because it was nearly dark and because he was exhausted after the long day. They climbed the far bank and circled the castle at a distance, moving among the camps of Lackmere's and Inchapter's men, some of whom were still coming in after marching for a night and two days. There seemed to be very many of them, limping and calling and crouching around new campfires in the darkness. The southern host was larger than either of the armies that had fought that morning. And Padry knew that this was exactly why the knights of the north had been so unwilling to wait for them. This was why the young Delverdis and so many others had gone to their deaths in the stream. Because tonight the King's victory rested on the south. The south had won, although only Lackmere's knights and those of the footmen that he could put on horseback had arrived in time to strike a blow. The south – Develin, Lackmere, Inchapter – would dictate the division of the spoils.

Padry knew this in one part of his mind – in the part that remembered the twisting and turning of the court and all the things he had once revelled in as chancellor. But most of him knew only that he was weary, stupid, sick, and could have cried aloud for comfort if there had been anyone who might comfort him. He walked on, following the mother of the King.

On a cart track that ran across grazing fields a few hundred paces from the castle walls, he passed a half-dozen large objects by the way. In the dark they looked at first like hollow tree trunks, balanced along the backs of carts that were sturdy but far too small for their load. They stood in a line, their open ends pointing towards the castle. He touched one idly as he walked by and found that it was not wood but iron. He could imagine that a faint warmth lingered in it and there was a scent on the air that he had never smelled before. Their mouths aimed a long, silent howl at the black shape of Trant.

Fifty paces further on he realized that they must have been Gueronius's cannon – those demon things from Outland that had lit last night with fire. Their servants were captured and their master broken. They were quiet now. And yet they had already changed the world.

He followed the lantern to where the King lay.

XXXIII

The Last Command

ain was coming. Cold gusts of air stirred the olive groves as Melissa rode with Atti in a cart, guarded by armed knights. Each time the wind rose it drowned out the grinding of the wheels, the muddy step of the horses, the clink of armour around her. She could hear only the roar in the branches. *Run, run!* it said. *Jump from the cart and disappear among the trees!* The night would hide her. The wind would cover the sounds of her movements. They might chase her but they would not find her. The arrows would miss her in the darkness. She heard it and did nothing. The stillness of Atti beside her made it impossible.

The manor stood among trees. It was a hall surrounded by a stockade and outbuildings. Some of the sheds had been stripped by soldiers for firewood and the animals had either been driven into hiding or taken for the camp-pots during the siege. Armed footmen warmed themselves by a brazier at the stockade gates. There were more guards and another brazier at the door to the house. The ground in the little yard was trampled and muddy.

The cart stopped. Atti and Melissa were made to get down. No one helped them. They were led into the hall. It was a small place, lit with torches, warm and close and sour-smelling after the ride through the windy night. It was full of faces that Melissa knew.

She saw the wolf-knight from the battlefield, still angry, still bloody. He paced restlessly and his face was that of his dead father.

She saw Padry, the chancellor, rubbing his hand across his brow. There were bruises on his cheek and forehead and a look like despair in his eye. And there were others Melissa had known from court, among them a woman who looked so tired and drawn that Melissa had to stare at her before she remembered Sophia, Lady of Develin, sweeping majestically through the corridors of Tuscolo on some visit from the south.

She saw Phaedra, mother of the King, dressed in a dull and shapeless gown with her bare feet peeping beneath its ragged hem. She saw them all. As in a dream, they turned to look at her – at her, and at Atti beside her. The faces ranged themselves in a close semi-circle around the pair of them. The room fell silent. Someone coughed, and a long low hiss came from the fire.

She saw the King.

He sat slumped in a plain wooden chair by the hearth. He was still in his armour but without either crown or helmet. His hair and beard were unkempt.

His skin was pale. His gaze was unsteady, as if he were drunk or fevered. Slowly he lifted his head and stared at Atti before him.

Atti looked round, proud in her silks within that circle of eyes.

'Well?' she said.

A man in livery cleared his throat. A herald. 'Lady, thou art charged before Our justice. Thou hast betrayed Us, thy husband. Thou hast committed adultery against Us, which is also treason. It is known to Us that thou hast done this many times.

'Also, with the traitor Gueronius thou hast now raised rebellion against Us, to whom thou sworest fealty as well as marriage oaths. Thou hast complied in the wrongful seizure of Our house and the murder of Our servants. Thou hast aided and abetted the raising of an army against Us. Thou hast ordered—'

'Enough,' said Atti.

The man stopped.

'Will the King not address me himself?' Atti said.

The King looked at his Queen. He did not speak. His eyes travelled past her and away to where Melissa stood. Melissa saw the moment when he saw her, with a sudden clarity as if he, too, were living a dream. He looked at her and she looked back. His eyes said, *Melissa. What will you say?*

Me? thought Melissa.

'Thou stand'st accused, lady,' said the herald. 'Wilt answer nothing?'

Atti bent slightly and peered at the man in the chair. She drew a long breath.

'Wilt answer nothing, lady?'

'I answer that your King is dying,' she said.

Dying! The thought lurched into Melissa's brain like a monstrous thing. She stared at Ambrose. The way he looked! The way he did not speak! She stepped forward, breathed deeply and – and . . . (No! Angels, please, no . . .)

'He is dying,' Atti repeated. 'I can smell it. So can you. His flesh rots. He has a poisoned wound. Look – he is at the edge of delirium. What judgement can he give now?'

It was there, in the air. Among the woodsmoke and the sweat smells there was something else: a foul scent of dark pus that weeps from wounds. That was not a hurt he had had today. That must have been done many days ago. It must have been festering all the while the armies had been marching. Wounds like that did not mend. Melissa knew that. They got worse and worse, and the sufferer went into a fever. And then he would die.

'Will you kill me, sirs?' Atti said. 'It will do you no good. You have already lost, because you are losing your King. Only Gueronius can claim the throne now. You will have to treat with him. Will he be the better pleased with you if my blood is on your hands?'

And the King was still looking at Melissa. Not at Atti, not at the lords and ladies and pages around him whose words seemed to be coming from so far away. He was looking at her as if there were no one else. His eyes were intent, fierce, gripping at her as if she were the last, the very last thing they could hold onto – as if he had been waiting for her a long time, and was still waiting even as his death sickened in his limbs.

'Why should we send to him?' a man grumbled. 'We have the whip hand. Should he not send to us?'

'Could we trust him to keep his word?' another said.

'What does it matter?' urged Atti. 'You are the stronger and he knows it. More deaths will achieve nothing.'

'At Bay I counselled a division of the Kingdom,' said Padry. 'Perhaps something along the same lines—'

'By my blood, no!' That was the knight of Lackmere, pushing angrily into the middle of the circle. And still the eyes of the King held Melissa, and they said, *What will you say?*

What *can* I? she thought. In another time, another place, we could have been . . . If we had had our years again, and nothing like this had happened! But I'm what I am, you are what you are, and now it's too late. Don't you see? What can I say that would change that?

'. . . I did not march my people here to see Gueronius crowned!' The knight of Lackmere was jabbing his finger within inches of the Queen's face. 'Nor did I have them spill their blood to put *you* by his side! And how long would it be before Gueronius grew itchy on his throne, and thought it better to be rid of me?'

'Gueronius is not caught yet, sir,' said the Queen coldly. 'Will you spill blood again tomorrow, for a cause that you know is lost?'

529

'After your doings, lady, do *you* tell me to spare lives? My King is dying, you say. What of it? We have all been dying since the day we were born. My King lives yet. He will live longer than Gueronius, I swear to it!'

For a moment Atti looked back at him. Then she turned to the Lady of Develin. Her voice was still cold, but now it shook slightly. 'Madam? Will you be counselled in policy thus? By – by a fratricide?'

'The fratricide speaks well, it seems,' murmured the Lady of Develin. 'He may speak for me.'

'There can be no peace with Gueronius,' said Lackmere. 'Nor can there be delay. We shall *not* send for a surrender! We shall *not* sit down and wait for Gueronius to starve! When it is light tomorrow we will climb the breach. And I claim the right to lead, since this is my counsel, and I would have Gueronius account for the blood of my father.'

'Well enough,' said another lord. 'But if we offer no quarter it will be a stiff fight indeed.'

Lackmere shrugged. 'We have a breach, and we have numbers. And tonight we will fashion ladders – as many as we can. I shall send my footmen to climb the wall. We shall come at him from every side.'

The footmen, Melissa, said the eyes of the King.

The footmen! Into her mind jumped the image of Puck, marching eagerly with his fellows in a leather cap and coat, and his silly face pursed up in a howl. And now she understood what they were talking about, even as their King died among them. Puck! Were they going to take him, too? Were they going to

530

take *everything*? She tore her eyes from Ambrose and looked around her.

'So tomorrow we begin again,' said someone.

'It will be bloody, in the breach,' said another. 'And worse still on the walls.'

'The price must be paid,' said Lackmere. 'With the strength he has left, I do not think he can guard all points. We shall have the castle soon enough—'

'Sir!' said Melissa.

The word was forced from her by her lungs and heart. She dropped to her knees before the Knight of Lackmere. 'Sir, please. There's no call for more of this, is there? You've won, haven't you? Why get more men killed?'

The man turned away as if he had not even heard her.

'Please, sir! Don't get them killed! Please!'

'Angels' Knees!' she heard him mutter. 'Get her off me!'

From behind, an armoured hand grasped at her shoulder. She shook it off and reached out again. She was following Lackmere on her knees, clutching at his armoured leg.

'Sir, if you must fight, then – then don't send the footmen! My lord – it isn't right! What are they? Young boys – that's all! They don't *know* anything. Don't send them to the wall! They'll just . . .'

Eyes all around the room were staring at her. Lackmere had his back to her. Someone in mail was pulling at her arm. 'Come,' said a voice in her ear. 'This is unseemly.'

531

Unseemly? Melissa did not care. She could see Puck – her Puck – in his leather jacket and little iron helmet, trying to climb a rickety ladder while men shot arrows and dropped stones on him from above, and the walls were painted in blood!

He mustn't go!

And all the eyes, all the world was watching her. She felt it. She felt almost as if she had broken into two people, one still Melissa, begging for what Melissa wanted, and one that was another woman, crying to another armoured man for a child Melissa did not know. Her words were coming with a force that startled her. As if they had started from somewhere far away, even before she had been born.

'Sir, there is one . . . He is not yours, sir, but I saw him with your men. He brought your father's message to you. *Please*, sir, don't send him!'

The knight looked at her for the first time. And although he did not answer her, she saw a moment's hesitation in his eye. She fought the arm that dragged her back, and her voice rose.

'He *isn't* yours. He's . . . he's mine. *I* sent him to you. Don't make him go tomorrow!'

'Quiet, damn you!' said someone, and cuffed her. Her head sang with the blow.

Above her she heard the knight say, 'I can spare none. I am bidden not to.'

'Sir!' she begged. But the knight shook his head. The brief flicker in his face was gone. In agony she cast around for someone who knew her – someone who could speak for her in that room. Atti was looking down at her. Her eyes were very hard and bright. Melissa lifted her hand in appeal.

Then she realized what she had said.

He brought your father's message. Atti had heard that. And *I sent him to you.* Atti would guess what that meant. She knew now who it was who had betrayed her; who it was who had been so close to her all the time, and yet had betrayed her in the end. She saw the knowledge settle in Atti's dark eyes. She saw Atti draw a long breath.

But she did not speak to Melissa. She spoke to the knight, in a voice that was stony and small. 'Sir? You have heard. Will you not spare even one?'

'Each will have as good a chance as any. But I may spare none.'

'Not one? Do you even know the man you condemn, sir?' said Atti.

'Lady, I know every face of every man who came with me from Lackmere. Aye, I mind the boy well enough. But if I hold back one, then another must fall in his place. And what shall I say to that one's sweetheart?'

'But he *isn't* yours!' Melissa cried again. 'He's not! He's the King's, if he's anyone's—'

The King!

On her knees, Melissa turned to him, arms outstretched. 'Your Majesty!'

'That's enough!' barked the knight. 'Get her out of here!'

'Your Majesty . . . Once you said you'd do something if I asked . . .'

The King was still watching her. And as she clutched at his armoured feet and looked up at him, she thought she saw him straining to hear, and that his head even bent towards her a little.

'*Please!*' she shrieked as the men seized her by the arms. 'Please – let him go!'

She was being dragged, wrestling and thrashing, across the floor. Something hit her on the side of her head. Everything went red-dark for an instant and sparkled with tiny stars. She heard the King cry aloud. When her sight cleared she saw him again.

He had hauled himself forward in his seat, gripping the arms of his chair as if in spasm. Now he was looking at Lackmere. His mouth was open. The room stilled.

Painfully the King lifted his arm. His finger trembled as he held it up. His mouth worked but no sound came.

No one moved. They were holding their breath, all of them, listening to the air that gasped in the King's throat.

'One . . .' he said to the Knight of Lackmere.

And again: 'One.'

At last Lackmere bowed. 'As you command.'

He straightened, and repeated: 'As Your Majesty commands. The boy may go.'

The wind moaned in the trees. It was as if the whole world had breathed out together at the King's word.

They carried the fainting man away. Guards clattered out into the night, calling for the surgeon. Others gathered around the Lady of Develin and talked

534

urgently about councils and parliaments. The Knight of Lackmere was speaking of ladders again. Melissa looked up and found Atti standing over her. Her face looked suddenly older, as if the great pain inside her were speaking at last through her eyes.

'It was you,' she whispered.

'Yes,' said Melissa dully. 'It was.'

Atti's mouth was a black slit. She stared at Melissa a moment more and then, as if she could no longer bear to look at her, she turned away.

'I knew it would be someone,' she said. 'It had to be. I never thought it would be you.'

Melissa did not answer.

'Why?' asked Atti.

(Why? thought Melissa.)

'For the King,' she said.

'But *why*?'

'Don't you understand?' cried Melissa. 'I loved him! Look at me, Atti. Look at me! I *loved* him! Can't you see that?'

Atti stood there for a moment, silent, with her back turned. Then she said, 'I don't know what you mean.' And she pushed the rough door-curtain to one side and stepped out into the night. In the glare of the brazier Melissa watched her slowly crossing the court-yard. Men cried aloud. Startled guards tumbled after her, clattering with iron as they hurried to prevent her walking clean away. The last Melissa saw of her was the side of her face, looking over her shoulder as they surrounded her and steered her towards the confines of an animal shed. And the first drops of rain were beginning at last, flashing in the torchlight as they fell singly and hissed in the brazier like arrows shot from the sky.

Melissa crouched by the doorpost, alone and hugging her elbows. No one was paying attention to her. The armoured men had gathered around the Lady of Develin by the hearth. Runners were being sent out with orders – for the storming parties, for ladders to be made, and yes, that a certain hill boy was to be found among the footmen of Lackmere and brought to Manor Gowden before dawn. No one talked yet of what would be done when there was no king in the land.

But as she listened Melissa began to realize that something had changed. They did not sound quite so tired now. It was as if a weight had been lifted from them. As if they could feel at last the glow of the fire on their skin, which had been cold for too long.

'. . . No, my lord,' the lady was saying. 'You have your tryst with Gueronius in the morning. Be content with that. But the Queen has done no bloody act herself. Surrender her to me, and I shall see that she is held in a convent in my lands where she may do no harm.'

The Knight of Lackmere was frowning. Watching, Melissa sensed again the struggle that had flickered in his eyes as she had pleaded with him for Puck. But his demons had lost their force now.

'As you wish,' he said tersely. 'Who am I to condemn her, after all?'

'And the Outlanders?' asked someone else.

'They shall have their lives, too,' he said. 'We will have need of what they know, I think.'

'Very well.'

The council was breaking up. Men left the room. The Lady of Develin remained in her chair, conferring in low voices with the Knight of Lackmere and Lord Herryce. At the fireside two other men had begun to play a game of chess. Melissa did not know their names. She had not seen them before.

Phaedra emerged from the inner room where Ambrose lay. Her face was tired and drawn, as if she had lost all hope of anything being good again. She came and leaned on the doorpost beside Melissa, looking out into the night and rain. Padry the chancellor saw her. He crossed the room to stand at her elbow.

'My lady . . .' he said in a low voice.

Oh, leave her alone, thought Melissa wearily. Can't you see how she's hurting?

'My lady, there is something I must ask you.'

Phaedra sighed. She looked down at her hands. 'What is it, Thomas?'

'You brought him the Tears, when we were at Bay.'

She seemed to think for a moment. Then she whispered, 'I did.'

'Why, my lady? For no sooner had you gone than he roused the camp! He had always been for peace. Yet he roused us and led us to a fight that we now know was useless. Why did you bring them to him? Forgive me but . . . I must ask.'

She looked at him wearily. 'You accuse me, Thomas? Of the deaths of thousands, and of my son?'

'Forgive me. But is it not so?'

'I brought him the Tears so that he might *live*, Thomas. I was on my knees to him. You heard me. He would have lived as I live, and as the princes have lived – it is a sort of life, and no sickness, no ageing . . . Yes, in his last fever I would have poured them down his throat. I would have done it whatever the price!

'But . . .' She drew a long, shaky breath. 'But he would not drink. Instead he chose this. He led us all to his death, when he knew that the goddess would hear him. Because he guessed that here, in the great eating of sons, there would be the chance to say what he has said. And now the hill boy has been saved by the last command of the King – by the last of the line of Wulfram, who killed the hill prince hostage at the beginning of his reign. She will depart. She is departing now. Don't you feel it? Already they have begun to spare lives they would have taken without thinking. Because he spoke the word she was waiting for.

'And her tears will dry. They will dry in the hearts into which they have fallen. Their power is going. They cannot save him any more. Even the princes will grow old and die as men. And only I will remain – because I must take her place.'

'I see,' said Padry softly. 'I see.'

He cleared his throat. 'I must beg your pardon, my lady. I am – more sorry than I can say.'

'Yes, be sorry for me,' she muttered. 'Be sorry for every mother whose son has died today, or will

538

tomorrow! What *right* have they to do this to us? But Thomas, Ambrose was no hapless victim. He knew what he did. And I knew that he would. In my heart I think I have known it all his life. Yes, I shall weep. But my tears will not be poison to the world.'

'Is there anything I can do?'

'*Do?*' she exclaimed. 'There is nothing you can do!'

She was silent for a moment. Then in a slightly steadier voice she said, 'Find me someone who can cut stone, if you can.'

'Stone? Yes. Yes, I – I will try.'

Neither of them said anything more. After a moment the man bowed and stepped out into the rain. Phaedra remained where she was.

By the hearth the chess pieces clicked and the counsellors murmured. Melissa watched them. But neither game had ever made sense to her. And now they never would. None of the things they were thinking about over there were to do with her any more.

'You going home, my lady?' she asked suddenly.

Phaedra looked down at her. 'In a little, Melissa. After this. Yes, I – I think I shall go home.' Her voice was hoarse and her cheek glistened in the firelight.

'Can I come with you? I don't think I want to stay here.'

Phaedra looked at her with hollow eyes.

'And – and Puck can sail us in a boat if you need him to,' Melissa said. 'He's told me so.'

'Yes,' Phaedra said at last. 'Yes, you will be welcome, Melissa. You and your hill boy, too. You will be a comfort to me. I see such ages of weeping in a dark place . . .' She sighed, and her voice strengthened a little. 'And yes, maybe we should go by boat, as far as we can. It will be easier for us to travel together that way, for you will not want to walk in my places. It will be safer, too, if there are soldiers on the roads.'

She looked out at the night again.

'I knew something of boat-sailing once,' she murmured. 'I wonder how much I will remember.'

XXXIV

Lakeshore

e died the next morning, while the battle raged on the walls.

Afterwards they carried him up to the castle where men were still counting the bodies and stripping the slain. In the chapel of Trant they lit the flame on the altar and laid his body on a trestle. The nobility of the land, limping and pale-faced, came at noon to hear the prayers for his soul. A priest spoke in words that echoed flatly around the stone. The lords bowed their heads and afterwards they departed. Guards stood about the corpse. Phaedra waited, with Melissa at her side, until the chapel was clear. Then she approached him.

He lay like a carved figure, motionless in his armour. His hands were folded across his chest. His face had lost its fever and his eyes were closed as if in sleep. Around him the guards stood silently and the sun from the windows glinted on their stained armour. The two women looked down on the man. Melissa wanted to say something but her throat was burning and she could not.

541

Phaedra reached forward to open her son's fist. There, clutched in his stiff fingers, was the white pebble.

'Give Mama,' she murmured. She prised it from him.

And she took it, and gripped it hard.

The light tock of a hammer sounded from an aisle as they made their way back to the chapel door. There was a man, crouching by one wall with tools in his hand. He was cutting something into the stone. Melissa could see where he had already traced the lines he was going to carve. But of course she could not read them.

'What's it say, my lady?' Melissa asked.

'Ambrose Umbriel, King,' Phaedra said, choking.

There were other names cut there – a whole line of them, done years ago. Melissa did not ask any more.

The sun was low, glinting on the far fringe of mountains and flaring along the lake. The olive groves above the shore were alive with the calls and clanks of soldiers settling to camp. The scent of cooking fires was beginning to creep through the trees. The wavelets lapped at the stony fringe of the lake where Padry paced, waiting.

Drawn up on the shingle was a small lake-boat. He had found it during the day at a little jetty by a hamlet Phaedra had directed him to. He had found and paid a crew to man it. (*He* was not going to trust the lives of its passengers to one inexperienced hill boy!) There had been no news of the owner. Perhaps the man had been one of the luckless settler-garrison of Trant, who now lay dead within the castle and whose bones had been buried beneath those of his killers, and of his killers' killers, as the last act of the King's reign was fought out within those walls.

The little wavelets glittered in the last of the day. The surface of the lake was lit with it. And Padry remembered another shore, with the sun setting on the waves of Velis and an arm pointing eagerly out to sea as a king surveyed his new toys. But Gueronius, too, had died that morning, caught between iron and the castle stones. He had fought to the last like a cornered beast. He would not have remembered or asked himself what it meant. He had never been one to ask for meanings.

All that was over. The house of Tuscolo was broken. The house of Baldwin had been broken long ago. And in Ambrose the last drop of Wulfram's blood had been spent. That great dynasty was ended. What was left? Not very much. Some good things: a few laws and charters, a new school, a bundle of good intentions for others to copy and improve upon. *We must leave them now*, Ambrose had said, *for those who come after us.*

Padry turned.

He had ordered the boat to be brought here from the jetty because this stretch of shore was deserted. Phaedra wanted no fuss about her departure. Now he was annoyed to see that he was no longer alone. A number of figures were picking their way towards him along the water's edge. He went to meet them, intending to send them quickly about their business.

They did not seem to be soldiers. They wore no armour, nor were they liveried servants of some lord. They wore robes and hoods and some of them moved strangely. And it began to puzzle him, as he approached, that they were so few. When first he had seen them he had been sure there had been half a dozen, certainly. But now he could see he was mistaken. They were only four . . . no, three . . .

Surely . . .

He stopped. The leader was a tall man, very tall and lean. He knew that shape. And now there was only one beside him, a small fellow who stooped. But he did not stoop as much as he had when Padry had first seen him, in the King's chamber more than two years ago.

He bowed. 'Your Highnesses,' he said.

Talifer, son of Wulfram, and Marc his brother bowed briefly in return. The others must have faded as Padry had approached, hiding their half-human forms in the shattered netherland of brown rocks. They would be watching him now. But he could not see them.

'I await the mother of the King,' said Padry.

'She comes,' said Talifer.

'Let us pray that she journeys well,' said Padry.

The princes were silent.

'I remember praying,' said Marc at length. 'I do not remember that I ever meant it for truth.'

People and horses were coming down through the olive groves to the lakeshore. There were armoured knights among them, leading their mounts. There were banners. Padry glimpsed the blue and white of Lackmere and the red-and-white chequers of Develin. He saw Phaedra and the Lady Sophia, too. And behind them were Melissa and a young hillman he did not know. A lucky young hillman, Padry thought. Lucky for all of us. *Vast things, things we cannot understand, may turn because a man helps an old widow with her load.* Who had said that? Lex? Because a man helps a widow with her load. Or because a king spares a foot soldier with his last command. Yes.

He bowed as the party halted at the lakeside.

'Now Michael guard you, my lady,' said Sophia of Develin.

'And you also,' Phaedra answered. 'And Raphael guide our ways.'

Heels splashed in the shallows. Wood scraped on stone as the crew pushed the boat out until it floated. Phaedra waded into the water and climbed, robe dripping, into the boat. Melissa and the hill boy followed her. A sailor held the stern, waiting. Another had his hand on the rope that would lift the sail. The passengers settled in the waist. Now the last crewman was aboard and the boat was free on the water. The sail rose up the mast. The craft heeled under the gentle pressure of the wind. It moved away, trailing ripples from its stern. Already it was beyond the reach of the mailed hands on the shore. In just a few moments more it would be beyond bowshot, beyond hail, gone altogether to a future unknown.

Padry watched it go.

'Now, Lord Lackmere,' he heard the Lady of

Develin say. 'Let us call council. And may we make a new beginning.'

He heard the armoured man bow. He heard Lackmere and the knights mounting their horses, the clash and the clatter as they started up through the olives to forge a new reign. He heard the lady's escort gather round her, murmuring in low voices, before they, too, mounted and followed.

They were going to council. They were going to discuss what must be done and to choose a new king. A Thomas Padry as young as yesterday's would have elbowed his way in among them. Whispered conversations by the tent-flaps, hurried deals in the horse-lines, a wink and a nod at the great table – yes, he would have thrown himself into that, shaping the outcome with the quickness of his tongue and mind. He would have urged a union of south and north, a marriage between Sophia of Develin and a northern lord – even Lord Herryce – and crowns for each, to bring the Kingdom together. It would not have been bad counsel. But it would not happen. For one thing, he would not be there to make it happen. For another, he knew already what they would choose to do.

They would set up the young Lackmere to be the new King. Lackmere was the maker of the victory and the man who had turned the council last night. He would show a strong face to Outland. That was what was needed. That was the kind of king men wanted – a king who could wield iron, and from it forge peace.

And as for wisdom, and compassion? Well, maybe

the man had them, more than Padry had allowed. Maybe he had learned something from his own young King, who had taken his terrible deeds from him. Maybe he would learn, too, from Sophia. Perhaps she would even give her hand to him? Would she? No, more likely she would not. He was already bound to her by bonds of blood and guilt as strong as any between men. And Lex, Bishop of Tuscolo, would set the crown upon his head in the high chapel where the eyes of the Angels blazed from the walls.

My pupils, thought Padry. Half their fates would still be before them. The dragon holds, the goddess departs, and the world is renewed.

The princes had vanished silently. They would be dispersing through the land, faithful still to the tasks the dead King had appointed for them. To the north the shoreline stretched before Padry like a long and desolate road. He, too, had a task ahead of him. He would return to Pemini, this time for good. He would take his limping band of townsmen home with such pay and promises as the treasury could afford them. And once back in those muddy alleys, he, too, would find a way to serve. Perhaps the almshouse was still looking for a porter to replace the man he had left lying in the pool. If not – well, there would be widows and orphans and cripples in plenty. There would be a thousand calls for help. He would answer those he could. Let only the Angels see.

He began to move, walking slowly northwards by the side of the lake. The shoreline unrolled ahead of him, a narrow, twisting path between the world and the deep water. To his right was the brown hulk of the castle where his King lay within the chapel walls. To his left were the glittering wavelets on which the boat rose and fell as it, too, pushed northwards, seeming with the distance to travel no faster than his own slow trudge along the shore. The little pebbles crunched beneath his toes. His eyes were hot and brimming. He could feel the tears on his cheeks. The boat was a blurry speck in his vision. And still he walked, and still he watched, as it passed from shadow to sun and its sail was filled with light.